CUTSLUT

KIM JONES

I'm that girl.
No.
I'm not.

This book is a work of fiction. Names, characters, places and incidents are of my imagination. I mean, really? You think heroes like this actually exist in real life? Well they don't. If they did, people wouldn't read about them, they'd go out and find their own real life book boyfriend. But honestly, it wouldn't matter if the fictional men in novels existed or not. Women would still find something to bitch about. They're too perfect. Too sweet. Dress too nice. Smell too good. We're miserable creatures—women. Can't be satisfied. Ever.

So keep being imperfect, gentlemen. Truth is, it doesn't really make it shit, anyway. But I do thank you. You're the reason I can continue to make a living doing what I love.

For Lacy:
I gave Jinx a big one just for you.

ACKNOWLEDGMENTS

Some of these are the same in all of my books. Some different. I should make a better effort at acknowledging people. But really, who the hell reads this anyway?

Last, last book.
last book.
THIS BOOK.

To **God** for giving me the gift of life, writing and an eternal love.

Reggie: All those nights spent in bed alone will be worth it one day. I hope. — Yeah... Still trying hun... **8 MONTHS LATER...STILL A SHITTY WIFE.**

Amy Owens: Don't replace me. I'm trying like hell to be a better best

~~friend. It's just taking a little while.~~ I dedicated this book to you, so I'm off the hook. **I'M STILL A SHITTY FRIEND.**

Parents: We're gonna get rich one day, I promise. — I know, I know. It didn't happen with the last book, but this may be THE ONE. **YEAH...THAT ONE WASN'T "THE ONE" EITHER. BUT....THIS MAY BE IT!**

Sisters: You'll be rich, too. ~~Maybe.~~ Definitely. **DON'T QUIT YOUR JOBS...**

Katy: Thank you for loving my ~~Cook~~ Marty. **JINX.** Your encouraging words help to breathe life into my characters. **STILL DO!**

Aunt Kat: I don't think I could've done this without your continued support. **I LOVE YOU!**

Uncle Don: I never would've mentioned Aunt Kat without mentioning you—after all, I am the favorite...author. Who are we kidding? I'm the favorite niece, too. **STILL THE FAVORITE**

Natasha: ~~You held my hand. Well, in spirit.~~ I'm not even sure you know about this book, but I'm keeping you here anyway. ;) **I FINISHED THIS MOTHERFUCKER!!!! YAY!!!!!!!**

Josephine: You owe me ~~87~~ ~~88~~ 89 drinks. BY THE WAY... Now that you're engaged, I'll never get the bastards. **STILL AIN'T MARRIED....SMH. STILL AIN'T GOT NO DRANKS.**

Sali: My first ever audiobook listener. I love you. I haven't read this one to you yet. But I will. **I DIDN'T READ THIS ONE EITHER. MAN... I'M SLACKING!**

HNDW: This may just be the one that gets that Bahama bottom rocker. Keeping my fingers crossed! **HELL, CROSS YA FUCKIN' TOES TOO. THIS SHIT AIN'T WORKIN'!**

Hang Le: The cover—perfection. Always!! **STILL AWESOME!**

Amy Tannenbaum: ~~Um...hang on. I'm checking my voicemail. Get back with you soon.~~ This is book number 5 with you and you still treat me like a redheaded step child. But considering I still have nothing nice to say about you in the acknowledgements section of my books, I guess I'll let it slide. **YEAH... I GOT NOTHING.**

Chelle Bliss: My a big thanks goes to you. For helping me figure out this damn Mac. You rock. I still can't figure it out. But you're always there to answer my call!! Actually, I'm talking to you as I write this. **STILL STRUGGLIN' WITH THIS MAC. AND YOU STILL ANSWERIN' THE PHONE!**

Paul Kirkley: You are too fine. Thanks for being sexy! **YOU DIDN'T MODEL ON THIS BOOK...BUT YOU STILL SEXY.**

Todd Jones: You make my life happy. Thank you for being here. And mixing me drinks, getting me drunk and way behind on my work. It's because of you I'm up all damn night doing this. **LOOKY LOOKY**

TODDY PODDY! I MADE IT TO NUMBER 11! SUCK IT, BITCH.

FORGY: THANKS FOR MAKING ME RE-WRITE THIS BASTARD AT 65K WORDS. :) LOVE YOU!

ROSE HUDSON: WHATEVER I SAY ISN'T GONNA BE AS AWESOME AS WHAT YOU SAY....SO JUST KNOW I LOVE YOU AND I THINK YOU'RE PERFECT!

JESSICA HAM: I LOVE YOUR FACE! I'D TOTALLY SHARE MY HUSBAND WITH YOU. ;)

SLOANE HOWELL: I'M MENTIONING YOU BECAUSE YOUR GROUP HAS LIKE 5K PEOPLE, AND I'M GONNA SHARE THIS SHIT SO THEY THINK WE'RE FRANDS AND HOPEFULLY THEY'LL BUY MY SHIT. CAUSE I'M ALL ABOUT DEM DOLLAS!!!!! AND 3 ICE CUBES.

HOUSE OF WHORES: KEEP BEING NASTY BITCHES!

OLIVIA BROWN: I CAN'T THANK YOU ENOUGH. SO I'LL JUST PUT YOU A LITTLE SOMETHING HERE. IT'S ALWAYS GOOD TO HAVE FRIENDS YOU CAN CALL ONLY WHEN YOU NEED SOMETHING. ;)

I'M FORGETTING SOMEBODY. I JUST KNOW IT. SO THIS ONE IS FOR YOU! PLEASE WRITE YOUR NAME HERE:_____

PROLOGUE

Jinx—One Year Ago

"Hey brother, can I get you a beer?"

I stare up at the hang around, fighting the urge to tell him I'm not his fucking brother. Instead, I shake my head and dismiss him with a look. It still amazes me how completely unrecognizable I am without my cut. To everyone here, I'm just another guy attending the party. Little do they know I am the enemy. They've let a Devil's Renegade come into their home just because he wore a white bandana and a hoodie that says, "I Support Madness MC."

Fucking idiots.

But as an added precaution, I've made sure to stay in the shadows. Seated out of sight. Knowing if I stand, I'll be a head taller than everyone else and draw unwanted attention to myself. Not that anyone would really question who I am. Even if they were brave enough to approach me, I'd just come up with some bullshit about being the dope man's nephew. They'll believe it. They're too stupid not to.

From my corner, I have the perfect view of the upcoming show. Madness's infamous cutslut will be making her appearance at any moment. Cocks will swell. Jaws will drop. Mouths will water. She's the complete show-stopping package. But I'm not here for a hard on. I'm here to collect. She took something that belongs to me. I aim to get it back.

The door opens and a hush falls over the crowd. Cain, president of Madness, walks in first. He doesn't have to speak to deliver the threat. With a warning glare, we all hear him loud and clear, "Don't fucking touch her." When he's confident the message has been received, he steps aside and there she is.

It's easy to get sucked into the thunderstorm of sex appeal she emits. With long, tanned legs, a slender waist and an ass you can sit a champagne flute on, she's the epitome of sexy. Her short sleeveless dress shows off her toned arms that are covered from wrist to shoulder in colorful tattoos—making her appearance even more erotic.

Endless waves of blonde hair surround her delicate face. Her nose is slightly upturned, chin raised, lips pressed into a permanent pink pout—an expression that says she knows her place. And you damn well better know yours. Some might say she looks proud. Snobbish even. But her eyes tell a different story.

The wide, soft, emerald greens framed in long, dark lashes are so striking I almost miss the imperfection. They're emotionless. Lifeless. Filled with a nothingness that has me temporarily forgetting why I'm here. For a moment, I want to pull her to me. Tell her I've got her. Take her away from this place. Then kill the men who stole her life from her.

Like she stole from me.

The thought is sobering. This girl is not innocent. My urge to protect her is just my natural instinct. I'd feel that strongly about helping any woman whose eyes held that same look of defeat.

Wouldn't I?

Cain's hand is at her hip and I bite my tongue to keep from growling at him like a fucking territorial Pit Bull. What the hell is wrong with me? This woman ruined my life. Took everything from me. I wonder if the years of my blood, sweat and tears she took paid for the Rolex on Cain's wrist. Or that expensive designer dress she's wearing. Those sky-high fuck-me heels.

No. This woman is not a victim. She's my nemesis. She's the same bitch who haunts my dreams. Fuels my anger. Quenches my thirst for revenge—a revenge I plan on exacting in due time. Not today. Not tomorrow. But in that moment when she least expects it.

Her name is Winter Tews.

She's my enemy's cutslut.

My MC brother's sister.

But very soon, she'll be *mine*.

WINTER

Standing outside room 421 at the Hard Rock Hotel in Las Vegas, Nevada, I ask myself, "Who is this irresistible creature who has an insatiable love for the dead?"

A guy stumbles out of his room just in time to hear me talking to myself and shoots me a confused look. But his confusion turns to desire when his eyes rake down my body—taking in my fishnet stockings, stilettos and satin bathrobe. I flip him the finger before answering my question.

"Me. Winter Tews. I have an insatiable love for the dead."

I mean, I must. Right? I'm here. At room 421. Visiting a man who may very well be meeting his death soon—depending on what I find out while I'm here. If that's the case, it won't be the first instance where a man living on borrowed time saw me minutes before he died. And just like all the other times, I'm not nervous or anxious. I'm just... here. I'm the girl in Rob Zombie's smash hit, "Living Dead Girl."

I swipe the keycard and wait for the light to turn green before pushing inside—leaving the card on the floor outside the door for Cain's men just in case something goes wrong and I need their help. They may not be here now, but in about ten minutes, they'll be in the room next to us—waiting for the signal if I decide to give it.

I make my way through the small entryway and into the suite. It's nice enough—overstuffed couches, pictures of rock legends, modern decorations, Aerosmith playing through the many speakers.

The bar is positioned in front of the floor to ceiling windows overlooking the top floor of a parking garage. Beyond it, I can see the twinkling lights of Vegas. Bright in color. Bold. Flashing. Designed to trigger the neurons in the brain that release serotonin. Leaving you with that happy, excited feeling. Too bad they don't have that effect on me.

"You're early," the voice says, moments before his reflection appears in the window. He's not nearly as big as I imagined him to be. Nor does he look anything like the ruthless gangster Cain claimed he was.

"Am I?" I ask, pouring a glass of scotch from the decanter. After scenting it, I take a sip and allow the smoky flavor to settle on my tongue a few seconds before swallowing. "Not bad."

"I got it for you. Heard Cain's little *cutslut* was a scotch drinker."

Over time, I've learned to control the urge to stab anyone who refers to me as Cain's cutslut. I still hate it, but I don't let it show. So instead of cringing or stiffening at the remark, I pretend what I find out tonight will result in his death. The thought has me smirking when I turn to face him and ask, "Is that so?"

He nods. "Yeah. They said you were sexy, too. Didn't think you'd be this sexy. No offense," he adds, flashing his gold teeth when he bites his bottom lip.

I shrug. "None taken."

We stare at one another a few moments. Me completely at ease. Him less so. Though he tries to hide it, I can tell he's nervous. He probably should be. This middle-aged, clean cut, chain wearing, gold teeth flashing bastard might very well be a notorious gangster, but if he wronged Cain, he's a dead man.

"Heard some other shit about you, too," he says, his eyes narrowing in suspicion.

"Yeah? Like what?" I take another sip of scotch. It's better than the last.

"That Cain either shares you with people he respects and trusts, or uses you to gain intel on people he doesn't." My brow furrows in confusion and he doesn't miss it. Who would have told him that? "So which one am I?" he asks in a tone that demands an answer. His confidence building now that he feels like he has the upper hand. "Am I someone he trusts, or someone he doesn't?"

Setting my glass on the bar, I notice the parking garage receipt and commit the level and lot number to memory before lifting an eyebrow at him. "You tell me, Mister." My hands move to the belt on my robe—the satin cool against my fingers as I slowly loosen the knot. "Does Cain have a reason not to trust you? Or are you as loyal as you say you are?"

His throat constricts as he swallows hard. I fight my smile at his reaction. *Who has the upper hand now, asshole?* His gaze drops to my hands, before travelling to the tops of my exposed breasts as I reveal the leather corset beneath.

"Jimmy," he rasps, his voice thick with desire. His hand moving to adjust his growing erection.

Men.

They're all the fucking same.

"Name's Jimmy."

"Well, Jimmy, I was told to come here and show you a good time." I slip the robe off my shoulders. "And I intend to do just that."

One foot in front of the other, I make my way across the floor to where he stands. In heels, I'm as tall as he is—making us eye level when I stop in front of him. I grab him roughly through his jeans, bringing him to his toes as he hisses through his teeth. The smell of smoke and whiskey lingers on his breath.

"Walk...Jimmy." With his cock in my hand, I urge him backwards—twisting my wrist and rubbing my palm against his crotch. His eyes flutter shut as his feet shuffle along the floor until he falls back onto the couch.

Straddling his lap, I grind my hips against him. His hands are on my breasts—squeezing. Rubbing. Pinching. Pulling at the fabric to reveal my nipples that are hard from his touch. I play the role and throw my head back on a moan. Rock harder against him. Pretend like I'm enjoying this, when really, I'm slipping my hand into the pocket of his jacket and retrieving his phone. He's too absorbed in my chest to notice. Too distracted by the feel of my body stroking along the length of his cock to pay any attention to what I'm doing over his shoulder—which is checking his phone for a passcode.

It's locked.

Of course.

"Shit," I mutter, slipping his phone back in his pocket.

His mouth on my neck, he mumbles, "You like that?" He gives my breasts another squeeze.

"Yes, but I meant, shit, I forgot to call Cain and tell him I'm here."

"He can wait."

"You know better than that," I say, fisting his hair in my hand and forcing his head back. I kiss him hard, biting his bottom lip. "If I don't check in, he'll think something's wrong. Might send someone over." That's enough to get his attention.

Reluctantly, he pulls away and reaches for his phone. I reach between us and work his cock through his jeans—making sure to keep him distracted. He's still careful enough to keep his phone angled so it's out of my sight as he punches in the passcode. Not that it really matters. Once it's unlocked, I'll make the call and get what I need before I hand it back to him. That's not the reason for the distraction.

While he's worried about me finding out the code to his cell, I'm stealing the keys to his Lexus. It's not part of the plan, I just enjoy taking shit that doesn't belong to me. With a twist of my hips and a steal grip on his cock, I slip his key fob from his pocket and tuck it beneath the thick lace of my garter.

A moment later, he's passing me his phone with absolutely no knowledge of my thievery. Or my ability to transfer data from his cell to mine with a few touches here and there. Just as I start to gather the info that will determine this man's fate, the door opens and in walks Cain along with three of his brothers—Rut, Swipe and Theo.

Cain's eyes are on mine. Those dead, midnight blues giving nothing away. As always, they're slightly narrowed—causing tiny crow's feet to crinkle at the corners. His big six foot three, two-hundred-pound body is relaxed. His thick, muscular arms hanging loosely at his sides.

Almost as if the heavy and worn leather cut on his back is weighing him down.

His damp, dirty blonde hair is combed back on his head. A shade lighter than the full beard covering his square jaw. His nose, slightly crooked after having been broken several times, is prominent yet complimentary of his face. Even sinister and evil, he's good looking. Strikingly so.

"Get my pussy off that motherfucker's cock," Cain growls, his hand tightening around his pistol. I slide off Jimmy's lap and sit next to him on the couch. Though I appear completely at ease, my gut is telling me something is off. And it's never been wrong.

"What are you doing here?" I ask with a practiced calm.

His expression doesn't change, but he tilts his head slightly. I can't tell if it's in warning or surprise. "You don't know?" Confused, I shake my head. My answer must not be the one he wants because his jaw tightens in anger. He stares at me as if contemplating whether I'm telling the truth or not.

When his gaze becomes even more lethal and cold, I know he's decided in his head I'm lying to him. The muscles in his jaw twitch. His nostrils flare. Hands curl into fists so tight, I'm surprised the skin on his knuckles doesn't split. Then he speaks a single word and it all becomes clear.

"Pierce."

My vision blurs. Stomach free falls. Heart hammers out a hard, unsteady beat. My throat tightens and my tongue feels thick. I'm paralyzed with fear. Stunned by shock. Gutted by memories. All at the mention of his name.

Pierce.

My brother.

The one I betrayed.

"That's right. Your brother. In my. Fucking. Town."

Pierce is not just my brother. He's the president of the Devil's Renegades MC West Coast chapter. And the one who forbade me to have anything to do with anyone involved with Madness MC. They were the bad guys. The rivals. The ones who gave MC's a bad name.

But not even the threat of being eighty-sixed from the Devil's Rene-gades or my brother could stop me.

I was eighteen. Young. In love. I didn't care what MC Cain rode with. To me, he was just Cain. But in the six years we've been together, he's changed. I can't remember the exact moment he became a stranger to me. The transition didn't happen overnight, rather over time. I

t was the little things I noticed at first—the lack of passion in his kiss. Desire in his eyes. Heat in his gaze. I became nothing more than a possession. A reminder that he owned something that once belonged to the enemy.

He found pleasure in my suffering. A sick sense of satisfaction in my humiliation. He wanted to express his power through me. He'd made the sister of a Devil's Renegade his cutslut—a girl he used to get what he wanted.

Cain's eyes slide from mine to Jimmy's. "And he's doing business with this backstabbing motherfucker."

Jimmy's hands rise in defense. "Cain, wait. I can explain." He starts to say more, but Cain cuts him off.

"You betrayed me." The words are barely past his lips before he pulls the trigger.

WINTER

The sound of a bullet exiting the end of a silencer is shriller than I ever expected it to be. It resembles more of a loud crackle like a bottle rocket, rather than the muffled "thump" I've heard on T.V.

I don't know why I'm not screaming. Panicking. Freaking out about the man whose body leans heavily against me. Whose head rests on the back of the couch only inches from mine. His open, lifeless eyes. Parted mouth. The small trickle of blood oozing from the tiny hole in the center of his forehead.

Cain looks terrifying, holding the still smoking gun in his steady hand. So different from the man one who once wore an easy smile. Had an infectious laugh. Blue eyes that had the power to melt me. Who was gentle and caring when I was upset. Rough and passionate when he made love to me. The man whose touch was my charge.

The Cain I fell in love with was young and free. Fearless. A bad boy with the desire to be an outlaw. A thirst for danger. A hunger for me. He was my everything. Now he's just a cold hard killer with a desire for blood and an appetite for revenge.

An icy fear runs through me as he glares at me once again. "You fuckin' knew, didn't you?"

I shake my head. "No, Cain. I swear..."

He lunges, grabbing my throat in his hand and placing the barrel of his pistol so close to my head I can feel the heat from it. "Don't fucking lie to me, Winter! You planned this, didn't you?"

His grip on my throat is tight, but not suffocating—allowing me plenty of air to speak. But it wouldn't do any good. He thinks I'm in on whatever Jimmy and Pierce had working. And when Cain gets something in his head, there's no truth I could tell him to convince him otherwise.

"I've been watching every move that motherfucker makes," he says, curling his lip in disgust. "Ever since you pulled that little stunt of yours." An involuntary shiver wracks through me at the reminder of that night nearly two years ago.

I'd escaped. Ran from Cain and made it all the way to San Diego—home of the Devil's Renegades West Coast Chapter. I knew my brother was on a national run, as was Cain, so I took the opportunity to break into Pierce's house and steal every cent he had in his safe.

I was going to use the money to get out of the country. Maybe Mexico. Some place warm. Far away from any MC. I barely made it to the end of Pierce's driveway when Cain found me. Under the impression that Pierce had given me the money, he lost it. Vowing to kill Pierce if I ever spoke to him or saw him again. And the price I paid for running was far worse than death. Cain promised me I'd never forget it.

I haven't.

I begin to realize that once again I'll have to endure a pain like that. I'd probably be better off if he just shot me. Because there's no doubt that very soon, I'll be praying for death. I guess that's what you get when you sell your soul to the Devil—a life of never-ending hell.

Now, I know what you're thinking. You're wondering why I don't just kill him. Wait for his most vulnerable moment—mid-orgasm, maybe. While he's too absorbed by the feeling of ecstasy to notice, why don't I just shove a pencil through his ear. Cut his throat. Drive a spoon into his heart. Something. I shouldn't be scared, right? It's not like I have anything to lose.

Well, here's the reason.

I lack balls.

Maybe someday I'll find them, but chances are I won't. Until then, I'm going to continue to be a coward. You continue to judge me. It's a free country. Being an asshole is your right. Just like being a chicken shit is mine.

"Cain," Theo says, coming closer to get his attention but making sure not to touch him. "Jimmy's guys are in the lobby. We need to bounce."

With a squeeze to my throat, Cain narrows his eyes. "I'll deal with you when we get home." I'm jerked from the couch and shoved toward the other room. "Get your shit. We're leaving."

It takes a moment for my legs to work, but I finally make it to where my things are. Cain doesn't follow, but I can feel his eyes on me as I slip my robe over my shoulders. Grabbing my purse, I discreetly tuck the key fob from my garter inside. I'd love another drink, but before I can pour one, Cain has me by my arm and is pulling me along beside him.

His grip on my arm tightens as we walk down the hallway. Theo walks in front of us. Rut and Swipe behind. Every eye is open and alert. Already anticipating signs of trouble. We don't find any until we're at the doors leading to the parking garage.

Standing in the breezeway is a small army of Jimmy's men. Cain shifts beside me and I notice his hand disappear inside his cut. The other tightens around my arm.

"Where's Jimmy?" one of the men asks, crossing his arms over his chest.

"Haven't seen him," Cain says with a shrug.

"He's supposed to be meeting with your bitch here." His eyes move to me. "Don't see how that's possible if she's with you."

"There a problem here?" Two security guards enter from behind us. Behind them, I can see more are on their way. Cain looks down at me and gives me a nod before releasing my arm. Understanding his unspoken demand, I cross the floor to where Jimmy's men are standing.

My walk is slow—deliberate. Crossing my ankles on every step, I wear a sultry smile until I've closed the distance and am standing only a hairsbreadth away from the one who was doing all the talking.

"Jimmy's sleeping it off," I purr, dragging my nail down the front of his shirt. "He proved his loyalty to Cain and in return, he got me. Do the same, and you'll get me too. Now..." I move my finger down his stomach toward his crotch—feeling his cock swell from beneath my touch. "Tell these nice men there's not a problem and I'll make it extra good for you."

His gaze shifts to over my shoulder and I know he's looking to Cain for reassurance. He must get it because in a throaty voice, he tells the guards, "No problem here."

"Good boy," I whisper on a wink. Turning to look over my shoulder, I flash a smile to the guards but it falters when I see additional security has arrived.

"I think it's time you guys called it a night," a guard says. Cain bristles when he claps him on the shoulder. My adrenaline spikes at the contact. I know what's coming.

"Get your fucking hand off me," Cain growls, his rage barely controlled.

The guard's hand curls around Cain's shoulder. "Come on. Get to movin'." Already anticipating Cain's reaction, I slide my heels off my feet while everyone else is watching Cain. When he turns and pushes the guard away from him, I see my opportunity and take it.

Ducking around Jimmy's men, I bolt through the door and into the garage. Behind me, chaos has ensued. Someone pulled a gun. The guards are radioing for backup. Jimmy's men are shouting threats. Theo is promising death to them if they take one step closer. And above it all, rings one word that is more chilling than any other.

My name.

"Winter!" Cain shouts, his wrath reflected in his tone. He screams my name again and again—throwing in a couple, "Get the fuck off me's" and some "Let me go's."

Heavy feet sound from behind me but I don't turn to see who it is. I keep running. Scanning the painted concrete columns in search of F17—the spot where, according to the receipt in his room, Jimmy's car is located.

I duck through an opening too small for Theo or any of Jimmy's men to fit through. My relief is short-lived when a car speeds toward me from the entrance of the garage.

It could be another of Cain's men. Or one of Jimmy's hoping to capture Cain's cutslut for leverage to use against him. Hell it could be a bookie Cain owes money to. The cops. Feds. The possibilities are endless.

"Shit. Shit. Shit. Shit," I pant, sliding between another barrier that's almost too narrow for me to fit through. Once I'm on the other side, I climb up a set of wire cables separating the levels to the next floor.

Though the footsteps have ceased, I can still hear the sound of screeching tires as the car turns the corner. Figuring I can climb to the top faster than he can drive there, I grab the cables and haul myself up several more stories until I reach F—a level below the roof.

The lot is eerily quiet and pretty vacant leaving me nowhere to hide. Only a handful of cars are parked up here and I jog toward the Lexus in the back of the lot. As I near it, I'm temporarily blinded by headlights. The high beams have me stopping in my tracks and throwing my hands up to block the light.

Before I can turn and run, I'm grabbed from behind. "Where you going, cutslut?" I struggle against the sweaty arms that trap me. "You promised me some fun." The voice belongs to Jimmy's guy who I'd spoken to downstairs. But his voice is drowned out by Theo's threat as his words echo across the empty garage.

"That doesn't belong to you."

That.

Me.

Like I'm an object instead of a fucking human being.

In my struggle to get free, I end up taking an elbow to the temple from Jimmy's guy. Sparks blur my vision and everything sounds far away for a few moments. I'm on my knees now. I hear gunshots in the distance. And the screeching sound of tires. Several men shouting. Then it's silent and I'm hauled to my feet. Thrown over a shoulder. Darkness starts to take over but not before the unmistakable scent of leather fills my senses.

Theo.

He's taking me to Cain. To where I belong. Where I'll no doubt live out the rest of my life being tortured and wishing I were dead. It's been years since I made that stupid decision to throw away everything good for a taste of something bad. And I got way more than I bargained for. Now there's no escape. No chance of redemption. This is my life. I sold my soul, and I'm paying the penance.

I, Winter Tews, living dead girl, belong to Cain Malcolvich. I am and forever will be his.

His property.

His possession.

His cutslut.

JINX

The stench of another man's blood permeates my senses as I take another pull from my cigarette. Even in the darkness, I can make out the dark stains on my hands. I should've killed those motherfuckers. But I knew my club would say it wasn't worth it. I think it was. And that's coming from the man who hates that bitch more than anyone.

Winter Tews destroyed me. What she took might've been only pennies to her, but to me it was a new beginning. A lifeline. A way for me to get the fuck out of the dark alleys I ran at night, cope with all the terrible shit I'd done and finally find some semblance of peace in a life filled with regret.

Maybe that's why I snapped. Because nobody has the right to hurt her more than me. It would explain why seeing Jimmy's guy put his hands on her, rattled my beast's cage. But when the piece of shit referred to Winter as *that*, the beast inside me shredded through the iron box I keep him locked in.

I sure as fuck hope it wasn't because I wanted to be the one to break her soul. That would make me just like them. A monster. I thought I'd left that life long ago. That I was better. But doesn't me wanting to hurt her, witness her fall, see her stripped of all that fancy jewelry and designer shit she likely purchased with my money make me a monster, too?

Even now, when she's tied up, gagged, unconscious and barefoot, I feel some sense of satisfaction. Like this, in my care, at my mercy, it's easy to imagine how she'll be in the weeks to come. How she'll act like a spoiled brat—fussing over her lack of luxury. Playing the role of entitled princess and demanding she be treated with respect. Threatening me with her big, bad boyfriend. I grow excited at the broken image of her—un-showered. Unkempt. Imperfect.

But I didn't see her as a privileged cutslut who'd fallen from grace in the arms of that man. She wasn't a cold-hearted bitch who'd been knocked unconscious and thrown over the shoulder of Cain's Sergeant at Arms. And it wasn't satisfaction I felt at the sight of her like that, either. It was sympathy.

As I made my way to them, my sympathy brewed to rage. By the time I got there, my wrath consumed me. So I gave them a taste of what they took from her. They may still be breathing, but it's not without pain.

Her head lolls from side to side and she whimpers—dragging me back to the present. To what has to be done. To what I've waited so fucking long for. She pulls at ties that bind her hands and I look down to find them visibly pale in the darkness. My thumb brushes over her fingers. They're cold.

I grab a knife from my pocket and pull on my gloves. After freeing her, I rub the warmth back into her hands while she continues to sleep. Listening to her soft moans as I do. Her muttered string of unintelligible words. Eyeing her long, blonde hair that's tangled around her face. Her thin, tattooed arms that are limp and lifeless. Her satin robe that barely covers the tops of her thighs, and offers an impressive view of her cleavage.

"Cain," she mumbles, crying out for that motherfucker. It's just what I needed to hear to get my head back in the game.

Immediately, any warmth I might've felt toward her vanishes. I smile as my plans for her resurface. Of course she'll have the option to make this easy for herself. But that's not who Winter is.

She'll test my patience—test us all. And she gives zero fucks about the destruction she'll leave behind. This selfish, cold hearted, beautiful betraying goddess will do whatever it takes to get ahead. Or at least she'll try. There's just one little problem.

One thing she didn't consider.

One play she hadn't anticipated.

One person she doesn't even know exists.

Me.

WINTER

W hen I come to, the first thing I notice is that my hands are free. So are my feet. But as I begin to fully wake, I realize something is in my mouth. I push against it with my tongue. It doesn't yield in the slightest.

I move to free my mouth as I lazily open my eyes. My hands freeze in the air when I make out a large figure across from me. His knees are bent with his elbows resting on them. His big, gloved hands dangle in the space between his legs. He wears nothing but black—including the ski mask that hides everything on his face except his eyes and his mouth. Even partially hidden from view, there's no denying that this man is *not* Theo. Which confuses me more because he isn't wearing a leather cut, either.

A bookie?

Jimmy's guys?

I survey my surroundings and find that I'm in the back of some type of cargo van. The only light comes from the two windows on the back doors. Beyond them is a concrete wall. My best guess is we're still in the parking garage. Is this the same vehicle that blinded me with its headlights?

My gaze moves back to the man across from me who hasn't blinked since I woke up. He just stares back at me. The only things I can really make out about him is that he's big, quiet and uber scary. I've seen my fair share of bad guys. Killers. Thieves. Gangsters and bikers. But none of them are as intimidating as this one.

In an effort to face my fears, I straighten my spine and lift my chin. My hands move slowly toward my face. When he doesn't object, I reach behind my head and untie the knot that holds my gag in place. After a few seconds of struggling, I manage to free it from my face.

"Who are you?" I ask, the moment I can speak clearly. Without giving him time to answer, I fire off another question. "Where am I?" He doesn't flinch. He's so still it's a little unnerving.

Hoping he doesn't notice, I inch closer to the door. There's a twitch above his eye. "It's locked, isn't it?" I deadpan, not needing an answer. Of course it's locked. Who the hell kidnaps someone, doesn't tie them up and keeps the door unlocked?

"Please," I start, trying a different approach—even though I'm not one to beg. "Let me go. I won't tell anyone." Nothing.

I shift, trying to find a more comfortable position. But the rigid, metal floor lining is unforgiving. So I give up and slump back against the wall. When I do, something presses into my hip. My purse. And inside are two very important things. A cigarette and a gun.

"Mind if I smoke?" I ask, not surprised when he doesn't answer.

Fumbling around, I open my purse and reach in for my cigarettes. My hand falls on the cool metal of the small .38 pistol inside. Without a second thought, I pull it out and point it at the man's face.

"Let me out or I'll kill you," I demand shakily. He doesn't seem the least bit threatened by me or my gun. "I swear I'll pull the trigger." His eyes narrow slightly in challenge. And even though I don't want to kill him, I know I have to. If I don't, I'll end up in the hands of someone who won't hesitate to kill me. Is his life worth more than mine? Probably. But I guess I'm just selfish that way.

"Last chance," I warn. I count to three then without giving myself time to think it through, I do something I never thought I was capable of.

I pull the trigger.

And nothing fucking happens.

So I do it again.

The loud click of the trigger and my heavy breathing are the only sounds in the van. His lips twitch as I stare between the gun and him. Wondering how one person could have as much shitty luck as me.

For the first time, he moves. My eyes are drawn to the movement and I see him holding something small and black in his gloved hand. The clip to my gun.

I snap.

"You son of a bitch! Let me out of here!" I beat my fists on the walls. The floor. Knowing it's pointless but not giving a damn, I scramble to the doors. He's faster. His arm reaches out and blocks the path forcing me back down. A surge of adrenaline rushes through me at the possibility that the doors might actually be unlocked.

I fight him with everything I have. Kicking and screaming. My fists wind milling into thin air. He hasn't even moved from his spot—using only his left arm to hold me back. Seeing an opening, I take it. Even if it is probably the stupidest thing I've ever done.

I slap him.

Hard.

The blow is powerful enough to jerk his head to the side. I'm so surprised that I not only had the balls to hit him, but that I actually did, that I'm frozen in shock.

Slowly, he turns his head back to look at me. I search his shadowed eyes for that heated anger I'm so used to. But there's no anger. Only amusement. So I hit him again. This time he's prepared and his face doesn't move. Actually, I think it hurt my hand more than his face.

When I try for a third time, he catches my wrist in his hand. His hold is firm but gentle. His big fingers wrapping easily around my wrist. With his eyes on mine, he slowly leans forward while pulling my hand to him. I flinch in preparation of what's to come. I know he's probably going to break my fingers. My hand. Wrist. Or worse, my arm. Surprisingly, he does none of these things.

I can feel his warm breath over my hand moments before he places a gentle, lingering kiss on the center of my palm. I stare back in shock, horror and complete disbelief as he crouches in front of me. Tenderly, as if I'm some priceless porcelain doll, he places my hand back in my lap. Then, he moves toward the doors.

I'm so confused about what just happened, I don't even attempt to escape when the door opens and he jumps out. A low voice speaks to him and he nods before turning back to me. One corner of his mouth turns up slightly and he shoots me a wink. I feel like it's some kind of unspoken promise. But I don't have time to dwell on it for too long. The moment he disappears from view, several more men take his place. One in particular has me seized with new panic.

This is my captor.

It might've been the man in the scary mask with the super soft lips that took me, but it was at this man's demand. He's not a bookie. He's not one of Jimmy's guys. He doesn't wear the colors of Madness, either. His stare might be cold and hard, but it's not sinister and evil. Yet he scares me more than the monsters I've spent the last six years of my life hating. More than the man in the mask.

When he addresses me, it's the hate in his voice, disgust in his tone and the malevolent nature of his shame-laced words that remind me of why I'm so threatened by him.

"Hello, little sister."

WINTER

"Pierce," I whisper in disbelief. His eyes seem to soften a little at hearing me speak his name.

He stands tall and strong. Confident and powerful. Handsome like my father. Humble like my mother, despite all his accomplishments—the business he built. The army of loyal men who surround him. The respect he's worked so hard to earn.

For a moment, he's the big brother I remember from when I was a child. The one who took care of me after my parents passed. Who missed out on his young adult life so that I may have one.

He held me when I cried. Grounded me when I broke curfew. He was involved in every aspect of my life. Too involved. Which is why I left. Why I betrayed him. Why I turned my back on the only family I had left in this world. And in the end, I became the enemy. The cutslut. Property of Madness President, Cain.

As if he's remembering too, his eyes grow cold again. Face hard, lip curled, he growls, "Get her out."

At Pierce's demand, two sets of arms reach for me. I slap them away—successfully using my foot to shove one of the men off balance. He stumbles but quickly gains his feet. With a harsh glare, he grabs my calf and jerks me roughly toward him. My back hits the floor of the cab with a loud thump nearly knocking the wind out of me.

By the time I'm standing on my feet outside the van, my robe is over my hips—exposing more than I'm comfortable with. A rage I haven't felt in a long time bubbles inside me. *Who the hell do they think they're messing with?* Cain may be an asshole. The Devil himself. But one thing's for certain, in the six years we've been together, nobody has ever laid a hand on me without his say so.

I jerk free of the man's hold and quickly straighten my clothes—cinching the belt of my robe tighter as I shoot Pierce a nasty look. He only smirks. "Don't be modest, Winter. It's not like everyone in Clark County hasn't already seen your ass."

"Fuck you," I snap, brushing the grit from my knees. "You into kidnapping now? Thought you were above that."

"I'm above kidnapping innocent people. People who actually matter. You're neither." If I wasn't so pissed, his words might actually hurt me—even though they are well deserved.

"What are you doing here?" With a raise of my chin I add, "This is Madness territory."

His brow rises in amusement. "Is that so?" Looking around at his brothers he asks, "Did any of you get that memo?" A low mumble of "no" echoes throughout the space. I look around and notice my masked captor isn't here. Then I realize we're in some sort of mechanic shop. Not the parking garage. How long was I out? Minutes? Hours? Hell, maybe we aren't in Madness territory.

Pierce glares at me with an icy smile. "That motherfucker may control you, but he knows better than to fuck with me."

"He doesn't control me," I lie, too ashamed to admit the truth.

"Not anymore, you mean." My brow wrinkles in confusion. "He did control you, but you ran from him."

"I didn't run from him." In the off chance this is some kind of rescue mission, I need to stop it before it ever gets started. I can live with Pierce hating me. But I can't bear the thought of him getting hurt because of me.

Entertained by my answer, he crosses his arms over his chest and cocks his head to the side. His tone dripping with mockery, he asks, "Well who were you running from, sweet pea?"

"The police," I grit, barely able to keep my tone even. "The plan has always been if one of us got pinched, the other fled." In an effort to act like he's not getting under my skin, I mirror his position and shoot him a smile. "Only because they don't have co-ed showers in county. Otherwise I'd be with him now."

He's unaffected. Possibly even more amused at my attempt to piss him off. I guess when you have a sister with a reputation like mine, you're not easily offended at the mention of her showering with another man.

"The threat in his voice and the way he screamed your name..." He shakes his head then leans in and whispers, "Damn sure didn't sound like a man encouraging you to do what you were told. Then again I'm not the kinda man who gets off on controlling women...so." He shrugs, pulling a cigarette from his cut and placing it between his teeth. "What do I know?"

I don't respond. I just stare back at him while he looks up at me from beneath his lashes and cups the flame to light his smoke. He doesn't believe me. Not that I figured he would. It doesn't matter if I'm telling the truth or not. Like Cain, Pierce believes what he wants.

"So you gonna tell me why you ran?" I don't respond. We're both silent a moment. Then a tiny crease forms between his eyes. "He hit you?"

"He doesn't hit me." My quick comeback is a stupid move on my part. Pierce smiles—almost as if he knew I'd take the bait.

"You don't have to lie, sweet pea."

This is the second time he's used that endearment. It was what he called me when I was a little girl. A nostalgic feeling tries to make its way into my heart, but I force it away. After all, he's only using it to try and break me down. I'm tempted to tell him to lay the fuck off. I'm already broken. No need to kick a dead horse.

"I bet the real truth's under all that makeup," he challenges. If I could prove him wrong, I would.

He pulls a bandana from his back pocket and grabs the bottle of water the man standing next to him is holding. His eyes never leave mine as he soaks the cloth, then passes it to me.

"What's this for?" I ask, staring down at the bandana in disgust.

"Your makeup. Take it off."

I huff out a laugh. "You're joking."

"Do I look like I'm joking?" Nope. He's serious.

"Why? What the fuck does it matter?" The tremor in my voice is a mixture of shame and anger. "I already told you. He didn't hit me. He's not the monster you think he is." *He's worse.*

Pierce stiffens. His playful, cocky attitude disappears. His eyes become glaciers. There's a chill in the air. The source? Cold fury. In one step, he's towering over me.

"I know exactly who he is and what he's capable of. I tried to save you from it. Went to fucking war for you, Winter. My club went to war for you. And in the end, you took that motherfucker's side. But tonight you ran from him. I want to know why. So for the last time, take off...the fucking...makeup."

With no other option, I bring the bandana to my face. Despair darkens Pierce's eyes as the truth is revealed. I know what he's thinking. He should have done more. Tried harder. Protected me. But none of this is his fault. I need him to believe that. Even if it means him hating me.

"Don't look at me like that," I snap, pushing him back a step. "I don't need your pity or your fucking remorse." His face gives nothing away, but I see his hands tighten into fists as he stares at the fading bruises around my eyes and cheek—the result of my latest beating from Cain because I "got an attitude" with him.

"I left San Diego because I wanted to. Not because he made me. Just like I ran today because it was the plan. Not because I wanted to get away from him. And if a few bruises are the only price I have to pay to stay away from the fucking cesspool I grew up in, then it's more than worth it." My chest tightens as I spit the hurtful words at him. I hate myself for being such a bitch, but it's either this or me breaking down in front of him. I refuse to do the latter.

Any softness he might have had vanishes. In an instant, Pierce transforms from the easy going, compassionate brother I once knew to the hard, callous man I've made him. With an evil glint in his eye and conviction in his tone, he says something that both wounds and relieves me.

"If one thing's for certain, little sister, it's this...not one fucking part of me, feels sorry for you." The harshness in his tone is like a punch to the gut, but it doesn't show. The scowl on my face hides it all. "I'm not here to rescue you. I'm here because of what you did."

My façade falters. I fidget nervously—feeling regretful. "Look," I breathe, meeting his eyes. "I know I stole from you..."

He holds his hand up to cut me off and quirks a brow. "What makes you so sure it was my money you stole?"

For some reason, the man in the mask pops in my head. I scan the crowd again to see if he's here, but none of them measure to his height or build. "Who?" I ask, the question coming out as a whisper.

Pierce shakes his head. "Doesn't matter. What matters is that someone trusted me with their money. I put it in a safe only two people knew the combination to. Me and my little sister who I thought I told to stay the fuck away from me and what's mine."

"I told you I'd pay it back."

He points at my face. "If that's what he does to you on a normal day, I'm sure the punishment for betrayal will be much worse. I need you alive for the next sixty days. After that, you can go to hell for all I care. But first I'm getting that fucking money, Winter."

Sixty days.

My twenty-fifth birthday.

Payday.

I was ten when my parents died in a tragic car accident. The vehicle at fault belonged to a shipping company who was more than willing to settle with us out of court. I still remember how angry Pierce was when the company sent a team of lawyers to our house the day of the funeral. At only eighteen he already had that lethal look about him. It didn't take long for the lawyers to retreat, continuously apologizing until Pierce slammed the door in their faces.

I'd been crying at the bottom of the stairs—watching the entire scene unfold. When Pierce turned to me, his anger instantly faded. "What's wrong?" he'd asked, pulling me to him. "Did those men scare you?" I'd nodded into his chest. "Don't worry, sweet pea. I'll make them pay for it." And he did.

Pierce set it up so I'd get three lump sums. One at eighteen when I graduated high school. One at twenty-two when I graduated college. And the final one on my twenty-fifth birthday—a time Pierce thought I'd be settling down and starting a family.

Like a fool, I'd given all my money to Cain. The first time because I loved him. The second time because he forced me.

He took the money I stole from Pierce too. Inside the safe, I'd left a note promising to pay him back. I thought I'd be free of Cain when I received that last sum of money. Even if I wasn't, I'd vowed to myself that no matter the consequences, I'd give Pierce back his money. I guess he didn't trust me to follow through on my promise.

"Did you orchestrate all of this?" I ask, plucking the cigarette from his fingers. "The meeting with Jimmy...having his men show up... hoping to catch Cain distracted so you could send your big ape to man handle me into the back of a van?"

"Does it matter?"

"Yes it matters!" I shriek. "He killed him. You know that, right?"

Pierce lifts a shoulder in an uncaring gesture. "Jimmy was a bad guy. The world is better without him."

I take a drag and study him. There's no way he knew it would work out like it did. But knowing Pierce, he's been planning this for a long time. His greatest strength is his patience. He's the kind of man who thinks everything through. Strategizes every move. Covers all bases. He is as skilled in life as he is at chess. And he uses the same tactics to play them both. But there's a kink in his oh-so-well thought-out plan.

"He'll come for me," I say, trying like hell to keep the quiver out of my voice. "And the first person he's going to go to is you."

An easy smile covers his face. "Oh, I sure hope so, sweet pea."

I don't. A face to face between Pierce and Cain will no doubt end badly. So I push forward, hoping my threat will be enough to convince Pierce to just let me go.

"He'll bring an army. He won't stop until he searches every square inch of San Diego."

"I don't give a shit if he looks under every rock in California. He won't find you."

My brow creases in confusion. "What's that mean?"

He smirks, his eyes dancing with laughter. His body language says he knows something I don't. And it pleases the hell out of him to enlighten me. "Because you, my dear, sweet little sister, won't fucking be there."

WINTER

I hate country music.

    I'm not talking about modern pop-country—where a guy in boots meets a girl in jeans and sings her a song on his tailgate. That shit is tolerable. I'm talking about real country—Merle, Waylon, Willie and George. The original men of country music who sing the most depressing fucking songs imaginable. I've never really thought about killing myself. But in this moment, I'm seriously considering it.

    Seconds after Pierce told me I wouldn't be going to San Diego with him, a black sedan rolled into the garage with two men who looked like cops inside. I was handcuffed, gagged and tossed in the back seat without any explanation as to where I was going or what the fuck was going on. Pierce just patted my head like a dog and said, "You're welcome," before sliding in next to me.

    You're welcome.

    Ha.

    Like he's doing me a favor.

    Fuck him.

    After all, he's the one trying to kill me. Or rather have me kill myself. He knows I hate country music. And that shit has been playing on a loop for the past twenty minutes. He's just sitting there, tapping his fucking foot to the beat and drumming his fingers on his knee. Next, he'll be playing a banjo and dipping snuff.

"Hey!" I yell past the gag in my mouth. Twisting in my seat to get his attention. He turns to me and lifts a brow. "Where are you taking me?"

He cups his ear. "What's that? I can't understand you." I narrow my eyes at him. His smile widens. "You said you wanted some Merle?" My glare hardens. "Hey man, you got Misery and Gin?" he asks, tapping the cage to get the attention of the men up front.

"Coming right up."

When Merle Haggard's Misery and Gin begins to play, I roll my eyes and groan. Outside the window, the sun is starting to set in the Nevada sky. We're literally in the middle of nowhere, on some deserted highway. A part of me wonders if Pierce is planning to take me out here and kill me. Another part of me hopes like hell he does. Then I won't have to listen to this crap anymore.

"Better get used to this music, Winter." I shoot Pierce a look. "This is what they listen to in the dirty, dirty south. By the way..." He touches my nose with the tip of his finger. "That's where you're going." The dirty south could be Louisiana. Mississippi. Alabama. Texas. Who the hell knows.

I look down at my torn robe and ripped stockings that are as dirty as my bare feet. "I don't have any clothes."

"Clothes?" he scoffs. "I didn't think a girl like you needed clothes. I mean, you do spend most of your time on your back, don't you?"

"Fuck you," I spit. I'm so pissed, I'd strangle him if my hands weren't cuffed behind my back. He laughs at me, and I have the feeling he knows exactly what I'm thinking. Or at least some of it. I'm sure he doesn't know that I'm also thinking his plan is fucking stupid.

If I was in Pierce's shoes, I could come up with a million different ways to get back that money. None of them nearly as risky as this. Does he really think sending me away is the answer? Cain will still come to California to look for me. And no matter the lies Pierce tells him, he'll be convinced he knows where I am. Then he'll do something stupid. Pierce will retaliate. War will commence. People will die.

But then again, this isn't about me at all. It's a standoff. A fight for respect. A battle over territory. A pissing contest between two MC's. I mean, if whose dick is bigger is really that important, one might wonder why they don't just whip the motherfuckers out and see? I'll tell you why. Because they're men. And men are stupid.

I stare out the window for the rest of the ride. It doesn't bother Pierce though. He sings. Tells the guys to turn up the volume when one of his favorites comes on. Nudges my shoulder to tell me how much he's enjoying our time together. Meanwhile I'm contemplating biting my tongue off in hopes of bleeding out. Banging my head against the window and knocking myself unconscious. Faking a seizure. Something.

Six songs later, Pierce announces, "We're here."

I straighten and look through the windshield as we pass through the gate of a private air strip. The driver pulls the car right out onto the runway and I look up at the jet waiting to take me to my doom. The name on the side of it informs me of exactly where that doom is.

Knox Companies.

Dallas Knox-Carmical.

Wife of Luke Carmical.

President of Devil's Renegades MC Hattiesburg, Mississippi.

I remember he came to my parents' funeral. I also remember him telling Pierce, "If you ever need anything, brother, let me know." I guess he called in that promised favor.

Mississippi. I'm going to fucking Mississippi. It's cold there in November. And I'm dressed like a poor, sidewalk tramp. Suddenly, I feel the urge to cry. I'm talking real tears. Real raw emotion.

I'm sad because of how Pierce is treating me. Disappointed that he would. Yeah, I deserve it. But he is better than me. Better than this. There's no quid-pro-quo with him. I shit on him. He doesn't stoop to my level. Therefore, he doesn't shit on me back. That's how it's always been. Or maybe that's just how it once was.

Stop it, Winter!

I blink back my tears and harden my stare as Pierce opens the door and helps me out. I refuse to look him in the eye. Instead, I stare at the button of his shirt. But he's not having it.

With his finger under my chin, he tilts my head back to look at him. "Don't worry, sweet pea. It's only a couple of months. Then you're free to go back to your old life. I'm sure Cain will welcome his little cutslut back with open arms. Or at least you better hope he does. Because who the fuck would want you now?"

My jaw tightens and my nostrils flare as I fight my emotion. Before I can pull away from him, he notices and the smile on his face falters. A look of regret flashes in his eyes. Clearing his throat, he steps to my side and takes my arm—escorting me to the plane.

He passes something to the lady standing on the bottom of the stairs. Then, with a squeeze to my elbow, he turns and walks away. I don't know if it was a gesture of reassurance, apology or him just being an asshole.

"Ms. Tews, I'm Shira," the flight attendant greets. She's short. Blonde. Pretty in that little girl kind of way. She doesn't seem the least bit concerned with my appearance. Makes sense. I'm pretty sure Luke is into that BDSM shit. He probably gags Dallas all the time.

I'm ushered inside and led to the main cabin. The carpet is so soft beneath my sore feet I almost moan. Luxurious white seats, lined with the finest leather are scattered throughout the cabin along with a couch, a few tables and a mini bar. A massive T.V. is mounted over the door—viewable from anywhere you sit. This is my first time on a private jet, and I must admit—I'm not disappointed.

"Let me get these off of you." She removes my cuffs and I immediately untie the gag from around my head. It's a bandana—the same bandana I used to take off my makeup. *Fucking Pierce.*

"You got any scotch, Shira?" I ask, working my jaw and rolling my shoulders.

"Of course, Ms. Tews."

"Winter," I correct, falling into one of the seats. "Call me Winter." She doesn't comment, she just smiles and hands me a glass filled with amber liquid. Without bothering to scent it, I take a sip and nearly melt in the seat at how fine it is.

"What are the chances that you'd have my favorite single malt scotch on board?"

Shira smiles. "No chance, Winter. Pierce's request for your accommodations was quite clear." I nearly laugh. I guess I'm supposed to forgive him now. Or maybe he was hoping I'd just get drunk and forget how he treated me. "We have about thirty minutes before we take off, if you'd like to use the bathroom or take a shower."

"Shower?" This time I do laugh. "You going to let me wear your clothes, Shira?" I rake my eyes suggestively down her body. She flushes from head to toe—quickly dismissing herself.

When I walk into the massive bedroom equipped with a king sized bed and private bathroom with a walk-in shower, I realize I won't be needing Shira's clothes after all.

There are four suitcases and two garment bags sitting open on the bed—filled with everything I'll need for my trip. Shoes. Clothes. Cosmetics. I have it all. In the center of them is a single piece of paper with a simple message.

-P

JINX

"How is she?" Pierce asks, trying like hell to feign nonchalance. I smirk at his shitty attempt.

I know my brother. I know he likely said some mean shit to Winter. The kind of shit you immediately regret. Now he's calling me, on headset, while I'm thirty thousand feet in the air, uncaring that I have a fear of flying, all in hopes I'll tell him something that will ease his conscience. And of course, I do.

"Bitchy."

I really wouldn't know. I'm in the cockpit. Out of sight. The only information I get comes from Shira, the flight attendant. But even though her last update was that Winter was simply drinking—a lot, I assumed she was still a bitch when she drank. So I don't feel guilty about my answer. And the relief in his exhale is evident—which tells me I made the right decision. Not that I ever make the wrong one.

"I found a new article on the internet," he starts. My eyes roll in my head. *Here we fucking go.* "It was published by this woman who was in an abusive relationship. She calls it, *the eight steps to knowing.*"

"Pierce..."

"There was a couple I'd never considered."

"Pierce..."

"Like, *compulsion to confess. The victim begins to acquire the beliefs and values the abuser has ingrained...*" He continues to read directly from the article. I cover the speaker and lower my headset.

"Can you hear this?" I ask the pilot.

My brother's business is just that—my brother's business. I don't need some asshat I don't know hearing it. I won't take the chance that this pilot might just encourage Pierce. Give him some story about his sister, or aunt or cousin who suffered the same shit. Or possibly the name of some other website or support group.

The pilot shakes his head and points to a button on the computer board. Like I know what the fuck that means. "Don't be listenin' in on this shit," I warn, shooting him a look that promises death. He lifts his hands in the air. I about have a fucking heart attack. *I hate flying.* Before I can tell him to put his hands back on the steering wheel, or handlebar or whatever the hell that thing is, he does.

I position the headset back over my ears. Pierce is still reading. The hope in his tone pulls at my chest. As infuriating as it is to have a brother obsessed with trying to find a reasonable explanation behind his only sister's actions, it's also admirable. The man is dead set on finding a solution to a problem that can't be fixed. But I have to give him props for trying. His loyalty knows no bounds.

"Pierce," I say, a little louder this time. He finally shuts the fuck up and I quickly start talking before he can start again. "She's a con-artist. A thief. A liar. If she wanted out, she would've found a way."

"What if he threatened to kill me if she left?" He's asked the question a million times before.

"For the last time, she's not stupid. A traitor? Yes. A bitch? Yes. But she's not dumb enough to believe that a scum-sucking, piece of low-life shit like Cain would ever be capable of taking out the most powerful, protected man on the west coast."

I pause to take a breath. My anger eating away at me. Anger toward her for torturing Pierce like this. There are many little sisters who would kill to have a brother like Pierce. She doesn't deserve him.

"She made her decision a long time ago," I say, my anger controlled. "Stop letting the ghost of that girl you once knew haunt you into believing she's still somewhere inside Winter's shell."

"What if you're wrong?" he asks, and I have to refrain from telling him I'm never wrong. Especially when it comes to his selfish, manipulative little sweet pea.

"Look, in two months, we'll know for sure. She'll have every opportunity in the world to make a better life for herself. If she's smart enough to take it, then I'll admit I was wrong. But if she isn't and she ends up going back to him, then you're gonna have to find a way to let this shit go, man."

It feels wrong for me to ask him to give up on her. But fuck... he's going to wake up one day and life will have passed him by. He's already spent so much of it obsessing over this. Which is the second reason I agreed to do this—give her one final shot for Pierce's sake. The first reason being revenge.

She's been given more chances than any man who wears a patch has been given. When she left, Pierce tried giving her time to make her own decision. Realize her mistake. Remember who her family was. Where her loyalties lie. When that didn't work, he went to get her. Rolled into enemy territory, his brothers by his side—ready to go to war for one of their own. To die and to kill. And she spit in the club's face.

She stood behind Cain. Refused her brother's outstretched hand. Spoke blasphemous words about our club that were unforgivable. It was then that the club decided to cut her loose. To this day I believe if it weren't for our bi-laws, Pierce never would've eighty-sixed her. Not that I'm judging. I don't have a little sister. If I did, I'm sure I'd be doing the same thing Pierce is.

"Two months," he says, his voice powerful. Strong. Pride swells in my chest at the sound. It's the voice of Devil's Renegades President, Pierce—not her big brother. "Don't show her any courtesy. We had to earn the right to belong. She sure as fuck will too." I smile at that.

Yes...she will.

WINTER

The girl in the mirror looks like me. The old me. Not the past twenty-four hour me. Makeup done, hair styled, short dress, tattoo showing, high heel wearing me. At five foot nine, I'm tall. With heels, I'm really tall. And my height makes me feel a lot less intimidated by the crowd of people standing on the tarmac just outside the window.

I glance back at my reflection again—noticing for the first time how glassy my eyes are. After I'd showered and dressed, I still had two hours' worth of flying time. I wasn't in the mood for T.V. I hate to read. I was too anxious to sleep. So I drank. A lot. And I'm feeling it.

"I'm taking this," I tell Shira, holding up the bottle of scotch as I walk out of the bedroom and into the main cabin. "You have a comment box?" She frowns. "Like a suggestion box?"

"Oh... no ma'am. I don't believe we do."

"Well tell Dallas she needs a smoking section on this plane." I hold my hand up. "Better yet, I'll tell her. Since I'm being forced to spend the next sixty days down here." I pull a cigarette from my purse and place it between my lips. Shira looks at it nervously but doesn't comment. "Did you know that, Shira? That I'm being held against my will?"

"I don't know anything about that, Ms. Tews," she says, wringing her hands. Her eyes on the lighter in my hand.

"Winter. Not Ms. Tews. Winter."

"Winter. Yes. Um..." She points at the cigarette a second then clasps her hands together and presses her lips into a thin line. I smile, knowing she wants to tell me I can't smoke but is too worried about how I'll react to do it.

"I'm not going to light it, Shira," I say. She visibly relaxes. "And I'm going to tell Dallas what an amazing employee she has in you."

She flushes. "Thank you, Ms...I mean, Winter."

"You're welcome. Now, where's my ride?" I follow her to the open door. She stops and gestures for me to go ahead. The cool air hits me and I pause on the top step—the effects of the alcohol hitting me hard. I light a cigarette before I look up and flash my best smile.

Eight of Hattiesburg's finest Devil's are here. Waiting for me. Dressed in leather from head to toe, standing tall and proud next to their steel horses, they watch me with curious expressions as I descend the stairs. And behind them, gathered in a circle of their own, is their ol' ladies. Shooting daggers at me—the cutslut.

As I make my way toward them, my eyes lock on the man in front who wears a President patch. He looks nothing like the Luke Carmical I remember as a kid. He's a hell of a lot hotter. "What?" I ask. "No marching band?"

He smirks, lifting a brow as he surveys me from head to toe. "Winter," he greets on a nod. "You've grown up."

"And not a moment too soon," I say, surveying the crowd of men. There's a few who return my lustful look, and I commit their faces to memory. They'll be the ones to help get me out of here. Judging by the eye fucking I'm getting from the VP, it'll be sooner than I'd thought.

"Plotting already?"

I slide my gaze back to Luke whose blue eyes hold a hint of challenge. "Nah. Just checking for wedding rings." I wink at the ol' ladies who've stepped closer to hear what I have to say. "You know, despite popular belief, us cutsluts do have morals."

He laughs and shakes his head. "Look, I know you're probably tired, but tonight is the grand opening of our newest night club. Since I promised Pierce I wouldn't let you out of our sight, you're coming with us. We're gonna be busy. Distracted. But there'll be eyes on you at all times. So don't get any ideas in that pretty little head of yours."

Unable to stop myself, I look over at Dallas and smile. She glares back at me. "Don't worry, baby," I say, pulling my eyes back to Luke before adding, "I'm all yours." His eyes narrow as he studies me—his lips fighting a smile. He knows exactly what I'm doing.

The man next to Luke laughs. It's deep and throaty and sexy as hell. It's the VP. I point my finger at him and smile. "Regg, right?" He nods. His wife, Red, takes a step closer. Might as well go ahead and piss her off too while I have the opportunity. "We should do a shot later. No hands." I lick my lips and drop my eyes to his crotch. "Blowjob style."

"Did she say blowjob? That bitch said blowjob." Red's tone gets louder with every word. She starts over and Regg must recognize the sound of her heels because he straightens and drops his smile.

Red stops mid-stride when Luke lifts his hand. He didn't even have to turn to address her. His power over this club and the ol' ladies leaves me with the feeling he's going to be my biggest obstacle in my attempt to escape.

In two steps, he's towering over me. Using the same move as Pierce, he puts his finger under my chin and tilts it back until I meet his eyes. They're as blue as the ocean. And hard as a rock. "I'm not gonna have any problems out of you, am I, Winter?" His says my name like the season. Cold.

"Nope. Just trying to make friends."

"Try harder." The warning can be heard loud and clear in his tone. After six years with Cain, it's going to take a lot more than a hard look and a verbal warning to intimidate me. He sees the challenge and smirks. "Don't underestimate me, Winter. If you play this game, you'll lose. You have my word on that."

I look at the stoic faced men surrounding him. The pissed off women behind him. Then I meet his eyes with a smile. I want to tell him he shouldn't gamble something as important as his word. Instead, I take a sip of my scotch and tell him, "Whatever you say, boss."

———

IT'S OBVIOUS THE OL' ladies are pissed at me after my show on the tarmac. So I'm not at all surprised to find myself riding alone in the backseat of a truck, driven by a man old enough to be my grandfather, just so they won't have to be next to me. Actually, I find it funny as hell. Especially when we arrive at the club thirty minutes later and I'm the only woman in the group not freezing her ass off.

It seems the women had no intentions of riding bitch tonight. After meeting me though, they decided they'd rather risk frost bite than be in an enclosed space with the infamous west coast cutslut. Unfortunately, they didn't think to take their purses with them. And I'm three hundred dollars, two tubes of lipgloss and a pack of gum richer than I was when I got here.

The Country Tavern is packed. I must say I'm impressed with these dirty south Devil's and their business. With wood floors and galvanized metal ceilings, it looks like a western bar. But the young crowd and pop music playing on the speakers proves that you can't always judge a book by its cover.

I'm escorted by Luke to the bar and seated in a less crowded area. "Remember, Winter. I have eyes everywhere," he warns, practically daring me to do something stupid. I offer him an indifferent shrug. He glares at me a moment longer before telling the young patch holder behind me, "Watch her."

Placing my elbows on the bar, I lean my back against it facing the crowd—my legs crossed forcing everyone that passes to walk around me. Looking over at the man to my left, I see him huddled over his drink. He's looking down, his face hidden from view. The flat-bibbed hat he wears pulled low over his eyes. He's dressed in a black sweater that molds to his muscular arms. Dark jeans that sit low on his hips— giving me a sneak peak of the boxers beneath. But what I find most attractive is the wallet that's visible from the front pocket of his jacket hanging on the back of his chair.

"What you sippin' on, good lookin'?" I ask, using my best southern accent. Slowly, the man turns his head to look at me. I still at what I see.

Son of a bitch.

He is undeniably the sexiest fucking creature I've ever seen in my life. A few days' worth of scruff on his tan jaw. Full lips accentuated by a deep philtrum. A perfectly symmetrical nose. And just below his flat-bibbed hat sits two silver orbs framed in long, black lashes. They seem to glow in the neon light. As if they belong to an immortal, supernatural creature rather than a living human. They're invigorating. Paralyzing. A little terrifying. Exotic, yet strangely familiar.

"Do I know you from somewhere?"

He shakes he head as he studies me with a heated intensity. Taking his time to examine every inch of my body from head to toe before meeting my eyes. Then he straightens in his seat and slides a glass down the bar. I catch it in my hand—the smoky scent hitting my senses and immediately making my mouth water.

I watch the man with suspicion as I take a tentative sip. It's delicious. Better than what I usually prefer. "I'm Winter, by the way."

"I know," he says, causing the hair on the back of my neck to stand up. His eyes twinkle at my obvious uneasiness. "I was listening when that guy walked you over here."

I let out a breath of relief and smile. "How very stalkerish of you." I take another sip, still feeling a strange sense of déjà vu. "Can I ask you a question?"

"You just did," he says, no trace of humor on his face. He just stares back at me with those striking, vampire eyes.

"It's a serious question."

"They always are."

I swallow, a little nervous about engaging in conversation with this guy. But his wallet sitting only inches from me is enough encouragement for me to follow through my attempt to lighten the mood.

"Did it hurt?" I ask, as serious as I possibly can. His lips twitch as if he's fighting a smile. I find it attractive on him. Even more than that brooding expression he wears so well.

"You mean when I fell from heaven?" I nod, my gaze zeroed in on his mouth. "No." *Damn he has pretty teeth.* "I can fly." I grin back at him.

"I bet you can."

His eyes crinkle a little at the corners in curiosity. "So what kinda name is Winter?"

"What kinda name is Jinxton?" I fire back, pulling a cigarette from my purse.

"I didn't tell you my name."

I wink. "It's on your credit card."

He looks down at the card the bartender laid in front of him only seconds ago. Smirking, he shakes his head. Then, as he lifts the glass to his lips, he breathes out a disbelieving laugh. "How very stalkerish of you." He takes a pull then adds, "Jinx. Just Jinx."

Sliding over, I move to the stool next to him. He turns in his chair, putting his wallet further out of reach. But the view of his chest is worth it. The man is huge. And he doesn't have to be naked for me to know that he's chiseled beneath his clothes.

The sudden flick of a lighter snaps my attention and I lean in for him to light my cigarette. When the scent of him is more pleasing that that of scotch, I decide it's time to seal this deal. Get out of here, get off on him then get the hell away from Hattiesburg, riding in his car with his money. He might be gorgeous, but all men think with their dick. Even the pretty ones.

"You know, *Just* Jinx, if I didn't have deputy dog breathing down my neck, maybe me and you could go somewhere a little quieter."

He glances over my shoulder at the patch holder. "And what are we gonna do when we get there?" he asks, lazily dragging his eyes back to me.

"You want to hear me say it, or are you just that innocent?" I tease, wanting to touch him but refraining.

His gaze sweeps my body again—pausing on my legs. He looks at me from beneath his lashes. "You a whore or somethin?"

I shrug. "Or somethin."

Studying me a little longer, he finishes off the scotch. Loud voices draw my attention and I notice a large group of rowdy college guys heading our way. As they pass, Jinx sticks his foot out tripping one near the end of the line. Bodies are shoved, drinks are spilled and tempers flare as the finger pointing begins.

Moments later, other arguments within the group start. Then people around us join in. The tension is thick. In a matter of seconds, someone is going to do something very stupid.

Jinx shoots a hard glare to the patch holder behind me. "You gonna do somethin' about this shit or you want me to?" At the question, the patch holder starts telling the men to break it up. I'm fighting a smile when Jinx turns his attention back to me.

"Please tell me that wasn't your grand plan to get me out of here." I laugh, shaking my head as the crowd starts to break up. If he was trying to create a diversion, it obviously didn't work. When he smiles back at me, my world rocks a little.

"No sweetheart, this is."

He stands suddenly—turning his shoulder into an innocent bystander and sending him flying into the patch holder's back. One punch is all it takes for the fight to turn into an all-out barroom brawl.

Grabbing my hand in his, Jinx pulls me from my seat. He tucks me close to his side as he barrels through the crowd that's gathered to witness the fight. Behind us glass is shattering, people yelling, cheering, screaming. I keep my head down—not wanting to get hit with a flying beer bottle or worse.

Seconds later, he's pulling me outside into the cold, night air. When the door slams behind us, the sounds become almost muted—making me aware of how hard I'm breathing. It could be adrenaline. Or fear. Or Jinx...

Letting go of my hand, he shoves his own in his jean pocket. Now that he's standing at full height, I'm surprised to find I'm nearly as tall as him—the top of my head coming to his chin. But what he lacks in height, he makes up for in width. He's much bigger than I'd thought. Wide across his shoulders. Broad and hard and a little scary.

Pulling his key from his pocket, he points it toward the back of the lot. A shiny black Escalade with blacked out windows and custom chrome rims purrs to life. I'm nearly bouncing on my toes at my stroke of good luck. If he rides in something like this, I bet that wallet of his is loaded.

"Backseat," he says, pointing to the passenger side as he rounds the hood of the car. He doesn't open the door for me, which I find I very much appreciate.

For years men have done that. Not because they were chivalrous, only because they were afraid to leave me alone for two seconds. For me, this is a taste of freedom. And I can't help but smile when I realize very soon I won't just be tasting it, I'll be devouring it.

WINTER

"That's a happy smile."

I jerk my head up at Jinx who sits next to me in the backseat. The intensity in his gray eyes as he watches me is as flattering as it is unnerving. It's like he's looking inside me.

"I wasn't aware there was another kind of smile."

He averts his gaze—snapping out of whatever trance he was just in. Something tells me he didn't mean to say those words out loud. My curiosity is peaked. But I don't have time for questions. I need to move this along. Luke will no doubt be searching for me very soon.

Sliding across the cool leather seat, I throw my leg over his and straddle his waist. My hands grip his shoulders for support—squeezing him hard. He's like granite. Usually, I'm not turned on by something as simple as touching another man. But there's something about this one that ignites a fire inside me.

My position is inviting. My dress riding high on my thighs. Breasts inches from his mouth. Pussy hot against his crotch. I'm readily available and expect him to fist my hair. Grab my hips. My breasts. Instead, he lays those big hands on my thighs in the most informal manner possible.

"Tell me what you want," I whisper, glancing up at him with that same sultry expression I use on Cain's clients. Shadows dance across his face. The darkness making his eyes shine even brighter. I try to read them like he so easily reads mine, but I only get a blank look in return. He's completely guarded.

Licking my lips, I drag my finger along his jaw—noting how square and hard it is beneath my touch. "Know what I want?" I ask, tracing his lips with my nail. *These lips...I feel like I know them.* "I want some music. Something sexy."

He reaches around me, bringing him closer to my face. The scent of his breath fills my nostrils. It smells like cologne and scotch. Scrumptious. He holds my gaze as he grabs a small remote before leaning back once again. With a push of a few buttons, Ty Dolla $ign's *Or Nah* sounds from the speakers. I lift my eyebrow in amusement.

"How fitting. So I guess you want to cut the small talk, huh?" He responds by turning up the volume until the bass hits hard enough to vibrate the windows. My eyes fall to his lips and I lean in slowly, seeing if he'll meet me the rest of the way. When he doesn't, I smile. Then my mouth is on his.

You wouldn't know the man kissing me back is the same man who was a statue only moments ago. Though his hands and body don't move, his lips melt beneath mine. He moves his mouth effortlessly, his tongue soft as satin when it strokes lazily against mine. There's something so erogenous about it, I moan. It's not forced, fake or for show. It's an involuntary reaction to the hottest fucking kiss I've ever had.

My fingers curl around his shirt. His lay lifeless on my thighs. My hips grind against him. He remains still beneath me. My chest presses against his—begging. Pleading for just a single touch. But there's no reaction from him. As if I'm not affecting him at all. It's infuriating. I want more. I want him to give it to me. Obviously, he wants me to take it.

I'm so absorbed in the feeling of his mouth fucking my mouth, I almost forget why I'm here. But as I tighten my thighs around him, I feel something hard against my knee. Dragging my hands down his chest, his stomach, the waist band of his jeans, I easily slide the key from his pocket and tuck it into my palm.

Seizing my wrists in his hands, he pulls his mouth from mine. I stare back at him frozen. Fear prickles my spine at the look in his silver eyes. It's not cold or hard. Just knowing. I've been caught.

Before I can start spitting excuses, he lifts my arms until my hands brush across the ceiling. Then, lazily, torturously slow, he drags the backs of his fingers down my arms. The sides of my breasts. My ribs. Over my hips. The tops of my thighs. Beneath my dress. He lifts it slowly, exposing the cheeks of my ass. I shiver beneath his touch—not out of fear. Out of pure ecstasy.

Gripping my waist, he flips me so I'm on my back. My arms over my head. His big body between my legs. Then he's kissing me again. Drawing circles on my stomach with his thumbs. His cock thick and hard inside his jeans—sending a surge of pleasure through me every time he rocks his pelvis against mine.

Fingers loop through the thin lace of my panties. He breaks the kiss to lean back and drag them down my legs. His eyes following their path. After freeing me from them, he pushes my knees apart with his hands. The scorching heat from my pussy alone fogs the windows.

I want his face there. His cock. What I get is his finger—eventually. He takes his time dragging it down my leg. Stopping sometimes to draw something. He waits until I'm writhing beneath him. On the verge of begging. I'd grab him and pull him to me if I knew I could do it without dropping his key.

With a touch as soft as a feather, he brushes his finger over my clit. My back bows. Throwing my head back, I squeeze my eyes shut—anticipating another stroke of his finger. When it doesn't come, I glance up at him. He stares back at me with that same patient, cool look he always wears.

"Touch me," I mouth, my nails digging into my palms. My heels burrowed into the expensive leather seats. A ghost of a smile touches his lips when he rubs his thumb against the inside of my leg with his other hand. I almost growl.

"If you want me to touch you, you're gonna have to be more specific than that," he says, his voice barely carrying over the music.

How the hell did I let this guy get me so worked up? When have I ever been so turned on, I was more worried about coming than anything else? Not just anything, but escape. Freedom. Important shit.

Swallowing hard, I try to rein in my desire. But the need is almost haunting. I need release like I need to breathe. And for some reason, I need it from him.

"Touch my pussy," I manage in a voice that sounds nothing like me. But I don't care. He's touching me. I'd have sung my request if that's what he required.

He traces the lips of my pussy with the tip of his finger. Then he sinks one thick finger inside me—just to the knuckle before pulling it out and spreading the wetness across my lips. I squirm. Shake. Can barely breathe. Waiting. Anticipating the touch I know will send me over the edge.

Every few strokes of his finger, he grazes my clit with his knuckles. The process is maddening—lips, finger, lips, clit. I'm so close. At this point, he could blow on my clit and I'd explode.

He's teased me and worked me up so much, a sheen of perspiration covers my entire body. The once cool leather is now slick beneath me. Wet with my arousal. My sweat. This—the buildup—is the best part. When he does let me come, it'll likely shatter me. And it'll be worth it.

I'm lost. So absorbed in the thought of my imminent orgasm, it takes me a moment to realize he's no longer touching me. I open my eyes and through the haze, I find he's no longer kneeling before me either. He's sitting beside me. And someone is knocking on the window.

"We've got company," Jinx says, matter-of-fact. His tone doesn't possess the slightest hint of anger or annoyance. He's not even slightly winded. Meanwhile, I'm panting. Gasping for air. Anger rising inside me. Whoever is on the other side of this glass is going to die. I'm going to kill them with my bare hands.

Hands.

I straighten, looking at Jinx out of the corner of my eye. He's focused on something in his lap. Slowly, so not to draw attention to myself, I lower my arms to my side. My hands tingle from me fisting them for so long. When I open them, there's nothing there.

"If you're looking for my key, it's behind the seat." He turns his head toward me. "That's where you dropped it." My expression matches his—blank. Stoic. I'm speechless. Appalled. Disappointed in myself. More so in him. But looking at me, you wouldn't know any of those things. Looking at him, you'd know he doesn't give a shit what I'm feeling.

He holds out his hand. Between his fingers is a crisp, folded hundred-dollar bill.

"What's that for?" I ask, glancing between the money and him.

"It's your payment. You are a whore... or somethin', right?"

A sense of something foreign washes over me.

Shame.

I am a whore. A *cutslut*. I sleep with people for money. Revenge. Respect. But it's never been my decision. I've always done what I had to do to stay alive. To survive Cain's wrath. This time somehow felt different. Clearly, it wasn't. My reputation has preceded me.

Another rap on the window has me quickly straightening my dress. I avoid Jinx's stare and the money he still holds in his fingers as I blink back tears and search for my panties. Before I can locate them, the door opens and Luke's face appears. He looks at me a moment before glaring over at Jinx. Something unspoken is passed through the air between them, but it only lasts a second.

With a hand at my back, Luke ushers me toward his truck. This time, instead of an old man riding behind the wheel, it's Dallas. Next to her sits Red. Climbing in the back seat, I slide to the middle, expecting Luke to follow me. But the door closes behind me and he says something to Dallas before walking off toward his bike.

What starts as a low rumble of pipes soon turns into a loud, reverberating noise that shakes the windows of the truck. We pull in behind the pack and out of the parking lot. When I see we're heading through town on a busy weekend night, I realize this is the perfect time for me to get away.

I could jump out and run when we're stopped at one of the many traffic lights lining the street in front of us. I could trick Red and Dallas into stopping somewhere. Hell, I could probably just ask and they'd willingly let me go.

But I'm too tired to plan. Too tired to run. My chest is tight. My eyes burn. I feel...low. The cause could be a number of things. Witnessing Jimmy's murder. Cain's rage. Pierce's hateful words. Travelling halfway across the country against my will. The sexual tension thrumming through my body. Or maybe just my shitty day in general.

I never thought I'd be the kind of girl who just gave up. Missed out on a perfect opportunity. Took advantage of a situation. I guess enough really is enough. Eventually, everyone breaks. I think I'm crumbling.

WINTER

Though the ride to the clubhouse is silent and completely uneventful, it's just not in the cards for me to have peace. Seems every time I get a taste of reprieve, it's snatched from me before I can savor the flavor.

Everywhere I turn, there's someone there to shatter what's left of me. Some job that needs to be done. Some bad news waiting to be heard. In this case, it's the familiar SUV that pulls in next to us that reminds me of why my life is shit.

"What's he doing here?" I ask, my eyes focused on Jinx as he rounds the hood of his car. He glances over his shoulder at me and smirks before continuing his walk to the clubhouse.

Red turns in her seat and shoots me a confused look. "Who Jinx?"

My blood runs cold. "You know him?"

"...Yes..." she says cautiously. "I assume you did too...considering." She smiles at that. Obviously pleased with my discomfort that's slowly simmering to a boiling rage. "Don't worry." She winks. "He's not married or anything."

"I don't give a shit if he's married, Red," I spit. "What's he doing here...at the Devil's Renegade's clubhouse?"

"Well *Winter,*" she drawls, as if my name tastes like sweaty balls.

"He's a Devil. Why wouldn't he be here?" Emotions guarded, I just stare back at her until she continues. "To be so damn clever, you sure are stupid." Rolling her eyes, she moves to get out but my hand on her shoulder stops her.

"How about you enlighten me on what the fuck is going on." She drops her eyes to my hand before looking back over her shoulder at me. I smile. "You know you want to. So go ahead. Because this may be the only opportunity you get to damage me."

I know Red's not an evil person. She doesn't want to break me. Not because she cares. It's just not who she is. But she owes me one.

"You stole from him. He's here to collect. Can't say I blame him."

Swallowing hard, I force out the question I really don't want to know the answer to. "Vegas. My kidnapping. He plan that shit?"

Her brow lifts. "What you think?"

Without giving her a response, I open the door and clamber out. My heels sink in the thick grass with every step. Even though it's freezing outside, my entire body feels like it's on fire. I'm beyond angry. I'm livid. And when I push through the door of the clubhouse, all I see is red.

Jinx is sitting with his back to the bar, facing the room. His cut is over his shoulders. A glass of whiskey in his left hand. My fucking panties dangling from the index finger on his right. His hat is pulled low over his eyes. And I couldn't be more convinced that he was the man in the ski mask if he was wearing it in this moment.

The bastard.

He took me.

Gagged me.

I pulled a gun on him.

He kissed my hand.

My lips.

He played me.

Me.

Winter Tews.

And I don't get played.

He's mid conversation when I approach so he doesn't see me. Or my hand as it cuts through the air and lands in a loud, satisfying smack across the left side of his face. The blow nearly knocks him off his stool. My hand throbs in response, but it's well worth it.

"You son of a bitch," I growl, ignoring the tiny prick of fear in my spine as he slowly turns his head to face me. The look he wears might be the most terrifying thing some people have seen, but I've lived with a monster for years. I'm not easily rattled.

"That shit's gettin' old, sweetheart," he says, a hint of a warning in his low tone. Just as I'd predicted, he's the masked man. Looking at him now, I wonder how in the hell I didn't see it before.

"If you're that hard up for cash, I'll get you the money. You didn't have to fucking kidnap me and send me halfway across the country over a measly three hundred grand," I seethe. He just shakes his head.

"It's not about the money. You know that." He's right. I know this isn't about money. It's about principal. Someone stole from him. A woman who was put out bad. If I were a man, I'd already be dead.

Steeling my spine, I glare at him. "Let me make something perfectly clear now that I have everyone's attention." I wave my hand around the room, motioning to the crowd that's gathered around us for the show. "I'm leaving."

Leaning back, he studies me with a curious expression. "You sure about that? Cause the way I see it, you have nowhere to go. That is unless you run back to Cain. And I guarantee you, you're better off with me than you are with him."

"Don't," I warn, pointing my finger at him. "Don't you dare tell me what's best for me. You don't know anything about me."

"I know you're not leaving."

I shoot him a sardonic smile and throw his words back in his face. "You sure about that?" He gives me a confident look that says he accepts my challenge. I wonder if he'll be as cocky about accepting defeat.

"You know," I laugh, turning to face the room. "They say it takes a village to raise a child. Seems you learned something from that ancient proverb. Considering it takes every fucking one of you to solve a problem. I steal from one and I find myself face to face with an entire chapter."

I cut my eyes to Jinx then drop them to his cut. "Cut one and we all bleed. I am my brother's keeper." Smirking, I lift my gaze and shake my head. "It's obvious you all live by those patches. But doesn't it get old? Constantly having someone else handle your problems? I know after years of living with Pierce, I got tired of it."

"Seems to me you didn't get enough of it," Dallas calls out from across the room. "Have you already forgotten whose team you've been on for six years? Or was that just a rumor?"

If this were my family, I might be proud to call such a ballsy woman my sister. But these people aren't family. She's not my sister. And she sure as shit wouldn't be that ballsy if it she didn't have that army standing behind her.

I shoot her my best smile. "Funny you should bring up rumors. I've heard a few myself. And now I have to question who is worse. Me? A simple cutslut who took a little cash. Or you? A woman who has murdered not one but five men."

"Shut up," Jinx warns. He's not yelling, but he's not exactly whispering either.

I ignore him and keep my eyes on Dallas. At just over five feet tall, you wouldn't think the multi-millionaire beauty was capable of any heinous crime. Word on the street says otherwise.

"How about you?" I move my finger to Red—ex-stripper. Ex-junkie. Ex-cokewhore. She bristles but remains silent. "Know where I can get any good heroin?"

"I won't tell you again." This time, Jinx's voice is lower. Deadly. I should heed the warning. I don't.

"Let's not forget you, Delilah." I turn my attention to the damaged girl who was once a whore, but now proudly wears a Property patch. *Traitor.* "You went from being a clubwhore who was a pain-slut, to a patch holder's submissive. How's that working out?" Delilah's smile suggests that nothing I've said bothers her. Good thing I'm not finished. "Oh...by the way, how's your brother?"

The last thing I see is her fearful, wide eyes staring back at me before Jinx dips and crashes into my abdomen. I'm lifted and thrown over his shoulder so fast, it takes my breath. When I finally catch it, I rain my fists down on his back and kick my legs against his stomach—

hoping to land a blow to his balls. I fight hard, but he doesn't slow his stride as he carries me down a hallway.

"Let me go!" I scream, calling him every nasty name I can think of. Just when my creativity starts to run out, I'm flipping through the air. Then I'm on my back on a bed. Jinx's big body straddles my waist. My wrists are seized in one big hand while he pins me to the mattress.

Gripping the sheet in his free hand, he pulls it to his mouth and rips it with his teeth. I still beneath him. *Maybe the son of a bitch is a vampire.* But when he starts to tie my hands with the scrap of material, I resume my struggle. It's pointless, but I refuse to give in.

I manage to kick him hard enough to make him grunt. He only presses his weight further down on me while he continues to tie my hands. Just as I feel the fabric tighten around my wrists, I pull hard against it. But not only is this bastard a master with his teeth, he's also good with knots. And the harder I pull, the tighter my binds become.

Quicker than I hope, I become exhausted from my fight. Instantly I'm aware that his knee is between my knees. The rough fabric of his jeans pressing against the heat of my pussy. I hate how good it feels. How my body responds. How much he's aware. How intensely he looks at me. How I can't hold his stare because my eyes keep moving from his to those fully, parted lips.

I remember how he kissed me.

How good it felt.

How bad I wanted it then...

...How much more I want it now.

JINX

This bitch is fucking with my head.

It started tonight when she got in the backseat of my car. The expression she wore threw me for a loop. Twisted me the fuck up and had me rethinking my entire plan. In that moment, I was ready to call Pierce and tell him I was out. All because she was happy.

Fucking happy.

When she smiled, it wasn't guarded or forced. It was genuine. Beautiful. And because I was so affected by it, it infuriated the fuck out of me.

When she showed up at the bar, she looked like the cutslut I knew. The traitor. The thief. The lover of my enemy. The girl I've been watching for years. When I asked if she was a whore and she didn't deny it, that hate that'd been simmering during our entire conversation surfaced.

It was almost too easy to get her to leave with me. I had it all planned out. I was going to fuck her. Use her. Take another piece of what she owed me. Then she smiled that happy fucking smile and I was floored.

Then it got worse. I made her feel cheap. Like the whore she didn't deny being. She looked conflicted. Shameful. Sad. Most of all, she didn't look happy. That bothered the piss out of me. I wanted to take it back. It was too late. The damage was done. Her happiness was gone.

But she wasn't the only one conflicted. I was one confused mother-fucker watching her walk away. For years I'd been anticipating how good it would feel to break her. Tonight, I finally got the opportunity to take something worthwhile from Winter Tews—her happiness. But instead of feeling good, I felt like shit.

My whirlwind of emotions sent me crashing to the earth and snapped me back to reality when the brazen little bitch walked through the door of the clubhouse. Put her hands on me. Opened her mouth and said shit she had no business saying. Once again, I was reminded of why I hate her. And it was time to remind her of it too.

But now here we are. Me on top of her. Her tied up beneath me. Glaring at each other. Seething with rage. Filling the air with our loathing. And all I can think is, damn I shouldn't want to kiss her crazy *or* fuck her hard. But damn I want to kiss her crazy *and* fuck her hard.

Someone like her isn't supposed to feel this goddamn good under me. Someone who intentionally hurt my family. Disrespected them. Said shit to their face that should've never been said out loud. No. This girl isn't supposed to make me feel anything. But she does.

I want her. Worse than I ever wanted any woman. Not to claim. Not to cuddle. Not to hold and pet and buy flowers and shit for. I just want to fuck her. Bury myself in the same pussy so many others have. Because I know when I fuck her, it'll be different.

That uncertainty in her eyes tells me she's never had a real man between her legs. Whatever clients, club brothers, gang bangers and pencil dicks she's used to riding don't quite measure up. She can control them. But not me. She knows it. It scares the fuck out of her. And turns me on even more.

My cock swells and her eyes narrow when she feels it press against her pussy. I bite back my growl when the heat there nearly scorches me. Son of a bitch she's hot. The only barrier between us is my jeans. Her panties are tucked into the pocket of my cut.

"I fucking hate you," she hisses, her chest heaving.

I give her a cold smile. "I fucking hate you too, sweetheart."

Then I'm kissing her. Angry. Hungry. Greedy...Crazy. Capturing what little breath she has. Keeping her powerless. Pressing my weight further into her so she's defenseless against my strength. Not that it's necessary. She yielded to me at *sweetheart.*

I check her wrists—making sure they're secure before I slide my hands down her arms to her chest. Then I'm fisting her dress. Ripping the fancy fucking material and exposing those big, fake tits I probably paid for. If I did, she can keep the money. I can't think of anything it would've better been spent on.

I drink in those pretty, perfectly round globes with light brown nipples and can't resist dropping my mouth to them. Sucking. Biting. Licking. Ravaging. Pissed because I want them. Pissed because she likes that I do. Pissed because I know if her tits have the power to turn me on this much, her pussy will be my undoing.

She moans. Throws her head back. Offers her chest to me. I press my knee further between her legs. Her cunt is wet—soaking through the thick denim of my jeans. She groans and tries to lift her hips. I shift so her legs are free and she immediately wraps them around my waist and pulls me further into her.

"If you want it, sweetheart," I say, kissing my way to her neck. "You gotta beg for it."

"Never," she breathes, defiant as ever. Turning her head and giving me better access to her throat. I smile against it.

I lick my way to her ear and whisper, "Beg."

She jerks her head away from me and I capture her mouth—absorbing her grunts of frustration. She finds my bottom lip and clamps it between her teeth. I meet her eyes and they're on fire. So are mine. So is my fucking lip. She bites harder and I growl—thrusting my hips in warning. Her entire body tightens when the movement strokes against her swollen, sensitive clit. But thankfully, her mouth falls slack and releases my lip.

I kiss her again—undeterred by her biting. Proving it's going to take more than a little nibble to scare me.

My fingers work the button of my jeans. Her heels are at my waist —impatiently shoving away the fabric that separates us. I break our kiss just long enough to tear a condom wrapper open, then she's soothing my swollen lip with her tongue. I'm punishing her with mine.

Shoving her dress up her succulent thighs to her waist, I get another glimpse of that pretty, pink pussy when she opens her legs wide in invitation. When I fingered her tonight, I was surprised at how tight she was. So I steel my resolve and prepare for how snug her little cunt is going to feel around my cock.

I line up the head of my dick with her slick pussy. When just the tip slips inside her, I have to fight against the pull as she squeezes around me. Trying to force me deeper. *Patience, sweetheart.*

Patience, Jinx—you over eager fucker.

"I hope you like it hard," I growl out, waiting for the moment her hips lift again in reply. When they do, I impale her.

Her mouth falls open wide in a silent cry. Her breath stuck in her throat. Eyes wide in shock. It's a struggle to keep from mirroring her expressions. I knew she was tight, but damn. And my cock is big, but it's not *that* damn big. Especially for a woman who fucks for a living.

I pull back, then plunge deep inside her again. My balls immediately draw up tight—heavy and throbbing as they slap against her. I keep my grip on her waist firm to hold her still as I thrust again. And again. It's rough. Merciless. And motherfucker it feels good. I can't get enough. So I drive harder—pulling her to me as I do. Surging impossibly deeper.

When her face pinches in pain, I still. Her eyes are squeezed shut. Her body wound tight. Stiff with tension but slowly relaxing as the pain subsides and is replaced with pleasure. But, I think I've hurt her. And for some fucking reason, that does *not* sit well with me.

This was supposed to be like it always is with a whore. No need for restraint. No reason to hold back. It's the best and worst thing about being with a loose woman.

But Winter isn't like other whores. Actually, I feel like a tool even referring to her as one. Judging by the vice-like grip she has on my cock, she may very well not be or have ever been a whore. It's either that or every man in Vegas has a tiny dick.

"Look at me," I tell her, my tone softer than I expected. Probably because, even though it's no longer there, that pinch of pain that was etched on her face still flashes in my head.

When those pretty green eyes flutter open, they're clouded in pleasure. Fucking bliss. Like she's never been this full. Felt this stretched. Like she never anticipated how much greater than expected the sensation would be. And like what she's feeling now was well worth whatever discomfort she suffered.

My cock thickens and now it's me who's feeling the discomfort.

I'm still buried to the hilt inside her. My pulse throbbing in my shaft. Her arms are stretched tight above her head. Her pulse likely throbbing in her fingertips. I contemplate freeing her so I can feel her hands on me. Her nails clawing at my back. But I decide to keep her tied and trapped beneath me. Mostly because I don't trust what she might do to me when I'm coming hard and have my guard down.

One hand on the head board, the other beside her head, I lean over her and rock my hips. Pulling and pushing a few inches out and in. She shivers with anticipation. Tightens her legs at my waist and stabs at my skin with her heels. Pleads in moans. Wanting more. Impatient. Unwilling to wait until I'm sure she can handle me—all of me.

"Lift your hips."

She instantly obeys. I ease further into her—the head of my cock sliding over that satiny, sweet spot hidden deep inside her fiery cunt. She throws her head back on a breath of pleasure—exposing her soft, feminine neck.

I want to wrap my hand around it. Squeeze. Control her breathing. Witness her eyes water. Redden. Push her to the point of panic and release her at the perfect time. Then watch as she experiences the high while she comes around me. But this close, I can make out a few fading bruises left behind by some other motherfucker's hands and decide against it.

My fingers curl tight around the wooden headboard. Both from anger at seeing the bruises and control over my desire to give her something to make her forget them.

I move inside her—slow at first. Working up a steady rhythm. Then I move a little faster. Teasing her spot. Then I pump a little harder. I shift my weight to my knees and move my hand from beside her face to her clit. Then I drive a little deeper.

When the pad of my thumb circles her clit, she melts beneath me. And I start fucking her just as fiercely and forcefully as I'd originally planned. Punishing and praising her with my cock that feels scorched from the heat of her wet pussy. In only three strokes, I'm witnessing the most erotic, rewarding, absolutely fucking beautiful thing in my life.

Her coming.

Maybe it's because I've never much paid attention to a woman's face when she came. Most of the women I fuck end up on their knees in my favorite position by the time they find their release. Selfishly, I'm too busy searching for my own to care too much about how they're affected by their orgasm. Whatever the reason, Winter Tews makes me wish I'd have paid more attention—although I doubt it would have been as sexy as this.

Her back is arched. Hips high. Head back. Brows creased. Mouth parted. A screaming cry escaping from between those pouty lips. It's not guttural or throaty. Not screeching or annoying. Definitely not fake and most definitely not forced. It's an involuntary, breathy, sweet as a box full of motherfucking kittens sound of pure ecstasy.

But the best part is her eyes.

They're open.

Wide.

Centered. On. Me.

A thin line of green circling dilated, black orbs that seem misty and faraway. Lost in some unknown abyss of pleasure. Fuck if I don't want to go there too.

I explode inside her—splintering the wood beneath my grip and biting my cheek to contain my roar. It ends up rumbling through my chest and sounding like a growl as my release powers through me. Temporarily weakening me. Draining me. Demanding every fucking ounce of my will power to keep from collapsing on top of her.

Her pussy still clenches and quivers around me. Awakening my dick that was just starting to soften inside her. Goosebumps cover her skin that's flushed in a pretty shade of red. All but her hands that have paled from the lack of blood flow.

Two breaths later, I pull out of her just as hard as I was when I went in. Not even the loss of heat can tame my erection. It's a struggle just to peel the condom off that's suctioned to me. It's a fucking mess too. You'd think I haven't fucked in years.

I shove my cock inside my jeans, pull my knife from my pocket and cut her hands free. She whimpers a little—flexing her fingers as she curls on her side. Her dress still around her waist. I pull off her shoes, toss a blanket over her and quietly leave.

In the hall, I close my eyes and take a breath. Without the scent of her sweetness, the sight of her perfect tits or the feel of that snug cunt of hers squeezing my cock, I can think straight. When I do, I wish I hadn't. Because thinking straight leads to only one thought.

What. In the motherfuck. Have. I. done.

WINTER

I wake up in the same position I fell asleep in. It doesn't take me long to remember where I am or how I got here. The events of yesterday flood my mind and immediately put me in a shit mood.

Swinging my legs over the side of the bed, I start to stand and become aware of every ache in and outside my body. Then I'm reminded of everything that happened last night. In this room. This bed.

I got fucked.

Royally.

Perfectly.

I don't think I've ever come so hard.

Even now, my body hums at the thought of him giving me that release I so desperately needed. I can still see him hovering over me. Intimidating. Dark. Dangerous. That leather vest covered in dirty patches only adding to his appeal.

He looked like he wanted to hurt me.

And he did.

When he speared me with no warning, I'd feared that what was happening between us wasn't lustful desire. I thought maybe it was him intentionally hurting me because he got off on my pain. But then he'd stopped. A fleeting look of regret in his eyes.

My chest warms when I think of how softly he spoke. He didn't ask me if I was okay or if he was hurting me. He simply said, "Look at me." I did. And there, in my eyes, he found the signal he was looking for.

I want to slap myself when I nearly sigh. There was nothing romantic or sweet about last night. So he's a good lay...big deal. Doesn't make him any more likeable. Or tolerable. Or smarter.

The dumbass should've known fucking me with that monstrosity of a cock he carries in his pants wasn't going to be like throwing a hotdog down a hallway. It's not like my pussy comes with a *one size fits all* label.

My shit mood is back now. Taking in my surroundings doesn't help lighten it either.

The room I'm in is small and very typical of a clubhouse bedroom. Plain walls. A bed. Dresser. Closet. A small bathroom. *No fucking towels....*

As much as I'd love a shower—even be willing to air dry for one—I settle for splashing some water on my face. Because not only are there not any towels, but my luggage isn't here either. Which means I have to settle for rinsing my mouth out because I don't have a toothbrush.

My now crumpled dress reveals more than it covers—thanks to Jinx and his mighty hands—so I remove it and search the drawers and closet for something else. They both turn up empty but I find a black button down shirt on the bathroom counter. Slipping it over my head, I inhale the thick cotton and an involuntary shiver runs up my spine.

It smells like Jinx.

Like smoke and whiskey and cologne. It doesn't appear dirty, but there's no doubt that he's worn this recently. I ignore that weird warm and fuzzy feeling his shirt gives me and tiptoe silently into the hall.

It's eerily quiet here. A surge of excitement bursts through me at the possibility that maybe somebody fucked up and left me alone. It quickly dies when I see Jinx sitting at a table to my left.

He's leaned back in his chair. Phone in hand. He wears a dark hoodie. Faded jeans. That same hat sits backwards on his head as he studies whatever's on his phone intensely. There's a steaming plate of food in front of him along with a cup of coffee. My mouth waters at the sight of both him and the food.

He looks up at me slowly, almost as if he can sense my presence. I try to read his eyes as I make my way over, but he's completely impassive. Then he seems to notice what I'm wearing and his gaze narrows a little.

"That's my shirt," he says, his tone bored as he watches me take the seat across from him.

"Good morning to you too, Captain Obvious." I shoot him a grin before looking around the room. "Where is everyone?"

"They left. They don't like you."

Unable to refrain, I laugh. It's as funny as it is relieving. *One chapter down, one patch holder to go.* "This for me?" Without waiting for a response, I slide his plate over to me and start eating—shoveling eggs into my mouth faster than any lady would.

The food is delicious. The eggs fluffy. Bacon crisp. Toast still warm and slathered in my favorite jelly. After I've had several bites of each, I reach for his coffee. He doesn't protest when I grab it, he only gives me a blank stare.

"Not a morning person?" I tease, scooping another big bite of eggs on my fork.

"Don't ever wear my clothes again."

"I thought guys loved the look of a woman in their shirt," I say around a mouthful of food. "Especially the morning after sex." I wiggle my eyebrows at him.

"About that," he starts, but I cut him off.

"Wait. Is this where you tell me last night was a mistake and it'll never happen again?" I take a sip of coffee and wait for his response. When I don't get one, I shrug. "Whatever makes you feel better, but you know as well as I do that it will happen again... And again... And again. Until you fall desperately in love with me.

"Then you'll start to regret holding me against my will. You'll slip up. I'll get away. And you'll spend the rest of your life wondering what might've been. Meanwhile I'll be sipping mojitos somewhere in the Caribbean. Waiting for that fated day when I see you walking toward me on the beach wearing white linen pants and a button down shirt." I pause and pull at the collar of the shirt I'm wearing. "Like this one. But it won't be this shirt. Because I'll have this one with me. I'll wear it every night as a reminder of what we once shared."

I look away and sigh dramatically, then laugh and take another bite of toast. He's not the least bit amused by my theatrics. The only reaction I get from him is the same one he's given me since I sat down—a void look that suggests I'm boring the hell out of him.

I continue to eat my breakfast until my plate is clean. After my last bite, he finally speaks.

"Last room on the right," he says, lifting his chin in the direction of the hall. "There's a door in there that leads outside. Since the only vehicle here is mine and I have the key in my pocket, you'll be forced to leave on foot. You won't make it down the driveway because I'll be standing there. So you'll try the woods. You'll get lost. You'll pray that I find you. I'll leave you to suffer until just before dark. Then I'll come get you. By that time, you'll be freezing. Hungry. Probably in tears. It'll make the trip back a lot easier for me because you won't have the energy to fight. We'll come back here. I'll tie you up. You'll beg me not to. But I'll do it anyway. Then tomorrow morning, we'll find ourselves back at this table."

He sits in confident silence waiting for me to comment. I'm trying to look calm, but my legs burn with the need to run. To show him I'm not his average captive. When I walk out that door, I won't be coming back. I almost feel sorry for him.

"So that's how the fairytale ends?" I ask, feigning shock. "No hearts and flowers or warm baths and sweet kisses? Where's the romance? Surely I'll get stickers in my feet or cut myself on a low hanging limb. You'll have to patch me up. Wrap me in your big, strong arms and whisper, 'I got you,' in my ear."

He smiles, but it doesn't reach his eyes. "This isn't a fairytale, sweetheart. It's reality. You run and you'll wish you hadn't. Or you could stay and live out the next two months doing normal chick shit like binge watching Netflix, eating chocolate and drinking scotch." Winking, he leans forward and whispers, "But where's the fun in that?"

I must admit, what he offers does sound tempting. There are several shows I need to catch up on. Chocolate is my guilty pleasure and I could never get tired of drinking scotch. But I'm not that girl. And he knows it.

"I think I'll take my chances," I say, pushing back from the table.

I watch him cautiously, waiting for him to leap from his chair and tackle me. But he only shrugs—crossing his hands behind his head and leaning back. "Suit yourself. I'll see you around dark."

"Only if you catch me," I correct, keeping my eyes on him as I walk backwards toward the hall.

"I'll catch you, Winter," he promises. "And you'll wish to God I hadn't." Something about his cold warning has me second guessing myself. It passes the moment his bright, gray eyes disappear from my view as I step into the hall. Then I'm sprinting to the last room— quickly scanning it for anything I can use.

I need shoes. Warmer clothes. Money. A weapon. But the room is completely empty. There's not even a bed. When I hear his chair scrape across the floor, I panic and bolt to the door that leads outside. I'll steal whatever I need once I'm away from here. Right now, I have to put some distance between me and this place. The longer I'm here, the better the chance of Cain finding me.

Adrenaline makes the bite of cold easy to ignore as I run full speed across the yard. The entire place is surrounded with tall pines. I'm tempted to try and circle around the clubhouse to the driveway, but I know he'll be waiting there—just like he said.

He expects me to run toward the highway. In an attempt to throw him off, and because last night I made a mental note of the huge wrought iron fence that surrounds the front of the property, I run in the opposite direction.

I don't break stride until I'm so deep in the woods, the clubhouse is no longer visible. Then I slow my pace to a steady jog—knowing I can't afford to fall and break a bone.

A thick blanket of pine straw covers the ground between the trees providing cushion for my bare feet. But I've been gone all of five minutes and they're already numb, so I doubt I'd even notice if there were sharp rocks and glass beneath me.

Since the area is pretty clear and lacks any cutover, I decide to once again quicken my pace while I have the energy. I'll slow down only when I'm forced to. By that time, I'll be so far away, Jinx won't have a chance at finding me—not that he could. Even if he knew these woods in and out, there's no way he'll be able to track me.

The thought has me laughing and shaking my head. I can already smell the salt of the sea, feel the warmth of the sun and taste the mojito on my tongue—if south is where I decide to go.

Meanwhile, he'll be here. Regretfully reliving this day over and over again. The day he underestimated Winter Tews.

JINX

"Where is she?" Luke asks, stopping to look around the room before leaning over the bar to grab a beer.

"Gone," I say, not bothering to look up from my crossword puzzle. Out of the corner of my eye, I can see him stiffen.

"Gone where?"

"The woods. What's a six letter word for rug?"

"Jinx."

"Yeah."

"Where the hell is she?" Luke's frustration is evident. I know the feeling. This puzzle is hard as fuck.

"I told you. She's in the woods." I slide my phone across the table where he's now seated—too absorbed in thirty-six across to meet his eyes and give him my undivided attention. "She's the blinking, red dot."

Carpet?

"You put a tracking device on her?" he asks, his tone incredulous.

"Something like that," I mumble, giving up and tossing my pencil on the table. Grabbing my beer, I lean back on the legs of my chair and watch him as he studies the phone.

"This is some advanced shit." Oh, now he's impressed. "Where'd you get it?"

"An old friend from Houston is a big tech geek. He settled down, moved to Barbados." I shrug. "He's bored."

"So you just let her go?" This motherfucker is full of questions today.

"She's barefoot and barely clothed. It's not like she can go too far. And there's not a soul around out here for miles."

The location of Hattiesburg's clubhouse is remote—centered in the middle of one hundred acres of trees. It's the perfect place to harbor a captive. And when Pierce called in a favor to Luke, he was more than willing to help.

For the past six months, the Hattiesburg charter's main focus has been the opening of their newest night club, which employs almost all of the local chapter members. To be closer to the business, Luke temporarily moved the clubhouse's location to one of his properties downtown. Now, the only two occupants in the old clubhouse are me and Winter.

Luke promised that last night was just a one-time thing. The brothers were curious. So were the women. They wanted to know more about Pierce's mysterious little sister who'd been eighty-sixed from the Devil's Renegades. I bet if they knew then what they know now, they would've stayed the fuck away from the mouthy bitch.

Truth is, I'm glad it happened. The guys needed some incentive to keep their distance. The last thing I need is one of my brothers falling for her crazy shit and unknowingly aiding in her escape. The plan has always been to keep Winter completely isolated from the outside world. I'm confident that it's the best and fastest way for her to come around to my way of thinking.

"She's five miles out," Luke says, in that same fucking disbelieving tone. This time though, I share his enthusiasm.

"Yeah..." I nod slowly, thinking about how I may have underestimated her will power. And stamina. "She's a tough one."

"She's a well-informed one, too. Dallas is still pissed Winter knew that shit about her. By the way, how did she know?"

I smirk at him. "You accusing me of something?"

"No, brother. But you know every move this girl has made in the past two years. Who she talked to. Who she had lunch with. I want to know which of those is responsible for sharing shit that shouldn't have been shared."

I could tell him that in the two years I watched her, she hadn't talked to anyone outside Madness and their affiliates. The girl had no friends. No outside connections. Not even a cell phone. It's all true, but for some reason, it's not something I want to share. So I give him another truth. One he should've thought of himself.

"Winter grew up around the club. She may not have known anyone from here personally, but she likely spoke to plenty of people who did. The shit about Red being a stripper, hell everybody knew that. She probably found out about Delilah from some whore who jumped ship and joined Madness. And Dallas...well, bad news travels fast, Luke. If your ol' lady capped someone, people in this world are gonna hear about it. And not just the people who wear our colors."

He considers that a moment before agreeing. Eyeing my phone, he picks it up and takes a closer look. "That dot hasn't moved since I've been here." He holds it up for me to see. I barely glance at the screen.

"My best guess is she's curled up trying to get warm."

"How do you know she's not hurt?" he asks.

"I don't." I shrug. Indifferent.

He lifts a brow. "Seriously?"

I nod once. "Seriously."

Shaking his head, he breathes out a laugh and stands. "Pierce won't be happy if something happens to her."

"Well Pierce ain't the motherfucker stuck here babysitting her either, is he?"

Luke really laughs at that. "Something tells me you're enjoying it more than you let on." *Funny fucker...* I know what he's insinuating. And he's right.

I enjoyed fucking her last night. But that was a one-time thing. Still, I can't keep that look she had in her eyes when she came all over my cock, out of my head.

"Call if you need me, Jinx," he says, starting toward the door. Still getting his seven fucking chuckles. "Oh," he adds, stopping at the door and turning. "Runner."

"What?"

He smirks. "Six letter word for rug. Runner."

Runner.

How fucking fitting.

WINTER

I hate fucking trees. I think I hate them more than country music. At least I can tell the difference between the miserable artists who make a living drowning people with depressing songs. But these trees? They all look exactly the same.

I should've left a trail. It couldn't have been with breadcrumbs because A, I don't have any, and B, if I did I would've eaten them by now. But I could've used something. Maybe one of these eighty-seven million fucking pinecones I keep stepping on.

As much as I hate to admit it, Jinx was right. I'm lost, fucking freezing, hungry, near tears and praying that he finds me. I've never wished for the sun to set more than I do right now. He said he'd be here just before dark, and I have to believe him. My sanity and my life depend on it.

I'm so stupid. He baited me with escape and I took it. Like a fool. If I'd have just made him believe I wasn't going to run, then I could've better planned this. Stocked up some food. Water. Warm clothes. A cigarette. Or maybe I'd have thought to hide in the edge of the woods until he went in looking for me. Then I could've ran down the driveway and to the main road.

Fuck my life.

Every few steps I'm stumbling. Sometimes I fall but I manage to always get back up and keep moving. But when my right foot disappears into a hole and causes me to head-butt a tree, I decide I've had enough.

Slumping against the same tree that nearly knocked me unconscious, I pull my shirt over my legs and tuck my arms inside. I curl them around my waist in search of warmth. There isn't any. My skin, scratched from head to toe from low hanging limbs, are as cold as my feet. Which are filled with stickers. And all I can think about is that warm bath that I'll never get.

I must be dehydrated. Delirious. Mentally unstable. Because I'm crying. And I don't cry. Ever. But here they are—big, fat tears streaming down my face. Worst of all, they're not even hot. They're like fucking icicles.

There's no way I'll make it until dark. That's at least an hour away. I'll be dead by then. Somehow, that's not as disappointing as I thought it would be. At least then Jinx will lose, too.

I've given myself whiplash from snapping my head up every time I hear a limb snap—only to find a squirrel, rabbit or bird scampering off in the distance. Eventually, I quit looking. Mostly because I no longer have the energy. I just sit and shiver and cry as time passes and I, regretfully, don't die. Instead I dream of pouring that hot coffee I drank this morning over my head.

"You made it further than I thought you would." The voice sounds far away but when I lift my head, Jinx is standing over me. A fresh wave of tears floods my face at the sight of him.

"You f-found me," I whisper, my teeth chattering so hard my jaw hurts.

"I told you I would." And just like he said, it's nearly dark. *Had so much time already passed?*

"How?"

Other than a smirk, he doesn't answer. Like he knows some big secret I don't. Which, obviously, he does if he could trek through this maze of fucking trees without so much as a footprint to lead him to me.

"If it makes you feel any better, you were about a hundred yards from freedom." He points in the direction I was heading. "Just a little bit further and you'd have been at the back entrance of a high school. Probably could've found everything you needed there. Clothes...food... Driver's ED car. Who knows? Maybe you'll get there tomorrow."

He's teasing me. He wants me to run. And damn if I'm not already plotting how I can make it that extra one hundred yards if given the opportunity.

If I had the energy to scream, I would.

"I h-hate you."

"So you've said," he says, kneeling in front of me. "Can you stand?" I shoot him a cold look. My vision is fuzzy, but I can make out his smirk, the jacket he wears in place of his cut and the beanie on his head where his hat usually sits.

"Even if I c-could, I wouldn't. If you want me to go b-back with you, you'll have to drag me there."

"I could force you to walk," he says, only a hint of humor in his voice.

A sob builds in my chest. I try and fail to choke it down before admitting on a cry, "I have stickers." For the first time, I hear him laugh. It's only a light chuckle, but the sound seeps warmth into my bones.

Reaching beneath my shirt, he guides my hands back into the sleeves. "I may be an asshole but I draw the line at stickers," he teases, placing my arms around his neck. He cradles me against his chest with one arm at my back and the other beneath my knees. I curl into him and absorb his warmth as he stands and starts walking us out of the woods.

We only walk a short distance before coming to a four wheeler. He climbs on—sitting me on the seat in front of him and keeping me pressed tight to his body. Probably because if I die of hypothermia, he won't be able to gloat in the morning.

Shrugging out of his jacket, he places it over my shoulders. It's so comfortable and inviting, I moan. And it makes it easier to endure the cold air on my naked legs. I still can't feel my feet and I'm too scared to look at them. Afraid I'll discover I've lost a toe or three.

"Seven miles," he says, the deep tenor of his voice reverberating through his sweater. "You made it seven miles through unfamiliar woods, barefoot, wearing nothing but a shirt."

"Your shirt," I correct, tilting my head back a little to look up at him. This close, I can see a small dimple in his chin beneath the few days' worth of hair there.

"Yeah. My shirt. That's ruined thanks to you. Stop wearing my shit." He hands me a bottle of water. "Drink. All of it."

I have no problem guzzling down the entire bottle. I'm still thirsty and am about to tell him that when he hands me another bottle. "Finish that before we get home." He gases the four wheeler then, forcing me closer into him. I tuck my arms and legs as much as possible and allow myself to snuggle into his chest.

The ride is smooth and I find myself dozing in between sips of water. Only when I'm lifted and carried inside do I fully wake. It's more to the scent of something delicious than the lack of cold air swirling around me.

"Is that soup?"

"Yep," he says, continuing down the hall. When he pushes open the door to the room I slept in last night, I smile. *Awe. Dinner in bed.*

Gently, he lays me down—straddling my waist. "Making a habit of this, are we?" I tease, allowing him to take my hands in his. He secures them quickly before standing and pulling my body until my arms are stretched tight. Then he has my ankles in his grip.

"Hey!" I try to pull out of his hold but my strength is no match and he easily binds me despite my struggle. When he straightens and meets my gaze, I stiffen at the unexpected harshness in his eyes.

"I told you what would happen if you ran." He snatches his jacket out from under me and instantly I'm cold.

"Wait!" I yell, just as he starts to walk away. "Where are you going?"

That stupid, blank look is on his face when he takes a step back to stare at me. "To eat soup," he says simply.

"What about me?" Swallowing hard, I give him my most pitiful expression. "Please. I'm hungry."

"Told you you'd beg. I'm a man of my word."

Scowling, I jerk against my restraints. They don't give. "You can't just leave me like this."

"You're lucky I didn't drag you out of those woods."

"Why? Because you draw the line at stickers? Well fuck you!" I scream, my anger heating my skin that's slowly starting to regain color.

Leaning down, he brings his face close to mine and growls, "You already did, sweetheart. That's what got you here in the first place." His voice drops. "And I'm not talking about last night. I'm talking about two years ago when you stole every-fucking-thing from me." With one last hard glare, he disappears from sight before cutting the lights and slamming the door behind him.

I'm left in the dark.

Tied up.

Dirty.

Hungry.

Tired.

Cold.

Just like he promised.

WINTER

When Jinx tossed me on the bed like an old sock, he made sure I was facing away from the door. So the only thing I have to look at is a plain wall and a window shielded by shades drawn so tight, I nearly miss the tiny sliver of light starting to filter between the cracks.

I have no idea how long I've been in here, but I lost my voice from screaming threats at him long before the sun came up. Now I wish I wouldn't have yelled so much. Then I could tell him that I'm about to piss on myself.

My full bladder, dry throat, growling stomach, lack of sleep and numb limbs have me nearly in tears when the door opens and I'm suddenly blinded by light. I tuck my head into my arm to shield my eyes but see a large figure that appears in my peripherals. Cautiously, I squint up at him.

"Sleep well, sweetheart?"

"I'm not your sweetheart," I whisper, turning my head back to get a full view of a smiling Jinx. Of course he looks good in his long-sleeved, black Henley that hugs his muscles and those baggy jeans. His hat low on his eyes. Jaw smooth. He smells good so he must be freshly showered. Meanwhile I smell like death.

He pulls a knife from his pocket and flips open the blade. "This is sharp. If you move, I might cut off a toe or a finger."

"Well since there's no blood there, I'm guessing my chances of survival are pretty good." His eyes flit to my pale limbs. He doesn't say anything, but he makes quick work of freeing me. I moan at the immediate relief then whimper in pain as the blood comes rushing back.

"That's gonna leave a mark," he says, twisting my ankle in his hand. I jerk away from him and roll to my side—groaning in agony. After my few failed attempts at sitting up straight, he rolls his eyes and lets out a loud breath.

He scoops me up despite my whispered protests and carries me into the bathroom. Once there, he unceremoniously sits me on the toilet and towers over me. Rolling my shoulders, I glare up at him.

"What? You want to watch or something? Get the hell out of here." The urge to pee has me curling my toes into the rug and squeezing my thighs together. I would like to use the bathroom in peace, but if he insists on watching, I won't be able to hold back for long.

He smirks down at me, obviously aware of my struggle. "Maybe."

"Asshole," I growl, no longer caring if he's in here. My entire body relaxes and my bladder thanks me for it.

When I'm finished, he hands me some tissue. I snort—half expecting him to demand to do that too. Before he can make some wise crack about it, I quickly wipe myself.

Without waiting for him, I stand on wobbly legs. He reaches out and wraps his big hand around my arm to steady me. I try my best to ignore how hot his skin feels on mine. *Probably because mine is still so damn cold.*

Making sure to avoid my reflection, I take the two steps toward the sink and wash my hands and face—clenching my jaw so hard my teeth hurt just to keep from biting the shit out of him.

"I can walk," I snap when he scoops me up once again.

"If you do, our breakfast will be cold by the time we get there."

I don't look at him as he carries me. I even hold my breath so I don't smell him either. Once we're in the main room, he sits me next to him and this time there are two plates of steaming food on the table.

"Eat up," he says, handing me a fork. "You're gonna need your energy if you decide to run again today. Although I doubt you'll make it out of the yard."

With shaky hands, I lift the fork to my lips, ignoring him as I shovel in bite after bite. The silence is welcome and I'm thankful he doesn't comment on the mess I'm making. If he did, I'd stab him in the eye with my fork. And the sight of blood would definitely ruin my appetite.

After I've cleaned my plate and some of his—which he offered to me—I reach for the pack of cigarettes on the table. He takes them from me wordlessly. I'm about to protest when he lights a smoke and passes it to me. I take it from his fingers, eyeing him cautiously when he hands me my coffee too.

"So do you plan to counter every horrible thing you do to me with an act of kindness?" I ask, taking a deep drag of the smoke I notice is my choice brand. *Coincidence?*

"You did this shit to yourself, sweetheart."

If looks could kill, mine would have him dying a slow death. "So what's the plan here, Jinx? You're going to keep me here? Locked away in your clubhouse in the woods for sixty days? Then escort me to the lawyer's office in San Diego, collect your money and send me on my way?"

"Something like that."

"And what happens when Cain shows up here?"

He gives me a lazy smile. "Why do you say that like you're positive he's coming?"

I snort in disbelief. "Because he's a greedy bastard. A prideful, greedy bastard. You took something that belongs to him. Rest assured he'll be coming to collect."

"Some*thing?*" he asks, amused. "You mean some*one?*"

I bristle. "You flew me out of the state on a plane that had Knox Companies boldly printed on it, from a private airport Cain has used more than once. Did you want him to find me? Because if your goal was to hide me, I can tell you now that you've failed. There's no doubt in my mind that he already knows where I am."

"Don't you think I know that, sweetheart?" He's smiling again.

Confident and proud as ever. "You're here because there's not a Madness affiliate within three hundred miles of this place. And if he plans to roll through my state with an army, *you* can rest assure I'll know about it long before he gets here. His club don't mean shit in the south. We outnumber him twenty to one. So...yeah..." Leaning forward, he rests his elbows on the table and fixes me with his glare. "I wanted him to find you. I'm fucking counting on it."

Of course he is. I'm the bait. Just an excuse to start a war. Battle for pride. A means to an end for a decade-old MC feud. Fuck that. Fuck Cain. Jinx. My brother. The clubs. I'm tired of being the goddamn rope in this tug-of-war match.

"You're an asshole," I mutter, stubbing out my cigarette and standing.

"Aw, come on now," he says, his voice as condescending as his grin. "If he does show up, you'll get to see your boyfriend sooner than you thought. I figured you'd be happy about that. I mean...it's not like you were running from him, right?"

Once again, he's trying to trap me into telling him more than I want to. So, I change the subject and tell him I'm going to take a shower. He doesn't respond, but I know he's watching—I can feel his eyes burning into the back of my head.

I limp toward the hallway even though I can walk just fine. My legs aren't nearly as sore as my arms and after moving around, the soreness in them has become pretty tolerable.

When I'm out of sight, I quicken my pace and dart back into my room. Stripping the bottom sheet from the bed, I tie it around my waist and collect the two water bottles I'd discreetly hidden beneath my shirt yesterday.

I fill the bottles and cut the shower on before peeking into the hall. Finding the coast clear, I tiptoe to the room with the door that leads outside. It opens silently into the cold.

Jinx is a clever guy. Chances are he's got the front covered. So once again, I sprint off to the back of the property with one goal in mind— to make it one hundred yards further than I did yesterday.

———

SINCE I DON'T HAVE access to pen and paper, and I can't write with my hands tied over my head even if I did, I've decided to start keeping a diary in my head. Today's entry sounds like this.

Dear Diary. It's now day seven of my captivity. For the past six days, I've attempted to escape this prison. And every attempt has been a bust.

Somehow, someway, I've been caught. Tracked down in the middle of the woods, hauled back to this godforsaken clubhouse, tied up and left to rot on a mattress with no sheet. See, I had a sheet, but it was taken from me after I used it to aid in my second failed getaway.

I'd made it only three miles when my legs gave out and I face-planted the dirt. The position was so inviting, I decided just to fucking stay there until he came to get me—hours later.

But I'm not a quitter. I pushed past the pain I fear may be perma-nent in my limbs and have ran as far as I could for six solid days. The last two haven't gotten me very far at all. Barely out of sight. But that didn't matter to my rescuer. That motherfucker made me wait until dark before he came for me no matter how close I was. Even when I gave up and made my way back, he locked me out so that I was forced to stay in the cold until the sun finally made its descent.

Oh, but he's a generous man that captor of mine. He feeds me breakfast every morning. Coffee. Cigarettes. He was even kind enough to supply me with my own toothbrush and allowed me some clothes out of my luggage—a T-shirt and underwear. Out of spite, I'm still wearing his shirt I found the first day I was here, just to piss him off.

He really hates that for some reason. Every morning he says, "Quit wearing my shit." Of course I ignore him. There's something satisfying about having my stench on his clothes—makes me feel like I've won some small battle with him. Even if he continues to win the war. And when I say stench, I mean it. I haven't bathed since I've been here. There's something deeply gratifying about that, too. And a little disturbing.

Other than failing to get away, I have another problem. Jinx seems to only get sexier every time I look at him. All I can think about is how good it felt when he kissed me. Fucked me. Made me come. Because he makes me have these thoughts, I hate him more.

But I can't deny my physical attraction to him. From his handsome face to his rugged hands and all the delicious muscle that lies beneath his clothes, he is, unfortunately, still the sexiest thing these eyes of mine have ever bared witness to.

Maybe I'm developing Stockholm Syndrome. I crave his presence. His touch. His scent. His company. I miss him when he's not around. Especially when I'm in the woods with nothing to talk to but fucking trees. I miss him here, too. When I'm tied up in bed. Alone.

My plan isn't working, obviously. So today I've decided to try something new. I need to rest up. Get my energy back. And pray Cain doesn't show up before I can get the hell out of here.

I'm going to see if Jinx makes good on his promise of "the easy life." He said if I don't run, I'll be rewarded with Netflix and chocolate and scotch. And, hopefully, a night of sleep that doesn't involve being tied up to this bed.

Who knows? Maybe I'll even get lucky. But if that's in the cards, I'll most definitely have to bathe first.

WINTER

"Sleep well, sweetheart?"

It's the same line I get every morning. My answer, like every other time, is the same—a grunt.

Jinx appears in my line of sight and I try not to focus on how good he looks. But dammit I can't help it. I think he looks better today than he ever has. Instead of jeans he wears black sweats that hang low on his hips. Where he usually dons a long sleeved shirt, today he wears a white T-shirt that shows off his muscular, tattooed arms. I find it hard to swallow.

Other than my mind having no problem running crazy, I can hardly function today. My shoulders feel out of socket. The tendons in my legs are pulled too tight causing a fiery pain to shoot from my calves all the way to my thighs. And this morning more than any other, I need his assistance simply getting out of bed.

Performing my usual morning ritual, I pee while he watches. Then wash my face and hands. Brush my teeth and refuse to look at the nasty creature that is my reflection in the mirror.

Deciding not to run today doesn't leave me feeling like a failure like I thought it would, it makes me feel triumphant. *I'll be warm*. That thought alone is enough to make me smile.

"Something funny?" Jinx asks, carrying me down the hall and sitting me next to him at the table. I glare at him over my eggs.

"What the hell could be funny about this?"

He shakes his head, spinning his hat around as he dives into his own breakfast. "Like I said, sweetheart, you're doing this shit to yourself."

I roll my eyes and stare into my coffee. "God, you sound just like Cain," I mutter, not really meaning to say it out loud. But he heard it. And his reaction causes the temperature in the room to drop.

"I'm nothing like that motherfucker," he growls, his tone icy.

I glance at him over the rim of my cup—his gray eyes steely glaciers. "Says the man who's left a woman tied up, cold, hungry and in the dark, all night...alone."

He studies me a moment before admitting, "I didn't leave you alone all night."

"Bullshit. I've seen you leave."

He quirks a brow. "Have you?"

Have I? No. I haven't. I've heard the door slam. I've even heard it open in the morning. But I've never really seen him leave. Doesn't matter though. He's done horrible things to me. And although it doesn't even come close to how Cain treated me, it's similar.

"He really do that shit to you?"

My head snaps up. I hadn't realized I was so lost in thought. "Well I sure as shit didn't do it to myself," I snap, stabbing another bite of eggs.

"You were running from him, weren't you?"

"No."

I can tell he doesn't believe me, but instead of calling me on it, he asks something different. "Why did you stay with him then. If he did that shit to you?"

I release a breath and regard him with the same stoic expression he gives me. "You wouldn't understand."

"Try me," he says, his tone a little lower.

For a moment, I contemplate telling him. Spilling all the secrets I've harbored for the past six years to this man I barely know. But no good can come of it. He may not care about what Cain did to me, but out of loyalty, he'll call Pierce and tell him. And even though he said things to me during our last conversation that left scars on my soul, my brother still doesn't deserve to carry that burden.

Clearing my throat, I leave my breakfast half-finished—suddenly having lost my appetite. "This conversation is over," I say, pushing back from the table. I wish I could stomp out but my limbs are like Jell-O and it takes me a moment to find my footing. Then I'm more sliding than walking toward the hall.

I finally manage to make it to the bathroom despite my muscles screaming in protest. Once I'm there, I turn and lock the door behind me. I know it won't keep him out if he really wants in, but maybe it'll be enough for him to knock rather than just barge inside.

Out of nowhere I'm hit with a cramp in my leg that's so painful, it knocks me to my knees. Sweat gathers beneath my arms and across my lip, but I manage to breathe through it pretty quickly. Being tied up six nights in a row, after hiking through the woods has definitely done a number on my body.

With one last look at the flimsy lock on the door, I reluctantly remove the shirt from my back. It takes me a minute to crawl inside the tub. Once I'm seated, I don't bother with the cold water, I just let the hot blast me to the point of scalding. When the tub is full, I draw my knees up, tuck my head between them and curl my arms around my legs as the steam rises around me.

Closing my eyes, I inhale deep and will the water to soothe my aching limbs. It would be smarter of me to lie back in the tub, but this position is most comfortable. Even if it does leave parts of me exposed.

The heated water calms me. I allow its warmth to seep into my bones and chase away the cold that still lingers from the past few days. But I've been cold for too long and even in the hot water, I shiver.

A knock sounds only seconds before the lock is picked and the door is easily pried open. It gives me just enough time to shift my body, grab the towel next to the tub and shield myself from Jinx's view. He stares at me with a mixture of shock and curiosity.

"Get out!" I yell, making sure to keep my back out of sight.

"What the hell's your problem? Not like I haven't seen them

before." His eyes fall to my chest that's covered by the towel. Normally, my body would respond to the heaviness in his eyes. But it's not my breasts or any other intimate part of me I'm worried he'll see, it's the evidence of my past. The one place I've managed to keep hidden from him—even when we fucked.

"Leave," I cry, panicking a little as I inch further back in the tub until I have nowhere else to go. That lustful look disappears from his eyes and is replaced with worry.

"Winter..." he starts, taking a step toward me. His look says he cares. I don't need him to care. I need him to leave. So I hide my true emotion and muster up as much anger as I can.

"You won't let me piss by myself but can you at least let me take a bath in peace?" His eyes narrow in suspicion. Good. Before he sees through my façade, I continue. "Fucking go!"

After a moment, he points a finger at me. "Whatever scheme you've got going, you better make sure it's worth the price you'll pay when I figure it out."

I don't allow myself to breathe until he's gone. When I do, I look down at the water and curl my lip in disgust. It's filthy. Not taking any chances of him coming in and seeing me again, and knowing I'll have to refill the tub probably a hundred times, I regretfully abandon my bath and opt for a shower instead—keeping my back to the wall just in case.

My arms are so weighted it makes washing my hair and body as exhausting as my hike through the woods. Time consuming, too. And when I have too much time, I think. Right now, I'm thinking why in the hell it matters so much to me that he doesn't see what I've never hidden before.

Is it because for the first time I'm in the presence of someone who isn't Cain, Madness or their associates? Is it shame? Or is it because I'm afraid that heat in Jinx's eyes when he looks at me will disappear once he sees it?

Nope. Not the last one. That's ridiculous. I'm just being self-conscious. Truth is, I don't want Jinx to look at me *any* way. I just want him to look *a*-way so I can run from this place. From him. Pierce. And leather...ugh. Whoever thinks that shit smells good hasn't smelled it after it's been worn in the sun by a sweaty man for a few days.

By the time I'm clean and my thoughts are clear, the hot water has long run out and once again I'm cold. Stepping from the shower, I towel off quickly and wrap it around my body.

Finding my reflection in the mirror, I cringe at what I see. My skin is red and splotchy—chaffed from the cold wind. Scratches cover my legs from low hanging limbs. There's also a few scrapes on my cheeks and neck. Nothing serious, though.

My eyes look too big for my face. A little hollow and sunken. That's due to lack of sleep and malnourishment. After a few good meals and comfortable nights of sleep, they'll appear normal. Hopefully.

Fingering through my long, knotty hair, I attempt to tame it. I could use a hairbrush. Like the one in my luggage that Jinx still hasn't given to me. Maybe once he realizes I'm not going to run, he'll allow me to have it.

In the bedroom, I notice there's another one of Jinx's button down shirts casually laying on the dresser. Beside it is one of the T-shirts Pierce bought me and a pair of plain cotton underwear. I roll my eyes, imagining Pierce telling whoever did my shopping to not get me any sexy lingerie.

For the first time in days, I dress in my own clothes and put on underwear. They feel weird after going commando for so long, but my shirt is shorter than Jinx's so I decide to keep them on.

Glancing over at the bed I've grown to hate, I feel like I'm actually seeing it for the first time. And it's completely disgusting. The mattress looks new except for where I've slept. There it's soiled in filth and grime from my dirty body. Maybe for good behavior I'll get a clean sheet.

Good behavior.

I snort at that and stumble my way silently down the hall on wobbly legs. Wrapping my arms around myself, I try to suppress the cold I just can't shake. The concrete floors beneath my bare feet don't help. When I arrive in the main room I find Jinx sitting with his back to me at the bar.

"Hey," I say, causing him to stiffen before he slowly turns on his stool to face me. "Can I get some socks and a sweater or something?" I jut my thumb toward the back room. "Ran out of hot water before I got clean and I'm freezing."

He smirks at me. "And make your trip into the woods a little more comfortable for you? Not a chance in hell, sweetheart."

Dropping my head, I stare at my feet as I begrudgingly admit, "I think I'm gonna hang around here today." I peek up at him and catch his surprise before he has a chance to hide it.

He stands slowly, looking me over with observant, cautious eyes as he makes his way to me. "You move from this spot before I get back and I'll tie you up outside in nothing but your panties."

Panties.

Son of a bitch why does that word on his lips send an electric charge straight to my clit.

Knowing he's never lied to me before, I stay rooted as he disappears down the hall. I look over my shoulder and find him walking into the last room on the right—the one with the door that leads outside. He's only gone a minute or so before he's back in my sights. He stops at another door and pulls a key from his pocket. Shooting me a look of warning first, he pushes inside.

Frowning, I survey my surroundings in search of what it is that has him so on edge about me escaping. Usually, he's so confident. Almost as if he wants me to run. Like no matter what direction I choose or where I end up, he'll find me.

When I glance down at my clothes, it hits me. *I'm not wearing his shirt.*

The wheels in my head are just starting to turn when he comes out of the room with an armload of shit. I immediately make a mental note that he doesn't lock the door when he leaves. I'll have to see what's in there later. Right now, all I care about is wrapping myself in that big fluffy blanket he carries.

"Follow me," he says, crossing the room to where a large, over-stuffed sectional sits centered in front of a massive T.V. "Sit." He points to a spot and I all but fall onto the soft cushions—sighing a little as the coziness envelopes me.

Tossing the blanket over my lap, he takes a seat next to me and grips my ankles in his hands. Instinctively I stiffen and try to pull back. He gives me a small smile that's one of the rare real ones he wears and pulls until my legs are over his thighs.

"Trust me."

"Seriously? You're asking me to trust you?" I ask, completely dumbfounded that he would even say such a stupid thing.

"Yeah. I am." His tone is serious. And despite the shit he's put me through, a part of me does trust him. Not a lot, but enough for me to relax.

He pulls a tube of something from his pocket and squirts a generous amount in his hands. "This will help," he says, slathering the cream across my calves before working on the tight knots with his big hands.

"Oh my god," I groan, my eyes fluttering closed. "That hurts so good." My skin heats from his touch and the orange scented lotion. "Why does this one smell so good? And why is it warm?"

"Because I knew you were cold." His simple, soft spoken answer has me opening my eyes to find him watching me. Then, as if he's afraid I'll read further into his act of kindness, he smirks. "Plus it doesn't work as good as the others."

I narrow my eyes on him. "You're such a dick."

He shrugs, not disagreeing. He just silently continues his massage until the tension leaves. Then he pats my leg and instructs, "Turn around and let me do your shoulders." I stiffen.

"No, I'm good," I say quickly. Still unsure of why I'm hiding. He studies me with an unreadable expression. Before he can fire off any questions, I point to the T.V. "You promised me Netflix. And chocolate. And scotch. So are you always a man of your word, or only when it's beneficial to you?"

He looks at me a few seconds longer before tossing a remote control in my lap. "Password's devil," he says, lifting my legs from his thighs and standing. He crosses the room and retrieves two bags, a bottle and a glass from behind the bar.

Handing me the bags, he places the bottle and glass on the table next to the couch. "I've got some calls to make. If you try something stupid, my promise from earlier still stands."

I give him a middle finger of acknowledgement as he walks away and start digging through the first bag. It's a huge assortment of candy bars. I settle on a dark chocolate one then pour myself a glass of scotch. I've consumed both and am working on my second serving when I remember the other bag. Inside are socks, a sweater, jogging pants and a beanie. All are from my luggage.

It takes me a few minutes to put everything on. Then I grab the remote and find the entire series of a show I've never seen. Starting the first episode, I snuggle beneath the blanket and curl up on the couch—really warm for the first time in days.

WINTER

"Shh!" I whisper shout at Jinx who's brought his phone call to my circle of solitude. I'm on episode three of Prison Break and this motherfucker is yapping all up in my ear, forcing me to pause the show for the second time in five minutes. He cuts his eyes at me but doesn't lower his voice.

Tossing off the covers, I figure now is as good a time as any for a bathroom break. Hunched over, I walk down the hall toward the bathroom. Glancing over my shoulder to make sure he didn't follow me, I pause at the door he left unlocked earlier and try the handle.

"Dammit," I mutter, finding it locked.

When I'm finished in the bathroom, I make my way back to the couch—my face pinched from the pain shooting down my neck and shoulders as I slowly lower myself to the cushions. Closing my eyes, I breathe in through my nose and out through my mouth while twisting my neck from side to side and rolling my shoulders.

"I can fix that," he says, his low voice causing me to still. I crack open an eye and see him observing me from the other end of the couch.

Smirking, I shake my head. "If I take my shirt off, you won't be able to resist, baby. And I'd rather suffer than have you salivating all over me." It's a shallow thing to say, but it's the only excuse I can come up with that might have him dropping the subject. Of course it doesn't work.

"You don't have to take your shirt off," he deadpans. "I won't use the cream. It'll hurt like hell, but you'll feel better when I'm finished."

"That's what she said," I quip, blowing the smoke from my finger guns.

He smiles at me. I don't like it. Not even a little bit. And that warm and fuzzy shit going on inside me? I don't like it either. Clearing my throat, I continue my head lolling and shoulder shrugging.

"Come here, Winter." The seriousness in his tone leaves no room for negotiation. It's so commanding and promising, my legs shake with the urge to carry me to him. He speaks like the guy from that movie—the one where he tells her to, "come here," right before he puts her over his knees and spanks her. For that, I'd gladly go to him.

"I have really sensitive shoulders," I breathe, the excuse as pitiful as it is ridiculous. Of course I have sensitive shoulders. I've been tied up like a fucking captive for six nights.

A fleeting look of apology flashes across his face. "I didn't think you'd take this long to break. You're incredibly strong, Winter." He drops his eyes then shakes his head as if to clear it. I'm still reeling when he looks at me again. This time, there's humor in his eyes. "And fucking infuriating."

"You didn't break me," I say, my voice strong.

He nods slowly. His voice a little sad when he speaks. "But if I have to, I will." He doesn't apologize for that, but the regret in his eyes is unmistakable.

What Jinx says is definitely true. He will break me, eventually. Expose me one layer at a time. That's the kind of man he is. He'll stop at nothing to get what he wants. He'll do what he has to, to keep me here. Call me crazy but I have to respect him for that.

Not many people are willing to sacrifice so much just to see something through. Even if it means giving up a piece of their soul. Maybe that's why I respect him. Because I'm like him. I'll stop at nothing to get what I want, too. Which is the fuck away from here. And I can't do that if I'm all stove up and hunched over.

"You'll stop if I tell you to? If it's too much?" A single nod is his only response. "And no funny business? No tricks or accidental nipple flicks?"

"Last time I checked, your nipples weren't on your shoulders. They were centered on those perfect tits of yours." *Perfect tits?* I mean, considering I paid eighteen grand for them they better be perfect. But he doesn't say it like that. He says it like he appreciates them. "Did I pay for them?" *Okay...maybe he didn't mean it like that.*

"For your information, asshole, I got these right out of high school. *Before* I took your money."

"And Pierce said you pissed that money away." He shrugs. "Personally, I think it was a good investment."

"You just can't help yourself can you? You go from decent to dick in one second. Must be exhausting."

"Not nearly as exhausting as you, sweetheart. Now come here."

I shoot him a disbelieving glare. "Fuck you."

His eyes harden. "Come. Here." *There it is again...that spank voice.* My pussy clenches and nipples tighten.

"Are you going to spank me?" *What? Mothershit. Assfuck. Dammit.* Why the hell would I say that?

He quirks a brow. "Do you want me to spank you?"

"Uh, no," I scoff, breaking eye contact because...*mothershit. Assfuck. Dammit.*

"You're a great liar until it comes to your body. I bet that little cunt of yours is soaked."

"No it's not," I snap, like a teenage amateur. Still unable to meet his gaze.

"I've always told you, Winter," he says, his tone that velvety smooth sexy one. "All you have to do is ask."

"Well, I'm not asking for that. Ever. So put the kink back in the closet."

"It's not my kink to hide." *I hate him. I hate him. I motherfucking hate him.* "Now come here and let me make sure your shoulders aren't out of socket. That turtle look you're wearing is starting to creep me out."

"That turtle look you're wearing is starting to creep me out," I mock, making my way over.

"Over my knee," he demands once I'm standing next to him. I still and look down at him in shock. His face breaks into a smile. "Kidding. Sit." He pats his thigh and I flip him the finger before taking a seat.

Immediately his hands move to my shoulders. Working. Massaging. Kneading the sore muscles there. I bite my lip to stifle my cries. Tears burn my eyes and my nails dig into his jean clad legs.

"Relax. You're only making it harder," he says. Then I feel his lips at my ear as he whispers, "That's what *he* said."

I release a small laugh and he takes that exact moment to press his thumbs firmly on either side of my spine between my shoulder blades. I cry out and try to pull away but he holds me in place.

"Relax, baby." *Baby? What the shit is that about? And why does it make me ease into him?* "Deep breaths."

I do as he instructs, breathing in deep, shaky breaths as I squeeze my eyes shut against the agonizing torture. Focusing on the pain rather than the way that word *baby* makes me feel all mushy on the inside.

Years later, I finally start to feel the tension subside. The pressure lightens. His firm touch softens. Becomes more of a caress. One that has my vagina waking up, looking around, finding him in those sweats, licking her lips and mouthing, "Fuck me."

"Thank you," I say quickly, standing too fast and having to reach out for something to steady myself. I realize he's given me his hand and withdraw before grabbing the bottle of scotch and pouring a glass. I down it in a single gulp and mutter an excuse about going to the bathroom.

I sit on the side of the tub and hold my head in my hands. This guy is getting under my skin. Which reminds me of what's on my skin. For years I haven't really given it much thought. Now that I'm suddenly trying to hide it, that awful night threatens to resurface.

A light knock sounds and I wait for Jinx to barge in. When he doesn't, I wait a few seconds longer before forcing a smile and pulling open the door. He stands there as indifferent as always. Hands in his pockets. Head slightly turned. Eyes appraising emotionlessly.

"You good?" he asks, bored. Whether he really is that uninterested in me or just pretending to be, I'm not sure. I'm thankful for his concern no matter the reason.

"Great," I say on a relieved breath. "Netflix and chill? Minus the chill?"

His lips quirk. "After you."

I lead the way, my socked feet silent on the floor. His boots loud as he follows behind me. In what I'm calling the living room—the couch and T.V. area of the main room—I curl up on the sectional under the blanket and he sits at my feet. I'm not cold, but you don't realize how much you miss covers until you don't have any for a while. So I'm taking advantage.

Jinx orders us pizza and it arrives by the time the third episode of Prison Break is finished. By the end of episode four, my stomach is full. Body relaxed and warm. Mind focused on the show and not on a trip down memory lane.

Settling further into the cushions, I pull the blanket up to my nose and stretch out my legs. My feet collide with something hard for only a second before Jinx lifts them into his lap—stretching the covers over the top of them.

"This is better than the woods." I stifle a yawn, refusing to give in to sleep because this show is just too damn good.

He chuckles. "Giving up already?"

I shrug. "Maybe."

"Smart girl."

"I mean, I like this. T.V. Covers. Food." I look at him. He's watching the T.V. but when he feels my stare, he turns his head toward me.

"And as long as you're here, you can have this. That is, if you don't run."

I smile. "Oh, come on now, Jinx." Shooting him a wink, I add, "Where's the fun in that?"

WINTER

"*Shit...*" I whisper, my anxiety rising by the second. "They're gonna get caught."

"Doubt that," Jinx says, completely calm. But the cigarette he's lighting suggests he's as anxious as I am—it's his fourth one this episode.

It's early morning. I have no idea what day it is. Since I started watching this show, I haven't moved from the couch. I've barely slept. Eaten. I haven't even been in the mood to drink. And I've finally made it to season one's next to last episode of Prison Break—the one where they escape.

Jinx has been with me most of the time. If he's not here, he's at the table with a laptop, outside or on the phone. I've yet to discover what he's working on, what he's doing outside or who he's talking to. Not that I've done a lot to figure it out. I've been too busy absorbed in this show.

I'm not even sure if he's slept. If he has, it had to have been while I slept, too. But I've never caught him. And he's changed clothes and showered twice. I haven't done either of those things. In my defense, though. I haven't really done anything to warrant a shower. My ass has been here. On this couch. And if I'm gross, who cares? It's not like Jinx has made a move on me. Not that I want him to.

"Give me that," I snap, snatching the cigarette from his fingers. I'm on the edge of my seat—literally. Covers, pillows, candy wrappers and empty water bottles surround me.

The Thai takeout container with last night's broccoli sits on the table along with a brand new bottle of untouched scotch—ready to be consumed and take me to that drunken state I dreamed about all those days in the woods.

"Twenty bucks says the big guy don't make it," I say, picking at my nails—a nervous habit.

"I've got three hundred grand on the old man."

Glancing away from the screen, I narrow my eyes on Jinx. He smirks back at me. "Not that I have anything to lose." I ignore his comment and roll my eyes back to the T.V.

Thirty minutes later, I slump back on the couch breathless as if it was me who just escaped from prison. Jinx mirrors my position, except he looks a lot more composed than I do. "Looks like we both win." I grin at him and offer up a fist. He looks at it then back at me before slowly shaking his head. "What? Too cool to fist bump?"

"I don't fist bump," he deadpans.

"You don't do anything."

"Says the girl who don't shower."

I frown, fighting the urge to sniff myself. "I shower," I say in defense. "Just not lately." Trying to be discreet, I pretend to stifle a yawn and press my nose into my arm and inhale.

"You don't stink," he says. "Because you're wearing my deodorant. And my shirt. Even though you have clothes of your own."

I look down at his shirt I'd found on the bathroom counter a couple days ago. After figuring there must've been something special about it, I decided to do some investigating. It didn't take long for me to discover exactly how he was finding me so easily in those woods. And why he was so nervous about me running the first time I wasn't wearing it.

The clever son of a bitch had disguised a tracking device as a button. The tiny button at the collar, where it was less likely to get torn off by a limb. Or discovered by me. And the bastard was pretending to hate me wearing his clothes, knowing I'd wear them just to piss him off.

"You really hate that don't you?" I tease, grinning at him. "Me wearing your clothes." His brows draw together a little and his nose scrunches just the tiniest bit.

"Yeah. I do. If I asked nicely, would you stop wearing my shit?"

I laugh and shake my head—finding his answer even funnier now that I know the real truth. "Nope."

"Didn't think so," he mutters, standing and pulling his phone from his pocket. He eyes it a moment before looking at me. "I have a call to make. Don't watch the next episode without me."

"Must be nice to have a life," I mumble.

"It is." His condescending tone matches his grin as he walks away.

I look over the back of the couch, watching him disappear out the back door. When he's gone I stick my head in my shirt, inhale and learn two things in that moment. Jinx is a liar and his deodorant is shit. Because I most definitely stink.

———

"SHE BATHES," Jinx says, nearly scaring the piss out of me when I open the bathroom door to find him standing on the other side. He eyes me in the white, cotton tank I'm wearing that's just long enough to cover my panties—pausing on my nipples that are visible without the protection of a bra.

"And he likes what he sees," I shoot back, crossing my arms over my chest.

His voice is gruff when he openly admits, "He does."

"Well, are you going to fuck me? Or are you going to stand here and gawk? I don't have all day."

"You seem impatient. Got somewhere to be?" He smiles that smile that suggests he knows something I don't. Then he holds up the butter knife I lifted this morning from the kitchen—twirling it between his fingers. I stare back at him blankly—giving nothing away.

"Let me guess," he starts, pausing dramatically to pretend to think hard. "You found the back door padlocked and figured since you couldn't pick it, you'd just use this to unscrew the metal plate from the frame." *Only after I found the doors wired with an alarm and the windows screwed shut from the outside....*

I shrug. "Or I planned to sharpen it with the file I found under the couch then stab you in the neck, take your keys and wallet and walk right out the front door." Winking, I whisper, "Never can tell about me."

He breathes out a laugh and licks his bottom lip as he studies me. "How did it take a clever girl like you nearly six years to figure out a way to get away from Cain?"

"Who said I was trying to get away?" I ask, bored by the question.

He closes the distance between us until his chest brushes against mine. Instead of cowering away, I look up at him with an amused expression. "You know what I think?" he says, his eyes on the dull knife as he drags it from my shoulder to my elbow. "I think you were running through that garage trying to get away from Cain and his men. Not because of some bullshit understanding the two of you had about what to do if the other got caught."

Needing distance, I place my hand against his chest and push. Surprised, he takes a step back. "You really shouldn't think so much, Jinx," I say, stepping around him and dismissing the subject. "It gives you premature wrinkles."

When I walked out of that bathroom, my head was everywhere. My solution was sleep. Curling up on the couch, I closed my eyes and slept on and off again for the next three days—only staying awake long enough to use the bathroom and eat the occasional meal.

Yesterday, I showered again. I'd hoped it would wake me up. It didn't. When I made it back to the couch, Jinx was sitting silently on the other end. He was absorbed in his phone and barely seemed to notice me. He made some smartass comment just as I closed my eyes. I didn't understand him and was going to ask him to repeat it, but I was already too far gone. When I woke up, it was a new day and Jinx was telling me breakfast was ready.

I'd noticed that this "clubhouse" sure seemed vacant a lot. When I asked where everyone was, Jinx reiterated that they left because they didn't like me. I was sure that was true, but it was still suspicious. Before I could demand more information, he told me the real reason.

He'd said a new clubhouse was now conveniently located closer to the bar where most of the club is employed. He also reminded me that there was only one way in and out—a perfect trap for any unwelcome guests. Oh, and he figured isolation was the best way to get me to cooperate. Obviously, it's working.

I haven't tried escaping in over a week. Not even thoughts of Cain showing up can force me to abandon the warmth of the clubhouse for the bitter cold outside. And on day fourteen of my captivity, I'm still warm. Cain has yet to show and I find myself sitting at a table across from Jinx, enjoying scrambled eggs and bacon like the obedient little captive I am. Since I took the butter knife, he makes me eat with plastic cutlery. I'm pretty sure I can melt it down and still stab him with it.

I yawn.

"Can you unlock that back door for me tonight?"

He pauses mid-chew and shoots me, what I swear, is a hopeful look. "Getting restless?"

"I'm getting lazy," I say, picking at my eggs. "I just woke up and I'm already tired. Maybe a day running through the woods will give me that energy I'm lacking." I wiggle my eyebrows at him. "Or we could fuck."

He's surprised but quickly recovers. "That was a one-time thing," he says, avoiding my gaze by lighting a cigarette.

I place my hand on my chest and feign shock. "But Jinx...we had that spark. That special energy coursing between us."

"No we didn't." He's so matter-of-fact, I can't help but laugh.

"Fine, no fucking. So can you unlock the back door?"

His eyes flit to my shirt a moment before resting on my face. "There's a trampoline out back. You should try that first."

I want to laugh at the uneasiness in his eyes at the sight of me in my own clothes. *No tracking device on this shirt, asshole.* Somehow, I refrain.

"Why is there a trampoline here? Nobody has kids, do they?"

He shakes his head. "Long story. I'll find you some pants."

Pushing away from the table, he makes his way down the hall. I'm guessing to his room where he's hiding all my fucking luggage. He returns a few minutes later with a pink hoodie, matching sweats and socks. I slip them on, aware of him watching me as I do. It takes more control than I thought I had not to shake my tits at him.

He leads me through a side door and into a covered, fenced area outside that's filled with workout equipment, a few exercise machines and, of course, a trampoline. Ignoring the cold, I climb on the trampoline and start jumping—cutting flips and doing air splits like I'm ten again.

But just being outside reminds me that there is life beyond these four walls. That soon, Cain will come for me. There's something about Jinx and being locked in the clubhouse that makes me feel so safe I forget. But here? Exposed and vulnerable? It kind of scares the piss out of me.

I hop down and join Jinx who's propped against the side of the building with his hands shoved in his pockets. I'm breathless when I reach him—mostly from exhaustion but a little bit of fear, too. There's a cramp in my side. My nose is running. My hands are like ice. And I want to slap that amused smug look right off Jinx's face.

"Shut up," I pant, grabbing my side and bending over.

"I can see why you're out of breath," he says, patting my head like a dog. I swat his hand away. "You've been out here all of ten minutes."

"Is that all?" I shriek, immediately regretting it when that pain echoes in my side. "Fuck this. I've got a better idea."

"Like what?" Jinx asks, bored as hell as he holds open the door for me to stumble through. When I reach out to hold onto the frame for assistance, the damn thing shocks me.

"First, I'm gonna lose these static clingers. Then I'm gonna get drunk." *And hopefully forget about Cain.* "Maybe I'll clean up some of that shit growing in the living room," I add when I see him watching me a little too intensely.

"That's a relief," he mutters. "Just don't trade in those static clingers for my shirt. Wear something of your own. There's some clothes in the bathroom. I've got shit to do."

I dismiss him with a wave and make my way down the hall—hearing the side door slamming behind him as he goes back outside. "Yeah, yeah, yeah," I mumble to myself. "Nobody wants to wear your shit, anyway."

Liar.

WINTER

My hair is on my head. I'm wearing Jinx's shirt. Dancing around the living room to Ariana Grande with a glass of scotch in one hand, a feather duster in the other and a cigarette hanging from my lips. That's how Jinx finds me when he comes back inside sometime later.

I have no idea how long he's been standing there. How long he's been watching me. It couldn't have been more than a second or two. Because if he's been there longer, I'm wondering how in the fuck I didn't notice him before now.

It could be the large amount of alcohol swimming through my system that has me overheating. I seriously doubt it though. I may by highly intoxicated—more like piss drunk—but even sober I'd have definitely felt heat at the sight of him. Considering he's naked from the waist up. Breathing hard. Sweaty. Earbuds hanging around his neck. Bright eyes barely visible beneath heavy lids. They move to the shirt I'm wearing and harden. Not darken in lust like in the books I've read. But harden. Like he really doesn't like me wearing his shirt. As he's said so many times before.

Hell, maybe he really doesn't like it when he knows I'm not planning to escape him. Maybe I like it because I know if I'm wearing it, I can't. And maybe it's this shirt that makes me feel safe—knowing if Cain showed up and I was forced to leave with him, that Jinx could still find me.

I'm crazy. Since when do I want help from this brooding bastard? Fuck his cold eyes. His mean look. My weird thoughts. I take a sip of scotch that I really don't need and move to more pleasant parts of his body. Like those beautiful tats covering his torso. The thick veins that protrude on his muscular neck from his recent workout. That inked, tanned skin stretched tight over bulging biceps and triceps and all the fucking ceps in his arms. His chest a slab of granite. Stomach like stone and chiseled in abs. A dust of dark hair trailing down, down, down and disappearing into his sweats.

Those damn sweats. Dark gray. Heavy cotton. High thread count. Little check mark on the pocket. Probably really fucking expensive. Hanging so low on his hips I can see that V. Which looks like an arrow. And it's pointing at that thick shaft pressing against those expensive fucking sweats that even heavy cotton and high thread count can't hide.

He waits for me to meet his eyes. Unhurriedly, I do. I see that same heat I'm feeling there. But the blazing inferno can't be nearly as hot as my pussy is right now. "You like me in your shirt," I say, my words clear but sluggish.

"I hate when you wear my shit."

I shoot him a lazy, drunken smile. Tilting my head a little, I bat my eyelashes—swaying as I do. "You're lookin' at me like you want to eat me."

"Do you want me to eat you, sweetheart?" Oh, he's using the throaty voice. How cliché. How sexy. How fucking crazy is it that me, a cutslut, a woman who does business on her back, can be affected by a tone. *It must be the alcohol.*

"Yes. But you won't." I give him a mock frown.

He lifts a brow. "Oh really?"

Nodding big, like the drunken fool I am, I say, "Yep. Cause you hate me in your shit. You don't find me sexy when I wear it."

He shakes his head, a small smile on his lips as he slowly stalks toward me. His movements fluid. Precise. Confident. His body even more massive now that he's closer. Towering over me. Looking down at my feeble form.

I'm all wobbly knees and shaky legs. Mouth hung open. Deer in the headlights. I'm going to be eaten. *Oh, god. Please let me be eaten.*

"I don't care how much I hate it. There's nothing about that shirt that's gonna keep me from devouring you. Just like there's nothing the Devil himself could do to keep me from fucking you into a goddamn oblivion once it hits the floor."

There's a feral need in his voice that's primal. Beneath all that calm is a beast—gnashing his teeth. Raging to break free from his cage. Roaring and pacing and letting everyone in the jungle know he's here and he's about to fuck shit up.

He's the king.

The lion.

I'm the gazelle.

No.

They're graceful.

I'm a clumsy zebra.

Or one of them baby giraffes that trips and falls on its face the first few steps of its life.

"You smell good," I whisper, my eyes falling half-mast as I inhale him.

I sway.

He catches my elbow.

"We have a connection. I *feel* it," I breathe on a sigh.

That spark.

That electricity.

Hot against my skin.

Too hot.

It's really more of a vibration.

A pulse.

But it's there.

Yep.

We definitely have a connection.

"It's my iPod, sweetheart."

My chin drops quickly—my forehead landing on his sweaty, warm chest. I blink a few times until my head stops spinning and narrow my eyes on what's pulsing. Sure enough, there's a white iPod in his hand. Pulsing with the heavy bass of some Metallica song.

"Well, *fuck* me," I slur, pulling in a deep breath and releasing it.

The lethargic feeling that comes with being drunk is a double edged sword. I love that my mind feels weightless, but I hate that my limbs feel like fucking concrete and move at a snail's pace. Like now, when I have to lift my hands to his arms and steady myself just so I can straighten. Which sucks because he feels really, really good in my hands.

"You always drink when you clean?" he asks, keeping his hand—and iPod—on my elbow when I step away from him.

"I drink all the time," I say proudly. "It's what you do when you're in prison. Well, not really but when you feel like you're living in one. George can tell it better than me."

"George?"

"George Jones. Country music legend." I grab the bottle from the table and top off my glass. Surprisingly, I do it without spilling a single drop. "Pierce loves him. He used to play that shit on a loop when I was a kid." Laughing, I lift the glass to my lips. "That's one of the reasons I left."

Sitting on the arm of the sectional, I cross my legs and pat the cushion next to me. "Sit." Jinx waits a few seconds before taking a seat. When he does, he sits two cushions down from me. I roll my eyes at him. But he doesn't notice. He's too busy putting a shirt on.

"Think that shirt's gonna protect you?" I ask, pointing to the red T-shirt he now wears with the arms cut out and ripped halfway down the sides.

He pins me with a promising look. "No more than the one you're wearing is."

My breath hitches. And for some reason, a fission of nerves course through me. This is unusual for me. I've only ever fucked Cain and the people he told me to. I've never had to actually make conversation without both of us knowing how the night was going to end up.

"George Jones," he says, pointing to the remote in my hand.

"Yeah, yeah, yeah. I'm gettin' to it." Shaking my head, I mumble into my glass, "So damn impatient." I finish off my drink. Pour another —smiling proudly when I don't spill a single drop.

It takes me a minute to find the song on the too-fucking-smart-T.V. app thingy, but eventually, "Still Doing Time" by George Jones filters through the speakers. We listen in silence. Him watching me. Me watching him. And the T.V. My glass. The floor. My fingernails. The couch.

"So living with Pierce made you feel like you were doing time." It's not a question. It's a statement. A fact.

"Yep. Couldn't wait to turn eighteen. To get the fuck out from under his watchful eye." I light a cigarette, giving Jinx the opportunity to comment. When he doesn't, I continue. "Do you know he ran background checks on all my friends, their family and their family's friends? Two people made the cut. A girl named Natasha who lived with her eighty-year-old grandma, had a six o'clock curfew and went to church religiously. She ended up graduating second in our class, marrying right out of high school and had three kids by the time she was twenty-two."

Nursing my drink, I think back to Natasha and how Pierce always told me I should be more like her. Little did he know his praise of Natasha is what ruined her in the end. She was in love with him and married a guy she barely knew just to get Pierce out of her system.

"You said there were two."

"I did." Nodding slowly, my eyes focus on the lamp across the room. "Mia. Another good girl. I was a bad influence. My own brother said so. Staying true to my reputation, I tainted her perfect little life. Talked her into going to a frat part our junior year. We got drunk. Flipped a quarter to see who was going to drive home. I won. She drove. Got a DUI. And her parents tried to sue Pierce saying I bullied her into it."

"Did you?"

Not meeting his eyes, I shrug. "Maybe." Stubbing my cigarette out, I eye the scotch. I'm pretty sure I'm an alcoholic. I'm okay with that.

Knowing is the first step, right? Right. And now that I've accepted it, I need to celebrate. Plus, nobody listens to George sober.

I take a drink.

"Why did you run from Cain?" Jinx asks, just as I'm about to take a sip. I study him—trying to see past that stoic face and find what he's truly feeling, as I take two, long swallows.

"That's the third time you've asked me that."

"Maybe this time I'll get the truth."

"Truth." I laugh and slide from the arm of the couch onto the cushions. "I've told both of you multiple times that I wasn't running from Cain. Yet there's a reason you and my brother are convinced I did. Whatever that reason is, should make the answer to your question pretty obvious."

"It doesn't."

Winking, I point a finger at him. "But you have a theory."

His lips twitch. "I do."

"It's probably bullshit."

"Probably." He shrugs, unaffected as he reaches for the bottle and pours himself a couple fingers before reclining back on the sofa—propping his ankle on his knee and stretching one, long arm across the back of the couch.

Forcing myself to focus on the topic and not on how sexy he looks, I snap my fingers and wave my hand in the air. "Well, let's hear it."

He's thoughtful a moment—nursing his whiskey as I do the same. "You left San Diego to get away from Pierce. Thought the grass was greener. Found out it wasn't. Tried to leave. Cain wouldn't let you. And he threatened you with Pierce. I'm guessing something along the lines of, 'I'll kill him if you speak to him' or some shit."

I smile at that. "Not even close," I lie.

"So tell me the truth." It's tempting—to tell him everything. But I'm too drunk. I'll likely say more than I should.

"One day," I offer, grabbing my glass. "Ask me something else."

He seems surprised by that. "Okay...let's say you get out of here and don't go back to Cain." He pauses as if to gauge my reaction. When he doesn't get one, he continues. "What if by some fucking miracle, and when I say miracle I mean walk on water miracle, you get away from me, where will you go? What you gonna do when you get there? What are you lookin' for? What do you want?"

"Geeze," I huff. "Who the fuck are you, Dr. Phil? I was thinking maybe you'd ask me something like my favorite color."

"I'm an overachiever."

"No shit you are," I mutter, finding the bottom of my glass once again dry. "Well, if I can't go back to Cain…I guess the first thing I would do is find a good bottle of scotch. Some sand and water. Get fucked up. Then have sex with someone who doesn't leave me waking up to a cold bed."

He lifts an eyebrow. "A snuggle partner?"

"Yeah. Snuggle partner. Cuddle buddy. I might even let him kiss me with bad morning breath."

"Wow," he says, humor dancing in his eyes. "You've got it bad for this guy. He your fairytale? Your happily ever after?"

I shrug. "Maybe. If he fits all the requirements."

"And what requirements must this dream guy meet?"

"Why so curious?" I wiggle my eyebrows. "Do you wanna be my dream guy?"

A devious smile on his lips, he shakes his head. "Not a chance in hell, sweetheart. You're not my type."

"Ditto, asshole. I'm sure your type consists of some meek, feeble minded bitch who does what she's told, praises you like you're some-thing fucking special and bakes cookies for the club."

"Nailed it," he says, fighting a smile. "Women like you are too much of a pain in the ass."

"Maybe to someone like you. But not to my dream guy." Laying down, I pull the cover from the back of the couch and struggle to cover myself. Giving up, I let it sit half-folded over my legs and place my hands behind my head. "He likes a challenge," I say, my words muffled by my yawn.

"Well, he'll definitely get one with you."

"Shut up," I snap, but I'm smiling when I look at him. He's smiling back. That genuine smile. The one that looks best on him. "He'll also let me hold the remote, rub my feet and pour my scotch."

"He sounds like a pussy."

"He sounds perfect," I mumble, my eyes returning to the ceiling. I stare at it a moment. My fuzzy brain drifting back to the original question—what do I want?

Ultimately...to be free.

To settle somewhere safe.

To maybe one day find that dream guy.

It's ridiculous, but I decide to humor him. And maybe myself.

"I want to go someplace where nobody knows me," I start, my eyes fluttering closed as I imagine the sun and the ocean and a beach full of strangers who don't give me a second look. "I want to have cocktails at a bar without looking over my shoulder or down at my watch."

Turning on my side, I pull the covers up to my chin and glance over at him. He's watching me. No smile. No smirk. He's serious. Attentive. Interested. "Is dream guy there?" he asks, his voice not condescending but rather curious. *He's obsessed with my dream guy....*

"Yes. And he rides a moped. Not a Harley." His lips quirk at my words.

I focus on a spot across the room—my mind drifting back to my perfect day. "He owns colorful clothes. Not just black. Wears flip-flops and shorts instead of jeans and boots. No helmet to hide his face. No patch. No club to answer to. No bi-laws to follow. He's his own man. Different. He's special."

My voice dips and my admissions become more serious. "He likes to hold my hand. Sometimes he kisses my fingers mindlessly. Like he doesn't even realize he's doing it. And when he kisses my lips, he holds my face in his hands. He controls the kiss, but it's not fierce and hard. It's gentle and passionate.

"I want a man who makes me feel wanted...not owned. One who wants me beside him...not behind him. Who knows when I need a hug and doesn't ask why, he just holds me. Who listens when I speak. Who doesn't tell me I'm stupid. Or ridiculous. Or that without him, I'm nothing.

"I want to watch the sunset on his lap. Laugh until the morning. Toast a new day over a shared glass of scotch. Dance to "Josephine" by The Black Crowes. Make love. Fall asleep to the sound of each other's breathing. Then wake up and do it all over again."

My heavy eyes have long been closed and my voice has become a whisper. I've gotten way too lost in my own fairytale. Caught up in the idea of something that doesn't exist. As I fade from reality and into sleep I realize and accept that even if this fantasy does exist, it'll never happen for me.

WINTER

"Cain...please. You're scaring me," I cry, pulling against the heavy chains that bind my wrists. It's dark here in this dank cellar. Cain calls it the pit. The coppery scent of blood that permeates the air is evidence that I'm not the first person to find myself strung up and at his mercy. It's his favorite place to be. Where he spends most of his time. He enjoys this—hurting people.

"You should be scared." The sinister look on Cain's face steals my breath. I search his eyes for some sort of remorse. But the dark, midnight blues are filled with evil. I've never seen him so angry. Fear grips me as tight as the binds that hold me because this isn't him taking his anger toward someone else out on me. No. This time, it's my actions that have caused his rage.

"I wasn't going to say anything, I swear." It's the truth. I had no intentions of seeing Pierce much less speaking to him. But Cain's not convinced. He just glares at me with simmering hate from his seat in front of me. A glass of whiskey in one hand. The other balled up into a tight fist. In the dim light, I can barely make out the patch on his cut that warns against times like these: SNITCHES ARE A DYING BREED.

I lick my lips, the tangy taste of blood and salty tears mingling on the tip of my tongue. He'd hit me before but was always immediately apologetic—wrapping me in his arms. Telling me how sorry he was. Promising to never do it *again. But tonight is different. Tonight I fear I'll need more than stitches to recover from what he has planned for me.*

"You were going to leave me. Go running back to him. Tell him my plans."

"No!" I cry, shaking my head back and forth. Begging for him to believe my next lie. "I just wanted to visit my mom on her birthday. I was coming back."

"Don't fucking lie to me!" Cain spits, his chair landing hard on the concrete as he lunges toward me. He seizes my neck in his hand and squeezes. I bring myself to my toes, trying to lessen the pressure he has on me. The tip of my big toe catches in something sharp and cold. The metal drain in the concrete floor. Convenient for easy cleanup when he's done with me.

"Not. Lying," I manage, my tears of guilt pouring from my eyes and pooling at his hand. I might've been planning to visit my mother, but it was going to be a quick stop on my way out of town. Seeing him like this, I know I'll never be able to tell him the truth. I'll claim the lie about visiting my mother's grave on her birthday until it is my cold, dead body lying in the ground.

He sears me with his glare. Burning me with it, then dousing me in icy terror when he promises, "I'm going to remind you who you belong to."

I'm spun around to face a wall. My breathing harsh. Chest rising and falling as I struggle to gain oxygen. Entire body shuddering with fear of what's to come. Lips parted. Mouth moving. Speaking. Begging Cain to let me go. Not to hurt me. Confessing love for him that doesn't exist. Reminding him that he loves me too. He laughs at that—a demonic sound that has me nearly blacking out from fear.

"Love ain't shit without loyalty, bitch."

The first crack of leather across my ass is heard moments before it's felt. Slowly, the pain surfaces as blood rushes to the affected area. The second blow overlaps the first and is hard enough to break skin. The agony is excruciating and I cry out just as the third lash is delivered. This one harder than the first two. Deepening the wound. The feeling coming faster. Blood flowing heavier. Just enough to trickle slowly down my ass, gather in the crease below it, slide over my thighs, trail down my calves, pool at my feet and disappear down the drain.

I hear the familiar buzz of a tattoo gun. I stifle my sigh of relief. Tattoos I can handle. Right now, it doesn't matter what he inks into my skin. I'll likely regret that thought in the future. But in this moment, I welcome anything that will stop him from hitting me.

"I thought about branding you," he growls in my ear. "But the scent of burning flesh is the one thing that nauseates me. So instead I'm going to permanently tattoo who you are on your back."

"Okay," I say quickly, sniffling and nodding in agreement. "I'll wear it. Proudly. I'll show you my loyalty. I-I'll prove it."

"What about Pierce?" he asks, his voice deceptively soft. "What happens in a few months when you get to missing big brother?"

Shaking my head, I force out the words. "I won't. He's dead to me. I'm yours. Always."

He fists my hair in his hand and jerks my head into an awkward, painful angle. I cry out—my eyes brimming with fresh tears and slanted from my skin being pulled too tight. "You fucking belong to me," he seethes, splattering my face in spit. "I'm gonna make sure you never forget."

Releasing me, he tells someone to start. I'm too absorbed in the throbbing ache in my temples to notice the sting of the needle at my back. It's comforting, despite the brand it delivers. The buzz of the gun and the slow drip of water from the pipes could actually lull me to sleep. But I know if Cain thinks I'm not suffering, he'll do something worse. So I force myself to cry and beg—pretending it's Pierce's forgiveness I'm pleading for. Not Cain's.

After the first letter, I'm given another three lashes. The pattern continues until I've been tattooed. Until the large, black letters are inked into my skin as if they were patches on leather.

Property of Cain Malcovich.

Twenty-three letters. Three lashes for each one. Every time on a different part of my body. My legs. Thighs. Stomach. Chest. Even the soles of my feet. Everywhere but my back, which is reserved for his name. My title.

I'm conscious the entire time. My body refuses to break. I count every crack of the strap. Saying the number in my head. My voice too occupied with my screams. My pleas that fall on deaf ears. But I know he hears me. Just like I know he's enjoying this. Giving me pain. Torturing me.

He stops only to trace the cuts with his finger. The salt in his sweat burning me as he smears the fine lines of blood across my body. Mixing it with the beads of sweat that pepper my skin. Then his lips are at my ear. Saying my name.

"Winter..."

No that's wrong. He doesn't call me Winter. I shake through the fog in my head and listen harder.

"Winter..."

Something's not right. It's not his voice. It's not his touch. It's not him calling my name.

"Winter. Come on, baby. Wake up."

My eyes fly open and I blink away the tears to find Jinx staring back at me. His face twisted in worry. A simmering anger in his eyes. "I'm sorry," I gasp, shaking my head. Telling him no. My mind confused as it lingers in that space between my dream and reality.

His rage vanishes and those bright, gray eyes, so different from Cain's deep blue ones, are just as reassuring as his words. "You're not sorry. You're safe. It was just a dream."

"No," I say, my voice shaky. Lip quivering. Eyes pooling with tears. "It wasn't." His face relaxes in understanding just as his fingers move across my back. I stiffen in his arms. Waking fully. Differentiating between what is real and what's in my head.

I'm on the couch. The cover pooled at my feet. My sweater next to it. He's sitting beside me—his arms around me, forcing me to sit up. Not just around me but on me. Touching me. One hand pushing the wet, matted hair out of my face. The other on my T-shirt that's soaked in my sweat.

"What did he do to you?" Jinx asks, his thumb trailing dangerously close to the inked flesh on my back as if he already knows.

"Stop," I choke out, trying to pull away from him.

He slides his hand to the side of my neck and curls his fingers around the back of it to hold me in place. "He did more than slap you around, didn't he?"

"Just...stop." My eyes roam the room to find something other than him to focus on.

His hands slip from my back and around my neck, but he doesn't move away from me. I drop my head and stare at my hands in my lap. Trying to clear my thoughts and control my emotions.

"I want to take a bath." I'm not asking for permission, I'm telling him I need space by dismissing him in the nicest way I know how.

He must get it because he nods and stands, offering his hand to me as I kick away the covers at my feet. I take it and absorb the comfort of his cool skin even though I shouldn't. This man is unraveling me. Comfort is the last thing I should feel from him.

Without releasing his hold, he leads me down the hallway and stops in front of the locked door. Only now it's not locked and he pushes it open before pulling me inside behind him.

I'm too engrossed in my own thoughts to really pay attention to my surroundings. Everything just seems gray. Fuzzy. Unimportant.

"I'll get you some clothes," Jinx says, releasing my hand and pulling the door closed behind him.

I barely notice that the bathroom I'm in is very spacious. That the tub is massive and already running with hot water. That the scent of pomegranate, my favorite, coupled with the low lights and rising steam should calm me. But it's not calm I feel. It's defeat.

I strip off my clothes, and discard them on the floor. Then I'm in the tub. Numb to the hot water swirling around me. The grainy bath salts beneath me. I draw my knees up. Lay my cheek on them. Wrap my arms around my legs. Expose my back. My past. My brand. Completely uncaring. Doesn't matter now. Who cares if Jinx knows? Pierce or anyone else. It won't change anything.

Will it?

Of course it will. I'd be stupid to think otherwise. And that inevitable change that's coming has tears leaking from my eyes.

Jinx is probably calling Pierce right now. Telling him about my nightmare. What he's discovered. Letting him know that what they'd assumed about me, might not be true at all. That maybe my staying with Cain wasn't a choice, but an act of survival.

My relationship with my brother will change. I'll become a victim. He'll become outraged. Blood will spill. People will suffer. Lives will be lost. And for what? Respect? Pride? Me? It doesn't matter whose name is inked into my skin below the words "Property of." As long as I'm alive, I'll belong to someone. That's just the life of the MC. It's a man's world. And if you're unlucky enough to be born or dragged into it, then you'll always be reminded of your place. Your role. Your title.

Property.

Little sister. Cutslut. Ol' Lady. Whore. Mother. Pass-around. House mouse. We all have something in common. We're beneath a man. Not above. Not equal. Always below. Some women get off on the idea of a man going to war for her. Expressing his loyalty. Willing to die for her. Kill for her. Bring hell to anyone who wrongs her. Those women are selfish. There's nothing good about losing someone you love. They don't die with honor, knowing they gave their life avenging the loss of a woman's respect. They just fucking die.

I know my brother. He'll let the guilt of the past six years eat away at him. It'll take over his life. Consume his mind. Brew to rage. He'll feel worthless. Less like a man. More like a coward. He'll retaliate against Cain.

I know my brother's club. Their creed. By-laws. Beliefs. They'll follow my brother into the pits of hell because that's what you do in a brotherhood. You charge. Fight. Kill. Die. Loyalty knows no bounds. Has no conscience. Respect is earned. Never forgotten. To the Devil's Renegades, revenge is air. And they all have to breathe.

Turning off the faucet, I lie back—sending water splashing over the side onto the floor. I float on top of the water and stare at the ceiling. Minutes later, I hear the muffled sound of knocking. I don't answer. Jinx calls my name. I don't answer then either. When he steps through the door, I pull my eyes from the ceiling and look at him. Wondering if it's his grave I'll be standing next to once the war is over. Or will he be standing next to me, shovel in hand, waiting his turn to toss a blade of dirt onto someone else's grave. Pierce's perhaps.

Tears blur my vision. He's nothing more than a fuzzy shape as he crosses the floor to me. "Why are you crying?" he asks. Such a simple question. Such a complex answer. One I simply don't have the energy to explain. So I stay silent.

He turns to leave, his boots slapping against the water and reminding me of the sound my hand made when I slapped him. Yet, he never slapped me back, even though I deserved it. Because he's not Cain. He's not evil. He's good. And this tug-of-war shit happening between me and the two clubs will be the start of a domino effect of terrible things in his near future. Things that, like Pierce, he doesn't deserve.

Sitting up in the tub, I call out to him. "Did you tell him?" I ask in a scratchy voice.

"Who?"

"Pierce. About the nightmare. About what happened. What did he say?"

"Nothing," he says, those bright eyes as void as ever.

"Nothing? Why would he say nothing?" I whisper, more to myself than to Jinx.

I'm dissecting Pierce's silence. Analyzing all angles. Wondering if it was silent rage he responded with, or silent remorse. Then Jinx speaks again. And his words change absolutely everything.

"Because I didn't tell him."

JINX

Winter's been here two weeks. That's three hundred and thirty-six hours I've spent alone with her. Every day she challenges my patience. Tests my will. Pushes me to a point that leaves me wanting to choke her or fuck her or do both to her simultaneously. But until tonight, I've managed to keep my shit together.

I can deal with her running. I can accept that she's a borderline alcoholic. I can cope with her attitude. Hell, I've even succeeded in not blowing a fuse when I see her in my shirt, or when I see her dancing, cleaning and singing in it. But her panicked, bloodcurdling, frightening screams—I can't handle that shit.

I was outside when I heard it. Nearly broke my fucking neck tearing through the door like a mad man—ready to kill who or whatever it was terrorizing her. Because a scream like that, like I've never heard, didn't happen simply because someone was hurt, pissed or had a bad dream. It came from someone in imminent danger. It was a cry for mercy from a torture too agonizing for the human mind to comprehend.

When I found her still on the couch, I felt relief—but only for a moment. Seeing her thrashing, covered in sweat, watching her body buck with guttural sobs...it was like someone had reached into my chest and squeezed the life right out of my fucking heart.

I grabbed her. Tried to shake her awake. She begged for me—or someone—to stop. At the sound of that, I no longer felt wrecked. I felt rage. Burning, furious, ready-to-rip-a-motherfucker's-spleen-out-through-his-throat rage. I wanted to kill the man responsible for this. Even if he only existed in her nightmares.

She finally snapped out of it. Opening those big, green eyes and turning them on me. They were filled with raw fear. Something I'd never seen in her. While I tried to assure her she was okay, she fought to breathe. To calm down. It took a minute for the fog clouding her mind to dissipate. Only then did she finally seem to understand that what she just experienced was only a dream. But something tells me that while it might've been a dream this time, it wasn't always.

My first instinct was to call Pierce. Explain the shit that happened and see if he could help me figure out what she refused to talk about. Problem with Pierce is, he doesn't know how to talk to Winter. His pride won't let him be the man he once was with her. He cares about her. Loves her. But only I get to see the wrecked man her situation makes him. With her, he just lashes out. Between the two of them, it's like a battle to see who can hurt who the most.

While she was in the bathroom, I paced back and forth—my finger hovering over the screen on my phone. This is something he'd want to know. Something he'll be pissed I didn't tell him about. I've decided, he's just going to have to be pissed.

Whatever she's hiding is monumental. There's a reason she's keeping it from Pierce. My gut tells me it's for the best. And this is the first time my gut has sided with someone who wasn't a brother.

So now I'm hiding something from one of my own. The price for my betrayal won't come cheap. She'll have to tell me her secrets no matter how much she doesn't want to. If I have to tie her up for days or pry it from her pretty pink lips, I aim to get the truth out of her any way I can. Even if I have to break her to get it.

WINTER

He didn't tell him...

I turn the question of why over and over in my head as I mindlessly scrub at my skin. Wash my hair. Drain the tub. Dry off. Brush out my hair. Clean the water off the floor. Until finally, anticipation gets the best of me. And in nothing but a towel, I slip out the door and into the bedroom—taking it in for the first time.

It's so much nicer than the one I've been staying in. Bigger too. A king sized bed centers the room with nightstands on either side. There's a sitting area to the left with an overstuffed couch similar to the one in the living room positioned in front of a gas fireplace that's lit and glowing a deep orange. Books line the top of it and a flat screen T.V. is mounted above it. There's also a massive dresser, vanity, walk-in closet and the bathroom.

Jinx is standing by the bed. Watching me with a guarded expression. His arms at his sides. His chest naked. Beautiful. Designed in tattoos. Sculpted in muscle. His head lacking a beanie or a hat. It's the first time I've seen his hair—short on the sides. Longer on the top. Brushed back in that classic, sexy, James Dean style.

Swallowing hard, I focus on his nose. It's the most unattractive thing on his face—only because it's a nose. "You said you didn't tell Pierce?" He nods. "Why?"

He studies me a full minute before answering. "Because I don't really know what you're hiding. And even if I did, it's not my secret to tell."

I keep underestimating this man and he keeps surprising me. Flooring me with responses that don't coincide with those of a man dedicated to his club. Maybe that's why he rides alone—nomad. Why he floats from chapter to chapter and refuses to have roots anywhere. Because with that comes responsibility. An entirely deeper level of commitment. Not to mention vulnerability.

Whatever his reasons for being different, I respect him all the more for it. It makes me trust him more. See him as a person—not a patch. Or a brother. Or another potential man ready to claim me as his own. Dictate what I should wear. Who I should hang out with. What I should call him.

"If you look close enough, you'll find scars all over my body," I say, refusing to ask myself why I'm opening up to him. "Most of them are small. No bigger than an inch or two. No more than a tiny white line, a small indention or a strip of raised flesh. Some are hidden beneath the art. Some are in plain sight. I remember how I got every one of them. Dates and times, too. Is that strange?"

"No," he says, his voice feather soft. Caressing me. Encouraging me to continue. The man should be a shrink, because I'm eager to tell him everything. My only anxiety comes from knowing that I should use this to my advantage. And deciding that I will.

I'll reveal myself to him one layer at a time. Make him think he's breaking me down. Getting in my head. Then when he least expects it, I'll make my move. I'll escape. In the end, we'll both get something. I'll get away. Maybe prevent any bloodshed between The Devil's Renegades and Madness. And Jinx will get a fresh reminder of why it's dangerous to get close to someone.

"I'm going to show you something I'm not ready for other people in your world to see. Not because I'm ashamed but because nothing good can from anyone knowing."

"Then why show me?" he asks, startling me. I'd assumed he'd be eager to hear what I had to say. Before I can catch myself, I'm giving him the real reason when I should be lying.

"Because I trust you." My mouth snaps shut but it's too late. I've spoken. He's heard.

I don't like how telling him this is making me feel. That's not part of the plan. Yet, some deep reaction is tugging at my heart. Tightening my chest. It's strange. And it kind of feels like friendship. I think. Hell, I haven't had friends in so long, I can't really remember what it feels like.

Clearing my throat, I quickly add, "And I want to avoid any surprise reactions in the future. Considering we're constantly together and you have no respect for my privacy."

His silence fills the room. He looks as unaffected as always. Like he could give two shits about what I say or what I show him. A part of me believes it's a façade. Especially the strain in his voice when he says, "Fair enough."

I lick my lips—not missing his eyes that break away from mine and lower to my mouth. I wait until our gazes are locked again before speaking. "I did something to Cain once that made him question my loyalty. He thought I'd forgotten my place. So he did something to remind me and everyone he shared me with who I was and who I belonged to."

I'm nervous. Nervous about his reaction. My reaction. Nervous that this will change things between us. That his lust will turn to distaste. That our undeniable sexual attraction will be severed. These things shouldn't matter to me. But they do.

"We all have scars, Winter," he says, his voice low. "Just because they're not on the surface, doesn't mean they don't exist."

I drop my head. Unable to look at him while all these emotions are swimming through me. Emotions I haven't felt in so long, yet with a few simple words, he can bring them to the surface.

My breathing is heavy. My heart racing to control my emotion. I blink rapidly to hold back my tears. I'm not going to breakdown. I refuse. I had my first moment of weakness in the woods. My second in the bathtub. He witnessed both. I can't let it happen again. I have to be strong. Independent. Stubborn and miserable and more trouble than I'm worth.

If I'm vulnerable, he'll want to protect me. If he sees I'm weak, he'll show his strength. The plan was to make him *believe* he was breaking me down. Not for him to actually do it. My act was intended to be a cover-up. I wasn't supposed to actually feel like this. But I do.

I'm not even aware he's standing in front of me until he cups my face in his hands. Then he kisses me. Gently. Passionately. Reverently. Those big palms warm and soft against my skin. Holding me to his mouth. Not possessively but tenderly controlling.

He presses his lips to each corner of my mouth before pulling away just enough to look at me. His hands still hold me in place as he pins me with his gaze. "I'm not your dream guy," he says, waiting a moment for me to absorb that before continuing. "I'm not your fairytale or your happily ever after. I'm not a monster, but I'm not a good man. Don't fall in love with me, Winter. You'll only be wasting your time."

His words are laced with conviction. His eyes are filled with determination. They race back and forth in his head, searching mine for understanding. He won't find anything less.

"Ditto," I breathe, needing this. Him. An escape from this reality of hell that is my life. I don't need a happily ever after. Just a small taste of the elusive fairytale is more than enough.

Two heartbeats later, his lips find mine again in that same heated, worshipping way. This is just how I imagined it would be. But not with him, with my dream guy—someone he clearly isn't or has any intention of being. Not that I mind. He might kiss good, but everything else about him is exactly what I'm not looking for.

The club.

The patch.

The possessiveness.

Him not being a good man.

But I'll allow this—a kiss. I'll even allow myself to get lost in it. Absorbed by it. I can be devoured without being owned. And most definitely without falling in love.

One hand around my waist, he lifts me just off my feet and carries me to the bed—keeping one big palm cradling my face. He pulls a low hanging string attached to the ceiling fan light and floods the room in complete darkness—unknowingly making this that much better for me.

In the dark, I don't have the anxiety that comes with knowing he can see all of me. My scars. My brand. My overwhelming emotion. I can be anyone. He can be anyone. Or we can both be no one. Characters from a book, perhaps—caught up in the magic of the moment.

Covering his body with mine, he pushes me to my back and kisses me softer than before, but just as thoroughly. Tongue sweeping lazily along mine. Mouth smothering all my moans. Hands on my face holding me sweetly.

In the moments that follow, everything happens almost in a blur. A dream. It's feels too good. Too right. Too soul shaking to be willingly involved in something so mystic.

His mouth breaks away from mine to trail tiny kisses along my jaw. Then his hands are opening my towel. Caressing the hot flesh beneath it. Sliding to the apex of my thighs and brushing across my pussy— testing me. Ensuring I'm wet. Ready. The evidence is on his fingers. In his mouth. He groans his approval.

He stands. I hear the sound of a drawer opening. Closing. The tear of foil. Feel the dip in the mattress. His body naked. Warm. Between my legs. Lips on my lips. Tongue on mine. Hungry, but tamed.

One hand cradles my head. The other slides down my side. Over my hip. My thigh. Gripping me beneath my knee. Drawing it up. Then he's inside me. Driving slowly. Long, delicious, thorough strokes that force him deep. He pulls out almost completely. Pushes in—going impossibly deeper. Over. And over. And over.

I lift my hips to meet him. My hands on his shoulders. His neck. Pulling him to me. My breathing staccato. Mouth accepting his lingering, lazy kisses. Body coiled tight. The tension nearly unbearable. Not just from my impending orgasm, but from something more. Bigger. Scary. Threatening to wreck me if it snaps.

Fear has me holding back. Refusing the peak that is so close. Whatever it is that's so tightly suppressed taunts me. I'm scared of what it is. What it isn't. What it will do to me. What it will reveal. What Jinx will think when it does.

"Give it to me, Winter."

I shake my head hard. My eyes squeezed tightly shut. I can't. I'm... scared. Overly aware of a plummeting pain in my chest. The kind you get when you hear horrible news. Or witness something terrible. I'm also aware of strong arms folded around me. A hard chest not over me, but beneath me. Warm breath on my cheek. Lips at my ear. And the softest words coming from the kindest voice I've ever heard.

"Quiet, sweetheart. You're okay," Jinx promises. It's then I realize I'm crying. Yet I have no idea why.

"I-I'm not. Something's wrong," I cry, shaking my head. Pulling out of his hold. Sitting up on his lap. Straddling his waist. Feeling him hard against me.

Sex.

It's something I can control. Something powerful enough to overshadow this...frustrating fucking feeling I can't decipher. I need it. The build...the anticipation...the release... God the release. I have to have it. Now.

Fisting his cock in my hand, I squeeze hard. He hisses through his teeth, but makes no move to stop me. He only grows thicker in my hand. His skin soft, warm, wet with remnants of my arousal, the pearl of come on the head of his cock signifying his and my infuriating tears that leak continuously from my eyes.

His groan is guttural when I lift my hips and sink down on top of him—burying him to the hilt inside me. I whimper through the pinch of pain. Moan through the slow spread of arousal as he flexes inside me. Cry out in ecstasy as I take everything I can from him. Riding him hard. Mercilessly. Selfishly. Absorbing the tingle of pleasure that comes from the contact my clit makes every time I slam his shaft deep inside me.

My nails dig into his stomach. Hips gyrating. Rocking. Searching for my body's release. My mind's. And once again, fear of that free-fall feeling doesn't let me find it. The part of me that wants it is overpowered by the part of me that is scared.

I scream out in frustration. But it's cut off when he sits up. Covers his mouth with mine. Cradles my face. Kisses me. Forces me to slow. To feel. But I don't want to feel. Not this. Not these emotions. I want to fuck.

I want him to fuck this feeling out of me.

Fuck me hard.

Fuck me crazy.

Fuck me into a goddamn oblivion like he once promised he would.

I'm flipped to my back. Our kiss broken. His cock still inside me. He's moving. Harder. Rougher than before. My mind clears—centered on one thing. My orgasm. And it builds rapidly. Taking my breath. Distorting thoughts. Pivoting me to new heights. But that fear breaks through the haze and I'm crash landing on jagged rocks again.

"Stop holding back," he says, still rigid and heavy inside me. He gives me no time to answer.

He slides down my body and replaces his cock with his tongue, impaling me before licking his way to my clit and sucking hard. My back bows. I cry out. The torture a mixture of pain and pleasure.

Two fingers easily dip inside my pussy. Pumping in and out several times before spreading the wetness to my ass—lubricating the tight hole while his tongue caresses my clit with just enough pressure to make me writhe.

The tip of his finger pushes inside me. Finding no resistance, he sinks it further until his finger fucks my ass as slowly as his tongue circles me. Building me up. Amplifying the anticipation. Touching all the forgotten places that make an orgasm that much more riveting. Then he stops.

"On your knees, baby," he instructs, his voice calm as if he has all the control in the world.

I struggle to my knees. My cries now a sob. My mind baffled by the reason—I'm broken. I know why I'm broken, I just don't know why now. In this moment. When I should be thriving, I'm failing. Could it be the nightmare? Was it a trigger? What about Jinx's kindness. His show of affection. Is that a trigger too?

Thoughts flee when his hands spread open my cheeks. His tongue presses against the tight ring—licking and circling and causing my fingers and toes to curl in the sheets. Something so forbidden shouldn't feel this good. Yet it does.

Millions of tiny sparks ignite inside me. Sending an electrifying shock of pleasure rocketing from every nerve. Blood rushes fervently through my veins. Causing every pulse point to pound against my skin. I'm so close...

Raising up, he runs a hand down my back. My body shakes from his touch. From the torment. The sobs. The uncontrollable sniffles and cries that have no place in a moment like this. "Shh," he soothes, his hands coming to rest on my hips. The thick head of his cock centered on my ass—pressing against the tense hole. "Relax and push back against me."

I do as he says. Knowing this is the best way to alleviate any discomfort. Remembering all the ways I taught myself to cope with the pain. The embarrassment. The years of unwanted sex and attention and the agony that came with it.

He's stilled behind me, but his hands are roaming my back. My sides. Comforting me. Soothing me. "Stop thinking and relax," he says, impossibly skillful and controlled considering his dick is halfway inside me.

I inhale on a ragged breath, exhale slowly and by my next breath, he's buried inside me. His stomach flush against my ass. His cock secured firmly, rooted within my ass. Filling me. Nearly overwhelming me. Causing a tingling sensation to flicker deep in my groin.

He presses his hand to the back of my head and applies a little pressure—encouraging me to place my head on the pillow. My ass rises slightly with the movement. I cry out into my pillow when his fingers begin a circular rhythm over my clit.

He fucks my ass with just as much practiced patience as he does everything else. Letting me feel everything. Experience the sensuality of it. He doesn't speak to me. He doesn't question my tears. He doesn't ask me if I'm physically okay, and I know it's because if I wasn't, he would be aware without me even saying so.

I'm pushed to the brink so many times I lose count. Each one worse than the last. I try to move against him. To touch myself. Force him to give me release that I'm sure will come this time. But my strength is no match for his and he easily stops my every attempt. Like though I believe I'm ready, he knows I'm not.

I'm sobbing loudly. Crying out. Pleading. Weeping. Wanting him to do more than just bring me to the cusp. But he is unrelenting. Giving me indescribable pleasure, just never enough. I'm at the peak once again. His movements have become more savage. I'm positive this is the moment. The explosion he's spent all this time working me up to.

Then he stills inside me—filling me with hot ropes of come that have his cock throbbing with every burst. His fingers have stilled too—leaving me incomplete and suffering.

"Please," I beg, my mind flashing back to all the nights I was left wanting. Feeling used and abandoned. "I need it. Jinx, I need it."

"Shhh," he says, gently rolling me to my back. Falling between my legs. Kissing my neck. My chest. Lapping at my nipples. My stomach. Spreading my knees wide. Then devouring me with his mouth.

I detonate around him. The sudden explosion can be felt in every limb. Every nerve. Every single fucking hair follicle on my body. It's the best high I've ever had. The greatest release I've ever felt. The most euphoric, rewarding, thrilling moment I've ever experienced. And it's never-ending.

I've heard of multiple orgasms. Experienced a couple in my life. But this is different. Bigger. Greater. A consistent increase of infinite skyrocketing pleasure that is so riveting, it's frightening.

The knot in my chest loosens. The tension in my body lessens. I feel as though I'm hovering in the air. It's foreign to me—to be this relaxed. Sated. Complete. The descent into reality comes at a slow, floating pace—a complete contradiction to what I've been feeling. And I know my mind won't permit me a moment longer of reprieve. It refuses my peaceful state and allows every demon in my life to rear its ugly head and replace the beautiful moment I just had with something poignant.

As I drift further from my reverie, the truth of my suffering is revealed. I'm broken. Shattered. Unfixable. Incurable. The knowledge isn't new to me, but it hurts more now. Because for the first time in six years, I've become aware of it without Cain or his actions to remind me.

The bed is cold now. The absence of Jinx leaves my body in shivers and my spirit bereft. But before I can process the why, he's back. Spreading my knees with his hands. Making me whimper in protest because I can't. Not again. Not tonight.

"Hush, baby. Just cleaning you up." And he does. Lifting my legs. Opening me up. Placing something warm and damp and soft against tender flesh that has me flinching—feeling the pain now that the pleasure has subsided.

He holds it there. Wordlessly stroking my stomach with his thumb as his warm semen pours out of me. Then he's holding me to his chest. Enveloping me in his heat. Covering us both. Burying my face in his neck. Rubbing my hair. Kissing my head. Hugging me.

The steel in my spine has stood strong against the evilest of men. Yet somehow this one has managed to liquefy me completely.

I shouldn't want his comfort. I shouldn't enjoy how he lazily rubs my back with his hand and strokes my cheek with his thumb. Damn I do, though. I crave it. Maybe it's because it's been so long and I'm starved for affection. Attention. Some semblance of security and protection even if it does come from my captor. Even if it isn't genuine or just a ploy to get me to let down my guard so he can destroy me all over again.

Whatever the reason, I don't care. In this moment, my heart needs this. My mind. My body. My soul yearns to just be that girl who needs to be held and comforted by a man. So I let go. I don't hide or shy away. I cry harder. Sob louder. Cling to him like he's my last thread of hope dangling from a busted spool.

The abandonment from my parent's sudden death. The remorse of leaving Pierce. The regret I harbor for all I've put him through. The hurt I caused just to get away from a family who so many would kill for. The pain I endured from that sadistic motherfucking Cain...I release it all. In a stranger's bed. My head on his chest while he holds me. Treats me like I'm someone. Not a piece of property, an object or a cutslut. A real person.

Without the light to reveal the real truth, this is my fairytale. In the darkness, this is my happily ever after. And he is my dream guy. But only in the dark. In the light, he is the guy whose wrath is well deserved. The one who has every right to hate me. To hurt me. To break me. He is this guy.

Jinx.

The guy I can't love.

WINTER

The tattoos that run from my shoulders to my wrists are very personal to me. Some of them hold a symbolic meaning. Like the date of my parent's death that's inked into the eyes of the sugar skull on my left forearm. Or the bunny rabbit on my right wrist —a drawing of the stuffed animal Pierce gave me when I was ten. And his tears which represent Pierce's grief that he never got to express because he was too busy putting on a happy face for me.

Not all of them are symbolic. Some are just things I like—flowers, a bottle of scotch, a smoking .357. Some are stupid—a toilet seat, a company's patented logo, an owl smoking a blunt. But no matter their significance, they're a part of me. Which is why I don't read too much into Jinx's tattoos as I trace them with my finger—he might perceive their meaning the same as I do.

We're still in bed. The clock on the table next to us says it just past seven thirty in the morning. He's asleep, or at least pretending to be. When I woke up about fifteen minutes ago and first touched him, his breathing quieted as if he was no longer in that deep sleep stage.

So I'm pretty sure he's awake and just avoiding the awkward "morning after sex" moment. Or perhaps he's worried if he opens his eyes and looks at me, he'll find me irresistible. Or he'll see a look on my face that tells him I read too much into us sleeping together and now I'm thinking he might be "the dream guy."

"I didn't steal that money for Cain," I start, unsure of why. I keep my eyes on his chest, my finger tracing the barbed wire wrapped around a tree inked on his bicep. I can't bring myself to look up and see if he's awake and listening. Somehow not being one hundred percent sure he is makes it easier for me to tell him the truth.

"At one time, I would have. But in the time we'd been together, he'd changed. He'd gotten meaner. Violent. Withdrawn. I knew I had to get away. I also knew he wouldn't let me go.

"When I heard about the national run, I knew it was mandatory for Pierce to go. I knew Cain would go just because it was mandatory he didn't. He thrived on being an outlaw. Took pleasure in flaunting it in other's faces. MC's would consider him showing up a disgrace. I found it a blessing.

"I guess he felt something was off. I'd been nervous for a few days, and thought I'd managed to hide it. But it showed. I should've known something was up the moment he left me unprotected. I was too excited at the possibility to care, though. I had a plan. One I thought was flawless.

"One of the whores drove a piece of shit Mercury. The kind you could still hot wire if you knew what you were doing. When Cain left, his pipes could still be heard and I was already in that car.

"I drove to Pierce's with nothing more than hope that there'd be something in that safe. I could pick pocket my way south, but it would take a lot longer. I needed money. I found it. Took it. But I didn't make it out of the driveway before Cain caught me."

Swallowing hard, I dig deep to find the courage to say the next part out loud. To tell the nightmare that still haunts me. To relive it like I had last night. The only difference is that I'm consciously deciding to re-experience it.

"Cain was convinced Pierce gave me that money. Accused me of selling Madness' secrets to him. In his eyes, I was a snitch. I'd forgotten my place. So he made sure I carried something to remind me and everyone else who I belonged to."

Goosebumps break out across my skin when the tip of Jinx's finger grazes one of the letters on my back. I thought knowing for sure he was awake would make this harder. But his touch makes it easier. It's like a reminder that I'm safe. Which I'd find ridiculous if I overanalyzed it. So I don't.

"He chained me up," I say, my voice strong. Matter-of-fact. Not a hint of fear lacing my words or clouding my mind. "Beat me. Tattooed me. And once I healed, he shared me. With everyone in the club just so he could show off his property. His *cutslut*. That part wasn't so bad, though," I add, grinning to myself.

Looking up, I find Jinx's lips tipped in a lazy, sleepy smile—his finger still trailing over the black letters. In this exact moment, the thing that matters most to me is that Jinx isn't repulsed by seeing someone else's name etched in my back. Instead, he looks like he might be remembering last night.

The heat in his eyes is unmistakable. He looks so delicious. So inviting. Without a second thought as to why, I'm straddling him. Dragging my tongue over one nipple, then moving to the other—licking it until it's as hard as the first.

His cock, thick and erect, strains beneath the covers. Pressing hard against my pussy that's already wet and ready for him. I rock against it —sliding back and forth a few times while I lick a path up his chest to his neck.

"I don't kiss on the mouth in the morning," I say, dragging my tongue across his Adams apple. Over the stubble on his chin. Then planting a kiss on it and meeting his gray eyes that are hooded with lust.

"Me either," he growls out, capturing me around my waist and slinging his legs over the side of the bed before standing.

I run my hands through his hair. Rake my teeth across his jaw. Press my naked chest harder against his as he walks us to the bathroom—jerking the covers from between us as he does.

I can't keep my hands or my mouth off of him while he moves around the bathroom. Starts the shower. Grabs a couple towels. All while keeping me pinned to him with one strong arm.

It feels good being here with my legs locked at the small of his back. So much that I frown when he steps into the large shower and sets me on my feet. He grins down at me.

"Wash me." He hands me a loofah already foaming with soap. I lift a brow in question. "Shut up."

"Mr. Badass uses a loofah," I tease, lathering his cock from base to tip, beneath, above and everywhere in between. He ignores my jab as he watches my hand work him. I follow his gaze and find the erotic act even more stimulating because I can see all of him. He's gloriously sexy naked. Flawless, chiseled, hardened perfection.

My mouth waters.

I drop the sponge and wipe away the soap as the water washes it from him. Before he's fully rinsed, I lower my knees to the shower floor and take him in my hand. Studying the thick veins lining his shaft. The smooth skin stretched over it. The head that's swelled and dotted with a drop of creamy, white pre-cum.

I flick my tongue over the small slit—anxious to know if he tastes as good as I think he will. He tastes better. His flavor just the perfect mix of salty sweet—not too strong or overpowering. I moan, squeeze his shaft and pump him in my fist in hopes of getting another taste.

"So fuckin' sexy," he mutters, staring down at me with his mouth parted. His eyes flashing. His hands gathering my hair and fisting it at the back of my head. My clit tingles when he drags a finger over my bottom lip. "I've been thinking about fuckin' this pretty mouth of yours for days."

Eager to please him, I lay my hands flat on his thighs and take him in my mouth. Only the tip at first, circling it with my tongue. Sucking hard. Then pushing a little deeper. Making sure not one inch of flesh goes untouched.

He pulls my hair a little to get my attention. "Look at me." I do and he cups the side of my head with his other hand—stroking his thumb along the underside of my eye. It's a gentle caress, but I have a feeling he's about to contradict it with something more harsh. So I relax my throat in preparation.

His hips pump slow at first. Giving me a little more on every drive until he's buried in my throat. He holds me there a few seconds. My eyes water. Burn from being open so wide, but I never break his gaze.

When he pulls out of me, I hear him mutter a, "Motherfucker," over my gasps for air. And it turns me on even more.

My nails dig into his thighs as he fucks my mouth—sometimes hard and rough and forceful like I like it. Talking in a tone that matches his thrusts. Grounding out dirty praises and rhetorical questions such as, "These lips are as pink and swollen as the ones on your cunt." And "You like having your mouth fucked?"

Then sometimes he fucks me easy and slow and sensual, which I also find I like. His tone much sweeter and spoken softer when he tells me, "You look beautiful on your knees with my cock in your mouth. Those pretty green eyes looking up at me." I'm so turned on, I could get off by just washing my pussy the same way I did his dick.

"Tell me what you want, baby," he says, fisting his cock and rubbing the head of it across my lips. Teasing me. Tightening his hold in my hair when I try to lean in for more. "You want me to come in your mouth then bend you over and eat your sweet pussy until you come on mine? Or you want me to fuck you hard against this wall and let you come on my cock?"

I whimper with indecision. Shiver beneath the hot spray of water that feels mildly warm against my fiery skin. I've never been given a choice. Now that I have one, the only conclusion I can come to is that I want it all.

I want to taste him and feel him. I want him to taste me and feel me. I want to be fucked hard and caressed softly. I want to be fucked softly and come hard. I want to stop thinking so fucking much and find that high I've been chasing since we got in the shower. I want to think about it forever and enjoy the build because I don't want it to end.

Either he's tired of waiting for my answer, or he has a solution to my problem, because next thing I know, he's pulling me to my feet. Turning me to face the wall of the shower. Lifting my knee. Spreading me open. Sliding his cock between the swollen lips of my pussy. Finding my wet, heated entrance. And impaling me in one, swift plunge that has my eyes closing, my mouth going slack and my toes curling.

Fingers dig into my hips and beneath my thighs as he holds me in place and fucks me hard and fast. The sound of our wet bodies slapping together can barely be heard over my cries of ecstasy. I scream for him to fuck me harder and without breaking stride, he angles his body a little to the left, lifts my legs a little higher and gives me exactly what I asked for.

I come so hard my knees go weak and his arms are all that hold me up. Millions of tiny sparks ignite inside me. Sending an electrifying shock of pleasure rocketing from every nerve. Blood rushes fervently through my veins. Causing every pulse point to pound against my skin.

While my body still hums from my release, I'm lowered to my weak knees. My matted, wet hair is smoothed off my face and fisted at the back of my head. He tugs and I look up. Open wide. Ready to take what I know he's about to give me. And pleasure begins to swirl and build deep in my belly at the thought.

"Play with your pussy," he says, guiding himself between my lips. "I want to see you come. Like the first time I fucked you."

The first time. When I was tied to the bed. When he fucked me out of anger. When I was angry too. When I told him I hated him. When he said it back. It feels like a lifetime ago. But I still remember how good it was. His expression when he witnessed me having one of the best orgasms of my life. And damn if I don't want to see his same reaction from that night too.

Vigorously, I circle my clit with my fingertips. Working the over sensitized nub with as much fervor as he works my mouth. Plunging deep. Stealing my breath. Causing my eyes to water. Forcing me to take him despite my throat that threatens to constrict.

I swirl my tongue. Hollow my cheeks. Rake my teeth down his shaft. Furiously stroke my clit. All while keeping my eyes on him. Watching as his stay centered on me.

His eyes flutter. Hands tighten. Hips jerk. Still. Then he's flooding my mouth. I'm desperately swallowing him. His heady taste coupled with my violent touch pushes me over the edge.

My vision clouds at the corners. Heart hammers an unsteady beat that's too fast. Heat pulses through me. Blood rushes to everywhere but my mind and I can't think straight. All I can do is feel. Ride this high. Experience this euphoria. Drift through the abyss of pleasure.

Until I slowly float back to reality. Only this time, it's as welcome as my escape.

Jinx is standing over me, looking down on me with a lazy, infectious grin. His sated look compliments him. He appears relaxed but composed and in control. Meanwhile, I probably look like a wounded, wet dog begging for a table scrap.

He pulls me up and keeps a grip on my elbow as he retrieves his loofah from the shower floor. I smirk when I see him holding the fluffy, black sponge that not even he can make masculine.

"Shut up," he says, smiling at me as he lathers it with soap. He holds it up and gives me a pointed look. "I don't share my loofah with anyone. But I'm making an exception for you."

I can't drop this big, goofy grin on my face as he begins washing my chest and arms as if the task required the deepest level of concentration and attention. "Awe..." I drawl, batting my eyes. "I feel so special."

He gazes at me from beneath his lashes. His eyes soft. His expression serious. And I know whatever he says next will most definitely have shit fluttering in my belly when it shouldn't.

"That's because you are special."

Damn butterflies...

JINX

This girl and her ability to make me say shit I never thought I'd say...

You're special?

What the fuck was that about?

Bitches like her are a dime a dozen. She's not special. She's a pain in my ass. A nuisance. A thief. So she's a great lay. As hot and sexy as she is beautiful and graceful. Has the most perfectly fat ass that shakes with the smallest movement. Big, gorgeous, flawless tits that I want to suck, fuck and come all over. And I could never tire of those long, shapely legs of hers wrapping around my waist. My hips. My back. My shoulders while I grip her ass and eat her until she's flooding my mouth with her sweet juices that I can't get enough of.

But special? Nah. Not even close.

So why the fuck am I bathing her with my very manly loofah, drying her off, letting her use my toothpaste, then kissing her good morning while I hold her face like that motherfucking dream man of hers? Because I'm a good guy.

She had a rough night. Me fucking her pretty mouth this morning probably wasn't the best way to show my appreciation for her opening up to me and giving me some truth. So I kissed her in a shitty attempt to make up for being an insensitive dick. That's all.

"You seem angry," she says, leaning against the door of the closet. I stiffen when I turn to face her. So does my cock.

What she's wearing isn't *special*. It's just a pair of them tight ass yoga pants. Coupled with a shirt that's short enough in the front to reveal her belly button. It falls off of one shoulder and I can see the top of her left breast. No bra. My eyes flit to the pants that cling to her like a second skin. No panties.

"I'm not angry." My tone is gruff. I sound like a liar. She calls me out on it.

"You're a shitty liar."

"You hungry?" I ask, wanting to change the subject. Get her out of my personal space so I can think.

"I could eat."

Fuck. Me too. Her. Right now. Grab her ass, lift her to my shoulders, rip open the crotch of those pants with my teeth and feast on her cunt until lunch. Then do it again. And again.

I clear my throat and turn back to my clothes hanging in a color-coded order in my very neat, very organized closet. I'm a little anal.

Anal.

"There's cereal and shit in the kitchen. Help yourself."

I don't allow myself to breathe until I hear her walk away. Even then, I can smell the distinct, lingering scent of her around me. Choking me. It's suffocating. I need some air. Some space. I need a break to clear my head before I lose track of what's important here. Or get attached to someone who's not important. Or at least who shouldn't be.

My phone rings and I'm so thankful for the distraction, I'm tempted to tell whoever it is that I love them. When I see Pierce's name, my chest tightens with indecision. I'm not sure what to tell him or if I should.

"Pierce," I greet, grabbing a black T-shirt and a pair of jeans from the rack.

"You ever heard of a riding club that goes by the name of Ten's Testament?"

"Nope." *Shit*. I left the empty hangers hanging in the wrong place. "They some Christian club?" I ask, forcing myself to get dressed and forget about the hangers.

"Doubt that. They're a Madness support club. Madness started with ten originals. Think that's where they got the name?"

"Maybe. Why are you suddenly so interested in them?" *Fucking hangers*. I give up trying to put my clothes on head toward the closet. But Pierce's words halt me.

"Because they're suddenly interested in Mississippi." I sit back down on the bed—giving him my undivided attention. "They stopped a couple hours north of you. Luke seems to think they may be making their way to Hattiesburg."

"Think they're here for Winter?" I ask, looking over my shoulder to make sure she's not listening. Come to think of it, it's awfully quiet in the kitchen. *Damnit...*

"What other reason would they be there? I swear I thought the fucker wouldn't show his face until her birthday. I thought he'd want the money. I knew we should've covered our fucking tracks better. Now he knows where she is. He's coming sooner than we thought. This whole motherfucking plan is going to shit. I need to relocate her. Texas. Oklahoma. Arkansas—"

"Hey," I snap, my voice stern. "Quit fucking rambling. He's sending some punk-ass riding club down here. He's not stupid enough to show his face this early. The plan is working. Stop overthinking this shit. She's safe." *Probably running through the woods right now.*

Pierce takes a few deep breaths. "You're right."

"Of course I'm right," I snap, pulling on some socks and grabbing my boots. "So stay where you are and don't do anything stupid. If you break away and try to come down here, Cain will get suspicious. You can bet your ass he's watching every fucking move you make." *Like I should've been watching your sister instead of stressing over the state of my closet.*

"You sound angry."

I roll my eyes. "I'm not angry. Just busy." Pierce laughs at that. When I find my wallet and keys missing and growl a low, "Fuck," he laughs harder.

"Sounds like you got outsmarted, brother," he says, his voice triumphant.

"She didn't outsmart me. But I gotta go."

He's serious when he speaks again—not a single trace of humor in his voice. "You gave me your word you'd take care of her, Jinx. And I gave you mine on what would happen if you didn't."

"Yeah, yeah, yeah. Shove it up your ass. Worry about keeping your head down and let me worry about your pain in the ass little sister." I hang up before he can say more.

I'm not at all bothered with this *Ten's Testament's* sudden appearance. They won't get to Winter unless they find her before I do. Because when I get my hands on her, I'm going to lock her up and throw away the key. But first, I'm going to put these fucking hangers in their rightful place.

WINTER

J inxton Marks
	Weight: 220
	Height: 6'2
	DOB: *Wow*...he's so young. Only twenty-eight if I'm doing the math right. I figured he was in his early thirties. Closer to Pierce's age.

I shrug, sliding his license back into his wallet and thumbing through his credit cards. My brows lift when I see a black AMEX hidden behind the Discover and Visa. Hot and good credit —impressive.

No pictures. No business cards. No amount of cash really worth stealing. But I bet I could get at least a couple hundred bucks just for this wallet. Freaking Christian Louboutin? This guy can't be a biker and carry a wallet worth more than what people around here make in a week, have excellent credit and a closet that's more organized than the First Lady's.

Poser.

Tossing the wallet on the table, I take another bite of cereal and eye the keys to his car.

Instincts had me grabbing both his keys and wallet ready to bolt.

But then his phone rang and my curiosity got the best of me. What I heard of the conversation didn't surprise me. Knowing I needed to find out more, I decided to hang around and get the rest of the story. And by doing that, I'd strengthen Jinx's trust in me. Which would make it easier to escape when the time was right. By the sound of that conversation, the time is right.

Pausing mid-chew, I watch in amusement as Jinx stomps through the clubhouse. He checks the kitchen first—passing right by me without noticing that I'm sitting only feet from him.

"Mother*fucker!*" he yells, and I can't contain my smile when I hear several pots and pans clatter to the floor.

Entertained by his theatrics, I take another bite. Seconds later, he emerges from the kitchen and walks behind the bar. He seems a little more in control now as he lights a cigarette and pulls his phone from his pocket—leaning his elbows on the worn wood as he studies the screen.

The sound of a car alarm blaring has him jerking upright and looking in the direction of the noise. His eyes pass over me quickly, then slowly drift back. Instead of surprise or relief, he wears his usual, blank expression as he stares at me.

"Hello," I say, my mouth spread in a grin so wide my cheeks hurt. He says nothing. "I got you a bowl." Still silent, he presses the screen on his phone and the alarm stops. "Wasn't sure what kind of cereal you like so I got both boxes."

"Seems I've misplaced my wallet and keys," he says a full minute later, his tone tight with barely suppressed anger.

"Oh." I set my bowl down and pick up his stuff. "You mean these? You didn't misplace them, silly, I took them." I'm struggling to hold in my laughter, but my smile is from ear to ear.

"That's not funny," he says, slowly coming closer.

"The hell it isn't," I mutter, dropping my head and digging into my cereal. "*Motherfucker!*" I mock his yell in a whisper shout. Then I can't help it. I'm laughing. And when I chance a look at him, he's shaking his head—the corner of his lips twitching.

He takes a seat across from me and pours some cereal into his own bowl. For the next several minutes, the only sound is the crunch of our chewing and the clanging of our spoons. When I'm finished, I lean back in my chair and fire off the first question of many to come.

"So what gave my brother the impression that I wasn't safe?"

"Nosey," he mumbles, lighting a smoke and offering it to me, then lighting one for himself. "You know who Ten's Testament are?"

"I do. They're one of Madness' support clubs. They only have a few chapters. All of them out west. Close to Cain. That was one of his little projects. An effort to spread his colors throughout his territory."

Where most MCs have a protocol when it comes to joining, Madness don't have any. Same goes for their support clubs. There might be cops and ex-cons in the same chapter. And from what I know of Tens, they mostly consist of bad guys who use their patch to gain entrance into illegal shit they normally wouldn't have access too.

"I'm guessing they're in Mississippi," I say to Jinx who seems to be pondering over the information I gave him. "Is that why you're worried Pierce is going to show up here?"

He eyes me thoughtfully a moment before giving me a nod—as if he's afraid of my reaction.

"So is he coming? Pierce?" There's strain in my voice when I speak his name. Jinx's eyes soften.

"Your brother loves you."

"I know that."

"Do you love him?" His question catches me off guard.

"Of course I love him," I whisper, my emotions evident. "He's my brother. I owe him my life." I shift in my seat and stretch my legs out in the chair next to me. Keeping my eyes averted, I take a drag of my cigarette—wondering if it's too early to start drinking.

"Is that why you stayed with Cain?" His words are as calm as his demeanor. "Because you feel like you owe Pierce your life so you stayed because you knew if he helped you and Cain found out he'd hurt him?"

"Don't give me that much credit," I mutter. "I wasn't trying to protect Pierce. I mean, of course I don't want him to get hurt or killed because of me. But Pierce doesn't need my protection. He's the most powerful man on the West Coast. Cain knows that. That's why he hurt me when he thought I'd traded some great secrets with Pierce instead of going after him." I shake my head in exasperation.

"Like Madness has secrets worth selling. Everyone already knows their business because they post that shit on their fucking social media."

Jinx nods in agreement.

"You really want to know the truth?" I ask, finally meeting his eyes.

"Only if you want to tell me."

Wow. Wasn't expecting that. I figured he'd jump at the opportunity to learn whatever he could about me, so he could share it with Pierce and they could dissect and analyze my every thought. Then again, he didn't tell him about the nightmare or the tattoo....

"I didn't want Pierce's help. To me, life with him was worse than a life with Cain." Jinx's eyes flit to where my shirt exposes part of my back. I shake my head and pull my shirt higher—already starting to regret opening up.

"I can't imagine a life with Pierce being worse than what that motherfucker put you through." His jaw clenches in anger and my own anger begins to simmer.

"It's so simple for you to see everything in black and white. Pierce is the good guy. My brother. My only living relative. Cain is an asshole. An outlaw. A man who used me for his own personal gain. To you, it's obvious that I should choose Pierce over Cain. But do you have any idea what it's like for someone else to have complete control over your life?"

"You mean Cain?"

"I mean MC life in general. I didn't leave Pierce because I thought the grass was greener. I left to get away from the MC." I hold my hand up before he can speak. "Yes, I know Cain was also in the MC, but he was supposed to help me get out. He had no connections to Pierce and I knew he had the resources to help me disappear."

He gives me a patronizing look. "So what happened? You fell in love?"

"Yes." He sobers at my admission. "With him. With the power. Growing up with Pierce, I was just the little girl who didn't have parents. So my brother figured the best way to ensure I didn't end up wasting my life was by not allowing me to have one. I didn't have a say over anything. My friends. My boyfriends. The classes I took. What I wore. He controlled every aspect of my life. Ultimately, he pushed me away."

"That's not fair," Jinx says, defensively.

"You're right. It's not fair for me to blame him. Just like it wasn't fair of him to treat me like a caged animal. Feeding me when I was hungry. Letting me sleep when I was tired. Rewarding my good behavior by allowing me to walk around the mall with him and his intimidating team of brothers flanking me."

I grab the pack of cigarettes and light one. I focus on inhaling and exhaling only. I don't want to fight or argue. I don't want this conversation to remind me of all the reasons Pierce and I don't see eye to eye.

"Why did you run from Cain that day, Winter? Did he hurt you?"

I peek up at Jinx. His expression is guarded. I fight like hell to keep mine the same way. "He was going to. He was confident I knew about Pierce being in town. I didn't want to meet the wrath I knew was coming. So at the first chance I got, I bolted."

"Why didn't you just tell me that? Why lie?"

I shrug. "Because I figured you'd tell Pierce."

"What's that matter?" he asks, his brow furrowed in confusion.

"How would you feel if you knew that your only sister had been living the past two years of her life in a situation she didn't want to be in? Who endured shit like being tattooed or beaten. Sure, Pierce knows Cain slaps me around a little, but he doesn't know the severity of what I've been through."

Jinx's jaw tightens but he doesn't comment.

"If Pierce believes I wasn't trying to get away from Cain, he'll just think I'm stupid. Some silly girl who somehow justifies my boyfriend's behavior. I can live with that. But I can't live with knowing he's miserable with guilt for not getting me out of there. For not doing more or trying harder. That's a burden he doesn't deserve to carry."

"Will you go back to him? To Cain?" he asks, thoughtful.

"That depends."

His eyes narrow. "On what?"

"On the circumstances," I say on a shrug. "I don't want to go back with him, but I will before I let anyone else pay for my mistakes."

"You know you don't have to, right? Pierce will protect you. The club will protect you."

"Really? How? By putting a bullet in Cain's skull? By starting a war? You can't just kill the President of Madness and not expect repercussions, Jinx. I have no doubt that the Devil's will prevail, but blood will definitely spill. And I don't want that on my hands. I don't want it on my brother's either."

"Like I said," he says, his voice lethal. Words slower. "We can protect you."

Shaking my head, I breathe out a laugh. *He just doesn't get it.* "I don't want your protection. I didn't run from one MC to be owned by another. I did that once already, remember?"

He looks like he wants to say more, but what can he say? That them helping me doesn't make me property? Because that would be a lie.

"I'm not stupid, Jinx. The only way for this club or even Pierce to help me is to make me one of you again. That's why you and my brother orchestrated everything that went down the day you took me. It's why you're using this bullshit excuse about me stealing from you to keep me here. In the end, Pierce is hoping that staying here for a while will persuade me to give up Cain for good."

Jinx doesn't deny it. Not that I thought he would. "Your brother may be a little overprotective. You shouldn't fault him for that. You should be proud to have a brother who wants nothing more than to keep his sister safe. The thought of someone hurting you kills him. Not because you're property. But because he loves you."

My eyes roll. "Forgive me for not groveling to him and expressing how proud it makes me to have him as a brother. But I'm not fully convinced pride isn't the reason he's doing this. Again."

"What the fuck is that supposed to mean?" he asks, angry at my blasphemy against the great and almighty Pierce.

"I know he loves me. That he cares about me and worries about me. It's who he is. What he does. But I didn't ask him to save me this time. Just like I didn't ask him to save me the first time when he came riding up, fifty deep with guns blazing ready to take on the entire Madness MC. You can believe whatever you want to, but that shit wasn't about his love for me. I was little sister to Devil's Renegades President, Pierce, and I was fucking Madness President, Cain. And they both wanted me for the same damn reason. Pride."

Standing, I grab the half empty bottle of scotch and tuck it under my arm—ready to end this conversation and drown all the memories it stirred in liquor. "Like I said, It's easy for you to see shit in black in white. Side with your brother and trust everything he says and does because that's what you're trained to do. So I'll try to explain this in a way you'll understand."

My lip quivers as I pull in a deep, shaky breath. "With a single phone call to Pierce, I could've avoided two years' worth of misery. I can make that same call right now and never have to worry about Cain again. But I won't. I didn't. I never will. I'll endure whatever my shitty life slings my way because it is *my* life, Jinx. And I don't believe it's any more valuable than my brother's. I refuse to have him risk everything he stands for because of my fuck-up.

"So, despite what you or anyone else believes, there is not a soul on this planet who loves Pierce Tews more than I do. Maybe that's why six years of hell with Cain didn't have the power to hurt me nearly as much as Pierce's words did the day he took me."

My admission puts Jinx in deep thought.

"You were right," I say, striding toward the hall before he can see my tears. "Some scars can't be seen."

WINTER

I've been here twenty days. It's been five since I've had a real conversation with Jinx. Other than the occasional small talk about what show I'm watching or what's for supper, we've kept our talks to clipped, one-word exchanges.

I figured he'd call Pierce at the first chance he got. But he must not have. Because if he had, Pierce would've shown up. Called. Something. He's done neither. For some reason, Jinx is keeping my secret. And somewhere deep inside me, I knew he would.

My head has been in a bad place. My thoughts dark, depressing and confusing. So I'm not surprised when I wake up sweaty and panicked from a nightmare. Gasping, I look around the living room and find it dark. The clock on the wall reads a little after three in the morning.

Like Jinx and Pierce, I'm confident Cain won't show his face until my birthday. Money is too important to him. He's in desperate need of cash to pay off some gambling debts. So I'm pretty sure I'm safe for now. But I still can't keep the thought of what will happen when he does show up out of my head. I'll be forced to make a decision between going with him willingly, or refusing, which will end in war. Needless to say, I'm fucked either way. Unless, I can get the hell out of here.

I throw the covers off, light a cigarette and head to the only room in the place that has some kind of access to fresh air. Just off the kitchen, there's a small pantry with a narrow window that slides open only a few inches. Standing on a bucket, I push it open and breath deep the cold, morning air.

My skin cools. Head clears. And by the time I'm finished with my cigarette, I feel much better. This is the time I need to plan. Plot. Find a way out of here and start down my long anticipated path to freedom. But for some reason, my mind keeps going to Jinx.

I wonder what he's doing. If he's asleep. How it might've felt to wake up with his arms around me. His mouth at my ear. His hands stroking my back. When the need to know and the aching loneliness become overwhelming, I tiptoe down the hall and pause in front of his door.

I glance behind me at the front door that is wired to an alarm. Then down the hall to the room with the door that leads outside which is now not only padlocked, but triggered with an alarm too. Behind me, is the side door that is also rigged to wake the dead in the event of my attempted escape. But what bothers me is how much more I want what's on the other side of *this* door, rather than the freedom that lies beyond all the others.

With a shaky hand, I curl the cool doorknob in my hand and give it a slow twist—a part of me praying it's locked so I can return to my couch and move past this stupid idea of mine. A soft click sounds when the knob easily turns and a bittersweet relief courses through me.

The room is much colder than the living room as if there's no heat at all. Stepping inside, I ease the door closed behind me and wrap my arms around my waist. The only light comes from a plug-in on the wall furthest from me, casting my creepy shadow above the bed as I move closer—my eyes never leaving the large, still form lying under the covers.

Afraid he might freak out and shoot me, I stand next to the bed unmoving in hopes he'll wake up and see me. When he doesn't, I tentatively place one knee on the bed and then the other. The mattress dips and his head jerks toward the movement. I stiffen and force out a choked, "It's me."

He stares at me but I can't make out his features or his expression. He's so still and uninviting, I'm positive he's going to tell me to leave. "I-I'm..." I clamp my mouth shut to keep my teeth from chattering. *Fuck it's cold.*

"You okay?" he asks, his voice thick-laced with sleep.

Am I?

No.

Not really.

My vision blurs and I shake my head—more to clear it than anything.

Through the misty haze, I see him sit up. One moment he's reaching for me, the next I'm in his lap. The heat emanating from his naked chest is like the sun—instantly warming me. His big hands frame my face. Thumbs rubbing across my jaw before tilting my eyes up to look at him.

"What's wrong, baby?" *Baby.* Dammit. Why does he do that? And how can one simple word decimate those iron walls I've built around me?

"I'm lonely," I whisper, my answer honest and pathetic and completely unlike me. Immediately, I regret my admission and start to crawfish. "Never—"

"Hush." He cuts me off as he moves his hands to the hem of my T-shirt. When he tries to pull it over my head, I allow it. When he lays back and tucks me into his side, I allow that too. Then he covers us both. Pulls my leg over his hip. Rests one hand on the small of my back. Cradles the back of my skull with the other. Holds me to his chest. Kisses my hair. And I more than allow it...I yearn for it.

———

"I THOUGHT ABOUT WHAT YOU SAID," Jinx tells me the next morning over scrambled eggs and coffee. I pause mid-chew and shoot him an expectant look. "About why you left Pierce. Why you thought staying with Cain was so much better. I can't understand it."

I shrug. "You can't. You never will. You're a man."

"So?"

Laying down my fork, I lean back in my chair. "So being a woman in the MC is tough, Jinx," I say, picking at my nails. "It's not the same for me as it is for you. I grew up in a man's world where cunts don't count. A world where women were to be seen and not heard. Told how to dress. How to act. What to do. I watched those women sit silently in the background for years. And it made me sick.

"With Cain, I knew who I was and where I stood with him. He controlled every aspect of my life. But in a weird, fucked up way, I had power over a lot of people. I could walk in a room and people would stand. When I spoke, people shut up to listen. I know it's not because *I* really had the power. They did it out of respect for Cain. But it still felt good. The more involved I became in the business and the decision making, the more addicted I became.

"I'm not proud of the things I did, but I can't feel ashamed about it either because at least I was more than those women who settled to just be property of some motherfucker who considered themselves superior because they wore a patch on their back and staked claim to a territory they didn't even own."

"Not all of us who wear a patch want that."

I lift my eyes to find his brows drawn in confusion as if he can't believe he just said that.

"Want what?"

He clears his throat and straightens as if he's uncomfortable. "A shell. A woman without a voice. Without an opinion or a backbone. Just like not all of us get off on using a woman as a punching bag or marking her body to stake our claim."

"Are you saying you're different from those men?"

"I sure as fuck hope so." His admission has the image of me wearing a patch with his name on it flashing in my head. I shake the ridiculous idea away. I don't want that—ever.

"You might be different in some aspects, Jinx, but I've been around long enough to know that ultimately, you all think the same. That's why you wear a CDC patch."

He lifts a brow. "You're pretty vain, sweetheart. What makes you think cunts don't count applies to you?" For the first time ever, I'm suddenly not fully convinced it does. "Judging by your strong expression of feminism in your claim that all bikers are opposed to women's rights, I figured you'd refuse to be considered a cunt."

"So who does it apply to?"

"Can't tell you." Smiling playfully, he winks. "You're a woman."

I scowl at him in an attempt to hide my own smile. "Funny."

I run my finger around the rim of my coffee cup. My mind taking me back to all those nights I dreamed of a different life—one that didn't involve any MC. I wondered what it would be like to grow up in a normal family. Have a brother who had normal friends—not bearded, gun-carrying, possessive ones.

"You know I've never been to a dance club or a bar and just had fun," I say, the sadness in my voice ringing through. "When I was with Cain, it was always about business. The few times it wasn't, during those first couple of years with him, I still couldn't let loose. If I danced too sexy, he thought I was doing it to gain attention from other men. If I was too quiet or wasn't as happy as he thought I should be, he'd swear to never take me out again because *every time he tries to show me a good time, I act like it's not good enough.*" I mock the last part in my best Cain voice.

"Even when I was a teenager, I couldn't have fun. I always had to look over my shoulder to see if I was being watched. Make sure Pierce hadn't caught me sneaking out and sent the cavalry to come get me."

I glance up at Jinx to gauge his reaction. It's the same as always. He isn't the least bit sympathetic or even interested.

"Cinderella," he says, after several more long moments of silence have passed. "Locked away in her tower. Hidden from the world."

"That was Rapunzel," I correct.

He shrugs. "Same shit."

"Actually...it's not."

"Who gives a damn what their names are. They were both young, beautiful girls who were refused something in life. You have that in common with them."

I grin. "Are you saying I'm beautiful?"

"I am." *Oh. Okay then.* "I'm also saying that despite how much I respect my brother, I kinda hate him a little for not allowing you those rights of passage all teenagers should experience."

"Who knows?" I say, lifting my hands and shrugging my shoulders. "It might've led me down a different path in life." I'm only teasing, but I can't help but wonder...

"Too bad you missed out," he says, but his voice is distracted as he studies me. As if he's thinking hard about something.

"Maybe one day. You know, when Cain is dead and Pierce has found something to obsess over in his life that doesn't involve me." *Like my shitty luck will allow either to ever happen.*

"Tonight."

My brows draw in confusion. "What?"

"Tonight. I'll drive you anywhere you want to go, within reason. Of course I won't be able to let you out of my sight, but I won't intervene no matter how sexy you dance. I won't tell you what you can and can't do or who you can talk to. I won't tell you how to dress or act or what to order when we eat. You won't have to look over your shoulder for Cain because I'll be doing that for you. Tonight. One night. You can be free...to a certain extent," he adds on a smile.

"You're serious?" I ask, not believing that he'd actually do what he says he will. Or that he'd actually do something that nice for me.

"I'm serious."

"You're not worried about Ten's?"

He shoots me a bored look. "Fuck no."

His answer makes my insides flutter. He's so...male. So powerful. So fucking cocky. I shift in my seat.

"I know that if something is too good to be true, it always is," I say, crossing my arms over my chest. "You're not just doing this out of the kindness of your heart, Jinx. There's a catch."

"There's a catch," he reiterates on a nod. "You can't run. If you do, I'll make the rest of your stay here as miserable for you as I possibly can without causing any permanent harm."

That...I believe.

"You'd really do all this. Just for me."

"No," he deadpans. "I'm getting something out of it too."

"Yeah? Like what?" *A blow job? Some kinky shit he's into?*

"An opportunity to prove that I really am different."

Reality is...I already know that.

JINX

I think I've lost my motherfucking mind.

I don't need to prove shit to this girl. And I really shouldn't risk taking her outside of these four walls because I want her to experience something as simple as a night of fun. Just like I shouldn't have held her in my bed last night. Kissed her good morning. Scrambled her fucking eggs. Felt happy and giddy and relieved that she was over whatever shit she'd been dealing with and was now talking to me and off that fucking couch.

If I wanted to be some thoughtful sap with the desire to make her happy, I could've just repeated my actions from last night. Or rolled us a blunt, played some blues and ate Cheetos while discussing all her personal woes like how bad it sucks to be a woman. Then, I'd not only still have my balls, but maybe some valuable information from her too.

But did I do that? No. After a few hours of working out, a shower and a lot of restless pacing and overthinking, I'm in here searching through my closet, very carefully so I don't disrupt the order of anything. I'm looking for an outfit that is appropriate for a restaurant —in case she chooses one that's nice—and also doesn't stain easily—in case I get the chance to kill Cain and some of his blood splatters on it.

I settle on jeans and a dark polo. Grab my leather jacket. My hat. Wallet. Keys...Cut. I'm going to wear it to whatever bar or club we go to. I'm going to prove that I can represent my club, protect her and not be a douche by controlling her night. Telling her what to do. How to act. Who to talk to. Just like I promised her I would. Like the fucking idiot I am.

It's after five. It's already dark outside. We agreed to leave ten minutes ago. She's been hulled up in *my* bathroom for hours. Well, I don't know if it's been hours, but it's been long enough that I had to use the other bathroom to shower in. The funky one that's dirty. The one I made her use. The one I swear that no matter what she does, I'll never let her use again. Luke should really hire someone to clean that shit.

She's probably dressing in something that will have me reneging on this deal before we even leave. I said I wouldn't tell her how to dress, but I can't have her going out in public looking like a tramp either. If that shit gets back to Pierce, he'll kill me. Although he'll probably kill me anyway if he finds out I let her out in public at all.

"You ready?" she asks, from behind me. I take a deep breath and steel my face. Prepare for the worst. Then I turn. And all my preparation for the worst wasn't necessary. But I am glad I filled my lungs with air. Because at the sight of her, she completely takes my breath.

Her green eyes are striking, framed in her long, black lashes. Lips big and pink and perfectly pouty. Hair blonde and wavy falling over her shoulders and spilling down her sides. Tits—those fucking tits—high and round and only partially hidden from view by the white shirt that's splayed open at the chest, cropped at her waist and split down the arms displaying her tattoos. The bright colors of her ink and the tanned hue of the exposed skin on her chest and stomach even more prominent against the white material.

Swallowing hard, my eyes trail down to her legs. They go on for days in those tight, black pants she wears that stop at her ankle. And on her feet are shimmering, gold heels that look as uncomfortable as fuck, but she wears them with ease. Twirls around in them gracefully to give me a view of her from behind.

Her ass is heart shaped perfection. Hips significantly wider than her tiny waist. Her back covered. She spins back to face me and lifts an eyebrow.

"So? Do you approve?"

Fuck yes I approve, I'm thinking. What I say is completely different. "You don't need my approval."

"What about your opinion?"

I shake my head. "You don't need that either."

"What if I want it?"

She does. Damn, she does. I can see the hope in her eyes. The bit of anxiety. The nervousness that I may not like what I see. Because whether she knows it or not, she dressed with me in mind. She wants to impress me. She has. But I don't want her to know that. So I shrug with indifference.

"You'll do."

Her knowing smile tells me that despite my attempts, she can see right through me. Or maybe she's learning me quicker than I thought she would.

Eyeing my cut that's folded over my arm, she smirks. "Representin' I see."

"Always."

"You do know you can't wear that *and* not act like a biker. You have a reputation to protect. How can you do that and keep your promise?"

"Like I said, tonight's not just about your right of passage. It's about proving you wrong. Let's go."

Spinning on her heels, she mutters something under her breath and walks to the door. I keep a couple paces behind her, let her open her own car door and slide into the driver's seat next to her. The car is already running, so it's warm inside—something I did for me. Not her. Or at least that's what I tell myself. And what I fear I'll be telling myself all night.

WINTER

"I can't eat anymore," I say, tossing my napkin on the table. Jinx eyes my plate of half-eaten food before looking at me. "I mean, I can but I'm not going to. I'd rather drink. And dance. And I can't do that if I'm miserably full." His response is a simple shake of his head and another bite of steak.

The place we're in looks like something out of a horror movie. There's farm equipment hanging from the ceiling. Dead animals mounted on the walls. Not to mention the strange, homely folks running the place. But Jinx promised the food was good. And it is. Maybe even some of the best I've had.

When we got in his car, I told him he could decide where we went since I didn't know anything about south Mississippi. He'd asked me what I liked to eat and I'd replied with the easily met demand of, "anything." I really didn't care to eat at all. I was too excited about having fun. Not to say this isn't fun, but...well, it's not.

"Why don't you belong to a specific chapter?" I ask, figuring a little conversation might help the time pass by faster.

He glances up at me, takes one final bite then tosses his napkin onto his plate. "Because I don't like conforming to one set of standards."

"But every chapter wears the same patch," I state, confused—eying the worn patches covering the front of his leather vest. "Don't you all have the same standards?"

"Each chapter governs themselves. Some people run their shit differently. Some things I agree with, some I don't. But I respect all of them. By not dedicating my time to one in particular, I get to come and go between chapters as I please."

"So when you get tired of one, you just move along." He gives me a nod. "If they made you choose a chapter, which one would it be?"

"They wouldn't." His response is dismissive, but I'm nosey.

"But what if they did?"

"They wouldn't."

I roll my eyes. "Well, let's say they would."

"They. Won't. And if they did, then it would be a violation of our bi-laws."

I give him a disgusted look. "You're impossible."

"No...I just don't make a habit of answering pointless questions for the sake of conversation."

"You're way too convinced they wouldn't. Sounds to me like if they did, it'd be a deal breaker for you." He doesn't deny it. Which makes me that much more determined to figure out why. "So are you going to tell me why you'd never belong to a chapter?"

"I already have."

I shake my head. "Not that bullshit excuse. The real reason." He quietly regards me.

"Fine," I say, after the silence becomes uncomfortable. "I'll guess."

Crossing my arms over my chest, I lean back and study him a moment. He stares back at me, his head slightly tilted. Body relaxed. Expression bored. Same shit as always.

"I think you can't fully commit to brotherhood and all it entails. Sure you show up when you're called. Help when you're needed. But there's some deep-seated issue that prevents you from really getting close to someone. Much like brothers in a chapter are. So..." I lean forward and ask, "is it daddy issues? Mommy? You come from a broken home? Only child or lots of siblings you helped raise by sacrificing your childhood only to have them turn out like thugs?" Pausing, I tap my chin as if I'm thinking hard.

"Or were you a child of the state? Jumped from foster home to foster home...never really fit in...quit school...searched for an outlet that would help you vent all that frustration and anger you have toward the parents that never showed you love. I bet your sob story is the same as all the others. You lost your way in life, the MC found you and now you feel like you actually belong somewhere. But the rebel in you just won't allow you to settle down and, as you say, conform to one certain set of standards."

I'm satisfied I got it right. My smile is victorious. But it doesn't last long.

"You're wrong," he deadpans. Now, I'm intrigued.

"So tell me the truth."

Smiling, he shakes his head. "No."

"Oh, come on. You know everything about me," I whine, suddenly thirsty for knowledge about this man. This sexy man in his black polo and dark jeans with silver eyes and pretty white teeth.

"I didn't come from a broken home," he says, surprising the hell out of me. "My mother and father are both alive and well. Together. They're supportive and loving and hardworking. I have a close relationship with my two younger brothers. Both are extremely intelligent. Both play football at an Ivy League University. Both are NFL draft prospects."

"Do I know them?"

He shrugs, putting his bottle to his lips. "Maybe." He takes a couple long pulls then sets the bottle down and lifts his eyes to meet mine as I fire off the next question.

"And you? Were you the outcast?" I shoot him a mock frown and pretend to wipe my eyes. "Poor little Jinxton. Never able to live up to his parent's expectations."

I'm being a dick to him only because on the inside, I'm hurting a little. And I don't like that I'm feeling bad for this guy. I meant it when I said I've heard this story a thousand times. After a while, it's hard to feel any empathy. Besides, he isn't offended by my teasing. He's fighting a smile. Probably at my theatrics.

"Asshole," he mutters, giving into that smile. "Actually, I was the kind of son any parent would be proud of. Academically, I thrived. I had my pick of Ivy League schools. Athletically, I was the highest ranked cornerback in the nation. Agents were calling my parents before I even graduated high school. Wanting to represent me even though I wasn't eligible for the NFL for years."

Wow. *Maybe he really is different. In more than one way...*

"That's enough for story time," he says dismissively, glancing at the check as he pulls his wallet out. "You're a cheap date."

Letting the subject drop, for now, I wink. "The night is young."

We stand and he shoves his hands in his pockets. I loop my arm around his elbow and lean into him as we walk out. "It's a good thing you got that black card, *sweetheart*," I purr, my lips at his ear. "Because you're gonna need it."

———

WHEN JINX first told me we were going to a blues bar, I protested. Then he explained that it was more than that. That it had something for everyone looking to have a good time. I was still doubtful, so he went on to explain that an authentic, Mississippi blues band would be there covering all the classics that the middle-aged and older genera-tion crowd enjoyed. But at eleven, the band would leave and the crowd would thin allowing room for the younger people to dance and party with the all-night D.J. That sold me.

Now, here we are—*Bee's*—a place that's off the beaten path and caters mainly to locals. Somewhere I never would've thought to come.

The building is unpretentious—muted lighting, several tables and chairs lined on either side of the spacious dance floor, and a large, curved bar highlighted in blue neon that sits opposite the small stage. But it's the atmosphere that makes me fall in love with this place. Everyone's happy. Swaying. Dancing to the sultry tempo. And I'm kind of sad that the band will be leaving soon.

I'm also kind of drunk.

Not only does this place have great music, but they have kick-ass cocktails. It totally made up for them not having any scotch. Actually, I think I've found a new favorite. A blackberry martini that's smooth and cool and fruity and potent as hell.

I'm in the middle of the dance floor. Drink in hand. My hips moving in tune to *The Thrill Is Gone*. Jinx, keeping good on his promise, has been at the bar. He ignores me completely. Has barely made eye contact in the few hours we've been here.

I've danced with several men—some whose hands they couldn't keep to themselves. It just went with the music, so I didn't mind. But I expected Jinx to come stomping over, demand the man keep his filthy paws off of me then tell me to, "Chill out." Or, "Cool it." Or, "Stop being an attention whore." He has yet to do any of those things. He doesn't even look mad. Not that I've been looking at him.

"Alright folks," the lead singer says, breathing hard into the microphone. "It's gettin' 'bout dat time." Everyone groans—none louder than me who boos like an idiot. "Y'all know how I like to do. Gotta save one dance for my lady. Gotta put my arms around her..." Catcalls ring out. "I gotta squeeze her..." More whistling. "I gotta hold her tight why dey *sang* her *song*." The regulars cheer, knowing what's coming. I cheer even though I don't because I want to be a regular too.

"Now, y'all get on ya feet. Grab ya a woman. We all dancin' to this one," he says, descending the stairs and never taking his eyes from the woman whose been standing center stage next to me all night. "Yo bartender. Give us some of dem Black Crowes...And let me dance with my *Josephine*"

The music starts. I stare at the couple next to me. Dancing to *my* song. Like it's *their* song. And all I can do is just shake my head. *Damn my shitty luck.*

JINX

Bee's is the kind of place you can spend a lot of time in. Judging by the amount of blackberry martinis Winter's had, money is another thing you can spend a lot of in here. I have to say though—it's been money well spent.

Seeing her move those fucking hips in those tight pants... yeah... it's worth every penny I've charged to that black card. But that smile... that laugh... the way she throws her head back, closes her eyes and loses herself in the moment... you can't put a dollar amount on that. It's fucking priceless.

I haven't talked to her since we walked in the door. Haven't touched her since she slid her tiny arm through mine at the restaurant. She thinks I haven't looked at her, either. She's wrong. My eyes have spent more time watching her than anything else. Moving those hips. That ass. Smiling that motherfucking smile I'm melting over.

"Crown. Double," I tell the bartender who lifts a brow at my request.

"Not the regular?" he asks, pointing at my empty glass.

I shake my head. "Nah. I need something stronger."

While he pours, I look back at the vixen standing on the dance floor. Looking around in confusion as the band makes an announcement. I've never paid much attention before or stayed long enough to hear it, but apparently, this is something they do regularly. I smile when she cheers along with the crowd despite her having no knowledge as to what the fuck's going on.

The singer calls out to the bartender just as he sets my whiskey in front of me. My glass is to my lips when I hear it.

Her song.

There's only a handful of singles in here. She's danced with all of them multiple times. Even some of the women. I've watched in disinterested silence. I'm not a jealous guy. Plus, she's not mine to be jealous over—even if I was that kind of man. But the thought of her dancing to this song with anyone other than me, bothers me.

I'm not pissed. Upset or the least bit agitated. It just... it fucking hurts. I don't like to hurt. So I down the shot. Watch as she politely declines an offer to dance. Then another one. Then I see her smile falter. Her shoulders fall. Her eyes drop to her fingers that fidget with the rim of her glass.

Fuck it.

Eight strides later, I'm behind her. Taking her glass. Setting it on the stage. Turning her in my arms. Lifting those long, tattooed beauties around my neck. Placing my hands on her hips. Pulling her flush against me. Staring down at her parted mouth, wide, green eyes and for the second time, telling her, "I'm not your dream guy, Winter. Don't fall in love with me."

"Ditto," she breathes, her cool, blackberry scented breath fanning my face.

Sliding my hand up her back, I cradle her neck in my hand. She instantly buries her face in my neck. I inhale her hair. The mixture of shampoo and her uniquely, sweet scented sweat is soothing. That pain in my chest at the thought of her dancing to this song with another man has long passed.

Josephine... I've never really listened to the song. Now, as I stand in for Winter's dream guy, I'm actually hearing it for the first time. And it describes us perfectly.

This—me and her—this is right. Wrong, but right. I'm telling this girl not to fall for me. That I'll end up only disappointing her in the end. She says the same, but neither of us can deny what's happening in this moment.

When the song is over, I realize I didn't pay attention to all the little things I was wondering about earlier. Like how she would feel against me. How her ass would move. Her hips would sway. Now that I am, I fucking want her. Desperately.

Hard.

Rough.

Fast.

Right. Fucking. Here.

And she just asked for a fucking drink.

While the band takes their break, another song starts to play. I move through the crowd of people dancing to some two-step shit with Winter in tow. "My regular," I tell the bartender. He nods once and turns his back away from the crowd as he discreetly fixes my drink.

"I think I'll have V's Special," Winter says, her eyes on the drink menu as she slides on the stool next to me. I take the plastic menu from her hands.

"You don't want that."

She snatches it back. "Yes I do. It's special." She points at the description. "It says so. Even has all those little stars by it."

"That's asterisks. Read the fine print."

Squinting her eyes, she tries to make out the warning. After a moment, she gives up and tosses it back on the bar. "Don't care. I want it."

"No."

The bartender hands me my drink, looking to me then Winter before coming back to me for approval.

"Hey!" She snaps her fingers in the air between them. "I'm grown, in case you missed that. I'll order for myself." Spinning to face me, she pokes me in the chest. "You promised."

I did. Besides, this might be interesting.

"Fine." I give her a shrug and nod to the bartender. He grins know-ingly and gladly fixes the drink—probably more excited about the gratuity he'll make off the fifty-dollar fucker than he is about the outcome.

When she has it in hand, she takes a moment to admire the sparkling blue liquid in the champagne flute before she proposes a toast. I grab my drink and happily oblige. "To a super fun and exciting night."

"Oh it will be," the bartender says on a laugh.

She shoots him a funny look then brings her smile back to me. "Thank you."

"No sweetheart, thank *you.*" I clink her glass and wink. She's oblivious to what she's getting herself into and I'm stifling a laugh when she tips her glass back and downs it.

"Mmm... that was like... the most delicious thing ever. I'll have another."

I shoot a why-the-fuck-not look to the bartender who tells her it's a two drink maximum. She's giddy at that.

"Must be some good shit. See?" She playfully slaps my arm. "And you didn't want me to have it. So selfish...."

"*So* selfish," I reiterate.

"You gonna hold my hair if I puke tonight?" she asks, draining half of her second glass before pausing to light a cigarette. When she crosses her legs, I drop my eyes to them. They travel up her flat stomach, to her bulging tits, her delicate throat, pink lips then stop on her eyes.

"No."

She grins. "Yes you will. You can't help yourself." Turning her shoulder toward me, she looks over it and bats her eyelashes. "Are you falling in love with me, Jinx?"

I take the cigarette from her fingers. "Nope."

"I love this song!" she screams suddenly. I wasn't prepared for it and nearly jump out of my fucking skin. She laughs at my expression, tosses back the rest of her drink and leaps from her stool. I watch as she saunters onto the dance floor and grabs one of the women.

The music comes from the speakers in the bar as the band joins the crowd to dance. I don't know what it is, but it's definitely not blues— likely a transition to what's to come. I cringe at the thought.

"How much do I need to pay the DJ to *not* play any of that techno shit tonight?" I ask the bartender who's still fucking smiling.

"No techno. Just pop and rap. Don't worry, I'll request some good, bass hitting hard shit." He leans in and drops his voice. "You'll need it to keep up."

"Yeah," I say, my cock already swelling at the sight of her dancing and the thought of what's about to happen. "You're probably right."

WINTER

S on-of-a-*bitch*.

For some reason, I'm so fucking horny I could dry hump a fence post. Or the leg of this really nice lady who is innocently dancing beside me. Unknowingly making me question my sexual orientation.

What I thought was only a slow build to my usual drunken-horny state, has exploded into a desperate need to be fucked like an animal. My tits feel heavy and just the feel of my bra rubbing across my nipples has me clenching my thighs. When I do that, I'm reminded of my pussy that is so wet, it has soaked through my panties and dampened my pants.

My clit feels like it's the size of a golf ball. And it's throbbing... pulsing. Pressing against my swollen lips. Trying to break free, find a rough surface and rub against it over and over until it finally gets release.

What the hell is wrong with me?

My thoughts are so fucked up. Next, I'll be naming my *lady parts* something stupid like Thelma for the right tit, Louise for the left and Tawanda or some crazy shit for my vagina. Not only that, I'm stupidly wondering how I can get off on this lady next to me, a hard surface or a fence post, when my very own wet dream is sitting on a stool merely feet from me.

Pushing through the crowd, I make my way over. As I get closer, I can make out the concerned look on his face. I don't stop walking until I'm standing between his knees. His hands reach out and grab my arms. Eyes roam my face. Then he's pushing my sweaty hair from my face and feeling my forehead.

"What's wrong, baby?" he asks, a little panicked. A lot of sexy. God he's so sexy. *Baby.* My pussy clenches.

I swallow hard and stare at his lips. Wondering what it would feel like if my golf ball sized clit were being caressed by his tongue. "I don't know," I breathe. Moan. Same shit. I grind against him. My fingers digging into his thighs.

"I do!"

I look over Jinx's shoulder to the bartender who's performing pelvic air thrusts. I moan again.

"I need you to break your promise," I say, my hands desperately seeking out his skin. Wanting to touch him. Wanting him to touch me more. The band begins a bluesy rendition of the song *Changes,* originally recorded by Black Sabbath, and I lean in closer so he can hear me —putting my lips against his ear.

"I need you to fuck me. Now. To this song. Hard. Harder than you've ever fucked me," I pant, nibbling his earlobe. Kissing his neck. Biting it. "To hell with our deal. Fuck me like I'm yours. Like I'm your property. A dirty whore. A bad girl. Spank me. Beat me...*Fuck... Me...Please!"*

He grabs my shoulders and pushes me back a step to look at me. His concern is gone. Replaced with pure amusement. Maybe desire. Fuck I don't know. Don't care. I need his dick. Not his facial expressions.

"Well..." His grin stretches across his handsome face. The face I want to sit on and ride like a Harley Davidson motorcycle. "If you insist, sweetheart."

I grab his hand. Spin on my heel. Pull him through the crowded dance floor and to the door beside the stage. My thoughts are choppy. Disjointed. I can't focus. I mean, I can, but only on one thing.

Sex.

Dick.

Cock.

Lips.

Hands.

Well, several things.

I push through the door. Find the nearest wall. Start to throw myself against it, but he beats me to it. Turning me. Kissing me. Holding me still. Forcing me to perform those pelvic air-thrusts just like the bartender.

Tearing my mouth away from his, I struggle from his hold and move backward—further into the room. He stalks after me. Slow. Predatory. Like a smirking fucking vulture. I'm trying to walk, get these tight ass pants off and keep some distance between us. Having him be close and try and take things slow is worse than him not touching me at all.

"Ever been on a road trip?" I'm rambling. Trying to distract him. "Stopped at a store. Bought one of those big gut-busting, kidney-infection-giving fountain sodas, knowing good and damn well you're gonna have to pee before you stop again? Forty-four ounces later, it hits you. You hide it for the first twenty miles, then some asshole in the car notices your struggle and tickles you. Ever had that happen?"

He shakes his head. My pants are now halfway down my thighs. He's still coming toward me. Still smirking. Still wearing that promising look of torture.

"Well, that's where I am. Kinda. I mean, I don't have to pee, but I'm forty-four ounces deep in arousal and if you tease me, I'm going to explode. So I'm asking—no, I'm begging you...please don't tickle me."

He lifts an eyebrow at that. My back hits a wall. He closes the distance. I moan when the heavy rise and fall of my chest has my nipples brushing against his cut. His hands move to his jeans. The buckle of his belt. He pulls it through the loops and holds it up. My legs shake in anticipation. Smiling, he drops the belt to the floor. I'm still watching it fall when he descends on me.

His kiss is quick. Thorough. A sweep of his tongue through my mouth. Then I'm spinning. My hands splayed against the wall for support. He presses his hand against my back and I bend over. Spread my knees wider. Bend deeper. Touch my toes. Cry out when the cold air hits my exposed pussy.

"Damn girl," he says, his voice thick. "You're fuckin' soaked." I shiver and make some strange unintelligible noise as he drags his fingers up my damp thighs to my dripping, weeping cunt.

He kneels behind me. "So swollen..." His breath tickles my sex and my knees nearly buckle. "So pink..." *Oh my God, I'm going to die.* "So pretty and wet and..." he trails off. Then his tongue is on me. Circling my clit. Lazily sweeping between my lips. Darting inside me. "Tastes so fucking good."

Know this: If a man uses his mouth in the same way he uses it when he gives you those toe curling, heart hammering, forget the world and fuck me now, kisses—he can eat pussy. And Devil's Renegades Jinx can most definitely eat pussy.

Problem is, I need more. Him. Inside me. Pounding the fuck out of me.

"You okay, baby?" he asks, standing slowly. Taking his precious damn time.

"Jinx..." It's a warning.

"*Fuck.*"

That was a bad *fuck*. A disappointed *fuck*. A we-have-to-stop *fuck*. Well... fuck that.

Struggling to stand upright, I glare at him over my shoulder. "What—"

"I don't have a condom."

"I don't care!" I yell, too loud. Too uncaring. I'm about to unleash the beast on him. I never get a chance. Obviously, Jinx doesn't care either. Because he's gripping my hips. My hair. Pulling. Pushing. Impaling me on a hard, deep, severe drive that has me on my toes.

"Hands on the wall," he orders through his teeth. It's accompanied by a groan when I shift to do as he says. "Straighten your arms." He moves back a step pulling me with him until my elbows are locked. "Be careful what you wish for, baby," he whispers at my ear, planting a soft kiss there before straightening.

He pulls out at an agonizingly slow pace until only the tip of his cock remains inside me. But the agony from him moving at a snail's speed is short lived. Because his next thrust and the countless after that, come at a rapid rate and are delivered in a beautiful, brutal fashion.

I'm coming hard. Screaming loud. My arousal flooding my thighs. His cock. The wet, slapping sound of our violent love making nearly overpowers the music in the other room. And I give zero fucks. So does he.

I move one hand off the wall to stroke my clit. His grip on me tightens—holding me in place. My head rolls with every pump of his hips. Breasts bounce roughly—spilling from my shirt. I can't count how many times I've come. Or if I've ever even stopped.

It's euphoric. Great. Mesmerizing. Consuming. But most of all, it's never-ending. That sated, blissful feeling is there, but the comedown isn't. I'm as high and horny as I was when we started—seventy-six thousand orgasms ago.

"Hush babe," he says, even as he reaches around to close his hand over my mouth. I knew my screams were loud, but I didn't realize how loud. I also didn't realize that the music had stopped.

"One more, sweet girl. Then we gotta go. The band will be in here any minute." I sultrily lick his hand. "I know, baby. Fuck I know." God I want to lick all of him. I bite down on the delicious pad of his thumb and he satiates me by thrusting impossibly harder. Then I'm coming impossibly harder. And it's impossibly better than the last time.

He swiftly pulls out of me and a second later, I feel him bathing my ass in his fiery come. Seizing my ass cheek with one hand as he pumps his cock with the other. When he opens his eyes, I'm looking at him. Still horny, but temporarily satisfied enough not to explode. More like a twenty-ounce fountain soda instead of a forty-four.

"Don't fall in love with me, Jinx," I say, my lips quirking.

"Ditto."

Pulling a bandana from his back pocket, I watch in amusement as he carefully cleans me. When he moves to drag it between my legs, I straighten. "I like being wet. Besides..." I grin at him. "If you touch me there, I'm gonna come again."

"Nothing turns me on more than an insatiable woman." He tucks the bandana back in his pocket and grabs his belt from the floor. "Behave tonight," he warns playfully. "Or I'll put this belt on your ass."

Wiggling back into my pants, I roll my eyes. "Promises, promises."

The moment my pants are up, and my tits are back in my shirt, the door opens and the band piles in—stopping mid-stride to stare at us.

Jinx smirks at me before turning to face them. "She had the special."

Everyone laughs and continues inside. I'm confused, but quickly become caught up in the conversation and greetings from several of the women I'd been dancing with—wives I presume.

"You smoke?" I hear one of the men ask Jinx. He politely declines, but I can tell he doesn't really want to. I can see the want in his eyes as the blunt is lit and passed.

"I'm going to the bathroom," I say, stepping around Jinx. He grabs my arm, sliding his hand down until it's holding mine. He regards me with a cautious look. Looking as if he wants to say something but not so sure he should.

"Use ours. Girl that one out there is nasty," one of the women says.

Jinx visibly relaxes at her request. *He thought I was going to run....* That's what I need to do. It's what I should be thinking about. Or maybe I should be thinking about how right now, running is the last thing I want to do.

WINTER

"Shut the fuck up," I say, my disbelief palpable. "You're joking, right?"

I'm in the bathroom, engaging in girl-talk bathroom conversation. Or, I was until the ingredients of V's special was dropped on me like a bomb. Now I'm staring at the lead singer's wife, Josephine, with wide eyes, repeating myself. "You are joking."

She laughs, her long black hair swept neatly off her neck as she fans herself. "Nope. That expensive ass drink is the only way they can keep the doors open here. Hell, by the time they pay off the ABC rep, they're still makin' a killin'." She winks at me. "I hear it's worth every penny."

It is. But I don't say that. I don't have to. Apparently, they heard me. I think they think I'm some sort of innocent, sweet girl who's never had sex in a bar. Now would be a good time to tell them I'm kind of a whore, so fucking is what I do. But I've never been fucked while jacked up on Viagra, so in a way, this is a first for me.

I can't believe there was Viagra in my drink!

"I'm going to kill him."

They laugh harder. "Yeah," one says, pointing her finger at me. "By fuckin' him to death." Unable to *not* find that funny, I join in on the laughter. Then my thighs involuntarily rub together and I'm reminded of why this really isn't that funny. I'm still horny as hell.

"Let's go," Josephine says, straightening her dress in the mirror one last time. "They probably high as hell and we in here missin' all the fun."

I fall in line with the five women and enter a smoke filled room packed with laughing men—Jinx included. I still and just stare at him. He's laughing. Like really laughing. Of all the times he could've chose to share that spine tingling, clit tickling laughter, he just had to choose the moment when I'm under the influence of one hundred milligrams of liquid Viagra—two times the average dose. *Where's that fucking fence post...*

Someone says it's time for a drink and next thing I know, the crowd is moving out of the room and to the main bar. Jinx, once again acting on his original promise, keeps distance between us—hanging toward the front of the line with the guys.

I flip off the bartender when he laughs so hard he can't fix my drink. Two martinis later, I'm sitting on the bar giving details of our Viagra sex and how the drug makes me feel to the women from the band, and a few younger people standing in earshot.

Periodically, I check on Jinx who is slamming back shot after shot. Laughing. Smiling. Having a really, really good time. It's obvious he's drunk and I'm glad he's letting loose. He's too damn uptight. And seeing him like this makes me smile. I'm happy for him. And of course, horny for him.

Feeling him look at me, I try to act nonchalant when my attention falls on a familiar face. *Well... I guess trouble has arrived.*

I know the guy by the door who drags his gaze from mine to watch Jinx. To everyone else, he looks like someone just hanging out having a beer. He's not. He's with Ten's Testament.

I discreetly lower my eyes, then scan the bar for any other familiar faces. I find two more—all posted in different areas throughout the room.

"Let's dance, sweetheart," Jinx says, suddenly appearing in front of me. He's outnumbered. Inebriated. Tripping and stumbling over his own feet. Sober, he could hold his own. Now? He doesn't stand a chance.

"Jinx, stop." I try to pull out of his grasp but he tightens his hold on my hand and twirls me around him. Bringing me flush against his chest, I look up into his hooded, blood-shot eyes. "Seriously, stop."

"Smile, baby. Have some fun." He beams at me. He kind of reminds me of a drunk college kid. And I'm not so sure I like him like this at all.

"Listen," I start, the thought of him being jumped, hurt or even killed has fear pricking my spine.

I pull in a deep breath, ignoring my warring thoughts as I prepare to tell him that what he feared has come. But before I can get another word out, one of the band members come up beside us and engages Jinx in conversation. I allow it for a few seconds then grab his face in my hands and turn it so he's looking at me.

I'm desperate to tell him. He has to know. Then my thoughts take a turn as I narrow my eyes on his heavy, bloodshot ones. "You smoked that pot, didn't you?" I ask, already knowing the answer. "You selfish fuck. That was some good shit too, wasn't it?"

His grin widens and he nods. "Best. Grass. Period." He sobers a little and nods. "Seriously, Winter. It's good shit." Then he's smiling again. Dancing off beat to some hip-hop song I don't even recognize.

"Jinx! Please!" I cry out. This time, he hears me.

Suddenly, he pulls me tighter to him. Dips me. Kisses me hard. I give into the kiss for a moment because I don't want to hurt his feelings. That's all. When he breaks away, my eyes are still closed—reliving the moment and the fact that even drunk, he's a great kisser.

"Winter," he says, and my eyes fly open at the sound of his voice. Not slurred. Not funny. Serious. Sober. Just like his face. His eyes are still blood-shot and slightly hooded, but there's no trace of drunken Jinx. Actually...

"Are you drinking apple something?" I ask, my nose scrunched up as I lean in and sniff the air between us. My body is still hovering just off the floor. He's bent over me. His face very close to mine. Making the scent of that damn apple something unmistakable. *He drinks martinis?*

"Apple juice." He blows out a breath and I inhale. "Me and the bartender have an understanding."

"What? Why? Wait... so you're not drunk?"

He grins. "No, sweetheart. I'm not drunk. I'm high as fuck, but I'm not the inebriated idiot I'm pretending to be. I'm aware of everything going on around me. And yes, I know they're here."

Well shit. Just when I thought I had one up on him. And just when I thought he was finally turning me off he goes and does some semi-heroic shit that has my body heating again. Shaking my head, I try to clear my thoughts and focus on what's important.

"Why are you pretending to be drunk?"

"To make myself an easy target."

"But there are three of them."

"Four," he corrects.

"What? Did you call Luke?"

His smile is cocky. Lazy. Hot. "You're funny."

I'm smiling too when I answer. "No. I'm not. Call him Jinx. You need backup."

"For four? Nah." He winks. I quiver. "I got this, baby. Now, I'm gonna let you up. Dance with me. Smile and don't do anything stupid like look at them."

I give him an apologetic look. "But I have to pee."

He rolls his eyes. "Of course you do." Standing us up, he stumbles toward the bathroom with me tucked against his side—yelling out that I'm ready for round two. It earns him an elbow to the ribs that he easily dodges.

"Make it quick," he says, standing outside the bathroom door—after he tries to follow me in. I play it off, like I'm saying "no" to him while he scans the bathroom for threats.

When I'm behind the stall door, I lean against it and release the breath I didn't realize I'd been holding. Closing my eyes, I block out the sound of the women coming and going. Chatting and laughing—enjoying a carefree life like the one I so desperately want. And something I regretfully don't have.

Tonight was perfect. But leave it to Cain to fuck up anything good in my life. Even from miles away, he has the power to control me. But for once, as if the universe is finally on my side, like it might actually understand that I'm fucked no matter what I do and is shedding a little mercy on me, I sniff the air.

"Hey!" I call out, praying like hell that's fresh smoke permeating my senses and not just a lingering odor from a previously smoked, bathroom blunt.

"You need some toilet paper?" *Josephine.*

"No," I say, opening the stall door and finding her and a couple other women passing a cigar. "I need some of that pot."

"Girl, if you fuck on this and Viagra, you gonna go to the moon."

I shrug, putting the blunt between my lips. After a long pull, I hold it deep in my lungs a minute, then release it on a loud breath. "Good," I say, taking another drag. "Never been there."

JINX

"**Y**ou smoked that shit, didn't you?" I ask, trying to narrow my eyes on Winter, which is fucking impossible to do when you're smiling. And smiling is inevitable when you're as high as me. Oh, and now her who's even fucking higher than I am.

"I was just so nervous, dude..." she says, dragging out the last word in her best hippy voice.

I laugh cause the shit's funny. Even though I should be acting a little more serious considering the circumstances. "You're so weird."

"Totally." She grins, pulling me onto the dance floor.

I hate dancing, but it's the safest place in here right now. And until these guys are finally convinced I'm too fucked up to kill them and they finally approach, that's where we'll be—in the middle of a crowded dance floor.

How they found us, I don't know. I'm guessing it's a mixture of shitty luck and coincidence. It doesn't bother me that they're here. Hell, I'm happy. Maybe they've already sent word to Cain and that motherfucker will show his face here too. But I'm pretty sure he's too much of a coward for that.

Winter, demanding my undivided attention and getting it, places my hat on her head and runs her fingers through my hair. Yeah. I'm high. I'd never let that shit happen if I wasn't. "Tell me you're gonna fuck me hard tonight," she says, looking up at me as I gaze down at her.

"I'm gonna fuck you so hard..."

"Tell me how you're gonna spank me."

"Beat the fuck outta you..."

"Tell me how good I taste."

"Like motherfuckin' Skittles..."

"The kind that come from a rainbow?"

"From heaven."

Her eyes squeeze shut and her mouth falls open. I have to blink a few times to make sure I'm not seeing shit. *This bitch having a stroke?* Then she pulls in a deep breath, and laughs so loud, people stare. After a few seconds of that, I'm laughing too. Asking her, "What's so funny?"

When she finally catches her breath, she tells me, "You said, 'from heaven'." I'm grinning like a damn idiot at her impression of me.

"Fuck you. That was a compliment."

She meets my gaze. Her arms around my neck. Eyes heavy and red. Still giggling every few seconds. "Are we gonna make it out of here in one piece?"

I give her the most serious look I can manage. "Yes."

"Well, I'm ready when you are."

"Patience, sweetheart. We need a plan."

She steps back and holds one hand out. The other behind her back. I think she may be trying to look like a gangster. "Oh... I gotta plan."

"Winter..." I threaten. "No." She takes one big step away from me. "Come here."

"Show me them football moves, Mr. Quarterback."

I point my finger at her. "I was not a quarterback. I was a *corner*back." *Yeah Jinx, because that's what important right now.*

"We bout to fuck some shit up," she yells. The crowd cheers. My high is lost. That ugly bastard coming up behind her looks confident. He shouldn't. I tense because he's closer to her than I'm comfortable with. She's looking at me. I shake my head. Put my hand at my back to get my gun that isn't there. Then she smiles and mouths, "I got this."

In the time it takes her to turn and face him, I'm at her back. My hand on her wrist. My gun trapped securely between us. I give the guy a lethal look. Winter leans her head back on my shoulder and gazes up at me smiling. I watch her out of the corner of my eye—keeping my focus trained on the man who's visibly shaken, but still too fucking close to her.

"God you're so hot," Winter says, grinding her ass against me.

Despite the stand-off, my growing temper and fading high, for some reason I respond. "Thank you, baby." My gaze doesn't falter from the guy as I kiss the top of her head and move my finger to the safety on the gun—afraid I'll get too damn excited and blow my own dick off.

"This your bitch now?"

Winter stiffens at the dumb fuck's bad choice of words. When she does, my anger becomes palpable.

"I'm gonna break your jaw for that comment," I promise, easily removing the gun from Winter's fingers. I push her behind me and tuck my piece back into my pants. "You want me to do it here? Or you want to tell your friends to meet us in the parking lot so they can watch?"

He smirks, but I know it's to hide his nervousness now that he realizes I'm not as drunk as he thought. After a quick look over my shoulder at Winter, he looks back at me and nods. "Lead the way."

I turn to Winter and wink in hopes of wiping that look of apprehension off her face. It works. She licks her lips and her eyes darken. I walk through the crowd with her tucked into my side. By the time we make it to the door, she's got one hand around my waist while the other is massaging my cock to life.

When I should be thinking about how I'm going to pull this off, I'm thinking about how I've never killed a man with a hard on before. I guess there's a first time for everything.

JINX

"Harder!"

Winter's demand is once again met and I piston inside her reaching a depth even I didn't think I was capable of. I guess she's not the only one who needs to blow off some steam.

Ten's Testament never followed us out. When I went back inside to try and find them, they were gone. So, I decided to take my frustrations out in a different manner. One I preferred. One Winter did too. And one that was a hell of a lot more rewarding.

I pound into her with the voracious drive she begs for. She screams so loud, the windows on my car rattle and shake with the vibration. She stills a second. Then comes hard. Her orgasm as violent as my thrusts.

It's her third one since I put her on her knees in front of me. Pushed her pants down her thighs. Pulled her panties to the side. Spread her open. And sunk my cock deep inside her dripping cunt.

I figure it'll take at least one more to sate her long enough for us to make it home. If not, I'll have to give it to her another way. My balls are already stretched to the point of pain. Heavy and swollen and demanding I find my own release.

Where she finds her strength, I don't know. But no sooner has she caught her breath, she's looking over her shoulder expectantly. Her fingers gripping the door. Back arched low. Ass high. Those green eyes half-mast and telling me, "More."

I oblige.

Sliding my hand over her hip, I reach between her legs and roll her clit with my finger. Loving how her eyes close and mouth parts at the contact. "Just like that," she pants, rolling her hips and squeezing her thighs around my hand.

"When we get home," I start, my voice a low, demanding growl. "I want you in the shower. On your knees. Your lips around my cock."

"Yes! More! Tell me more!"

"I'm gonna fuck your mouth hard. Bury my dick in the back of your throat. Make you take all of it—"

"What happens if I'm a bad girl and bite you?" she asks, cutting me off. I smirk. *Dirty girl. Guess the kink's out of the closet...*

Fisting her hair, I slow my thrusts and pull her back so my lips are at her ear. My voice deepens. "Bad girls get punished."

"I'm so bad..."

I tighten my hold on her hair to silence her. "Yes, you are. That's why I'm gonna drag you to the bed. Bend you over. Take my belt. Wrap it around my hand and spank that pretty little ass of yours..."

"Ah!" She stiffens around me. Squeezes me so hard I groan. Then she's pulsing. Coming on my cock. And this time, it's my undoing.

I pull out of her and work my shaft with my fist. Watch her fingers between her legs, rubbing her pussy as she stares at me over her shoulder. I move my eyes on hers as I bathe her ass in ropes of fiery come.

The sensation is overwhelming. The sight a sexy fucking thing to see. And just like her, I can't get enough. Already I'm thinking of the next time I can have her. How I can make it different. Better. Even more perfect—if that's even fucking possible.

WINTER

I remember the Viagra commercials. I know what they said. According to them, I should call a doctor. My lady erection has exceeded four hours and shows no sign of decreasing.

Jinx fucked me at the bar. In the car. Gave me at least twenty orgasms. Promised to sate my hungry appetite for as long as it takes. I took him up on his offer. Now, he's fingering me in Waffle House. My eyes on the syrup bottle. My hands fisted on the table. When it becomes too much, I bury my face behind his shoulder. My teeth biting down hard on his leather cut to stifle my moans.

"Come for me, baby," he says, his voice a low, desperate demand. His use of the word *baby* sends tingles to my chest while his fingers have me tingling in other places.

I come apart. Somehow managing to find the decency to twist further into him and hide my reaction. Smother my cries. Do my very best to not bring attention to myself in the packed restaurant.

When the fire inside me dies down to only a simmer and I catch my breath, I tentatively ease my head from behind his shoulder. His hand slides from my pants. When he puts them in his mouth, I'm ready to go again.

Shaking away the thought, my eyes scan the restaurant to find the drunken three a.m. crowd paying us no attention. Thankfully. But my relief is short-lived—replaced with a fiery, jealous rage when I notice the waitress making them pathetic googly eyes at Jinx. *I'll annihilate that bitch.*

"You don't have a girlfriend, do you?"

Jinx lifts a brow. "You fuckin' serious right now?"

"Yeah." I shrug, averting my gaze.

"If I had a girlfriend, I wouldn't be finger fucking you in Waffle House, sweetheart." Relief. Unwanted relief floods through me. "Hey..." He tips my chin to look at him. His eyes are narrowed and serious. "You think I'm that kinda guy?"

"Well...I don't know. That's why I asked."

He smirks. "Well...now you do know." His tone drops. "I'm not that guy."

"Pecan waffle?" My gaze shoots to the waitress. She's undeterred by my threatening look—batting her eyelashes and smiling suggestively and shit at someone who doesn't belong to her. I mean, he doesn't belong to me either, but... still.

"*Mine,*" I snap, my emphasis on the word directed more toward the man sitting next to me than the waffle she all but shoves in my direction. My temper flares at her obvious dismissal of my warning. "The scent of my pussy is fresh on his fingers... his mouth... and his cock..." My hand flies out, gesturing to the room. "So find someone else to flash them crooked ass, cigarette stained teeth at."

Jinx drops his head to hide his grin. The waitress, *Wanda,* looks like someone just shit in her tip jar. And I'm three seconds from shoving her face in the deep fryer when she very quickly, very smartly, puts the rest of our order on the table and disappears.

"Thirsty bitch," I mumble, covering my waffle in syrup.

"If I were alone, I'd have gotten her number." I glance up to find an amused Jinx smiling playfully at me.

"Yeah?" I fork a bite of waffle and pop it in my mouth. I'm still chewing when I tell him, "Well, if the rabbit hadn't stopped to piss, the dog wouldn't have got him."

He laughs at that—a loud, uncaring, genuine laugh. It's infectious and I find myself laughing at my own joke along with him. "My Dad used to say that same shit all the time."

My ears quirk up at the mention of his dad. I'm hungry for knowledge about his personal life, but I don't want to push him. Lucky for me, my silence works and he continues. "He hated excuses. And every time I'd say "if" an excuse followed it. By the time I was in high school, I finally understood that excuses didn't work for him. It was better to just suck it up, agree that you were wrong and move forward."

I point to the NO EXCUSES patch stitched on the collar of his vest. "I bet he was proud to see you wearing that." I know the patch means something different in the club world, but I want to find out what his family thinks about who he is. What he gave up. If they agree with his lifestyle.

"Wouldn't know," he says so dismissively, I'm surprised when he elaborates a few moments later. "He's never seen it."

Waffle forgotten, I turn in my seat to face him. *Now who's the thirsty bitch?* "He doesn't know about the club?"

"You catch on quick." He winks at me before turning back to his food. Cutting and chewing and making me wait for more. "My parents are simple-minded, hard working people. They're also pretty naive. They'll assume I'm out robbing liquor stores and killing people because that's the kinda shit that happens on Gangland. I figured it best not to tell them about this part of my life."

"Part of your life?" I blanch. "This *is* your life. It's who you are. Every day. It's not some hobby. Right?"

He points at me with his fork. "You're two for two." I'm not sure why he's so passive about this. *Maybe he really does have daddy issues or some sob story.*

"So what do they think you do?"

"I own a company that provides security for wind energy towers."

I scrunch my nose up. "What the hell is that?"

"Wind energy... windmills. My company protects the transportation and delivery of them from vandalism and theft."

"Who would steal a windmill?"

"You'd be surprised," he mumbles.

"Wait, so you really do own a company that does that?" He stares at me like I have three heads and nods slowly. "Have you always done that?"

"No." His short response coupled with the obvious tension in his neck piques my curiosity.

"Are you going to elaborate?"

"No."

"Butthole..."

He grins and grabs the check from the corner of the table. "You finished?"

"Yeah." I rub my stomach and look down at my half-eaten waffle. "I'm full. I think it was the liquor."

"Well," he starts, standing and holding his hand out to me. I take it and allow him to pull me into his chest. "If you get hungry later..." His hands move to button my pants I'd forgotten was open. "I got something to feed you."

Those dark, dirty, whispered words have me suddenly aware of that lingering, insatiable feeling that's been hovering inside me. Immediately, my body heats. My control is lost. I want to fuck his leg. His face. This table. That ugly ass waitress who really isn't ugly at all.

I'm squeezing my thighs together. Inhaling his scent. Blatantly rubbing my nipples that are hard and visible through my shirt across his back. I don't give a shit who's watching either. No woman can blame me. Because I'm pretty sure, there's not a bitch in here who isn't wet at the sight of Jinx.

We're in his car. His cut is off. His forearms visible. Tattooed and tanned and muscular. He drives with his left hand on the wheel. His right elbow resting on the console. I'm breathing hard. Squirming in my seat. Watching him. Waiting... Impatiently willing him to look at me. Say something dirty. Do something even dirtier.

"When we get home..."

He hasn't even finished and I'm whimpering. Fingers pinching my nipples. Legs opening and closing. Head back. Mouth agape. Eyes fluttering. He shifts to adjust his hardening cock and I start to cross the barrier separating us and put my mouth on him. Lick him. Tease him. Suck him. Take him deep.

His phone rings loud through the speakers of his car. I want to smash the motherfucker into a million pieces. He must feel the same because when he presses the button on the steering wheel to answer it, his tone is clipped and angry.

"Yeah?"

"Either you've got a death wish, my sister has a twin or whoever sent me this picture is one talented, photo-editing motherfucker, because I *know* it's not Winter I see getting trashed in a bar when she's *supposed* to be locked up tighter than a nun's cunt, secured and safe but miserable and alone and under your watchful eye. So which one is it, *brother,* because I'm two seconds away from flying down there just to kill you and do the job myself."

Jinx shoots me a lazy, questioning look along with a smirk. I roll my eyes and mutter, "Hello, Pierce." I swear I can feel the tension radiating from his silence. After a few seconds, he speaks, but it's through gritted teeth.

"Take me off speaker, Jinx. Now..." he adds, the threat clear. Jinx doesn't look the least bit intimidated but does as Pierce says.

"What?" Jinx asks, bored.

There's a lot of shouting. A few unenthusiastic "yeah's" from Jinx, then a more stern, "I got it" before the call is ended. The moment he hangs up, he looks over at me. "Too bad we don't have anymore of that cush. I could use some right about now."

"Who says we don't?" I grin, then pull the baggie I'd lifted off of Josephine without her knowledge from my bra.

"Damn woman," Jinx says, a playful growl in his voice. "I'm gonna fuck around and fall in love with you." He's only kidding. His smirk says so. But only one word comes to mind at the mention of him falling in love with me...

Ditto.

WINTER

Ding-a-ling-a-ling... Ding-a-ling-a-ling... Ding-a-ling-a-ling...

"Answer that motherfucker or eat it!" I croak, groaning when my own voice has my head throbbing in pain.

I keep my eyes closed against the bright light streaming through the curtains, but can feel and hear Jinx as he removes the battery from the phone and throws it across the room. It crashes against the wall with a satisfying, yet ear splitting, sound.

He cradles the back of my head in his hand again. Softly massaging my scalp with the tips of his fingers as he caresses my arm that's thrown over his stomach. When he kisses my hair, I think it's unintentional. Which makes that butterfly-wing-flapping in my belly even more excited.

After we made it home last night, he rolled us a blunt. It took him a couple of tries because I couldn't keep my mouth off of him. He ended up stopping so he could feed me what I was hungry for, took his turn eating me until he was full and then we finally smoked that blunt neither of us needed.

As if that wasn't enough, we finished off a bottle of scotch. Watched the sun come up. Fucked like animals when we got in bed.

Then I curled against his chest. My legs tangled with his. Naked and finally fully sated.

Five seconds later, I was bolting from the bed. Hugging the toilet. Puking my guts up. He'd said he wouldn't hold my hair. He totally did. He even helped me take a shower. Dried me off. Carried me back to bed—naked. Because my clothes were in the other room. And he sure as shit wasn't letting me wear his.

When I woke up only moments ago to the incessant ringing of his annoying fucking phone, I found myself in the same position I went to sleep in—tucked into his side. And once again, I'm drifting because the comfort of his embrace just does that to me.

Bang. Bang. Bang.

"Jinx!" *Luke.*

With lightning speed, Jinx grabs the sheet and pulls it over my exposed back. Then his large hand is covering the side of my head—protecting my ear from the loud crash of the door as it hits the wall. Thank god he's got good reflexes, because I'm too tired to even think straight, much less move.

"What the fuck, man?" Jinx snaps, his voice quiet despite his palpable anger.

"Why aren't you answering your phone?" Luke roars. I cringe. Jinx's hand rubs my head in a soothing gesture.

"Keep your voice down. I was asleep, obviously."

The room is silent and I feel like they're communicating in a different way. A look. A sign. Something. Anything to keep me from hearing the exchange.

"You owe me," Luke finally says, his voice soft as the light click of the door when he closes it.

"Owe him for what?" I mutter, licking my dry lips.

"For running Ten's out of town. And for handling Pierce. He's still pissed."

"Fuck Pierce."

"That's what I said."

Jinx continues his tender rubbing. Fingers gently kneading. Touching. Soothing. Caressing. His lips kissing my hair. His words a whisper. "Go back to sleep, baby."

And I do.

———

IT'S BEEN a week since we got hammered and stoned out of our minds. It took the first three days to recuperate from our hangover. Most of our recovery was spent on the couch watching T.V. Rehydrating. Eating food that we could actually stomach, like Jell-O and pudding cups.

Our routine hasn't changed much since then. But things between the two of us have definitely changed since that night. Like when we watch T.V. we do it curled into each other. When we shower, we shower together. When we sleep, it's in his bed—together. And it doesn't feel weird or strange but perfect and right.

Worst part is, I can't even blame our obvious attraction on the sex. Because since he fucked me seventeen ways to Sunday the night we went out, he hasn't touched me. Well, not like that. It's not that I don't want him to, but we both seem to be satisfied with the intimacy that comes with cuddling, showering and sleeping together.

Besides, yesterday was the first day I could walk without wincing. My aching pussy felt battered. Clit swollen and raw. Thighs bruised. Ass cheeks sore from his hard pounding when he took me on my knees. Breasts tender from his harsh kneading and sucking. But damn, I'd loved every second of it and my body ignited with every painful reminder.

When I hissed out a breath as I crawled out of bed and made my way slowly and painfully to the bathroom that first day, I figured he'd smirk. I was prepared to give him the finger and tell him to fuck off, but he wasn't cocky about it. He looked uneasy. A little regretful. And my chest had tightened at his concern.

I'd assured him I was fine. But he'd stopped me in the bedroom and held me at arm's length. His brows had creased and worried eyes traveled across every inch of my naked body—the corners tightening every time they scanned a bruise. Eventually, he met my eyes. Stared at me for the longest moment. Then, he cupped my cheeks. Kissed my head. And every day since then, has treated me like I'm something precious.

Now I'm terrified of this shit happening in my chest. This damn heart of mine that flutters every time he smiles. Swells when he walks in the room and deflates a little when he's not around. The bastard skips a beat when he calls me *baby*. Yearns to hear it instead of the snarky *sweetheart* he uses when he's being a dick.

Yep. This heart of mine is fucking with my emotions. Destroying my plans. It's forcing me to feel things for Devil's Renegades Jinx....

Not my dream guy.

———

"Happy Thanksgiving," Jinx says, tossing a creepy rubber chicken at me. I nearly spill my scotch trying to catch the damn thing.

"It's Thanksgiving?"

"It was Thursday."

"What's today?"

He shoots me a look that says I should know this. Like there's a fucking calendar posted on the wall. Or I have a phone I can look down at to verify the date. "It's Saturday. Get dressed. Club's annual feast is tonight." He sounds as excited about going as I feel.

Another week has passed with it being just him and me. Fucking when we want to. Sleeping when we want to. Talking when we feel like it. Ignoring each other when we don't. The last thing I want is to be cooped up in a house with a bunch of people I don't like, who share the same feeling about me.

"Eh..." I shrug my shoulders. "I'll pass. Besides, this show is pretty damn good." I pick the creepy chicken up with my finger tips and sling it across the room then settle back into the couch and press play.

Jinx, in all his half-naked, sexy as shit glory, blocks the T.V. with his big body. "You're goin'."

I give him a hard look. "No... I'm not."

Ignoring me, he turns off the T.V. then saunters over. My breath hitches. Panties dampen. Heart does that weird shit it's been doing lately.

"If you're hungry..." I trail off, licking my lips as he parts my legs and sinks to his knees between them. Pushing my shirt up my stomach, he trails a finger across the hem of my panties. When those bright, gray eyes peek up at me, I nearly come.

"As delicious as you are, baby, a man's gotta eat real food every now and then." *Baby... It just... gets me.* And he's been saying it so much here lately. And I've been swooning like crazy every time he does.

"Then I'll cook for you."

He lifts a brow. "You cook?"

"No... but I can figure it out." My hips buck. He smiles.

"Tell me why you really don't want to go." He turns his head and places a kiss on my right thigh. Then my left.

"You know why," I breathe, my eyes already falling closed. Ready for him to do what he always does—fucking devour me and leave me wet and sated and floating.

"I really don't." *Damn his serious voice...*

Cracking open one eye, I glare at him the best I can. "They don't like me. I don't like them. Why the hell would I want to spend my holiday with them?" Settling back, I dig the heels of my feet into his ribs, urging him closer. "When I could stay here with you and do something a lot more exciting."

"Well, I'm going so that's not possible."

"You can stay," I fire back. He chuckles. It's deep in his chest. The echo vibrating my pussy that's so close to his mouth, I can feel his breath on me.

"Sorry, sweetheart." *Sorry sweetheart...ugh.* "I've gotta go. Which means you do too. Get up. We leave in twenty."

I narrow my eyes. "I'm. Not. Going."

Pulling some Chuck Norris shit, he flips me to my stomach and swats my ass hard. Then he's on top of me. His cock digging into my still-stinging ass. His lips at my ear. "How about this," he whispers, rocking his hips against me. "We'll have dinner with them..." His tongue traces the shell of my ear. I shiver beneath him. "And I'll have *you* for desert."

Done.

JINX

I 'm sitting at the table smoking a cigarette. It seems I'm always waiting on Winter for something.

In the shower, I have to wait for her to shave her legs before I can rinse the burning fucking soap from my eyes, because she needs the hot water and refuses to shower alone.

In the morning, I have to wait for her to wake up before I can eat breakfast, because she likes to eat with me.

At night, I have to wait for her to get sleepy before I go to bed, because she doesn't like sitting up alone.

When we fuck, I have to wait for her to come at least three times before I do—that one is my preference, but still. I'm waiting. All the time. That's not the most annoying part, either. I actually *like* it. That's what's so fucking crazy.

I like that she needs me. That my day consists and revolves around nothing but her. That every-fucking-thing I do is done with her in mind. With Ten's out of the state and eyes on Cain confirming he's still in Vegas, I've been able to let my guard down. So for the past two weeks, we've been acting like a couple on their honeymoon—hidden away in some romantic retreat in south Mississippi without a care in the world. It's unnerving. But I guess I fucking like that too.

She'd asked me if we were taking the bike. When I told her no, she looked a little disgusted. Shook her head. Then said, "You're the only fucking biker I know who doesn't ride a bike." Now I want to prove it to her. Put her on my Harley, ride off into the sunset, stop for gas, fuck her on my bitch seat and then keep heading south. Just me. Just her.

I'm losing my goddamn mind.

"You ready? I'm hungry."

"I've been ready," I snap, keeping my back to her. Making her wait as I finish my cigarette. I've never waited on a bitch. I don't know what makes this one so special.

Movement catches my eyes as I stub out my smoke. When I glance up, what I find has my anger dissipating—immediately replaced with a raw, primal desire to pound into her until she's screaming my name while she comes around me.

She's naked.

All long legs and tattooed arms.

Bare pussy and big, fake tits.

Curled hair.

Perfectly made-up face.

Hooded, bright green eyes.

Painted pink lips part and her tongue darts out to lick her bottom lip. They're full. Pouty. But I want them swollen from being kissed too hard. Her lipstick smeared. Her mouth around my cock. Hear her crying my name. *Fuck.*

"Sometimes," she says, her bare feet padding silently on the floor as she closes the distance between us, "I like to have dessert before dinner."

"Yeah?"

She's still nodding when I reach out and wrap my arm around her waist—pulling her on top of my lap. She straddles my thighs and moans when she feels my cock already stiff for her. The fucker sprang to life at just the idea of having her. Like I haven't fucked her a hundred times already.

"I want you," I ground out, my hands on her waist. Thumbs circling the skin just below her breasts. She squirms in my lap and I have to choke out the next words. "But we don't have time."

We should've left thirty minutes ago. If I didn't have church, I wouldn't care. But I do. And I can't be late. Well...I can but then I'll have to pay a fine. Penalty fee. Fucking five-thousand-dollar charge for being late without a legitimate excuse. And pussy, is not a legitimate excuse.

Winter slides off my lap. I'm thinking she gets it and isn't going to argue. Then she drops to her knees. Pushes mine apart. Worms her body between my thighs and starts working the button on my jeans.

I groan at the sight of her on the floor. Licking those lips. Salivating for my cock. Hungry to have me in her mouth. I've never had a five-thousand-dollar blow-job. This would be my first. If I let it happen. I shouldn't let it happen. But I can't find the will to tell her no. The moment she frees me from my jeans and fists her hand around my shaft, I'm a goner.

My fingers thread into her long, blonde hair. Hands tightening around her skull. Guiding her. Applying just a little pressure to encourage her to take me deep. She doesn't disappoint. Her eyes flutter. She moans. Her fingers slipping between her legs. Playing with her pussy. Her other hand reaching inside my jeans. Cupping my balls.

"Fuck...baby," I hiss through my teeth. She mewls—loving it when I call her baby. I'd call her anything. Just as long as she keeps that silky, wet, hot mouth around my cock. That tongue of hers licking up my shaft. Those pink cheeks hollowing. Wide, watery eyes looking up at me.

My balls swell in her hand. She squeezes just hard enough for my legs to stiffen. Then, with her lips on my zipper, my cock down her throat, she swallows—tightening those muscles at the very back of her throat around me.

Hips jerking, spine tingling, fucking chest on fire...I come so hard I see spots. My head swims. Heart hammers. I'm fucking panting. And she's still sucking. Massaging. Swallowing every. Last. Drop. This damn girl...*fuck*.

When my eyes flutter open, they find her immediately. Hell, they have to. She's the only thing I see when she's around. Everything else is a mist. A dark haze. Overshadowed by her presence. Not just her beauty, but the whole fucking package that is Winter Tews.

Tightening my hand in her hair, I have to pry her off my cock. She moans her disapproval. Her body rocking against her fingers. Cheeks flushed. Eyes so damn green and rimmed in red. Lips still as perfectly pink as they were when she first parted them.

"My turn," I say, voice hoarse.

Fisting her hair, I give it a tug. When her feet are planted, I wrap my hands around her slim waist and sit her on the table in front of me. Pushing my chair back, I toss her legs over my shoulders, grip her fat ass in my hands, pull her to the edge and dip my head between her thighs. "Watch." Her eyes flutter at my demand.

Leaning back on her elbows, she watches me as I spin my hat around and inch closer—her legs spreading wider to accommodate my broad shoulders. "Prettiest fuckin' pussy," I mumble, my eyes drinking in her wet, pink flesh. Her lips soft and bare. Clit swollen and peeking out at me from beneath its hood.

Placing my thumbs on either side of the tiny nub, I expose it completely. I love how close I am to her. How I can see everything. How the pink stains her cheeks with embarrassment at me seeing her like this. How she pulls in a sharp breath, then exhales on a whispered, "Please."

Parting my lips, I close my mouth over her bared clit. Knowing how worked up and oversensitive she is, I keep my touch soft. My wet tongue feathering her clit in a circle. When I suck slightly, her legs spasm and she releases a pleasure-pained cry.

My eyes lift to meet hers. They're half-mast. Focused on me. Mouth slack. Golden hair messy and draped over her shoulders. Elbows trembling to support her weight. Flat stomach rising and falling in harsh breaths. She's fucking beautiful.

I sink a finger into her dripping cunt. Curl the tip. Watch her head fall back as she cries out. Her pussy squeezing my digit. Juices soaking it. I pull out and drag the wetness over her ass. She tenses and I pause.

When she doesn't look up or relax, I flatten my tongue against her clit and press hard. That instantly has her body loosening and I take advantage. Pushing the tip of my finger past the tight barrier, I don't stop until I'm knuckle deep in her ass.

She stiffens again, but I just keep working her with my tongue until she slowly melts around me. Then, as my tongue works her clit, I pump my finger in and out of her. Not too deep, just enough to give her all the sensation she can possibly stand.

Seconds later, I know she's close. Her head lifts. Gaze centers on me. I flick her clit hard with my tongue, and she explodes. Crying out. Nails scratching at the wooden table beneath her. Her hips lifting to meet my face. Grinding against my mouth. Legs tightening around my head. Ass inching further down—forcing my finger deeper.

I don't stop until her strength gives out and she collapses. Her back hits the table and her breath leaves her in a whoosh of unmistakable pleasure.

Kissing my way down her flaccid legs, I slowly unwrap them from around me. Leaning back in my seat, I take a moment to just look at her. Appreciate every inch of her naked body. From her hard, pink nipples to her pink painted toes. But a moment is all I have.

Then I'm on my feet. Picking her up. Carrying her sated body to my room. Planting her in front of her clothes that are laid out on my bed. Pushing her hair over her shoulder. Kissing her neck. Leaving her to get dressed. Making my way to my safe. Retrieving the five grand for the most expensive pussy I've ever eaten.

And not giving a single fuck.

Because it was worth every cent.

WINTER

Regg and Red's home is located in the middle of nowhere. Literally.

There are no signs on the narrow roads that lead us there. No other houses. No sign of life other than a few stray cows littering the endless, open fields.

We've been riding for over an hour when we finally turn down a narrow driveway. At the end sits a beautiful, old, three-story, Victorian style house that looks like a picture ripped from the pages of The Amityville Horror.

Bikes are lined in the yard out front. A massive porch surrounds the first story. In the distance, I can see row after row of chicken houses, an old barn and then nothing but pine trees. I might find it serene under different circumstances.

"Let's go, sweetheart," Jinx says, grabbing the small black bag he'd brought from the house and climbing out of the car. With a deep breath, I follow him out and inhale the cold, fresh air that's tainted by the faint scent of chicken shit.

"Ugh. How do they stand that?" I ask, placing the cuff of my sweater over my nose.

Jinx pauses his step to turn and look at me as I check the bottom of my boots—making sure I didn't step in anything. "Regg says it smells like money." I glance up at him to find his eyes roaming over me.

"What?" I snap, following his gaze down my Tiffany blue, oversized sweater that hangs mid-thigh. Then to the flash of cream colored leggings before trailing down my brown, knee high boots. *I don't see anything.*

"Nothing," Jinx whispers, a warm smile on his lips as he takes my hand and tucks it into his. "You look good, babe. That's all."

Before I can respond, he gives my hand a tug and I follow him up the stairs to the porch, finding my lady nuts by the time we make it to the door. I'm most definitely going to need them with this crowd. The women hate me. The men don't much like me either. And a pit of dread and nerves have my stomach tightening in anxiety.

Without knocking, Jinx pushes inside and immediately I'm hit with the scent of something delicious. Whatever's baking in the kitchen, has my mouth watering as we make our way through the foyer and up a flight of polished, wooden stairs.

The walls are all weathered, white wood scattered in pictures and paintings. Sixteen foot ceilings span over us. The banister is wrapped in garland decorated and lit for Christmas. For a moment, it reminds me of home. The home I had as a child before my parents were gone. The last time I remember being really happy. Then my brow wrinkles when I realize that's not entirely true.

Because when I think of happiness now, I think of Jinx. Of the past couple of weeks we've spent together in complete isolation. Of how he mindlessly held my hand in the car. Kissed my fingers. How comfortable the silence was and how happy it made me.

Happy.

I, Winter Tews, am... happy.

Then, I hear the sound of women's chatter and the memory fades when reality surfaces.

I yank on Jinx's arm pulling him to a stop. "Don't leave me with the bitches!" I hiss on a whisper. An amused look claims his face when he lifts a brow at me.

"You scared?"

My spine stiffens. "Fuck no. But I'm not exactly looking forward to baking cookies and shit with them either." He smiles at that.

"Never know..." He winks at me. "You might even learn something." I narrow my eyes on him and snatch my hand from his. I didn't realize I could go from liking him to hating him so fast.

Without any other option, I follow behind him—stomping my feet unnecessarily hard. By the time we reach the top of the stairs that open up to a massive den on the second floor, I'm wearing my best bitch face. Spine straight. Shoulders stiff. Eyes assessing the room that's bare other than a few furnishings. Including the card table in the middle of the room, surrounded by three women—the same three women I'd called out weeks ago. *Great.*

Jinx gives them a chin tip then turns to me and smirks. "Have fun, sweetheart."

"Eat shit," I mutter. My words have him laughing as he brushes past me and back down the stairs. I listen to every stomp of his heavy boots. Keeping my eyes on everyone, but no one in particular as they all stare back at me.

I drink them all in. Red and her fiery hair. The dust of flour on her left cheek. Tough demeanor that's betrayed by her kind, hazel eyes. Dallas with her supermodel good looks. Aura of superiority. The confidence she possesses and portrays. Then Delilah. She looks happy. Maybe not in this moment, but the story in her eyes tells it all. She finally feels of value. Knows her worth. Of the three, she is most like me, yet there's still a world of difference between us. And I can't help but feel a pang of jealousy that this ex-clubwhore has a peace about her that I will never know.

When the footsteps cease and a door shuts from somewhere downstairs, Red speaks. "You play?" she asks, tone bored. Head titled. Brow lifted. Eyes studying my clothes. Hair. Face. Stance. Then finally meeting my gaze. "It's three card poker. Loser matches the pot."

I glance at the pile of money and personals in the center of the table. A thought springs to mind and I shrug. "I'll give it a try."

Dallas, looking overly confident, kicks a chair out. "Take a seat."

Taking the offered chair, I lift a brow at Red who offers me a glass of Scotch. The hair on my neck stands up when I notice it's my favorite. No doubt information that Dallas got from her flight attendant, Shira. I shouldn't take the bait, but I nod anyway. Because who the fuck am I kidding? It's scotch.

Red pours a glass and I accept, taking a sip as I cross my legs and lean back. With all eyes on me, I pull out the wad of cash stuffed in my boot. I make a show of removing the rubber band and flipping through the bills.

Some of this money I lifted from strangers when Jinx and I went out the other night. The rest of it is what I stole from their purses when I first arrived—the last time I saw them. By the daggers they're shooting me, they know it too.

"You enjoy taking shit that doesn't belong to you?" Delilah asks, her arms crossed over her chest as she glares at me.

"I do," I admit, meeting her harsh look. She's taking this personally —even though it wasn't her money I stole. It says a lot about her. My best guess is she's struggled for money before. And my nonchalance about stealing pisses her off.

For some reason, her anger pulls at my conscience and I find myself peeling off three one hundred dollar bills and tossing them on the table. "The thrill is taking it. Not keeping it."

"So that makes it okay?" Delilah scoffs, shaking her head. Her anger growing.

"I didn't say that."

"What about putting our business on front street for the whole club to hear? Did you think that was okay?"

My lips press together to keep from saying anything. I want to tell her to fuck off, but I hurt her that night. Unlike Red and Dallas's situation, Delilah's wasn't something very many people knew about. Well, at least not the brothers. The whores knew everything—especially about each other. If the men were smart, they wouldn't let them inside their clubhouse at all.

For example, Loose-Lipped Lindsay. She was a clubwhore from Lake Charles who moved to Vegas not long ago. Looking to find an easy place to turn tricks, she came to the MC. I quickly befriended her —per Cain's request so he could gain some more intel on the Devil's.

It's how I learned that shit about Red and Dallas, too. But what she told me about Delilah was much more disturbing.

Delilah used to be a pain slut. Believed she deserved to be hurt to pay for her "sins". She would let her brother beat the hell out of her just to feel some semblance of normalcy. It was some real fucked up shit.

Then she found Bryce. He helped her in a different way. Gave her pain in a controlled manner by using BDSM tactics. Spanking, orgasm control and all that kink. But mentioning her brother was definitely a trigger. And judging by the way she's shifting in her seat, it's one her ass has paid for.

Guilt is a feeling I've learned to ignore in my line of work. But in this moment, I simply can't ignore it. I shouldn't have said those things to her. It was wrong. Even if I believed it was better in the end for all of them if they hated me and could somehow help in getting the club to let me go, it was still wrong.

"I shouldn't have said that, Delilah," I tell her, my words sincere. "And I'm sorry that I did." She nods. Her face relaxing. The anger and sadness fading marginally from her eyes.

"What the fuck about me?" I shift my attention to Red. "You told everyone I was a heroin addict."

"And that I killed people," Dallas adds on a whisper. I roll my eyes. *Like not saying it out loud is going to change anything.*

Reaching for the pack of smokes thrown in the pile in the center of the table, I retrieve them and put a twenty in their place. Lighting one, I inhale deep—blowing the smoke over the top of my head. I hadn't asked Red if she smoked in her house. Forgiveness over permission and all that....

"So?" Red prompts. "Are you gonna apologize to us?"

"For what?"

Dallas stiffens and speaks through gritted teeth. "For calling us out. For stealing our shit."

I point to the money I threw on the table. "I paid you back."

There's a kick under the table. Judging by the eye exchange, it was from Red to Dallas. *Subtle.* The invite... the scotch... suddenly I have the feeling that I'm being played. And there's another reason they invited me to sit at the table other than to beat them at poker.

"Yeah," Dallas says, her nerves evident in her tone. "You paid back the money. But about what you said...?"

"What about it?"

"I know how you can make it up to us."

"Who said I wanted to make it up to you?" I counter, tilting my head as I shoot her a challenging look.

She glances to Red then Delilah before coming back to me. With a deep breath, she admits, "I need something." *And there it is—the real reason I'm here.* "And since you're so good at taking things that aren't yours, I thought maybe you could help."

"No." My quick answer confuses them. I don't elaborate, I just smoke and drink and wonder if we're ever going to play cards because I really could use that extra cash.

"I'm asking you nicely."

I smile at Dallas. "And I'm *nicely* telling you no."

The silence is thick. Tension palpable. Who the fuck do these girls think they're messing with? I'm not your average whore. I'm not easily intimidated by ol' ladies or pretend to be nice to them in hopes of one day earning their respect. I don't need their approval. Have no desire to be one of them. So if they want my help, they'll need a damn good reason. And I need to be in a great fucking mood. Which I'm not.

"You're not the only one who did your research, you know."

My glass stills on my lips as I look over the rim to a smirking Delilah. She might've appreciated my apology, but this girl lives by the "Eye for an Eye" code. And she's hungry for her revenge.

"Is that so?" I ask flatly.

Her pretty head nods. "What I don't know is if, like me, you're a *pain slut,* or if he beat you regularly for a different reason."

I have to fight to contain my laughter. So she thinks she's got me with *that?* I'm property of the infamous Cain Malcovich—known for his evil temper and demonic way of life. Slapping his bitch around wasn't some new-found knowledge. Everyone is aware of my abuse. Maybe not the extent of it, but they know he put his hands on me.

"Maybe it's a little of both," I offer, flashing her an easy smile. "We all have our own way of dealing with shit life gives us. Right?" I don't push further, but if she doesn't drop this shit, I have no problem hurting her feelings again.

Leaning forward, Delilah rests her elbows on the table and clasps her hands. Her cold eyes meeting mine. "I'm gonna grant you a courtesy you never offered me." She motions to Red and Dallas who are watching me closely—confusion marring their faces. "Some things they know. But they don't have any *inkling* about the real shit."

She knows about the tattoo.

I still. *Fuck. What else does she know?*

"Are you blackmailing me, Delilah?" I ask, hoping my calm expression and cool attitude are convincing.

"I don't like that particular word, but yes." She nods once. "Help Dallas, or I'll tell everything I know. Not just to the people in this room, but to the entire club. I won't hesitate to do to you what you so easily done to me."

I take a sip of scotch. Light another smoke. This little bitch is something else. I'm not sure of all she knows or if she has it in her to actually out me. Beneath her hard exterior is still that lost, conflicted girl who's a victim to the darkness. But whatever Dallas wants from me can't be extreme enough to make it worth the gamble.

"What do you want?" I ask Dallas—keeping my eyes on Delilah. She sags in relief a little at my question. I almost smirk. She wouldn't tell on me. Sluts before cuts. She might wear that ol lady patch now, but she'll never forget where she came from.

"I need Luke's book from inside his cut."

My head jerks to Dallas. "What?"

"Luke's book," she repeats. "I need you to get it for me. Tonight."

I breath out a humorless laugh. This ol' lady was asking me to steal *the* book. The one that held contact information to every ally and enemy, known and unknown the club had. Every MC president had one. And they guarded it with their life.

"Wow," I mutter, shaking my head at Dallas in disbelief. "You really think I'm that stupid?"

"If anyone can get it, you can."

"Cut the shit, Dallas." She draws back at the aggression in my tone.

"That book is as classified as the Daily-fucking-Brief. So what could you, an ol' lady, possibly want with it? And why the hell would you want someone like me...your husband's enemy's cutslut, who's been eighty-sixed from this club, to get it?"

Without meeting my eyes, she says, "I just need it. It's important."

I smirk. "You're gonna have to do better than that, sugar. Cause it sounds to me like you're setting me up for a trap."

"It's not a trap," Red snaps. Slowly, I turn my attention to her. "We need some answers about a situation one of our sisters is involved in. There's only one person who can give us those answers and the only known contact information for him is in that book."

Confused, I ask the obvious question. "Why not just ask Luke? If she's your sister she's his. And judging by my own personal experience, the bastard loves getting into other people's shit."

"Because the situation is sensitive. She wants to handle it herself." Red levels me with a look. "You seem like the type of girl who can appreciate that."

She's right. I am. Whoever this sister is, I understand her wanting to handle this on her own. If Luke got involved, it would no doubt turn into a club issue. They always do shit in an extreme manner—taking something simple and blowing it out of proportion just to show their strength. To prove they can.

What they're asking me to do can be done, but if I'm caught, the blowback will be detrimental. Pierce... Jinx... they'll lose their minds over this. Pierce will hate me even more than he already does and Jinx...well...Jinx won't like me anymore.

My stomach tightens in fear at the thought and I meet Dallas's eyes —ready to tell her no. That she'll have to find another way. But upon seeing my expression, she visibly slumps. The light leaves her eyes. Blood drains from her face. I owe her nothing, but I find that I'm affected by her reaction.

"This sister..." I start, my voice low. "Who is she?"

Dallas is quiet a moment before admitting, "Maddie. She's not just my club sister. She's blood."

"Where is she now?"

"Away." The way she says it tells me I won't be getting any more than that.

Before I can think better of it, I'm speaking. "Okay." Hope blossoms on her face. I hold my hand up. "But I'm gonna need some help. And you're not gonna like it."

"Anything. I'll do anything," she quickly adds. *Damn... this really is important to her.*

"Good." Draining my glass, I try to mentally prepare for what's about to go down. "Cause you're the bait."

EVERYONE IS PACKED inside the small, busy kitchen waiting for food. Pouring drinks. Talking. Laughing. Paying little attention to me as I scan every single body and prepare for the mother of all thefts. The best part? I'm not even going to steal Luke's book. He's going to give it to me. Well, to Red anyway.

Dallas, Red and Delilah have no idea what I'm about to do. When they asked about the plan, I just told them they'd figure it out. That didn't sit well with them, but they agreed. It was for the best and so far, things are working in my favor. As long as I stay away from Jinx.

He's been suspicious of me since I came down the stairs. When he asked how it went and I replied, "Great," he shot me an inquisitive look. When I told him I was going to help the bitches in the kitchen, he pierced me with a questioning gaze. And when I tried to walk away from him, he caught my elbow and gave me a low warning. "Whatever you're doing... *don't.*"

Yeah, yeah, yeah... save it for someone who listens.

We're standing in a near perfect line getting food. Dallas stands in front of me. Luke in front of her. Red directly to our left. Delilah to her right. Jinx is toward the very back of the line but I swear I can feel him watching my every fucking move. Knowing I need to act before he gets even more suspicious, I decide it's time to set things in motion.

Shoving Dallas hard, she crashes into Luke's back—the contents of her full plate smears onto Luke's cut just before it falls to the floor and shatters. Sticky yams and buttery corn drip from the reaper on his back. He immediately pulls his cut off and brings it around to look at the damage. But when he catches Dallas glaring at me, her confusion mixed with anger, he quickly passes it off to Red and turns to us.

Perfect.

"You didn't think I'd actually help you, did you?" I taunt, my voice cold. Her cheeks redden as confusion dissipates and her temper flares. "Aww..." I shoot her a mock frown. "You did."

"You bitch," she hisses, taking a step closer to me. She cranes her neck to meet my gaze. My body tightens in preparation for her words. Fists clench. Adrenaline pumps. She's going to try to say something to hurt me. And I'm ready.

Then a fleeting look of recognition flashes in her eyes. It's quickly followed by an evil glare and a sinister smile. Before I know what's happened, she flattens her tiny palms to my chest and shoves me hard. I'm still finding my footing when my vision clouds with black just as a sharp pain rockets through my head.

She hit me.

The little bitch hit me.

Punched me right in the fucking eye.

I'm so shocked by her surprise attack, all I can do is hold the side of my face in my hand and stare at her.

"That," she says, breathless and panting—more from the rush of adrenaline than anything as she points her finger at me, "Is for talking shit about my sisters."

The room is completely silent.

Every eye on us.

Jinx to my left ready to intervene.

Luke next to him—cock rock hard.

Dallas tilts her head to the side and shoots me a look. Silently asking me if we're good.

I don't give a fuck if I hurt her feelings when I called her out. I don't care if she hates me. But she didn't hit me because of what I did to her. She hit me because of the pain I caused her sisters. I've got to give props to the bitch for that.

Smirking, I give her a single nod. Then I walk through the crowd of people to the freezer, take my time grabbing a bag of frozen peas, then make my way to the porch—tucking the bottle of scotch I'd brought from upstairs under my arm.

Dallas and I aren't friends.

We're not family.

I'm still a cutslut.

She's still an ol' lady.

But if my brother ever taught me anything, it's this—respect is earned.

And Dallas Carmical had most definitely earned mine.

JINX

She did something.

I fucking know it.

The diversion. The fight. Her not ripping Dallas's head off after she hit her. Not to mention she's been smiling to herself the entire ride home. Yeah... something's up. I knew it the moment she looked focused and conniving instead of pissed off and annoyed when she walked in that kitchen.

"What did you do?" I ask, my eyes leaving the road to watch her. But she never meets my gaze.

"I didn't do anything."

"Bullshit."

Her shoulders rise in an indifferent shrug. "You were there. Watching me like a hawk. If I'd had done something, you'd have seen it."

She's right. I need to think outside the box on this one. She knew I'd be watching. Knew she couldn't get away with doing anything herself. Which means...

Slamming on breaks, I jerk the car to the side of the road. She grabs the dash and shoots me a furious look. "What the—"

"Luke's book," I snap, cutting her off. "Where is it?"

"How the hell am I supposed to know?" She looks genuinely confused. But beyond the act, the bewildered facial expression, the wide eyes, there's a hint of panic. Anyone else would miss it. I don't miss anything.

"You've got one chance to come clean. If you don't, I'm calling Luke. And so help me Winter, there'll be hell to pay if you're lying to me."

Stiffening, she narrows her eyes at me. "Like I said, I don't know where his *book* is."

I can't save her once I call him. But she's not budging. She's acting like she doesn't even know what the book is. And she's fucking lying. Some things I can keep my mouth shut about. This isn't one of those things. That book is like the holy grail. If she has it, or information from it, she could hurt the club. I can't let that happen.

Dialing Luke's number, I give her one last look of warning. She rolls her eyes and leans back in the seat—sealing her fate. Hitting send, I wait for Luke to answer. Tension mounting as it rings. My anxiety heightening.

"Yeah?" *Fuck... he answered.*

"Check your pockets," I growl, my eyes on Winter who crosses her arms and lifts a brow at me.

"What?"

"Your fuckin' pockets, Luke. You missin' anything?" I hold my breath as I wait for him to check. With every sound of movement, my heart beats heavier.

There's a pause and then, "That bitch!" Luke's roar echoes through the speakers in the car.

Unable to stop myself, I reach out and fist her sweater in my hand, pulling her halfway across the console until we're face to face. She lifts her hands in surrender, that fucking smirk still on her lips.

"Where... is... it..." I snarl, my teeth clenched. Jaw tight. Rage evident.

"It's in the freezer," she says on a grin.

"Check the freezer."

"I fuckin' heard her," Luke snaps.

She's beaming now. Holding in a laugh. Not at all affected by my anger. My lethal fucking glare. The sound of Luke's heavy footsteps as they stomp through the house—pounding loud enough to rattle the windows in my car.

He opens the freezer.

Mutters, "Thieving little shit."

Slams it shut.

"It's here. So is the Prospect's."

I frown, confusion trumping my anger. The Prospect didn't have a book. "What?"

"How the fuck did she do that without me noticing? And when was she around the Prospect?" Luke asks, more amused than angry. "You got yours?"

"What the hell are you—"

"Don't worry, baby," Winter whispers, reaching down in her boot and pulling out my wallet. "I got it."

Luke's mumbling something about how all his shit seems to be there. I'm not really listening anymore. I just hang up and stare at her. Realizing I still have her shirt fisted in my hand, I release it and she slides back into her seat.

"No need to apologize for overreacting," she says, opening my wallet and pulling out a hundred-dollar bill. "This will suffice." Stuffing it in her bra, she shoots me a smile. "You good now? Or should I expect a spanking when we get home?"

I nearly lost my shit on her. I thought she stole something much more precious than a goddamn wallet. I was so confident, I'd grabbed her. Put my hands on her in a way no man should ever touch a woman. She's not hurt, but it doesn't make me feel any less of an asshole.

But I'm not the kind of guy who apologizes. I'm also not the kind who spanks women. Now I'm thinking that maybe I want to be that guy. So as I pull on the highway, I decide I will apologize to her—after I spank her ass and make her come so hard she loses consciousness... just as I say the words.

WINTER

I'm spent.
    Sated.
    Blissfully content.

You know... all those awesome things you are when you've just been fucked hard. Kissed softly. Held tenderly... Good romance novel shit.

That's me.

Lying on the bedroom floor.

Unsure of how I got here.

Not giving a damn.

Focused on the scruffy jaw that nuzzles my neck. The rough hand that slides up and down my hip. That massive arm-pillow beneath my head.

"There's a club party this weekend," Jinx says, his mouth close to my ear. "Starts at the bar, then everyone is coming here for the after party." I suppress a groan.

He lifts his head to look at me. Raising a brow, he studies me with those half-mast gray eyes. "You gonna play nice? Or do I need to find a cage to lock you in?" I know he's referring to my bullshit fight with Dallas. It's the first time he's mentioned it since we left Regg's three days ago.

I knew Jinx could never find out that I assisted in taking Luke's journal. So I decided to take something less important, because he was watching me so closely. It was too easy to slide his wallet from his baggy jeans. Then the Prospects. And it was Dallas who'd stolen Luke's and passed it to me. I hid them in the sleeve of my sweater. Left them in the freezer when I got the frozen peas for my eye and now everyone believes it was just a joke. Not the girl who committed an unforgivable sin—like taking, "the book."

But he'd overreacted. Grabbed me. I wasn't angry. I'm still not. I'm pretty sure guilt over him losing his shit and fisting my shirt is the reason he's avoided the topic up until now. And since I'm dealing with some guilt of my own, I can't hold what he did against him.

"Me and Dallas are good. It's Luke who I think is still pissed at me."

Jinx smirks, his eyes falling to my lips that he traces with the tip of his finger. "He's not pissed. His pride was hurt, but he's over it." Thoughtful, he drags his finger to the fading bruise at the corner of my eye. "You say the two of you are good. I'm not so sure I believe that."

Rolling my head so I'm looking at the ceiling, I shrug. "Believe what you want. I'm not lying. She hit me. I deserved it. As far as I'm concerned, the shit is squashed."

"What shit?"

I shoot him a sideways look. "I called her out."

"That's not why she hit you though, is it?" *He's a smart fucker.* "You told her you wouldn't help her. That's what pissed her off." *An observant one too...* "What was that about?"

I could tell him. But there's a bitch code all women within the MC live by. It's unspoken but understood. It doesn't matter if you like the woman or not. You don't rat each other out to the men. Even the smallest, most insignificant thing can be taken out of context. But something like this? Stealing *the book?* That shit will start a fucking war.

"Nothing really. She thought I owed her an apology. Wanted me to do something to make up for calling them out. It was bullshit. Just a test to see if I would. I didn't." It's not a complete lie.

"What did she want you to do?"

I smile. "Wouldn't you like to know?"

"Yes. I would."

Releasing a breath, I untangle myself from beneath him and stand. "Sorry, sweetheart. Some things just aren't any of your business." Even if it was, I wouldn't tell him. There's something satisfying and warming about having this secret with Dallas. It makes me feel like, for the first time, I actually have a place in this life. A respected place.

Rolling to his back, he crosses his arms behind his head and looks up at me towering over his deliciously naked body. A crooked smile plays on his sexy as sin lips. "I can fuck the truth out of you."

No. He couldn't. But my body still heats at his promise. I want more of him. I can't get enough. So I give him an offer I know he can't refuse and I won't regret.

"You're more than welcome to try."

———

SPENDING the rest of my life with Cain was my greatest fear when I arrived here. Now, six weeks later, my greatest fear is a life without Jinx. Maybe that's why even though the clock is ticking and I have less than two weeks left here, I can't find the will to leave.

I should be long gone, or at least have some sort of plan in place. But every time I try to focus on getting away, Jinx looks at me. Like he's looking at me now. Causing my temperature to rise to dangerous levels.

It's the night of the club party. He's wearing his cut. Low hanging jeans. White long-sleeved Henley. His hat backwards. The chain around his neck has a silver, diamond shaped pendant hanging from it —the number thirteen embossed in bold letters. And as I drink him in, he's devouring me.

He starts at my pink heels. Moves up my naked legs. Pauses at the hem of my shimmering, gold dress that is dangerously short. To the low neckline that scoops beneath my breasts. Across my collar bone. My lips that match my heels. Then finally to my eyes.

When he holds my gaze without blinking for longer than I'm comfortable with, I shift on my feet and brush a wayward strand of hair from my face. "What's wrong?" I ask, almost innocently.

Biting his bottom lip, he surveys me from head to toe one more time and shakes his head slowly. "Not a motherfuckin' thing."

My thoughts go crazy at the possessiveness in his tone. His stare. I lick my lips. Suppress a moan. Thinking of all the places he's going to touch me tonight. Kiss me. Lick me. *Fuck* me. *Why the fuck do we have to go to this damn club? And why the hell do they have to come back here?*

He's in front of me now. His knuckles grazing the side of my breast. His lips pressing softly against the corner of mine. His scent— that masculine, rich, heady, expensive cologne infused scent of his, permeating my senses. Making me drunk. Dizzy. *Wet.*

"I don't want to leave," I whisper, barely stifling a moan.

Taking my hand in his, he brushes my knuckles with his thumb. Pulls me along side him as he moves toward the door. His strides fluid. His eyes focused. His voice reluctant and regretful as he mumbles under his breath.

"I know, baby. I fuckin' know."

THE NIGHTCLUB IS PACKED. The music is loud. The drinks flowing. The atmosphere electric. And all I can think about is ripping the face off of every bitch who gives Jinx a onceover as they pass. When I steal a look at him, I'm pretty sure he's thinking the same thing about all the men who are openly ogling me.

Jaw tight. Teeth clenched. His barely contained rage is obvious in the thick veins that pulse in his neck. When a guy says something about my legs being around his neck, I swear I hear Jinx growl. And it only makes me that much more possessive of him. That much hotter. *Hornier.*

Though the place is crowded, people seem to move out of our way as we walk through the room and toward the VIP section that's roped off in the very back. This, I'm used to—that aura of power that demands respect. Only this time, I feel butterflies knowing that, in this moment, I belong to the man who has my hand firmly clasped in his.

"There the fuck you are!" Dallas yells, pulling at the hem of her tight, black dress as she clambers off her stool. The Prospect who unclasps the velvet rope to let us in, pales when Dallas nearly loses her footing. When she straightens, he lets out a relieved breath.

"You good?" Jinx asks, his mouth at my ear. *Shivers. Motherfucking shivers.* I nod because I can't seem to find my voice. "I'll get you a drink," he says, giving my hand a squeeze before releasing it. I turn and watch him walk back through the crowd, my body instantly missing the warmth of his.

"I *never* thought you'd get here!" I look down at Dallas's small form and smirk. She's pretty buzzed. And it's barely ten.

Grabbing my arm, she pulls me past the overstuffed couches and flashing neon tables to a small crowd of women—all ol' ladies or club affiliates.

"Winter, this is everyone. Everyone, this is Winter." I get a few nods from Dallas's introduction but most of them ignore me—too caught up in some shitty gossip or talk of a pencil dick none of them will be allowed to fuck, because these women belong to the club.

"How's your eye?" Dallas asks, screaming at me over the music—no doubt in hopes others will hear. And ask. And she'll get to tell the story of how she punched me in the eye. Whatever makes her feel better.

"It's good. Thanks." I manage a smile. It widens when I feel a hand on my back and a familiar cocktail is offered to me.

"Blackberry martini. Exclusive only to you." I turn and Jinx's arm instinctively wraps around my waist. Taking the drink, I wink at him over the rim. "Any surprises in this one?"

He grins. "No beautiful. Just lots of alcohol. You're gonna need it." He arches his eyebrow toward Dallas who is chanting along with the song, "Shots." Meanwhile, I'm still reeling because he called me beautiful. And to hide the effect that word has on me, I take a gulp of my drink. It's perfect.

"When you need another one, let him know." He points to one of the Prospects who meets my gaze with a nod.

I frown. "Where are you going?"

"You get to party, sweetheart, but I actually have to fuckin' work." Even through his playful tone, I can hear the hint of disappointment. "Luke needs me out back. I'll check in on you in a little bit. Have fun."

His eyes narrow a little and his voice hardens slightly. "Just don't do anything to piss me off."

I grin at that. "Like what? Run?"

"Exactly," he mutters, fixing me one last time with his hard look before disappearing back into the crowd.

Run? In this overly-guarded clusterfuck? I wouldn't get past the door. But there's some fun to have that doesn't involve that. Like getting drunk. Dancing my ass off. *Stealing everyone's shit.*

"Yo!" I yell to the Prospect. He jerks his chin at me and I lift my glass. "Make it a double."

JINX LIED. There's something special in this drink. There's got to be. Because I'm fucked up like a lab rat. Granted, I have been throwing back doubles for the past couple hours. But I'm a professional! I should be able to handle my shit.

When my buzz started to kick in, the need to steal something intensified. I got bored just as quickly. It was the same shit—keys to a Chevy. Wallets with little or no cash. Bic lighters. Chapstick. And I had more cigarettes than was smoked in Vietnam.

So I started training Dallas and Red to pick pockets. That was more fun. Especially when they got caught. Swore their innocence to the club and we got to watch as the victims were ushered out in a not-so-nice manner.

"Welp..." I slur, tossing an arm over Dallas's shoulder. "Did ya get it?"

She slumps in defeat and looks out at the man on the dance floor who still has his wallet. "No...fucker caught me."

I turn to Red whose kickass leather dress makes my nipples hard. "Whatta bout you?" Red holds her fist out, opens it and a set of keys dangle from her middle finger. We all cheer.

"MY FEET HURT," I groan, contemplating taking the bastards off like almost every other woman in the club had already done. I glance long-ingly over at the couches that have filled up since I've been here.

"You wanna sit?" Red asks, not waiting for my answer before bull-dozing her way through a few girls and glaring daggers at the people seated on the couch closest to us. When that doesn't work, she calls in reinforcements. Soon, a patch holder is offering some kind of coupon to the people who quickly un-ass themselves.

We swoop in and immediately fall back onto the cushions—prop-ping our feet on the glowing table in front of us that changes colors every few seconds from purple to blue to green. A waitress brings us each a glass of ice water and we greedily accept. I lift mine to the camera in thanks, knowing Luke and probably Jinx are watching.

Looking around, I notice Delilah is missing. Actually, I haven't seen her in a while. "Where's Delilah?"

"It's after midnight, which means it's Sunday, which means she's somewhere with Bryce, getting her ass spanked," Dallas explains. We all nod in understanding. And a little bit of envy. "Hey..." Dallas's head rolls to the side to face me. "I'm really glad you came. I mean, not just tonight. But...you know."

I cut my eyes at her. "I didn't have a choice."

"Yeah, but I'm still glad. I like you. Not just cause you got me the book, either. Thank you for that, by the way." I nod once. She'd told me Maddie had found what she was looking for and managed to resolve the situation before it became a real situation. *At least I've done something worthwhile since I've been here.*

"I agree." Red peeks her head around Dallas and shoots me a genuine smile. Drunk, but genuine. "Pierce made it sound like you were a complete dick. Hell, he had us hating you before you got here."

Gulping down the rest of my water, I try not to focus too much on what she said, but Red has diarrhea of the mouth tonight. "He said you couldn't be trusted."

"And that you were a selfish fuck who cared about no one but your-self." *Apparently Dallas has diarrhea of the mouth, too.* "Nothing but a whore lookin' for a dick to help you get what you wanted."

My blood cools.

"A cold-hearted *trashy* whore," Red clarifies.

My stomach sinks.

Dallas continues. "Who would fuck our ol' man at the first opportunity."

My eyes sting.

They continue. Telling me shit my brother told them about me. They're laughing. Not realizing it's tearing me to shreds. Probably because I'm laughing along with them to hide the pain. When one of them says he hated for me to be a burden to them like I was to him, I decide I've had enough.

"I've got to pee," I lie, standing so fast I have to reach out for something to steady myself. My hand lands on the shoulder of some chick who offers me a smile and a knowing look. But she doesn't know. Doesn't have a fucking clue.

Unaware of the turmoil I'm feeling, Dallas and Red continue their excited chatter and follow behind me. I snag a cocktail from a passing waitress as we stand near the ropes and wait for a patch holder to escort us. Before she can protest, I've downed it and handed her back the empty glass with a look that dares her to say something. She doesn't. Although I wish she would. I'd do just about anything to distract my mind and my heart from Pierce.

My blood.

My brother.

My enemy.

His hatred toward me. His bitterness. His malicious intent. Sure he'd said some mean shit before. But how could he force me to be a prisoner of the very people he blasted me to? Had I really wronged him enough to deserve that level of evil?

I can feel the roll of emotions coursing through me—the ones leading up to my inevitable fall that will undoubtedly shatter me to pieces. I don't want to cry here. I don't want to show my weakness. Expose my broken heart. But I'm dying inside. And everyone will soon know it, because I'm not sure I have the strength to hold it in.

What I need to do is sober up. Get the hell out of here. Stop drowning my sorrows in whiskey, kick these fucking heels off and bolt. Somewhere along the way, I've lost sight of who I am. Why I'm here. What I've done and what I still have to do.

I've allowed myself to get too close to these people. I've made friends with Dallas and Red, who I'd vowed to keep at arm's length. Tonight, I partied with the Devil's Renegades—a club I'm not only eighty-sixed from, but who are holding me against my will. They'll be returning to the clubhouse tonight. A place that's supposed to be my prison, but has somehow turned into my sanctuary. And then, there's...

"Hey baby." *Jinx.*

He's here.

In front of me.

Disrupting my thoughts.

Looking at me with his brows slightly furrowed.

Knowing that something is wrong.

And I didn't have to say a damn thing.

Just like my dream guy...

I nearly lose it. The urge to be *that girl* I promised myself I'd never be is almost overwhelming. I don't want to run away. I want to run to him. I want him to hold me. Hug me. Be silent and strong. For once. Just for the moment. Only tonight, I want to be the girl who falls. And I want him to be the guy who catches me.

"We're leaving," he says, and my entire body sags a little with relief. Keeping his eyes on me, he tells the Prospect, "Tell Luke he can get me on my cell." Then his hand is at the small of my back and he's gently guiding me toward the exit.

Everyone is a blur as we weave through the crowd. I blink furiously to clear my vision—unsure if it's tears or the alcohol. The moment we're outside, I'm pretty sure it's the alcohol. Jinx has to tighten his hold to keep me from toppling over. What the hell is it about fresh air?

After a minute of just standing—me trying not to face-plant the sidewalk—I finally find my footing. With one hand on my hip, Jinx kneels at my feet and starts to remove my heels. Gripping his shoulder, I stare down at him and slur, "You don't have to leave."

"Hush." The demand is firm, but not harsh as he straightens with my heels dangling from his fingers. "Can you walk? I don't want to carry you in that dress." I follow his gaze to my short dress that will reveal more than just my legs if he picks me up.

Looking over at the long line of people waiting to get in, who will definitely see my ass if he carries me, I shake my head. "I can walk."

He nods once and holds me close to him as we head to the back of the parking lot to his car. His stride is determined, yet he keeps a slow enough pace that I don't have to struggle to keep up. I deeply inhale the cold air and soon my body that was hot only minutes ago from dancing, shivers from the frigid temperature.

Jinx helps me inside the car that is already running. It's so warm in here, but I let down my window afraid if I don't get some fresh air, I'll die. Or worse—puke. Tucking my legs beneath me, I curl up on the seat and lay my head on the door.

"I d-don't want to see them t-tonight," I stammer, the moment Jinx is in the driver's seat. "Can we g-go somewhere else? A motel?"

"Already handled, babe," he says, rubbing his warm hand up and down my thigh as he drives us away from the club. From the party. From the girl's. From Pierce's words.... All because he looked at me and knew I needed to leave.

He's my dream guy. Or at least he's acted a lot like him over these past few weeks. I doubt he has a moped, but I've never seen him ride a Harley. He's proven he's different which also makes him special. He doesn't always wear black. He holds my hand. Kisses my fingers mindlessly. My lips passionately. Everywhere else heatedly.

I've watched the sunset with him. Watched the sunrise. We've laughed. We've drank. We've danced to "Josephine". I sit beside him. Walk beside him. Lay beside him. Fall asleep in his arms. He listens when I speak. He's never called me stupid. Never told me I was less.

I never thought moments like this would happen to me. Yet they already have. I never thought my dream guy existed. I was sure my fantasy was only a fairytale. That I could never love again. Especially not a man who wore a patch. Now...I'm not so sure.

JINX

One fucking look.

All it took was one look in those mesmerizing green eyes of hers and I knew something was wrong. I didn't know the reasons. I didn't care. All I knew was I had to get her out of there. So I did.

I didn't care that Luke needed me. That my brothers were depending on me. That walking out with her forced me to go back on my word that I'd be there—hell or high water. But I didn't factor in Winter. I didn't plan to see her like that—broken. Gutted. Looking completely normal to everyone else. Yet utterly devastated to me.

Whoever hurt her or whatever happened to her, happened in that bar. With my club. And that thought shook me to my fucking core. So I took her away. Booked us a room. Carried her unconscious body inside. Stripped her down. Laid her next to me. Knew it was the right thing to do. Thought it would be over by morning. Forgotten once she woke up. But before the night ended, she unveiled the secrets to her misery. And her truth had me questioning not only my brother, but my patch.

"Why does he hate me?" she'd cried. In her sleep. In my fucking arms. There's never been a question I didn't have the answer to until that moment.

It took little coaxing to get Luke to find out from his ol' lady what had happened in the moments right before we left. He was eager to find out himself. So he questioned his wife. His VP's wife. What he found upset him. And set my motherfucking blood to boil.

I'd heard Pierce say plenty of nasty shit about Winter. I'd said my fair share about her too. But seeing how it broke her...watching her crumble like that... it did something to me. I'm still reeling from it—five days later.

I still haven't called Pierce—afraid of what I might say. Winter has yet to bring it up—afraid of reliving it, I assume. At first, I thought maybe she didn't remember. But that was only false hope. She remembers everything. And it's changed her. She's different. Distant. It's not like it was between us. I hate that more than I should.

For the first time ever, I'm considering breaking my bi-laws. Find myself wanting to do everything in my goddamn power to give this woman some semblance of peace in her life—this woman who has been labeled an enemy. A woman I should hate. Refuse to help. Keep for a few more days, take back what she stole from me and walk the fuck away. Problem is, I'm on her side.

That's why I'm taking her home.

To Cumming, Georgia.

To meet my family.

My parents.

My brothers.

One minute we were sitting on the couch, the next I was asking her to spend the weekend with me at my parents' place. She didn't ask why. She didn't complain. I think she was too numb in that moment to really feel anything. But I was giddy for some damn reason.

I've got to be out of my motherfucking head.

Or at least I keep trying to convince myself I am. Truth is, I'm not anxious about them meeting. I'm not nervous about what she'll think of my family or what they'll think of her. I want her with me. On my arm when we walk in. Next to me at my parent's dining table. In my old bedroom. In my fucking bed.

I look over at her sleeping soundly in the seat next to me. She's a beautiful sight. Hair styled messy on her head. Pink lips. Leather jacket. Tight jeans. Barefoot with her feet on my dash. Knees pulled up. Her body curled and turned to face me.

Unable to resist, I reach out and take her hand that's laying limply across her stomach. Her skin feels smooth beneath the pad of my thumb as I stroke her knuckles. I press the tips of my fingers into her palm and she instinctively curls her tiny hand around them.

I'm thinking shit. Shit I don't need to be thinking. And I'm more than relieved when the sound of a phone ringing echoes through the speakers. Pierce's name flashes on the screen in my dash and I press the button on the wheel to answer. Knowing if anyone can shake these feelings and thoughts from me, it's Winter's brother.

"Hang on," I say in greeting, pulling my hand from Winter's so I can take the call on my cell. She catches my wrist. Intertwines her fingers with mine and shakes her head. Her sleepy eyes dancing from the screen to me. "Yeah?"

"Where the fuck are you?" Pierce's tone pisses me off. He's not my fucking keeper. He's not Winter's either. But you can't tell him that.

Reigning in my temper, I force my eyes to the road. "I'm twenty miles south of Cumming." I can feel Winter's smile.

"Well, we're four days from sealing the deal on this shit. So she's definitely going to have it in her head to run. You watch her, Jinx. Don't let her out of your fucking sight."

"She's sitting right here, you know," Winter says, her eyes closed when I look at her. I'm not sure if it's to hide emotion or if she's so used to being spoken about, that she's bored with it.

There's a long pause from Pierce then a clipped, "Winter."

"What's the matter, Pierce? You act like you're afraid to talk to me now. Hell, you had plenty to say when you gagged me and threw me on a plane eight weeks ago." The smirk on her face doesn't hide the sadness in her eyes.

"Well... *sweet pea*... I wouldn't have talked to you at all if two years ago, you would've kept your sticky fucking fingers to yourself and out of my safe," he says, his malice palpable. He sounds nothing like the desperate man who called me on the airplane. Not that I figured he would. He's too fucking stubborn and prideful to show any weakness toward her. And she's the same damn way when it comes to him.

"Don't worry, *brother*," she snaps, her eyes narrowing as she stares at the screen as if she's looking right at him. "You'll get your fucking money. Then you won't have to worry about ever seeing me again."

"Thank fuck for that... Jinx," he growls my name. "Watch her."

The line goes dead and we're both silent. Both of us lost in our own thoughts. Her looking out the window. Me staring at the road trying to keep from looking at her. Out of the corner of my eye, I can see her chest rising and falling as she tries to calm down. When she drags in a deep, staccato breath, I know the emotion she's trying to control is not just anger.

I think back to the shit Luke told me the girls said to her. Then back further to when Winter told me about how Pierce's words had cut her the day he took her. How they'd scarred her. How a life with Cain wasn't nearly as hurtful as what Pierce had said.

Club creed has always been that your brother is always right. Even when he's wrong, he's right. But not this time. I can't side with him on this. He's hurting her. And I don't fucking like it.

I don't care if she deserves it. If she gives it back tenfold. He's a man before he's anything. Her brother above everything. It's his place to make this right. Reel in whatever shit he's dealing with and fix what's fucked up between them. To hell with pride. It doesn't have a place in the club, so why the fuck should it play a part in their relationship?

WINTER

"My baby!"

I lift a brow at Jinx who rolls his eyes at me over his mother's shoulder. Her arms are locked around his neck. His big body bent slightly so she can reach him. With one arm around her waist, he grips the handle of our small suitcase with the other hand. When she doesn't let go, he gives in and releases it to wrap his other arm around her. Even though he acts annoyed, I can see he's enjoying this.

"Momma... I want you to meet someone." That snaps her out of whatever spell she's under and she quickly releases him to turn to me.

She's a tiny thing. The top of her head barely meeting the center of Jinx's chest. Her brown eyes are warm with small wrinkles in the corners. She pulls off her gardening gloves then adjusts the crooked sun hat on her head—revealing light brown hair that's streaked in silver.

"Well I'll be damned," she says, her disbelief evident as she looks me up and down as if I'm not real. "It's a girl."

"For fuck's sake Momma, you make it sound like I'm queer or something."

"For fuck's sake Jinx, it's the first time you've brought one home since high school." I'm shocked at her language that sounds even more foreign because it's said in such a sweet, southern tone. But strangely, I like her a little more because of it.

Since Jinx told me he was taking me to meet his family, I've been a nervous wreck. I'd tried to refuse, but he wouldn't allow it. He pulled the whole, "I miss my family," card on me and I caved. I'd give anything to see my parents again. I wouldn't deny him that right, either. Besides, sitting around the clubhouse being depressed wasn't really all that great.

But I don't do... family. Especially southern ones who live in the Bible belt and say words like *darlin'* and *bless your heart*. But his mom? Yeah, she doesn't seem like one of those backsliding Christians who will damn me to hell for having tattoos. Actually, she seems pretty awesome.

"Hi," I say, finding my voice and extending my hand—because that's what they do in the south, right? "I'm Winter."

She takes my hand, shaking it slowly. "Winter... what a lovely name." With a genuine smile on her lips, she pulls me to her chest in a warm embrace. My eyes widen at Jinx who's fighting a smile. Not wanting to be rude, I pat the center of her back awkwardly.

"I'm Lynn," she says, pulling back and holding me at arm's length as she surveys me once again. "You're beautiful. And tall. And Jinxton is going to have his hands full keeping Clayton and Payton away from you."

"Clayton and Payton?"

"His younger brothers. They're inside. Come on, I'll introduce you." Looping her arm through mine, she practically drags me through the door. I look back at Jinx who follows behind us.

"I'm gonna take this up. I'll be back in a few," he says, ignoring my pleading look as he turns to go up the stairs—leaving me alone with his mother who steers me in the opposite direction.

The house is like a step back into the seventies. All wood paneling and shag carpet. Outdated furniture and boxed T.V. Framed pictures of her boys covering every wall in the living room—ranging from toddler age to college. It smells like cookies and feels warm and cozy. It's the kind of place that makes you want to take your shoes off and curl up on the couch.

We step into the kitchen and she releases my arm. I'm surprised to find that the kitchen still has all the original appliances. I mean, it must. Unless they still make olive green stoves, refrigerators and sinks.

"Babe!" Lynn yells, running around the kitchen opening cabinets and drawers. "Jinxton's here! Got a girl with him!"

"Shut the fuck up!" I whip my head around in search of the deep, thunderous voice that echoes from another room. But the kitchen is closed off and I can't see anyone through the open door aside from a dining room.

Then a glass is thrust in my hand, I'm all but shoved onto a barstool and I look down at the counter to find a perfectly arranged plate of sweets and snacks sitting in front of me.

I give a beaming Lynn a nervous smile. "Thanks," I say, lifting the Mason jar in my hand. I look down and guess it's sweet tea. Taking a tentative sip, I nearly moan and gulp down half the glass.

"Good, huh?" she asks, nodding knowingly.

"Yes. Delicious."

"Damn, it really is a girl." The room seems to shrink in size as a man who looks like an older version of Jinx strides through the door. He moves to the sink to wash his hands—his look as disbelieving as Lynn's and his eyes the same shade of gray as Jinx's.

Heavy footsteps sound above me. I look up but the sound has moved to the stairs. Seconds later, I feel a presence behind me.

"Who the fuck is this good lookin' thang?" I turn toward the voice of the young guy with the body of an athlete who slides up next to me. Falling down on a stool and leaning heavily on the counter, he eyes me with appreciation. *Those eyes.* Same color as Jinx and his dad. But his hair is blonde. Messy. Lips in a wide, lopsided grin revealing dimples. He's like Barbie Ken.

"This is Winter," Lynn offers. "Jinxton brought her."

"Our Jinx? Brought a fuckin' girl?"

Lifting my chin, I meet another set of grey eyes on my left. Then I look back at the guy on my right. Then back up. The one standing winks. "We're twins." Yes. They're identical twins, obviously. I don't know how anyone could tell them apart.

"Y'all are going to scare her half to fuckin' death," the dad says, leaning across the counter to offer me his hand. "I'm Lyle." My trembling hand reveals my nerves as I place it in his huge, calloused one. His warm smile relaxes me a little. "Don't be nervous, Winter. You came with the only one who bites."

Winking, he backs away to stand next to Lynn who is leaning against the refrigerator watching me. Her smile wide. She's so happy. There's a softness in her eyes that makes me feel uncomfortable. She thinks we're together. As much as I don't want to hurt her, I don't want her to get the wrong idea either. I start to tell her Jinx and I are just friends, but the smoldering, gray-eyed twins have moved in closer.

"I'm Clayton," the one on the left says, reaching around me to grab something from the plate. He points to the guy on my right. "That's Payton." I nod at Payton and give him a small wave. His eyes drop to my lips and he licks his.

"You can tell us apart by our hair," Clayton says, demanding my attention again. I'm quick to look back at him and away from the lip licking little devil on my right. "Mine's shaved on the sides." He smooths his hand over his short hair above his ear. "Payton's ain't."

"Nice to meet you." I glance around the room in hopes of finding Jinx. *Where the hell is he?* "All of you," I add, nodding to his parents. "I guess by now you know, I'm Winter."

"You should be Summer," Payton says, shamelessly eyeing my cleavage. "Cause you hot as fuck."

"Payton Murphy Charleston Marks!" Lynn snaps, her tone icy and filled with warning.

Payton's eyes lazily lift to mine. "Sorry, Momma," he says, then mouths to me, "No I'm not."

"I told you idiots to stay the hell out of the kitchen." My body tingles. Heat engulfs me. Just at the sound of his voice. Familiar to his brother's and father's voice, yet distinctively different.

Lyle is attractive for an older man. Clayton and Payton are cute— sexy even. But none of them hold a candle to Jinx. He's so male. So masculine. So commanding. He has that hint of danger about him.

That aura of power. Although none of the guys seem to be lacking in confidence, Jinx exudes it in a way that isn't cocky, but more predatory.

I watch as he embraces his father. Smiles tenderly at his mother. Glares at his brothers. Finds me and winks. I'm an instant pool of lava. "Move," he growls, elbowing Clayton away from me and dismissing Payton with a look before claiming his seat. "Like a bunch of goddamn vultures."

"Hey!" Lynn yells. "Watch your mouth! We don't say the Lord's name in vain in this house. You fucking know better."

These people sure do love the word fuck.

Obviously reading my mind, Jinx smirks at me and mutters, "Sorry, Momma." What is it about this man calling his mother, Momma, that makes my heart melt?

"Come on, boys," Lyle says, herding the two horny toads out of the kitchen. "Let's give them some space." He glances back over his shoulder at Lynn who hasn't moved. "You too, wife. Quit picturing grandkids and come on."

She follows dutifully as does the twins and soon it's just me and Jinx. Staring at each other. Kind of smiling. Kind of processing.

"My family is a little crazy. My mom's an over eager hopeless romantic. My dad's a deacon of the church. My brothers are obsessed with pussy and they all think the word fuck is lucky. Draft's six months away and they believe if they say fuck and pray enough, the twins will get picked."

It's the most ridiculously awesome thing I've ever heard. "What do you think... *Jinxton?*"

"About what? Them getting drafted or fuck being a lucky word?"

I grin. "Both."

"They'll get drafted. Not for any other reason than they're just that damn good."

"And the luck?"

He shrugs. "I think if something good happens, they'll believe it was all their cussing and praying. And if something good doesn't happen, then they'll just cuss more and pray harder."

"Why do they think that's lucky?"

"It started with my mom. My entire life I'd never heard her cuss. She swears she never had before she was at a game last season. It was a college football game and they were losing so the word was said by people around her on every breath. It was in her head. Last play of the game, she spilled coffee down her shirt, yelled out 'fuck' at the same time Clayton caught an interception and ran it back seventy yards to win the game."

"Seriously?" I throw my head back on a laugh.

"Oh, it gets better," he says, propping his arm on the back of my barstool—bringing him closer. "She probably would've chalked it up to coincidence, but the very next week, the same shit happened. Only this time, it was Payton."

My eyes narrow. "Are you pulling my dick?"

He laughs at that. "No, baby. I'm not pulling your dick. You can't make this shit up. Fourth quarter. Eighteen seconds on the clock. Fourth down. Forty-yard line. Payton's got the ball. He's looking to pass and can't find an opening. This linebacker who'd sacked his ass three times already is closing in. Momma, scared as shit that he's gonna get his head knocked off, freaks out and cries, 'fuckin' get rid of it, Pay!' The linebacker trips over his own feet. Takes out two more guys in the process. Opens up a hole in the line and Payton breaks through. Runs it in for a touchdown to win the game."

He's beaming at me. Shaking his head in disbelief as if he's not even fully convinced it was possible. I'm speechless. It's the best story I've ever heard.

"So Winter," he says, tucking a strand of hair behind my ear. His voice soft. Lips still smiling. Gray eyes caressing my face. "Now that you've heard the story, do you think it's lucky?"

Smiling at him, I nod. "Abso-fucking-lutely."

JINX'S ROOM is exactly as I'd imagined.

Posters of athletes, women in bikinis and several floating shelves displaying trophies and medals cover his walls. His queen sized bed is made—the navy blue comforter matching the blue shag carpet. A wooden dresser showcases a football signed by someone of importance. There's a nightstand with a lamp. An alarm clock. And a baseball bat propped against the corner of the bed.

There's no clutter. No dust. And absolutely everything seems to have a place. I guess growing up, he was just as anal about shit as he is now.

"This is nice," I say, when I turn to notice him watching me.

"My parents may or may not be cool with us sleeping together. If they're not, you can sleep in here and I'll sleep on the couch."

"Are your brothers staying here too?"

His lips thin. "Yeah. And they'll be downstairs with me."

Grinning, I strut toward him and run my hands up his chest. "Worried I'll want a little ménage action with the Hollywood twins?"

"It's not you I'm worried about," he mutters, his hands at my waist. Dipping his head, he presses a soft, but brief kiss to my lips. His forehead against mine, he says, "Thanks for coming."

"You didn't give me a choice, remember?" He'd practically said I was going. Not in the mood to argue, I'd agreed knowing I didn't have another option. I'm glad I'm here, though. But I don't tell him that. Instead, I say, "I can tell your mom needed this."

"My mom thinks we're a couple."

"What did you think she'd think?"

His lips tip. "I guess I hadn't planned that far ahead. Hell I don't even know what we are." Voice husky, he asks, "What are we, Winter?"

I fidget with the hem of his black shirt—fighting the urge to run my hands under it and touch the hard, hot muscles beneath it. "We're... friends."

He lifts a brow. "Friends don't fuck like we fuck." *True.* "Friends don't sleep naked together. They don't end every night together... start every day together. So no, sweetheart. We're not friends." *Well... when you say it like that...*

But I'm not his. He's not mine. This isn't a relationship. We're just two people spending time together. Brought together by a fucked up circumstance. We've been living in solitude together for nearly two months. Of course we'd be close. But we're not... *together.*

"What do you think we are?" I ask, my nerves evident. My pulse quickening. Heart skipping a beat when I realize whatever this is—

whatever we are—is only temporary. I want a life that doesn't involve the MC. He's the kind of man who won't give it up. And already, it hurts at the thought of leaving him.

"More," he says simply. "More than friends, babe."

"And when you're gone? Then what will we be?"

"Do you want me gone?"

I drop my gaze. "It doesn't matter what I want."

Tilting my head back, he forces me to look at him. His gray eyes are soft. "What you want is the only thing that matters."

His words melt me. Since when had anyone cared about what I wanted? Even asked? And never had anyone thought that what I wanted mattered.

Until now.

Until this man.

Until Jinx.

The man I...the man I think...the man I'm pretty sure...I...

"Yo bitch!" The door swings open and I jerk away from Jinx just as Clayton walks in. Our moment shatters. My thoughts clear. I look at Clayton. But can feel Jinx's eyes on me even as Clayton comes up and throws his arm around him. "Come on, big bro. Let's see if you still got it."

My brow lifts in question. Jinx smirks. "You know I still got it."

"Um..." Clayton starts. "No...I don't. Ain't seen your ass in months. Looks like you got fatter, too." He pats the wall of muscle that is Jinx's stomach.

"Jinx," Payton says from the door. We all turn to look at him as he leans heavily on the frame. His cocky smile in place. Those eyes on me. He's as tall as Jinx, but not nearly as wide. Definitely the body of a quarterback. "Momma wants you."

"I'm over here, Pay," Jinx rumbles.

"I know. But she's better to look at." He tips his chin at me. "Wanna put on something sexy and cheer for me, darlin'?"

"She's out of your league, pretty boy." Jinx grins down at me as he wraps his arm around my waist and pulls me to his side. "Trust me... you couldn't handle it."

Both Jinx and I shake my head at him. He's cute, but I'd break him.

Ruin him for any other woman. I'm not like those college girls he fucks around with. I'm the real deal. I could have him coming in his pants by just playing with my tits.

"Oh, you don't think so?"

"Sorry sugar," I breathe on a shrug. "Maybe in a few years."

"My dick's bigger than his." I laugh at that. Then sober when I notice no one else is laughing.

"That," Jinx says, a little defeated, "is actually true."

No fucking way. Scanning Payton's crotch, I move down his thigh, wondering where the fuck he stores that big bastard.

"I strap it to my leg." He winks, licking his lip. His face smug. I flush scarlet and a wolfish grin spreads across his cheeks. Then he's barreling down the stairs, trying to escape Jinx. But not before his offer.

"Wanna touch it?"

WINTER

"**B**lue forty-two...what I could do to you...red twenty-seven... make you think you're in heaven...set...get you real wet—"

"Would you just hike the fuckin' ball!" Jinx roars.

Payton winks at me from his position behind Clayton.

I laugh—shaking my head at the horny little idiot whose dirty talk has his mother threatening him with a switch. Whatever the fuck that means.

"Hut!"

Clayton snaps the ball. Payton catches it easily. Takes three steps back. Then with a grace as fluid and precise as any pro, he hurls it through the air. My eyes move to Jinx who is running full speed across the huge lawn. In those hot ass shorts, I can make out the muscles in his legs flexing and hardening as he quickens his pace.

Head up, looking over his shoulder, he watches as the ball starts to fall from the sky. Then reaching one, long, tattooed, strong arm out, he snags it with just the tips of his fingers. Pulling it to his chest, he slows and circles back—jogging straight toward me.

I'm sitting next to his mother in a lawn chair. To her right is his father. And I want to kiss them both for creating the perfect, flawless specimen that is Jinxton Marks.

As he nears, I focus on his naked, tattooed chest that rises and falls with his deep breathing. We both seem to ignore everyone as we look at each other. Me gaping. Him grinning. Just like we've been doing for the past forty-five minutes we've been out here.

"That the best you got?" he asks, tossing Payton the ball as he completes his jog to me.

"You big fucker," Payton calls out. "Ain't no way you should be able to run that fast."

Reaching me, he scoops me up in his arms and falls down in my chair—planting me on his hard thighs. I'm still reeling as he takes the water bottle from my fingers and guzzles it down. I can smell his sweat. I want to fucking lick it. I want to grind my pussy against his hard thigh.

Shit, Winter.

"I'm going to finish up dinner," Lynn announces, standing and placing a kiss on Jinx's head before ruffling his sweaty hair. "Show Winter the lake... fuck," she adds, like she just realized she hasn't said the word in a while.

"That's private property, Momma." Jinx narrows his eyes playfully. "Are you asking me to break the law?"

"No son, I'm *telling* you to show Winter the fucking lake. It's only private property if they have a sign."

"My Momma's a fuckin' outlaw!" Clayton shouts, throwing his mother's small body over his shoulder like she's weightless.

"Put me down you damn Neanderthal!"

"*Fucking* Neanderthal, Momma. Get your shit together."

"Fine...Put me down you *fucking* Neanderthal."

"So," Jinx says, pulling me away from the chaos that is disappearing into the house. "Wanna break the law and trespass on private property to see a body of water that doesn't belong to us?"

I laugh because it's funny. Because it's a little strange. But most of all, I laugh because I'm happy. "I'd love to."

"Wow," I say, only a hint of sarcasm in my voice.

Jinx shakes his head and tosses a rock in the water. "I know."

So the lake really isn't all his mom made it out to be. It's pretty small. Like the smallest lake in history. Dried up in some places. The banks overgrown with weeds. And the pier we're sitting on looks like it could collapse any minute.

But I don't get to see a lot of sites like this where I'm from. Vegas is mostly dry dessert or flashing lights. Here, it's serene. Quiet. Peaceful. Nice. I'm happy he brought me. Besides, I've never ridden a golf cart before and that alone was worth the trip.

"I like your family," I say, leaning my head on his shoulder. It's cold out, but his body immediately warms me.

"They're fuckin' crazy. Really superstitious. A little old school, but they're good people."

"When you say old school, you must be talking about that shag carpet," I tease.

He laughs. "No doubt. Momma's motto is, 'if it ain't broke, don't fix it.' Dad's threatened to fuck shit up just so she'll update. But I think he likes it. Reminds them of old times. When me and the twins were back at home."

"Those twins..." I trail off, unable to find words to even describe them.

"Clayton's two minutes older. And he's about that much more mature than Payton. They're both loud and obnoxious, cocky and horny. But damn they're talent..." A mystic look crosses Jinx's eyes as he stares out at the water. "It's unbelievable, babe. And smart? Don't let their idiocy fool you. They're both brilliant."

"I can see that." *No fuck I can't...* But if Jinx believes it, then that's good enough for me.

"I should want what they have. What my parents have," he says, breathing out a laugh as he runs his hand through his hair. "But I hated it. Hated being perfect. Walking into the grocery store and people pattin' me on the back. Those same people sittin' next to me at church on Sunday. Then gossipin' about me on Monday. Sayin' I'm not all I'm cracked up to be. That the perfect Marks family of five will one day fall. And how they can't fuckin' wait until it does."

He's not sad. Just matter-of-fact. And though this conversation is serious, I can't hide my smile at his accent now that he's home. He notices and grins—eyes dropping from my eyes to my lips.

"What?"

"Nothin' honey," I drawl.

His eyes roll. "Shut up."

"So you left your perfect world and crossed over to the darkness."

"Something like that. I left. And for the first time in my life, I didn't know who I was. How to act. Didn't take long for me to get in trouble. I refused to bring that shit to my parents, so I made my own way out of it.

"I'm good with numbers, so I turned to gambling. Soon, I was approached by someone who showed me how to take it to the next level. Make some real money. Get the fuck out of the casinos."

He looks at me. I have the strange feeling he's wanting me to guess who that someone was. I don't have to guess. I already know. "Pierce." He nods once.

"He introduced me to some people. Through that, we got close. I found myself missing the power I had back at home. The way people looked up to me. How they struggled to speak around me. They were intimidated by my skill and my inevitable fame. I never thought I'd miss it, but damn I did.

"Hanging around the MC, I noticed they possessed that same kind of power. I also missed my brothers. My dad. Our bond. The relation-ship within the MC was similar. So I prospected. After I patched out, my connections grew and I got into some deeper shit. When things got bloody and my bets became dangerous, I knew I needed to get out of the bookie business.

"I had a friend from back home who worked for an energy company. Said they could never find enough security, so the demand for it was high and the pay good. I needed startup capital so I got the money the best way I knew how. By doing something I was good at. So I took a risk... bet big... got paid..."

"And got out," I finish, my smile proud. It falters when he gives me a distant look and shakes his head.

"No. I got fucked."

My entire body goes rigid. My heart free falls. Stomach flips. I'm the one that fucked him. The money I stole was his startup capital. His new beginning. I feel sick.

"Jinx..."

"Don't, Winter," he says, a little exasperated. "I don't want to go there. Not now."

Problem with that is, we're already here. I've ruined our trip. This perfect day. Possibly everything.

"What did you do? How did you get the money for your startup?"

"The old fashioned way." He winks. "I stole it."

Before I can decide if he's lying or not, he moves to stand and I grab his arm. When he looks at me, I have to swallow hard before I can speak. "For what it's worth, I'm really sorry."

Tucking a strand of hair behind my ear, he roams my face with his eyes before settling on mine. There's no anger. No sadness. Nothing. Those silver marbles are completely impassive. When his lips quirk, the pressure in my chest lightens.

"Eight weeks ago, I'd have told you to eat shit. But now that I know what I know, I'm good with it. You needed that money a hell of a lot more than me. For what it's worth," he adds, throwing my words back at me. "I'm really sorry it didn't work out for you."

But for the first time ever, I'm glad it didn't. Because if it had, I wouldn't be where I am now. And that thought saddens me more than the past two years of my life.

WINTER

"Lord we know it is your will that must be done," Lynn continues, blessing the feast spread out on the table before us like she's been doing for the past forever. It's so strange —listening to a woman bare her soul to God only moments after telling everyone, "Shut the fuck up so I can say grace."

I lift my eyes to Jinx who sits across from me with his head dutifully bowed. Feeling my stare, his lids flutter open and those shocking grays seize me. He watches me throughout the rest of the prayer—both of us fighting to contain our smiles. When his mother asks God to please bless Jinx and his new significant other whose title has yet to be revealed, he loses the battle and his lips curve up on the sides. Moments later, after she's asked God for forgiveness of their many, many, many, many sins, she finally says, "Amen."

"Amen," everyone says in unison. Almost immediately, the cussing begins.

"Pass the fucking turkey."

"Give me that, you selfish fuck."

"Nobody does dressin' like Momma does fuckin' dressin."

"I sure am glad Jinx missed Thanksgiving," Clayton, who sits on my left, says. "Now we get to eat it twice." I feel a pang of guilt for Jinx missing the holidays with his family.

"I missed Easter, too," Jinx quickly adds, his gaze on me as if to reassure me it's not my fault. I smile in thanks, but it doesn't really ease my conscience.

"Well, at Easter we didn't get a do-over. We just got fuckin' sandwiches," Payton says, glaring at Jinx who sits next to him.

Lynn clears her throat then swings her eyes to me—her face a bright smile. "How about you, Winter? Did you make it home for Thanksgiving?"

Clayton nudges me. "Yeah... where do you live, by the way?"

"You sure don't sound southern," Lyle laughs.

It's innocent. I know that. But I can't fake a smile for them. I can't lie even though it's on the tip of my tongue. I can't tell them the truth, either. And I can't fucking stop these eyes of mine from filling with tears.

Before I can embarrass myself or Jinx further, I stand and quickly rush out an, "Excuse me." I pray for the sound of chatter to resume or the clanking of forks. But I hear nothing. And I can feel every set of eyes burning into the back of my head as I leave the room and bolt up the stairs.

Inside Jinx's room, I pace the floor—my hands alternating from my hips, to wiping my cheeks until I finally cross my arms over my chest.

So... stupid! Why didn't you just lie? Why couldn't you keep your shit together? Who are you and what have you done with Winter Tews?

The moment I hear the door click shut behind me, I know it's Jinx. Spinning around to face him, I stifle a sob and manage, "I'm sorry."

He's standing with his hands shoved in the pockets of his shorts. His feet bare. Hair messy. Head tilted. Eyes burning me. He's the blank man. The stoic faced Jinx I met weeks ago. I want to thank him for hiding the pity. The concern. I don't want it. Not from him.

"I've never had that," I say, gesturing toward the dining room before turning my back to him to look out the window. The sun has set, but I can still make out the outline of trees that border the massive yard. "I mean, I did when I was a kid, but every year I get older, those memories seem to fade more and more."

Closing my eyes, I try to imagine what it was like. Sitting around a table with my family. My mother at one end. Father at the other. Pierce across from me. Both of us smiling. Laughing. Happy. Telling the other to pass the fucking turkey.

"Sometimes, I forget that there's normalcy outside of my fucked up life. That there are families who sit down for dinner together. That there are houses that aren't run by men in leather and don't reek of cheap pussy and pot. That sibling rivalry doesn't end in war and blood-shed. That there are people who love because they want to... not because there's some bi-law that says they must."

Sitting on the end of his bed, my shoulders slumped, I lift my eyes to him—relieved to find he remains impassive. "You once asked me what I wanted." Waving my hand around the room, I give him a sad, watery smile. "This. I want this, Jinx. Normal."

Soft, warm eyes regard me. Waiting patiently for me to continue. But there's nothing else to say. I want something I can't have. Not with him. Not with Pierce. Definitely not with Cain. Not in this life. Or ever.

Wordlessly, he walks toward me. His stare processing. Watching. Studying. Appraising me with an intensity that doesn't make me uneasy, but instead has me feeling like I'm slowly crumbling under his gaze.

When he's standing in front of me, he grabs my hands. Hauls me up. Wraps my arms around him. My body molds to his. My head burrowing in his neck. Fingers gripping his hair. Absorbing all of his heat. Strength. Comfort.

He cradles the back of my head in one massive hand. Holding me closer. His other arm wrapped around my waist. Keeping me to him as he sits on the bed. Lays back. Pulls me on top of him. And just lets me lay on his chest and cry.

It's all so much. The memories. The pain. Pierce. Cain. Jinx... thoughts of him are the worst. Hurt the most. Where will I be when I'm not with him? Who will I be? I said I want normal. Or do I just want him? What we have?

I cry it all out. Let it all go. Break. Crumble. Shatter. Like I knew all along I would. How can I not when I have this man beneath me?

Rubbing my hair. Keeping me safe. Making me feel so fucking good even when I'm so sad.

The tears have dried. My breathing steady. I'm not sure how much time has passed, but it doesn't seem to have much meaning in moments like this. The peaceful silence is comfortable as I trace the tear stains on Jinx's shirt. The one I love—the red one with the arms and neck cut out. The one that shows off his tattoos. His muscles. His beauty.

"I want to show you something," he says. I nod and he drags us both from the bed. Holding my hand, he leads us out of the room. Music filters into my ears as we descend the stairs. Something bluesy. Slow. Beautiful.

The music gets louder as we move through the kitchen. Past the dining room that is now empty—the table cleared. I have little time to feel bad about what happened before I'm pulled through the sliding glass doors that lead to the back patio.

There, endless strands of miniature light bulbs are strung above us. Orange flames dance and blaze from the fire pit centering the concrete porch. And around that fire, are seated his family. His parents sit together on a love seat—wine in hand. Lyle's arm is draped behind Lynn. Her head is on his shoulder. They offer us a smile. I give a small wave before turning my attention to the twins.

Payton doesn't notice us as he continues to play the sweet melody on his guitar. Clayton sits across from him—a guitar in his lap and some sort of tambourine attached to his foot. The twins sing in perfect harmony. I've never heard the song, but I'm instantly in love with it.

"Dance with me," Jinx rasps, his lips at my ear. Without waiting for my answer, he turns me in his arms. Places my hands around his neck. Puts his hands on my waist. Pulls me in and leans down to rest his forehead against mine.

Closing my eyes, I breathe in his scent. Follow his lead. Sway in his hold to the song. When I open them, he's watching me. From the corner of my eye, I can see his parents have joined us. The twins effortlessly flow into the first verse again—repeating the song without breaking melody.

"They do this every night," Jinx says so only I can hear him. "When everyone is home, this place is complete chaos. The arguing. The joking. The praying. The cussing..." He smiles at that. "The twins are always fighting. The three of us are always trying to outdo the other one. Momma's always trying to make peace. Dad's acting like he don't hear shit then loses it when Momma gets overwhelmed. But this?"

He pulls back and looks around. I follow his gaze to the brothers getting along. His parents lost in their own private moment. Us dancing. The only sounds are the lyrics. The music. The crackle of the fire.

"It's everything. It's where we come together. It keeps us humble. Lets us remember what's important in life. How blessed we are." Wrapping one hand around the back of my neck, he gives me a look so deep, I swear my heart stops beating.

"What you want is so much more than normal. Because this is fucking extraordinary. It's special. I can't give you this life, Winter. But I can make it possible for you to start your own. I'll give you what Pierce refused you. What Cain promised you. If it's really what you want, I'll help you disappear. I'll set you free."

My brows draw together. I stare up at him in confusion. This goes against everything he believes. He'd be turning his back on his brother. His club. Swallowing hard, I force out the shaky words. "Why? W-why would you do that?"

Stroking my jaw with his thumb, he gives me a small smile that contradicts the sadness in his eyes. "Because nobody deserves an extraordinary life more than you."

WINTER

He promised me freedom.
Freedom.
Freedom.
I keep saying the word, but I feel like I have no idea what it means. I wanted to ask him, but our moment was interrupted. I ended up dancing with his father. Him with his mother. Then we were all in the kitchen—Jinx and I eating leftovers. The parents reliving moments from Jinx's glory days. The twins swearing theirs were better.

It was around midnight when everyone started to head to bed. I was anxious as I climbed the stairs. Ready to continue our conversation from the patio. Get Jinx to tell me in detail what he meant by granting me my freedom. By helping me disappear. But his mother made it quite clear that he would be on the couch tonight.

It didn't matter to her that we were both consenting adults. She'd prayed too hard for the Lord to punish her for allowing us to sleep in the same room together. She feared he'd frown upon her for enabling our sin. Or at least that's what she said.

I glance at the clock and see it's after two. Jinx is probably asleep. But I can't lay here one moment longer without knowing. So with one last look at the clock, I creep from the bed and tiptoe down the stairs.

It's dark in the living room. Bodies are scattered all across the floor. Jinx had demanded the twins stay down here with him. And since they were all too tall to sleep on the couch, they'd settled for a king-sized air mattress on the floor.

Squinting through the darkness, I try to locate which one is Jinx. Knowing he won't be in the middle, I start at the one closest to the couch. When I lean down to get a closer look, three sets of gray eyes meet mine. I nearly scream at how bright they are in the dark. *Fucking vampires.*

"If she's here for a gangbang, I'm gonna have to go last," Payton says, his voice a husky whisper. "Cause I'll ruin her for y'all—oww! Fuck Jinx!"

"Keep talkin' shit and you'll have to learn to throw with that moth-erfucker, cause I'm gonna break your arms," Jinx threatens, his tone making the hair on the back of my neck stand up.

"How about you both shut the fuck up before Momma comes in here," Clayton whisper shouts. I stifle a giggle at these three grown men, scared of their five foot four mother.

"Who the fuck asked you, shit breath?" Payton snaps, and the arguing begins. I'm surprised to find that Jinx is in the middle of them and I'm pretty sure it's because he's been playing referee all night.

"...Goddamit... would the two of you stop!"

"Boys...!"

Lynn's voice is accompanied by the sound of a door opening which is quickly followed by her slippers sliding across the floor. I panic. Look to my left. My right. The assholes on the floor are playing dead. With no other option, I dive under the covers.

Pulling the blanket over my head, I come face to face with Jinx. "What the fuck are you doing?" he asks, his voice barely a whisper.

"What does it—" I'm cut off when Jinx pushes me to my back and rolls his body half on top of mine. I can barely breathe. When the light flips on, I'm not breathing at all.

"Is everything alright?" Lynn asks, a hint of worry in her voice. The answers come in a chorus of mumbles that include *yeah Momma, it's all good,* and *Clayton farted.*

"Did not!"

Son of a bitch they sound like little kids. Yet... I'm smiling through my panic.

"Same shit, Momma," Jinx says, his voice like honey. "I got it covered. Go back to bed."

Silence for the longest minute of my life then, "If you little fucking idiots wake her up, I'm going to beat the daylights out of you. She's had a rough day. Last thing she needs is to be startled awake and get scared and come down here to this fart smelling room...I swear you boys—"

"We got it, Momma," Payton chimes in. "Nobody is gonna wake sleeping beauty up." I feel a hand on my hip that doesn't belong to Jinx. I'm desperate for air. Desperate to remove Payton's hand before Jinx breaks it when Clayton decides to put in his two cents.

"And if she gets scared and comes downstairs, I'm sure we can make room for her under the covers since we obviously have so much of it." He pushes against Jinx who must be lying half on him too. My body is shoved further into Payton and I close my eyes. *That better be his arm...*

"Jinx, give your brother some room. Stop being a fucking bed hog."

"Yeah Jinx." I can hear the smile in Payton's voice. And feel the temperature drop with Jinx's glare. "Scoot over here. I have plenty of room."

"I'm good," Jinx grounds out.

"Boys...don't make me come in here again. And I mean it. Don't wake her up."

They mumble an acknowledgment and the light goes out. There's the shuffle of slippers. A door closing. Then I'm finally able to breath as the tank that is Jinx rolls off my chest. He flips the covers from over my head and I inhale deeply. Then stop and wrinkle my nose.

"Damn...it does smell like a fart in here."

"Welcome to our slumber party, baby. You just won the turtle championship," Jinx teases.

"That's where you fart under the covers—"

"I know what it is, Clay," I snap, jerking away from Payton and folding myself into Jinx. I kick at Payton's leg, trying to untangle it from mine. After a few failed attempts, I let out a breath and meet Jinx's stare. "Tell your brother to move his leg."

"What makes you think it's my leg?" This time, instead of Jinx lashing out at his perverted brother's comment, he laughs. The deep rumble in his chest can be felt all the way to my toes.

"Guys," Jinx starts, his tone sincere. "Mind giving us a little privacy?"

"Yeah, brother."

"No problem."

I'm more than surprised by their response. Then there's some moving around. Seconds later, I can hear the faint sound of music coming from their earbuds. I have something snarky to say, but Jinx speaks before I can.

"Hey baby." *God...that voice. So deep. So male. So...focus!*

"Hey..."

"So what brings you down here at two in the morning? You miss me?"

I sigh. I did miss him. But that's not why I'm here. "I'm curious."

"'Bout what?"

"What you said. Your promise." He nods slowly. "Did you mean it? Is it possible? Why would you do that? I mean, you said why..." I heat at the reminder. *Because you deserve an extraordinary life...* Damn. *Be still, my heart.* "But I want to know why you're willing to betray your club."

"That's a lot of questions," he teases. His hand brushes my hair from my face and he kisses my head. "Yes, I meant it. Yes, it's possible. I'm doing it because it's important to me that you're happy. And I'm not going to betray my club. You're eighty-sixed. So actually, making you disappear will be helping them."

I only heard one part of that. The part where he said my happiness is important to him. "I told you not to fall in love with me," I whisper, the words out before I can stop them.

He grins. "Lucky for you, I didn't."

"What does that mean?"

"It means if I had, then I wouldn't let you go."

Oh.

Why does that hurt? I should be happy he's helping me. Happy he doesn't love me. But suddenly, I feel like this freedom he's promising isn't nearly as rewarding as his love.

Idiot.

I shake away the thoughts of love and happily ever after's. "Tell me how it works. What you'll do."

"I'll call in some favors. Get you a new identity. Make sure you have no problem getting to wherever you want to go. And if you need me to, I'll help you get settled when you get there."

Swallowing past the lump in my throat, I struggle to ask the next question. "W-what about Cain?"

"That's up to you. I can kill him or I can keep an eye on him and make sure he doesn't come near you."

"Yeah...but for how long? He'll never stop searching for me."

"For as long as it takes. Or, like I said, I can just kill him."

That wouldn't work. That would start a war for sure. Which is exactly what I've been trying to prevent. "I don't want you to kill him," I whisper regretfully.

"Then I'll keep an eye on him. You're overthinking everything, baby. It's really not that hard. If you want this, I'll make it happen."

"When?"

"As soon as the meeting with the lawyers is over."

My stomach sinks and I close my eyes to hide my disappointment. Of course Jinx doesn't miss it. "You have to face him, Winter. Even if you don't want to." He's talking about Pierce. But my distress is caused by something completely different.

Pressing my head against his chest, I wrap my arm around his waist. He pulls me in tighter and kisses my hair. "I don't want to go back to bed," I admit.

"Then don't."

"Your mom would kill you."

"Some shit's worth dying for."

There goes my heart again.

I relax into him. Sleep coming fast. His breathing is deep. Body lax. A telltale sign that he's fast asleep. "I'll miss us," I whisper to the darkness.

I'm fading in and out. But I swear I hear him reply, "Ditto."

JINX

I *'m a liar.*

It's something I've never wanted to be. Something I've prided myself on avoiding. I don't lie. Ever. Or at least I didn't.

Something inside me shifted the moment we walked through the door of my parents' house. I was happy to be home. See my folks. My family. But it was more than that. Stronger. And I knew it was because Winter was with me.

Seeing her in the kitchen with my mom had me thinking crazy. Like marriage and kids and shit.

Hearing my dad tell me, "She's a keeper," after learning she knew a thing or two about American muscle cars, had me thinking about moving into a little house down the street. White picket fence and a dog and shit.

Having her next to me at the dinner table, on the patio, at the lake, on a deflated fucking air mattress, next to my brothers who'd already threatened to kill me if I ever hurt her, had me thinking about forever —a forever with her. Filled with happiness and kittens, rainbows and sunshine and shit.

I'm a liar.

She wants normal. She wants the life I took for granted. She wants the marriage. Kids. The little house. White picket fence. A dog. A forever. Happiness. Rainbows and sunshine and all the shit that comes with it. She deserves it. And now she has me thinking I might want all of those things, too.

But I've lived the normal life. It wasn't for me. So I gave it all up for something bigger. Something I thought was better. Something I've never regretted. Something I never will regret. Because it brought me to her—this girl. Winter Tews. Who's...*everything*.

I'm a liar.

I'm going to give her what she wants. Set her free. Unlock the shackles the MC has bound her with her entire life. She thinks I'm doing it because I don't love her. Because that's what I told her. I know she believed it because that look in her eyes fucking gutted me.

But, like I said, I'm a liar.

I'm not letting her go because I don't love her...

I'm letting her go because I do.

WINTER

I wake up on the deflated air mattress alone. Yawning loudly, I stretch and crane my neck to find Lynn sitting on the couch staring at me. She's still in her robe. Her legs crossed. One slipper dangling from her left foot as she bounces her knee.

"I was watching you sleep," she says, matter of fact. "Is that weird?"

I nod. "A little."

"Hmm." I wait for more but she just keeps staring. Finally, she smiles. "Coffee?"

"Please." Trying like hell to get off the floor as graceful as she stands from the couch, I pull myself to my knees and struggle to stand.

She eyes my shorts and T-shirt, seems to approve then jerks her head toward the kitchen. "I'll make a fresh pot."

"Sounds good." I clear my throat and point to the bathroom. "Is Jinx in trouble?" I ask. She says nothing. "Okay...I'm just gonna..."

"Of course."

Dropping my head, I move quickly toward the bathroom. Wondering what I feel most anxious about—her watching me, or me not really giving a shit that she was. After my face is washed and my teeth are brushed, I feel a little more normal. Actually, I feel great.

That is, right up to the moment she points at the barstool and says, "Sit."

I have a strange feeling I'm about to get *the talk*. And where the hell is Jinx?

"They guys went for a run," she says, answering my unspoken question as she hands me my coffee.

"Oh." It's the best I got.

"He's a storm, you know."

Frowning, I still my cup at my lips. "Excuse me?"

"Jinx. He's a storm. Unpredictable. Incorrigible. Capable of bringing mass destruction, yet you anticipate him." A faraway look flashes in her eyes for a brief moment. Then she smiles. "You know that feeling you get right before the rain starts? The smell of it in the air...The sound of it on a tin roof...The thought of curling up to a good book on a cozy couch with a warm blanket...I find those things peaceful. Do you?"

"I guess..." *What the fuck?*

"But then you hear that first rumble of thunder. See lightening in the distance. Next thing you know, you're fucking power is out. You're scrambling around trying to find candles and flashlights. Worried a damn tree is going to fall through the roof. Or a tornado is going to rip your house to shreds."

"Is this a metaphor or something?" I ask, starting to get a little nervous. "Because I'm not following."

Reaching her hand across the counter, she grabs mine and gives me that sweet smile of hers. "There's a little bit of fear with every storm. A whole lot of mystery. And you could never appreciate the beauty of the sun without the devastation of a storm."

"So you're saying that if Jinx didn't fuck shit up, then we wouldn't be able to appreciate things when they aren't fucked up."

Throwing her head back, she lets out a loud laugh. But as the seconds pass, her laugh dies out and then she completely sobers. "Shit...it does kinda sound like that, huh?"

I nod. "Yeah. Just a little."

"Well, that's not what I mean." She grins and shakes her head. "Mother of the fuckin' year right here. What I'm trying to say is that

Jinx is strong. Powerful. He's a force. He can bring such happiness..." She trails off and I can tell she's searching for the right words.

"Like to a farmer who needs rain," I offer. "Because he's a storm."

She points a finger at me. "Exactly."

"But he can also fuck up his property, kill his crops and put a tree through his house."

"Yes."

"But even then, the farmer can collect insurance and probably get out of farming all together because it sucks balls and nobody wants to do that shit anyway, but they're too invested to get out...Until this huge *storm* comes, blows their shit away and gives them that out because..."

I hold my hand out for her to finish. She doesn't disappoint.

"Because farming sucks balls."

"Yep."

She stares at me in mock awe. "I knew you'd understand."

"How could I not?" I ask, animatedly. "You explained it so well."

Buffing her fingernails on her robe, she looks down at them and shrugs. "It's what I do."

Laughing, I finally take a sip of my coffee. It's perfect. Almost as good as scotch. And this conversation is perfect. And Jinx is perfect. And I feel perfect. And I really hope I get to spend the rest of the weekend with these people. In their home. With Jinx. Because in a few short days, this perfect feeling I have will only be a memory. So will they.

So will he...

"A FUCKING STORM?"

I laugh at Jinx's disbelieving expression and nod. "An unpredictable, incorrigible storm, no less."

After the guys returned from their run, I offered to help Lynn cook breakfast. I broke two dishes, burned a carton of eggs and set a dish towel on fire before she demanded I take a seat. But at lunch time, I made some kick ass ham sandwiches that earned me a slow-clap, standing ovation. Dinner, I just poured the wine. Drank most of it too.

Now, we're back at the lake that could definitely benefit from a rainstorm. The thought makes me smile.

"There's that happy smile again," Jinx says, tracing my lips with his thumb. "Mama says there's something magical about this place. I'm starting to believe it."

"Yeah? Me too." I look back out across the shallow water. Down at the rickety pier. Along the overgrown edges. "I think it might be the most perfect thing I've ever seen. What about you?"

Jinx just shakes his head. His eyes on me. Voice barely a whisper when he speaks. "Not even close."

I KNEW the sleeping arrangements were going to be the same the moment we walked back inside the house.

On the floor in the living room, was a brand new, king sized air mattress and twin sized air mattress already inflated—giving the guys a bed and a half to sleep on. Standing next to them with a pointed look was Lynn who simply nodded her head toward the floor and said, "Boys."

"Winter sugar," Payton started. My grin was already forming, knowing he was going to say something completely inappropriate and funny as hell. "If you want to cuddle, just let me know and I'll come to you. No sense in me having to fuck up Jinx's ugly face when he tries to steal you from me."

"It's sweet of you to offer, Pay," I said, my tone serious. "But it'll be nice to sleep solo tonight. I think I've had all the cuddling I can handle."

I wasn't serious.

I was lying.

Because it's just after two, again, and I'm tiptoeing down the stairs. I recognize Jinx's large form in the middle. His tattooed arms out from under the covers and on display for my greedy eyes. As if he'd anticipated me coming, or someone, there's a small nightlight casting a faint glow over the entire room.

Wordlessly, I slide under the covers. My head falling on Jinx's shoulder. My arms around his waist. His around mine. Our legs tangled. And that unfamiliar hand that is becoming more and more recognizable curls around my hip.

"Payton!" I whisper shout.

"Let me touch youuuuu..." Payton cries in a creepy tone. Clayton starts making those weird throaty noises from that freaky movie with the little dead kid. Jinx laughs. I just shake my head.

"You know Mama's gonna kill us, right?" Jinx asks, pressing his lips in my hair.

I sigh. Swoon. Snuggle deeper into him and admit, "Some things are worth dying for."

WE'RE LEAVING TODAY...

It was my first thought when I woke up this morning. That quickly faded when I found the guys gone and Lynn watching me sleep—again.

I joined her in the kitchen for coffee where she tried to come up with a different metaphor to describe Jinx. It too was an epic failure that ended in us both laughing. Finally, I just told her what I think she'd been wanting me to say all along. "I think he's perfect."

Because I did.

I do.

She cried. We hugged. It was some real Brady Bunch, Full House, Hallmark card shit. But I liked it.

When we said our goodbyes, Lynn hugged me again. Lyle was curt. Clayton was overly dramatic. Payton copped a feel of my ass—I let it slide.

Jinx offered to take me to the magical lake one last time. I refused. Not because I didn't want to go, but because I was afraid if I did, I'd cry. He'd told me I'd see it again. I didn't respond. But I think we both knew I wouldn't.

The entire ride home, I worked on blocking out my emotions. Putting up my walls. Preparing myself for tomorrow—the big day. The end of my captivity. The day I see Pierce. Meet with a lawyer. Give Jinx back what I took from him. Say goodbye and start my new life of freedom—something I wasn't allowing myself to get too excited about.

Jinx claimed he had it all figured out. He planned to hide me away for a few days after the meeting tomorrow. Somewhere safe. Secure. Once he had my new identity, he'd put me on a plane to wherever I wanted to go. Even offered to go with me and help me get settled if I wanted—practically insisted it.

I didn't say anything.

Because Jinx is forgetting one major detail in his oh-so-well thought out plan.

Cain Malcolvich.

He's yet to show his face, but I know he's somewhere close. I swear I can feel his evil in my bones. He'll come for me. Just like I always knew he would. And if he demands I go with him, I will.

I won't poison Pierce with my problems.

I won't burden Jinx.

You don't do that to the people you love. And God, do I love them. Both of them. Pierce I've loved for as long as I can remember. Jinx stole my heart in the back of that van two months ago. When he kissed my palm. When he showed me tenderness when all I'd felt was pain. I didn't know it at the time, but I'm sure of it now.

I'm in love with Jinxton Marks.

And as good as that feels, it hurts just as bad.

Now, we're in bed. Back at the clubhouse. *Home.* And I can't fathom the idea of going to sleep without him. Of waking up alone. All I want is to touch him. I know if I do, it'll only make leaving that much harder. But I'm tired of denying myself. My mind. My body. My *heart.*

"You know," Jinx says, his voice cutting through the silence and making me tense. "All you have to do is ask." *How did he...* "For the past few minutes, you've been rubbing your pussy against my hip every four and a half seconds." *Oh...that's how...*

I search for his face which I can't make out in the darkness. "Four and a half seconds? That's pretty precise."

"I've been counting."

"If you knew I wanted it, why are you making me ask? Why not just give it to me?"

"Because I like when you beg." His tone might be playful, but he's serious as hell. As is my need. So I don't hesitate a moment longer.

"I want you to make love to me."

He's silent a few long moments before he speaks. "You say that like this is goodbye."

"You never know," I mumble, wondering if this truly is goodbye. If this is our last night together. Or if fate might actually cut me a little fucking slack and give me the future I want.

"Yeah," he says, rolling over on top of me and pinning my arms above my head. "I think I do." It's the only thing he says. Then he's kissing me. Rocking his hips against me. Teasing me until I do beg before he gives in and gives me what I want.

My panties are ripped away. Legs over his shoulders. His hands beneath my ass—lifting me. His cock sliding between the wet, swollen lips of my pussy. Once...twice...he's inside me. Sliding into me slowly. Filling me. Completing me.

We make love—just like I asked. Passionate. Unhurried. Sweet and sensual love. Our kiss only breaking when he asks, "You okay?" When he demands, "Spread your legs wider so I can see that pretty pussy." Or when he says, "You feel good, baby. You're fuckin' perfection."

Perfection—I'm not even close. Yet my heart swells when he says it. My body responds. I come hard around him. He comes with me. I'm not one to refer to an orgasm as beautiful, but this is. Or at least I can't think of a better word to describe it.

I cry myself to sleep in his arms. Silent tears of guilt. Sadness. Pain. Remorse. Each one shed with a different emotion. The last just as heart breaking as the first. And every last one of them for Jinx.

The man I love.

WINTER

I'm up early. I've showered, dressed and consumed two cups of coffee and smoked a half of a pack of cigarettes before Jinx joins me on the couch.

He doesn't sit next to me. Instead, he sits opposite me on the sectional. Fully dressed. Coffee in hand. Expression stoic. Voice blank when he announces, "Pierce is here."

I nod. My reaction gives nothing away. I'm calm. Composed. I have my emotions in check. I've had all morning to prepare for this moment. I'm ready.

The door opens.

Closes.

Footsteps.

Pierce appears before me. Dressed like the business man he is by day—shiny black shoes. Perfectly tailored gray slacks. Bright white button down. The sleeves rolled up his strong forearms. Rolex on his wrist. Dark, unruly hair styled messy and just long enough to brush the top of his crisp, overly starched collar. He's freshly shaved. Expression cool. Blue eyes appraising.

To women, he's a dream. To his enemies, a nightmare. In the eyes of his brothers, he's a leader. In the eyes of his partners, a force. But all I see when I look at him is a distant memory. He's like a stranger to me. And all I feel is heartache. Because he'll never be anything more.

"Winter," he greets. Formal. Polite. Detached.

I respond in the same manner. "Pierce."

His gaze sweeps over me. Taking in the outfit I know he wanted me to wear just for this occasion. White silk blouse. Sensible, knee length black pencil skirt. When he gets to my red high heels, he frowns. He wanted me to wear the other pair he'd provided—the black ones with the thin, short heel. But he doesn't say anything.

"If you don't mind, Jinx. I'd like a moment alone with my sister."

I can feel Jinx's eyes on me. Almost hear his unspoken question. But I keep my gaze trained on Pierce. I don't need my brother getting the idea that I'm attached to Jinx. Or that he has any kind of feelings for me. It will only complicate things.

After several seconds, Jinx leaves us. Pierce takes his seat, stretching his arm across the back of the couch and propping his right ankle on his left knee. His fingers curl around his leg and I notice he's wearing my father's ring—the one that was supposed to be mine. I ignore it—assuming he wore it just to get under my skin.

"You look good," he says, his mood friendly. Posture relaxed.

I gesture toward him with my finger. "Ralph Lauren suits you."

His lips twitch. "It's Armani."

I gasp. "Wow. Business must be good."

"Always."

That, I was sure of.

Pierce had invested all of his money from the settlement we got from our parents' accident in some oceanfront real estate property when the market was shit. Now he owns the only high-rise condominium on La Jolla Beach in San Diego, along with several other properties on Mission Bay. He's living proof that stereotypes are bullshit—especially when it comes to bikers.

"So..." I trail off and give him an expectant look. Steeling my spine for what's to come.

He shrugs. "What?"

"You wanted a minute. You have it. What do you want to say?"

"Nothing. I just thought we could talk."

I laugh. "Talk." Shaking my head, I reach for the nearby decanter and pour a glass of scotch. I knew I'd need it. I just didn't expect it to be this soon. Taking a sip, I meet his stare. "You don't want to talk to me."

"If I didn't, I wouldn't be here."

"Fine," I say, taking another drink. "Talk."

"How are you?"

"Great."

"Did Jinx treat you well?"

"He was the perfect gentleman."

"And the club? Were they good to you?"

"I couldn't have asked for better hosts."

Pierce releases an exasperated breath. "I'm trying here, Winter."

"Me too. I'm answering all your questions aren't I?"

"Only with what you think I want to hear."

I feign shock. "Oh...you want the truth?" His lips thin and he nods once. "The truth...hmm...let me see." I tap my finger on my chin as if I'm thinking hard. "Well, you asked how I am. I didn't really lie. I'm great. Considering this will all be over very soon. You asked about Jinx, I didn't lie about that either. Except for the first week when he tied me to a bed for seven days straight, tried to starve me to death and forced me to stay out in the cold for hours a day."

"What?" Pierce asks, his voice a little disbelieving with a hint of anger.

"Come on, big brother." I shake my head. "You didn't think he'd be nice to me, did you? Treat me like a queen? Actually, I remember you saying I was supposed to be tied up, uncomfortable and alone, but safe. Right?"

"I didn't mean that literally. I expected him to take care of you and treat you with respect."

"What about the club? Did you expect the same of them?"

"Of course," he says, his tone soft. His expression even softer. Almost innocent. It only pisses me off more.

Slamming my glass down, I lean closer to him. "Well then why the fuck would you tell them I was nothing but a trashy whore? Someone who couldn't be trusted? A fucking burden...," I have to look away from him for a moment after choking out the words. When I turn back, he's thoughtful.

"I was angry. It was wrong. I apologize."

I lose it.

"Fuck you and your apology!" I scream, sending the decanter and my glass to the floor with the sweep of my hand. There's something pleasing about hearing it shatter. I want to throw something else. Somehow, I refrain and settle for just walking away—my feet crunching the broken glass.

"Winter, please." Pierce is suddenly behind me, his hand wrapping around my wrist. I don't fight him. I don't think I have the energy or the will. "I know I pushed you away." I stiffen in disbelief at his admission. "I have a problem with control. I need it. My brain doesn't function right without it. I never meant to hurt you or stop you from living your life. But I did. And I'm sorry."

I turn to face him. For the first time in my life, I see my strong, powerful brother completely trounced. It's heart-wrenching. Guts me. I hate seeing him like this. I want Devil's Renegades Pierce back. Not this defeated man in front of me.

"We should go," I whisper, unable to look at him another moment.

I pull out of his grasp and he easily releases me. I find Jinx standing by the door, his brows drawn tight over his gray eyes. Confused. Angry. Sympathetic. I avert my gaze and stride through the door, knowing the shit I'm feeling is only the start of what I'll experience today.

Outside, the Devil's Renegades Hattiesburg chapter sits patiently on their bikes. Black full-face helmets hide their identities. But I recognize Luke by his President patch proudly displayed on the front of his cut. He lifts his chin at me. I offer him a small wave—noticing the flat-black, monster of a machine next to him. The seat is empty and immediately I know who it belongs to.

I stop at Pierce's SUV and watch as Jinx strides purposefully across the sidewalk to his bike. He's in full leathers. His helmet already on but his visor up so I can see his eyes. After straddling the seat, he meets my gaze while he pulls on his gloves. My lips twitch. When he gives me the finger, my face breaks into a smile.

I guess he really is a biker....

Pierce clears his throat and I notice he's holding the door open for me. I duck around him and slide inside—too busy watching Jinx in all of his leathered-up glory to care that my brother is strapping me in like I'm a child—another one of his weird, overprotective measures. As if I'm too stupid to buckle my own damn seatbelt.

The windows shake with vibrations as the Harleys rumble to life. A surge of excitement sweeps through me. It quickly dies when I realize I won't ever feel the wind in my hair or my body pressed against Jinx's from the back of his bike.

With a wink, he closes the visor on his helmet and gracefully guides the massive machine in line with the others. Pierce and I pull out behind them—passing several more who wait for us before falling in line.

The car is silent. Both Pierce and I lost in our thoughts. Outside, the bike escort is loud. Yet somehow, soothing. But the moment we arrive, my nerves start to get the best of me. I manage to play it cool as Pierce leads me inside. I ignore Jinx and his inquisitive look as he follows in behind us—leaving the rest of the guys in the parking lot scanning the surroundings for threats from Cain.

This small law firm we're at isn't the same one we've done business with in the past. But money talks. And with the right amount of cash, you can get just about anything. Like the most prestigious attorney on the West Coast to fly nineteen hundred miles just for you to sign some fucking papers.

Pierce has that kind of cash. And he's arrogant enough to use it. Which is why I have to stifle my grin when he all but growls at the young woman shuffling papers around on a desk.

"Where's Clinton?" Pierce barks.

"Mr. Clinton had a family emergency to deal with, so he won't be here today," she says, not bothering to look up. That only pisses Pierce off more.

"Then who the fuck did I pay fifteen thousand dollars to have flown in here?"

"That would be me, Mr. Tews." She looks up and stills. I nearly roll my eyes at the look on her face as she blinks furiously to make sure Pierce is actually real.

"And you are?" he asks, his tone curt. His hand gesturing impatiently for her to continue.

"Gianna. Gianna Marcel."

"Are you a secretary, Mrs. Marcel?"

She bristles at his comment. Her pretty lips pinching together. "I'm an attorney, Mr. Tews. And it's *Miss* Marcel."

Pierce clears his throat. "My apologies, *Miss* Marcel. I assume you will be handling everything today?"

"That is correct. But first, I need to speak to Miss Tews alone."

I start to follow her out but Pierce stops me with his hand on my elbow. Eyes narrowed, he shoots Gianna a suspicious look. "For what?"

"With all due respect, Mr. Tews," she starts, removing her glasses and squaring her shoulders. "That's none of your business. Winter is the client here. Her name is the only name on this account, yet you are the one calling our office and making all the demands. I'm not sure of your relationship with Clinton, nor do I care. But today, Winter is *my* client and I'd like a moment to speak with her alone about *her* trust and the arrangements that have been made. So if you will excuse us."

She steps around him and opens the door. I give a very pissed off Pierce a smirk, ignore Jinx once again, and follow her out.

As we walk down the long corridor toward another private office, I feel dread deep in the pit of my belly. My palms are suddenly sweaty. My pulse racing. Every hair on my body prickles.

He's here.

The realization comes too late. Gianna has opened the door to my doom. She leans in and whispers something to me about being back in a few minutes. Her voice sounds far off—distant. But the click of the door behind her sounds so loud, I flinch.

Then I'm alone. With him. Standing face to face with my own personal hell. Watching as the Devil himself slowly stalks toward me. Disguised in a suit. Boasting a charming smile. Sporting a recent haircut and a clean shaven face. But there's still a wicked sparkle in those ice-blue eyes.

He stops in front of me. The scent of him fills my nostrils. Many women would find the aroma of his designer cologne delicious—intoxicating. I find it repulsive. It doesn't smell like the woodsy, marine fragrance that it would on anyone else. It smells like pain. Hate. Power. Evil.

I shiver when he slides his hand up my arm. Not from desire or the drop in temperature that results from his presence, but out of pure fear. He continues until his hand is possessively wrapped around my throat—tight enough to press down on my windpipe. But loose enough for me to still breathe and speak.

His lips are on mine—punishing and harsh. I don't kiss him back, but I don't pull away. When he growls in warning, I open my mouth to him. Let him claim me. I try to ignore the nausea. Push back the fear. Because I know this kiss. It's not a kiss of love. A kiss that says he misses me. No—this, is a promise.

He finally pulls away leaving both of us a little breathless. He wears a sneer on his face as he glares down at me—obviously pissed. "Who do you belong to, cutslut?"

A stronger woman would tell him to go to hell. A weaker one would scream for help. I'm neither. I'm numb. I effortlessly slip back into my role as his property. Because I made a decision before I got here. A selfless one. Stupid, but selfless.

So without further hesitation, I look up at him and say, "You, Cain. I belong to you."

When Gianna walks back into the room a few minutes later, Cain immediately releases me. He shoots her a charming smile before pulling out his cell and walking across the room to make a call.

I quickly straighten my clothes and look like I have my shit together when I turn to face her. But inside, I'm screaming.

Screaming at Cain for years of misery.

At Gianna for leaving me alone with him.

Pierce for pushing me away all those years ago.

Jinx for making me fall in love with him, which makes this moment that much harder.

"Winter?"

I snap my head up to see Gianna frowning at me—the papers she's organizing on the desk forgotten as her eyes flit from me to Cain. He's standing next to the window. Watching me. His phone still attached to his ear.

Swallowing hard, I force a smile and meet Gianna's wide, worried eyes. *Maybe I don't look like I have my shit together after all.* "Sorry...long day." I glance down at the papers and pick up a pen. "Where do I sign?"

"Winter..." she says, her shaky voice just above a whisper. I can hear the apology in her tone. It only confirms my suspicions that she's somehow involved in all this. Although I doubt she knew the extent of what she was really getting into.

I shoot her a tired look. "I just want to sign the damn papers, Gianna. Okay?"

After a moment, she glances back at Cain then nods. "Okay."

Page after page, I scribble my name on the line. A simple task, considering I'm about to inherit two million dollars by just flicking my wrist a few times. But by the time I get to the cashier's check for three hundred thousand dollars, I feel exhausted.

"What the fuck is this?" Cain asks, placing one, long finger on the check and dragging it across the desk.

"Pierce had them set it up. It's the money I owe him,' I say, my tone bored.

Cain huffs out a breath of disgust. "Not anymore." He crumples the unsigned check in his hand before shoving it in his pocket. "Way I see it, he owes me." His sinister glare hardens. "Since he took my property without permission and kept it from me for two fucking months."

His *property.*

Not his woman.

Not his ol' lady.

Hell, not even his cutslut.

His property.

Pierce had kept *it* for two months.

I've always heard you had to hit rock bottom before you found the strength to get back up. Well, I must have finally found the darkest pit of my existence. Because although I'm tired...so *fucking* tired of living this life, I suddenly, for the first time in six years, have the will to do something about it.

Cain's focus is trained on the documents spread out on the table. When Gianna tells him that information is private, he silences her with a look. She stands scared and quiet as he leans closer, surveying the details on every page. Committing every account number and dollar amount to memory.

Meanwhile, I'm eyeing the bulge at the small of his back beneath his suit jacket—visualizing the gun I've seen so many times. Imagining how the steel handle will feel in my hand. How heavy it will be. If it'll take both hands to hold it or just one. If I'll kill Cain quickly with one shot, or if I'll unload the entire clip before his lifeless body slumps to the floor and he vanishes from my life for good.

I came here today prepared to meet my fate. To willingly go with Cain in order to avoid bloodshed. I would do whatever I had to do to keep my brother alive. To keep Jinx alive. But what about me? If they found my life worthy enough for sacrifice, why couldn't I?

I've been so absorbed in keeping everyone else out of my life that I never considered standing up for myself. Until this moment. And despite the adrenaline rushing through my veins, a sense of peace surrounds me.

So many times, I've considered this—taking his gun. Shooting him in the foot. Or the face. But there's always been someone in the room or right outside the door. Right now, it's just me, him and Gianna. It's the perfect opportunity and likely the only one I'll ever get.

I'm taking my life back today. And if I end up losing it in the process, I'm okay with that. Because death is better than this. Better than being a prisoner. A piece of property. Being referred to as "it," or "that."

Fuck that.

Fuck it.

Fuck life.

Fuck death.

Today, one way or another, I'm going to reclaim my freedom from Cain. All on my own. Without the help of a motorcycle club, my big brother or my dream guy.

My name is Winter Tews.

I'm not a fucking cutslut.

I'm not your fucking property.

I'm just a girl who found her balls. Flipped her middle finger to the world. Grabbed her crotch and screamed to the universe, "Suck my dick!"

WINTER

"Did you just tell me to suck your dick?" Cain asks, staring past the gun in my hand to give me that signature look of his that used to make me feel stupid. Not anymore. Because right now, I feel like a motherfucking ninja. I have ever since I grabbed his gun and turned it on him thirty seconds ago.

"Yeah. I did. Now move."

Slowly, he lifts his hands up and backs away. "Okay, baby. Just calm down." I nearly laugh at his attempt to woo me with his charm. But he's about five years too late for that.

"I'm out, Cain," I tell him, my voice calm despite how amped I am. I've never felt this alive. This powerful. No wonder the men in my life love being assholes. It feels good.

"Out?" he asks, a hint of laughter in his tone.

"Yes. Out. As in, I'm done. I want you to leave me alone. I'm not yours. Not anymore."

That easy, charming look of his melts away—replaced with the hardness of the Cain I know. "Who the fuck—"

The sound of a bullet slicing through the air cuts him off. It takes me a moment to realize it was me who fired. It takes Cain just as long to realize he's been shot. I stare wide-eyed at the blood slowly staining the side of his jacket.

He stares at me in disbelief then stumbles back into a shelf and slowly slumps to the floor—clutching his side. Face pale. Breathing ragged. This sight of him should make me feel confident. Instead, I tremble as fear slowly takes over. My gut churns with sickness.

I shot him.

The door busts open and Jinx storms into the room, Pierce on his heels. They both look at me. Then Cain. Back at me. I frantically search their faces—unsure of what I'm looking for. When I meet Pierce's eyes, I can't look away.

"Hand me the gun, Winter." He's so calm. So in control. But I'm holding the gun. I'm in control. I shake my head. He ignores me and steps closer. "It's okay, sweet pea."

Sweet pea.

My childhood nickname.

Tears blur my vision but I blink past them. "I shot him."

Pierce nods. "I know."

"Me. I did it on my own."

"I know, baby. Now hand me the gun."

He doesn't wait for me to hand it over. In one fluid movement, he has my wrist in his hand. He easily removes the gun from my shaky fingers. Tosses it to Jinx. Then his arms are around me. My head on his chest. His hand cradling my skull. Lips kissing my hair.

"Shh..." he soothes. And I realize I'm crying. Crashing from the adrenaline rush. Panicking over what I'd done. Trying and failing to deal with the storm of emotions I feel at being in my brother's arms.

I'm ten years old again. Just a lost, little girl without parents. At the time, I didn't understand Pierce's controlling nature. And in this moment, I just don't care. It feels good to let him carry the weight of my problems. To feel protected. To just fucking cry and let someone else deal with all the bullshit.

After years of feuding. After all the hateful words. The betrayal. Lies. I'm right where I should be. I don't want to stay here forever. I still want my freedom. But in this moment, I need Pierce to be Pierce. And I just need to be his little sister.

"Winter," Pierce says, sometime later. He tries to pull me back from his chest, but I cling tighter. "The police are here," he whispers into my hair. "Just tell them the truth, understand?" I nod and he kisses my head. "Good girl."

When Pierce is in control, he's relaxed. Focused. He exudes power. Under any other circumstance, I might find it fascinating—watching him give orders and bark out directions as if he's in charge rather than the police. But all I can think about is the paramedics hovered around the body across the room.

Is he dead?

Alive?

Am I a murderer?

"Go with Jinx," Pierce says, shifting me toward Jinx.

His arm around my shoulders, Jinx guides me from the room. I breathe in his scent—immediately feeling better. Where Pierce has the power to make me feel vulnerable and dependent on him, Jinx makes me feel strong. Like I can conquer anything.

I love him.

The police ask me the same questions over and over. I don't lie. After my story, Pierce, Jinx and Gianna's all line up, they're convinced that Cain was shot in self-defense and we're able to leave.

Three hours later, we're back at the clubhouse. Me and Jinx sitting next to each other on the couch. My head on his shoulder. His fingers absently stroking my arm. Pierce is pacing as he talks on the phone with a detective getting more answers—something he's been doing since we got here. I was impressed with his ability to find out shit by just lowering his tone.

It was Gianna who'd contacted the police. She'd ran from the room after I pulled the gun on Cain, barricaded herself in an office and dialed 9-1-1. She'd also been the one who told Cain about where the meeting was taking place, gave him access to the back door of the building, and arranged the alone time between me and him.

I wasn't angry at Gianna. I knew how manipulative Cain could be. But I'd be lying if I said it didn't make me feel better to know he'd promised her money she never got. And that she'd pissed herself after hearing the gunshot.

My thoughts are suddenly interrupted with Pierce's newest announcement. "He's going to live." He sounds disappointed. Jinx grunts his disapproval. I, on the other hand, am relieved. I hadn't killed anyone.

"He has some outstanding warrants in Clark County. Once he can travel, they'll be picking his ass up and locking him away for a while." Pierce's gaze lands on me. "We won't have any problem out of his club either. From what I hear, they're more relieved than anything."

I nod. Still taking it all in. Trying to process that I'm here. Alive. I shot Cain. He's still alive. I'm free. *Free.*

"Our flight leaves first thing in the morning," Pierce says, pouring a glass of scotch. *Okay. So maybe I'm not free.*

"I'm not going to San Diego with you." I sound more confident than I feel.

Pierce doesn't bother to even look at me. "Yes. You are."

"No... I'm not."

"Until this dies down and I'm confident Madness isn't going to do something stupid like retaliate, you'll be staying with me in San Diego."

"You just said—"

"I want to be confident. I won't risk your life at someone's word."

"You just want to control me." He doesn't deny it. "I can take care of myself, Pierce."

He rolls his eyes and loosens his collar. "Don't be ridiculous, Winter. Just because you shot a man doesn't mean you can take on an entire motorcycle club."

I flinch at his words. Jinx stiffens beside me. "Pierce," he warns.

Pierce snaps his gaze to Jinx. He takes in the two of us sitting close on the couch. My head against Jinx's shoulder. "Don't go there with me, brother. She's not any of your business."

"I'm sitting right. Fucking. Here!" I yell, losing my shit. "I'm not your business either. Stop treating me like a child."

Pierce lifts his brows in amusement. "Stop acting like one."

"Goddamn control freak," I mutter, standing and stomping out like the petulant child I'm not.

"Flight's at six, sweet pea," he calls after me.

I flip him the finger. "Go fuck yourself." Then I think to myself...

I won't be here.

JINX

When I hear the bedroom door slam behind Winter, I shift my attention to Pierce. "You're doing it again," I say, drilling holes into him. He doesn't look the least bit concerned.

"Doing what?"

"Being an asshole."

He laughs and lifts his glass to me. "Cheers to that, Jinx. Not all of us get to be the hero in this story."

"You're gonna push her away. Again."

Pierce shakes his head. "No. Not this time."

I lift a brow. "You sure about that?"

"Yes. Because I'm not letting her out of my fucking sight."

I just stare at him. Wondering how a man as smart as him can be so stupid when it comes to women. I know he needs control. That it's somehow ingrained in him. But why the fuck doesn't he find a woman who enjoys that shit? Who wants to be told what to do. And leave people like Winter, who deserves some fucking slack, the hell alone.

A part of me died a little when I heard that gunshot. Not just because I feared I lost the woman I love, but because of the look on Pierce's face. He was completely broken. In that moment, he aged ten years. I don't want to ever see that look again. But some shit he'll just have to figure out on his own. I've tried to help him, but I'm not getting anywhere.

Because of him, I was going to let her go. I was going to lose the woman I love because her brother was hell bent on controlling her life. She wanted freedom. I was going to give it to her. Even if it ripped my fucking heart out.

Sacrifice.

Because I'm a hero and shit.

But I'm selfish, too. She's not going anywhere. Not because I want to control her like Pierce, but because I know what it is she really wants—to be with the man she loves. And that motherfucker is me. I'll give her the choice, though—always—but I'm pretty confident she'll choose me. Like I said, I know my girl.

My girl.

Fuck that feels right.

"Winter stole that money to buy a new life away from Cain," I start, ready to get this shit over with so I can be with her.

Pierce's back stiffens. I wait for him to turn around and look at me before continuing.

"He caught her. Tattooed his patch on her back. Beat the fuck out of her. Held her against her will for two years. Made her do shit with men for his own personal gain. Belittled her daily. And treated her like an object instead of a person." I pause to catch my breath. Trying to reign in my anger.

Pierce hides his reaction well. But the skin on his knuckles is bone white as he grips the glass tight in his hand.

"Today she finally got away from that sadistic motherfucker. Stood up to him. All on her own because she knew if she asked for your help, you'd give it no questions asked. She didn't want you involved. Was scared Madness would retaliate and something bad would happen to you.

"Remember how it felt the first time you killed somebody?" I hold my thumb and index finger and inch apart. "Well, she came this close to killing a man today...her fucking birthday. Something you haven't even acknowledged."

I stand and close the distance until my boots touch the toe of his shiny fucking shoes. He struggles to hold onto his pride as he glares at me and asks, "So I'm supposed to just let her go so she can end up with some other piece of shit? I want more for her. I always have."

I shake my head. "Don't make this shit about you."

"Well what the fuck are you asking for, Jinx?" he asks, his temper rising.

"Asking?" I shoot him a cold smile. "I'm not asking for shit, *brother.* I'm telling you. Cut her some fuckin' slack."

Something in my expression has his eyes widening. "You son of a bitch," he whispers in disbelief. "Are you in love with her?"

Not wanting to hear a lecture on his sudden revelation, I walk away. But not before telling him the truth.

"You goddamn right I am."

WINTER

"I'm taking this...and this...," I say to myself, stuffing random shit in a duffle bag I found in the closet. I'm getting the hell out of here. Even if I have to pistol whip Pierce to do it. I've held a gun. Shot a man. I can handle it.

"Hey baby."

Baby.

It still gets me.

Like someone flipped a switch, all my anger dissipates. God, I love this man. Now I'm going to leave him. Like a dumbass. But if I stay here, Pierce won't leave me alone. And I'll end up resenting Jinx for being so amazing and making me fall in love with him.

Releasing a breath, I force a smile and turn to face him. That smile spreads into a wide grin when I see the look of disgust on his face as he surveys the damage in his closet.

"I was just getting some stuff together," I say, trying to hold back a laugh.

"You couldn't do that shit without doing...," he says and gestures with his hand around the small space. "This?"

Eyes on me, he then drags them up and down my body. "Really?"

"What? It makes a cute dress!" I'd put on one of his button down shirts. Accessorized it with a thin, pink belt at the waist. Pulled on some pink Converse and piled my hair high on my head. Hell, I thought I looked good.

"Stop wearing my shit."

"Did you come in here to fuss at me?"

"No." He clears his throat. "I came in here to give you this." From the inside pocket of his cut, he pulls out an envelope. "Happy birthday."

My birthday...how had I forgotten?

Curious about my present, I look from it to him before taking the envelope. I catch a whiff of something masculine. Bringing it to my nose, I sniff.

"Smells good."

Jinx rolls his eyes. "Just open it." I'm not sure why he's so damn annoyed. I sniff it again just to piss him off. It's some kind of men's cologne. Definitely not Jinx's though. The scent is familiar, but I can't place it.

Sliding my finger beneath the flap, I open it up and find several things inside. The first is a plane ticket to Barbados. For tonight. I look up at Jinx in disbelief. I know he said he'd help me, but I never thought...

He nods toward the ticket. "I got a friend there. Him and his wife will be there to pick you up and help you get adjusted." He studies me a moment before lifting his chin. "Keep going," he says, his voice low. Almost sad.

I look down at the other items. A house key. Bank account information. Passport...I flip open to my picture, then smile at the name beneath it. "Summer Payton?" I grin up at an annoyed Jinx. "Payton makes fake passports?"

"Him and Clay. They played paper-rock-scissors for your last name." He flicks his finger at the document. "You see who won."

I sniff the envelope again. Yep. That's Payton's cologne. Hard for me to forget it after having him spooning me two nights in a row.

"I thought they were good kids," I tease.

"They are. But they ain't saints, sweetheart."

Sweetheart.

My eyes burn. "What about you...? Us?" I ask. Sadness filling my voice. My gut. My heart.

"I told you not to fall in love with me, Winter," he says softly.

"I didn't," I lie. Because my pride won't let me say otherwise.

"Bullshit."

I smirk. "What? You think I'm in love with you?"

"I know you are."

"How?"

"'Cause I'll be damned if I ain't in love with you too."

I stare up at him with wide eyes as he closes the distance. Tucks a strand of hair behind my ear. Studies my eyes. Drops his gaze to my mouth. Rubs his thumb across my bottom lip.

"You said you wanted your dream guy to wear something other than black," he says, gray eyes meeting mine. "Well, I own thirteen different colored shirts. I have six pair of flip-flops. I like holding you when I kiss you. I like holding your hand. I'll pour your scotch if that's what you want, and you can have the remote." He pauses and the corner of his lips tip up a little. "Breathe, baby."

I suck in a breath at his command. Then I pull in another. My heart pounds furiously in my chest. I stand on wobbly knees. Trying to concentrate on breathing. On not passing out. On the gentle sweep of his fingers across my cheek. My jaw. Then back to my lip.

"I'm a package deal, Winter," he says, his brow furrowing. "My club is a part of me. But it's not all of me. There's plenty of room for a challenge." He smirks at that. "I'll never take your voice from you. I won't treat you like you're less, tell you how to live your life or make decisions for you. I won't let any other motherfucker treat you that way, either. Not even my brothers...not even yours."

Pierce.

He's the reason I'm running—now that Cain is out of the picture. But isn't running from him just as cowardly as letting him control me? And if any man can stand up to Pierce and put him in his place, it's Jinx.

"So here I am," he says, his bored tone teasing. "Your fucking dream guy. Your fairytale. Your happily ever after. Standing in my destroyed closet, confessing my love for you like a goddamn book hero."

He takes a step back and runs his hand through his hair. I've never seen him nervous. "I'm offering you a life with me, Winter." He nods at the passport I'm clinging to in my hand, "Or a chance at another life entirely. It's your decision."

Something in his tone tells me it's really not a decision. I can leave, but he'll follow. He's the kind of man who gets what he wants. No matter who he has to pass through to get it.

I could tell him I want to leave. Force him to abandon his family. His club. His entire life just to make a new one with me. But when you love someone, it's not always about you. And I refuse to suffer or allow Jinx to suffer just because my brother is an asshole.

Although there is one thing I want to request....

"Moped," I say, my face serious.

"What?"

"Moped. You have to ride a moped."

He shakes his head. "I'm not riding a fucking moped."

I poke my lips out. "Not even for me?"

"Nope."

"But you said you'd do anything for me."

His brow lifts. "I didn't say that."

"But I'm your dream girl," I whine.

"I didn't say that shit either. I said I love you. Which translates to: you'll do until some better bitch comes along."

"Say it again."

"You'll do until some better bitch comes along," he repeats. I narrow my eyes. He smiles. "I love you, baby."

I beam like an idiot. He watches me with amusement. He's waiting for me to say it back. He'll just have to wait. I want to live in this moment just a little bit longer. After all, it's my fucking fairytale.

This isn't about Cinderella and her strange feet that are different from everyone else's feet in the kingdom.

This isn't about Rapunzel and her super strong neck muscles that can support the weight of a grown man.

This isn't about Snow White and her seven little men kink—although I'm more like her than the others.

This story is about me—Winter Tews.

So cue the music.

Light the fireworks.

Pour the scotch.

Because this shit is really happening.

This is the ending to a fairytale I never imagined could be mine.

I give Jinx a pleading look. "One more time?"

"For fuck's sake," he rushes out, exasperated.

He cradles my face in his hands. Kisses me crazy. Doesn't pull away until I'm breathless. Then he says it again. "I love you."

I only have one thing to say.

"Ditto."

And we lived happily ever after.

AFTERWORD

Reader!! Thank you soooo much for reading Cutslut! I hope you enjoyed it! I smoked like, 50,000 cigarettes and drink a few hundred cases of Mountain Dew to finish this fucker, but hopefully you're smiling and my hard work paid off!

You're perfect!

-Kim

ALSO BY KIM JONES

ABOUT THE AUTHOR

Kim Jones is just a small town Mississippi girl who loves writing, dogs, Merle Haggard, long vacations and never doing laundry. You can keep up with her meaningless, silly videos on Facebook. Follow her on Twitter, where you may possibly find one tweet a month. Instagram, where she posts pics of her Bloodhound. And her website that she never updates because she's too lazy and ignorant.

And be sure to check out The Snobby Author!

Because that's me. And I'm awesome.

www.kimjonesbooks.com
twitter:@authorkimjones
Instagram: kimjones204
Snapchat: kimjones204
www.facebook.com/kimjonesbooks
www.facebook.com/kim.j.jones.7
www.facebook.com/thesnobbyauthor

Made in the USA
Middletown, DE
06 December 2019

80158940R10170